STANDING STILL

STANDING STILL

An Anderson and Costello Mystery

Caro Ramsay

This first world edition published 2017
in Great Britain and the USA by
SEVERN HOUSE PUBLISHERS LTD of
19 Cedar Road, Sutton, Surrey, England, SM2 5DA.
Trade paperback edition first published
in Great Britain and the USA 2017 by
SEVERN HOUSE PUBLISHERS LTD

Copyright © 2017 by Caro Ramsay.

British Library Cataloguing in Publication Data
A CIP catalogue record for this title is available from the British Library.

ISBN-13: 978-0-7278-8697-2 (cased)
ISBN-13: 978-1-84751-806-4 (trade paper)
ISBN-13: 978-1-78010-870-4 (e-book)

This is a work of fiction. Names, characters, places and incidents
are either the product of the author's imagination or are used fictitiously.
Except where actual historical events and characters are being described
for the storyline of this novel, all situations in this publication are
fictitious and any resemblance to actual persons, living or dead,
business establishments, events or locales is purely coincidental.

All Severn House titles are printed on acid-free paper.

Severn House Publishers support the Forest Stewardship Council™ [FSC™],
the leading international forest certification organisation.
All our titles that are printed on FSC certified paper carry the FSC logo.

MIX
Paper from
responsible sources
FSC® C013056

Typeset by Palimpsest Book Production Ltd.,
Falkirk, Stirlingshire, Scotland.
Printed and bound in Great Britain by
TJ International, Padstow, Cornwall.

PROLOGUE

24 December 1989

They had been aware of the scent of wood smoke as they strolled home from midnight Mass, gloved hand in gloved hand. Rosemary was sticking out her tongue to catch the falling snowflakes, while Ronnie, full of mulled wine and Christmas cheer, sang an inappropriate version of 'While Shepherds Watched Their Flocks'.

The explosion made them jump.

Rosemary reacted first, jogging round the corner into Marchmont Terrace to see the flames. She ran up the neatly slabbed path to the blistering front door of the burning house as Ronnie went in search of a phone.

She was only halfway along the path when the heat hit her, like the power of a blast from an open oven door. She paused to pull her scarf up round her mouth to protect her from the choking air; jerking her hood closer to her head and ramming her hands deep into her gloves. She stretched through the searing heat in front of her, painfully aware of the biting chill of the night air behind her. Her hand approached the blackening glass panel of the front door, its handle tantalizingly close.

She reached out.

Beyond the glass she recognized the flash of a limb, a dark face through the shadows and patterns of swirling grey clouds. An open mouth, shockingly pink amongst the smoke, appeared then vanished, leaving a bloodied smear of skin on the blackening pane. But Rosemary had seen the torture in the face, the desperation for breath, for life. She turned her own face away from the heat, and stretched out her hand to reach the handle. She tried, standing tense while the heat bit at her ankles, melting her shoes onto her toes. She felt her lips burn and eyebrows singe.

They were two people separated by a few feet, one in the

snow, one in the flames. Their eyes met. As Rosemary braved another step forward, she saw the figure crumple into the flames. Above the cracking and crashing from the belly of the inferno, she heard a cry.

Then she was knocked sideways, pushed onto the front lawn and its carpet of melting snow. A yellow firefighter's glove reached past her to the door handle. She watched, willing them to reach. They did. She willed the handle to turn. It did not.

Rosemary was pulled back down the path. She heard the axe smash the glass and the answering roar of the flames, as if the inferno itself had been wounded. The rush of heat punched Rosemary forward. The flames, thriving on their gift of fresh oxygen, flew skywards, hissing and spitting, now at war with the water jet from the hose.

Rosemary turned and looked. The body had surrendered to the flames, merely a small black shadow behind the glass. She heard the hiss and click of the breathing apparatus as two firefighters walked slowly into the inferno, bulky automatons that then returned, half-carrying, half-dragging their prize past her to their colleagues, the oxygen, the stretcher, ice-cold sanctuary. And life.

Rosemary jumped as an oxygen mask covered her face. She had been unaware of how laboured her breathing had become, how blackened her face was, how burned her clothes were. Her husband slipped a blanket round her shoulder, his hand caressed her back.

She looked up to see the woman dancing on the first-floor windowsill, still wearing the black dress that she had probably bought for her Christmas Eve dinner party; the beautiful, expensive dress now being ripped apart by the frantic hands of the screaming woman as fabric melted onto her skin. The torn ends floated out in the wind, black flags in the orange flames against the glittering silent night. Her face was ugly; features twisted with fear, lipstick smeared, pale skin blackened by smoke. One tenacious hand held on to the sandstone bricks, steadying herself against the force of the flames that streamed out the window behind her and curled round her legs.

Rosemary watched in macabre fascination as the woman composed herself, then relaxed. For an instant she was beautiful, her dark hair caught the snow and she smiled. Then slowly, imperceptibly, she took a step forward. She hung for a moment in the night sky, a dark angel in the circling smoke, and then she joined the snowflakes falling through the air.

Falling.

Falling.

ONE

Sunday 5 June 2016

I t had taken Stephen Pickering about a minute to decide he didn't like his Christmas present from Jackie, a tiny fur ball of West Highland terrier. As he opened the puppy cage on Christmas morning and lifted little Murray up, the puppy had shown his disdain for his new owner by peeing on him.

Three weeks later, to add insult to injury, Stephen opened the credit card statement and realized that the £800 had come off the joint account. Seemingly, he had agreed to get the dog. He just didn't remember. And while it was Stephen who walked Murray, fed Murray and cleared up Murray's mess in a multitude of little, coloured plastic bags, the dog saved his adoring eyes for Jackie.

Six months and two chewed carpets later, man and dog were fully engaged in a silent war of attrition. At the moment Murray was holding the most disputed territory: the marital bed.

And that was where Murray had been when Stephen got home from The Curler's Rest at one o'clock in the morning of the 5th of June. The dog had leapt out of bed, yapping loudly enough to waken the neighbours, again. So Stephen had dragged him out for a walk.

The walk was always the same route. It had been deathly quiet in the small hours of the morning, but now, at the back of ten, Stephen could hear the thud thud of the parade preparations. Despite being two streets away from Byre's Road and the buffering effect of the four-story buildings on either side, the noise still jarred his hangover. The whole West End would be jumping soon and he intended to be jumping along with the best of them, all he needed was – he looked at Murray strutting along with his own sense of self-importance, tail in the air – the hair of the dog.

Stephen had been planning to take Jackie to watch the

parade, then a nice boozy lunch out in the sunshine somewhere, maybe take in some open air jazz, watch the world go by, a snooze in the park and a Vindaloo from the Wee Curry Shop to round off the evening.

Jackie had put the mockers on that the minute Murray pulled his sad face. *Oh what about wee Murray, we can't leave him in the house all day.* Stephen's solution that they could lock him in the shed had not been well received.

So man and man's best friend walked along in silence, tenements high to the left and right, the sun painting patchwork patterns on the concrete of the lane. Murray pulled on his lead, swaying from side to side as if his nose was scanning for underground treasure.

They walked round the dog-leg halfway down Athole Lane, meandering back to Saltoun Street. Home for a cup of strong black coffee, get Jackie out her bed and . . . Murray stopped, nose twitching. Then he started to bark. Not his usual 'yap yap' that accompanied the inane jumping around and running in circles. This was a solid bark from somewhere deep inside; a warning. The dog gave Stephen a quick look then fixed his eyes on an old tea chest sitting neatly against the bright white plaster of the new build. Stephen had passed this way at one o'clock that morning. Had he been so drunk he had missed it? No, Murray would have reacted at the time.

Stephen pulled the lead in tight and approached the box, looking up and down the lane, thinking that somebody must have left it there to be picked up. It didn't look damaged. It had been placed there, neatly in line with the wall, but not at a particular garage or garden door. The top was nailed down. He ran his fingertips over the nails, banged in any old way. Murray kept back, lead at full stretch. His lips pulled over his sharp little teeth and a pyramid of erect hair erupting over his shoulders.

Stephen felt a little apprehensive. It was quiet down here in the lane, in the shadows, among the trees. And cold despite the early morning sun. He placed a hand on the rough corner of the chest and nudged it; too heavy to budge. He slid four fingers under the first panel and snapped it open. Crouching down, he could see red padded lining. Then the smell hit him.

Like his own bathroom after a heavy night. Stephen knelt beside it, his nose in the crook of his elbow and peered in to the dark interior, catching sight of a single curl of blonde hair. He smiled. Somebody was asleep in there. Typical West End Festival prank, some poor bugger had gotten drunk and his mates had nailed him in a box and he had shat himself. He pulled off the other two slats of wood, then placed his hand on the shoulder of the curled up man, giving him a little shove to waken him. There was something odd about the way his hand pushed the shoulder way too far with the grating noise of a car tyre on gravel. And it was cold. The fabric of the black jumper was so very cold it felt damp to the palm of his hand.

Stephen Pickering took a step backwards. Then he did what he always did when he had no idea what to do. He phoned Jackie.

Partickhill Station was gearing up for a busy day. The first day of the West End Festival, the day of the big parade. Twenty-four hours of madness when the cops turned a blind eye to offences against public order. Within reason.

ACC Mitchum trotted down the stairs at Partickhill, all Brillo pad hair and shiny buttons. He took a sharp left into the toilet, hoping to stop the persistent stream of consciousness spouting from the mouth of the local MSP, James Kirkton. Mitchum's hopes were in vain.

He needed to wash his hands. There was something about being locked in a small room with any politician that made Mitchum feel unclean. He had first noticed it when he worked in Vice; a need to empty his bladder, to scrub under his nails, to stand under a shower so hot it was nearly scalding. It was the fear that bullshit might be contagious.

The meeting with Kirkton had consumed an hour of his life that he wasn't going to get back. All the politician's promises reinforced the ACC's long held belief that it was different words but the same crap. No difference what party was in charge. Mitchum's view on policing remained sensible, effective, but never worthy of the sound bite. Most crime was caused by poverty. Work on the poverty, and crime figures improve. But those views never got an airing. It was easier to blame the unemployed. Or immigrants. Or unemployed immigrants.

Mitchum closed the toilet door behind him and turned on the tap.

Kirkton followed him in. 'So what about this DCI Anderson? Is he still working at this station?' he asked, standing behind Mitchum, fixing his tie in the mirror before turning sideways to check his outline in his new suit. A run of the third finger through his long, floppy fringe. God, the man was vain.

Mitchum answered in the affirmative and walked over to the urinal.

'And do you think there should be some limit, some agreed protocol on what is acceptable behaviour in the private life of a detective serving at that rank. I mean, considering the scrutiny of social media these days.'

This had been accompanied by the smile of the great white. As Mitchum emptied his bladder, Kirkton then went on to question why a DCI was living at one of Glasgow's most expensive addresses, although if he knew that, then he also knew damn well why.

'Sir?' The toilet door opened a couple of inches.

Mitchum zipped up and turned round.

'The press office is on the phone and they want you to switch your mobile back on. The photographers are outside. The children have arrived.' PC Graham saw Kirkton and quickly closed the door.

Mitchum went back to the sink and ran the hot tap until the water steamed up the mirror, obliterating Kirkton. He was proving as impossible to brush off as dandruff. James Kirkton. Klingon Kirkton as he was known in Police Scotland circles. He was here to soak up the media coverage of the West End Festival parade, allowing himself little speeches here and there about his campaign for the Safer Society. Nobody would take any notice, they had all heard it a hundred times before. And Kirkton never said anything once that he could say twice, and nothing that had not been penned by his speechwriter. Kirkton was the worst kind of media whore, a man who really would put allegations into the mouth of alligators.

It had always been Mitchum's policy to pay polite attention to what any politician said before disregarding every single word. So far it had proved effective as they all wanted to be seen to be doing something about 'this', then they would move office and suddenly become an expert in 'that'. But this petty point scoring about private lives seemed a new low. And Mitchum couldn't really see the point, until he recalled Kirkton having a rant in the press about the ever increasing numbers of cold case initiatives, maintaining it was not an effective use of police resources, given the current statistics.

Of course, DCI Colin Anderson was hotly tipped to head CCAT, the Cold Case Assessment Team. The success of the Partickhill Major Investigation Team as a small functioning unit made it ideal for a new initiative. But what the hell did the private life of Colin Anderson have to do with this over-dressed prat?

Mitchum dried his hands again, the noisy blast of hot air drowning out the hot air coming from Kirkton. He left the toilet, his companion following him so close that he felt the politician's breath on the back of his neck. The narrative ploughed the usual furrow; law and order, family values. Kirkton saw himself as a self-appointed Police Service czar, making an impact on his Safer Society ticket. It should be a Safer Society for today, not yesterday. If anybody had a good case for review, they could get a lawyer.

ACC Mitchum didn't trust him an inch. Even the Police Scotland PR would have stopped the Safer Society initiative, if only for the unfortunate initials. But Klingon Kirkton had one huge talent. He was an expert at multitasking; he could walk and talk shite at the same time.

As Mitchum placed his hand on the internal keypad of the station door, Kirkton started up again. 'And what was the exact nature of the relationship between DCI Colin Anderson and Helena McAlpine? I mean, was their relationship acceptable in the police service these days?'

'That kind of relationship was almost compulsory at one time,' muttered Mitchum with a hint of nostalgia in his voice, as he keyed in his code. Thinking back to the good old days before ball breakers like Costello came along. That reminded him, he needed to phone Archie Walker and see how Pippa was doing. She'd been in the care home for a fortnight now. A wife with dementia and now being pally with DI Costello? That man made life hard for himself. 'As you know,' Mitchum said over his shoulder, 'Helena McAlpine is dead. Has been for well over a year now, and Colin is still married, so the simple answer to the question is that it's none of our business. Anderson's daughter and Helena McAlpine, Helena Farrell as you might know her, were very close.' Mitchum held the door open for the politician to follow.

'The artist, yes I know. I have some of her work.' Kirkton straightened his jacket one last time in preparation for the cameras. 'Not really my thing but the investment potential is huge. Now that she's passed away.' He smiled to the waiting press, going down the stairs slowly. Like a minor royal.

The door swung closed on Mitchum's face and the politician was blissfully silenced. Mitchum could no longer catch the words but he could see Kirkton's mouth opening and closing. The ACC thought fondly of Johnny McConnell, a vomit-covered drunken flasher, with BO so bad it peeled the paint off the cell walls. McConnell was a piece of walking bacteria, but infinitely more amiable company than this piece of tactless political shit.

Mitchum joined Kirkton, walking down the external steps into the cauldron of heat, envious of PC Graham on desk duty in the cool, quiet station.

The ACC looked out at the gathering press and gave them a hands-up. Kirkton now placed a hand on his shoulder. Mitchum shivered, there was only so much shite a man could take. 'We will be with you in a minute,' he called out to the crowd as he turned back to his companion, his words a mere breath from his lips. 'Helena McAlpine's relationship with Colin Anderson has no effect on our plans for him to head up this team as part of our cold case initiative. Content yourself that it will be a dead end for his career. And while I have a lot of respect for Colin Anderson, if I was stuck in a lift with DI Costello, I'd take my chances, climb down the shaft naked into a tank of piranhas. But they function well as a team.'

Mitchum was surprised at the glow of pride he felt. He

pulled his shoulders up and was flattered to hear a few cameras fire. He wished he could remove Kirkton's hand with unreasonable force, but the pictures on the front pages of *The Scottish Sun* would be bad PR. 'We are here,' he continued, 'putting on a united front and getting our photograph taken with the children before they join the parade, so cut the crap.'

Right on cue a couple of children dressed as Munchkins came forward. Mitchum watched as they were organized for the picture. A pretty teenage girl pushed her way through the cameras, and staggered up the steps to the station, either very happy or very drunk, much to the merriment of the onlookers. Her cream dirndl skirt, half gathered up in one chubby fist, dragged on the ground behind her. The photographers stepped aside to let her through.

The group fell silent in expectation of drama.

Mitchum seized the PR opportunity, holding the station door open for the garlanded girl, making a grandiose gesture of tipping his hat. She paused as she passed, asking him, in a perfectly clear voice, if Colin Anderson was in. Mitchum tried not to catch Kirkton's eye as he indicated that she should go through the door, 'Look after this young lady will you, PC Graham?' he called inside, loudly so that the press could hear that she was getting personal attention, a living example of good practical policing.

At the door she turned round to Mitchum, regarding him with big hazel eyes, pupils like huge black holes. She was on something. 'I have been abducted by aliens and they wanted me to tell him.'

'Oh well,' answered Mitchum benignly, 'you pop in there and we will find Colin for you.' He closed the door behind her.

'Aliens?' mocked Kirkton, loud enough for the nearest reporter to hear.

'We will make sure that she is OK.' Mitchum spoke a little louder as the press closed in. 'Her welfare is our priority. She will be cared for and a doctor will be consulted if we have any concerns.' He smiled for the camera. 'We are a police service after all, and it is the day of the big parade. Time to be happy and enjoy a wonderful day, in this wonderful city and keep

safe! Enjoy your drink responsibly. I know I'm looking to a
nice cold pint the minute I'm off duty.'

'First round on you then!' shouted a journalist and there
was a ripple of laughter.

Mitchum took off his hat. The chief liked them to do that
so the photographs would show off their eyes, rather than have
them obscured by the dark shadow cast by the peak. He walked
towards the group of children, a Munchkin girl ran forward
and he placed the hat on her head. The cameras fired.

James Kirkton moved up alongside him to get in the shot
and smiled. 'And we hope this beautiful day is enjoyed by
all here in this glorious city. The police service and the
council have worked closely together to ensure that the . . .'
And he wandered to the front of the group, and the front of
the picture, as the children regrouped behind him.

ACC Mitchum threw a quick look over his shoulder, a glance
at the front door of the station. He had been a good detective
in his day. He still noticed anomalies. A young pretty teenager
with her blouse buttoned up incorrectly. Deftly, Mitchum took
his phone out of his pocket and turned it on, noting it was six
minutes past ten. He dialled the desk that was only a few yards
behind him.

Safer society my arse, he thought. *It was a bloody jungle
out there.*

Sandra Ryme slid into the driver's seat of the Panda, the back
of her nylon blue uniform sticking on the plastic. She plonked
the Lidl bag into the passenger footwell before leaning over
to open the window. The air in the car was hotter than
a tropical greenhouse. She had been up most of the night and
the daylight charred her tired eyes, the plastic seat was now
burning her skin through her trousers and she was going to
be late for her work, again. She'd never get through this bloody
traffic. It had been a clear run from Govan, but from here, on
the south side of the Clyde Tunnel to the secure living facility
on the north side where she worked, it would be chaos. The
parade was diverting the traffic up tiny side streets and through
folk's front gardens. Every single year for the last twenty years
it was the same havoc. Well, except for the first year when

nobody bothered and then again more recently when they couldn't find the funding for the parade at all.

Sandra had been late setting off from her council flat on Copland Road, but then she had a brainwave and nipped into Lidl to buy some Italian cake to appease the Duchess. She could always blame the traffic for her tardiness. Sandra had also bought four salted caramel fudge doughnuts for herself. Pulling an all-nighter always made her hungry, but she had her prize in the boot. Her prize.

She pulled down the vanity mirror and wiggled her face about a bit. Make-up never stayed on her skin, it seemed to have a more 'free range' approach, mascara spidering on her cheek, lipstick staining her teeth and blusher that sat in two round blotches making her look like a clown. She pulled a paper tissue from her uniform pocket, spat on it and rubbed at her face. Instead of blotchy and red, it was now blotchy, red and streaky. And covered in spit. She took out some rose Vaseline and smeared that over her lips. It didn't help the overall look. The overall look was less boho chic, more chronic hay fever.

One day.

One day, she would be beautiful. When she had money.

She stuffed a whole doughnut in her mouth and slurped down some Irn Bru, burped loudly and wiped her lips on her forearm, the Vaseline leaving a sticky snail trail on her white skin.

She put the Panda into gear and pulled into the queue heading out the car park, licking bits of doughnut from her fingertips before pressing play on the CD. The warbling of an operatic soprano filled the car.

It was rumoured the Duchess had been an opera singer. Like Sandra, the Duchess was not pretty and never had been. She was 'strong featured' with a long nose and broad chin. People said her face was 'full of character'. Sandra reckoned if she didn't achieve 'beautiful' she could be, at least 'full of character'.

She needed to leave this crappy life behind. On her birthday, her last boyfriend had bought her a gift all wrapped up in pretty paper. Inside it was a brown paper bag. He had presented it to her in the pub and, not being in on the joke, she had opened it in front of everybody. They had all laughed. Sandra had laughed. At the time. Sandra had waited a month then keyed his car.

The Panda inched forward by one car length, then stopped. The car was now full of the sound of a tenor, singing like he was in need of a laxative. She looked at the mirror again, pulling at her eyelashes, looking into the red-veined rims of her eyes, the irises of dishwater brown that could never be the deep velvet brown of romantic heroines. Even the Duchess's eyes had a touch of drama about them, the blue of a faded watercolour seascape framed by jet eyeliner to give her the look of Cleopatra. Hours later, the Duchess's eyes would still be bordered by a precise line, unlike Sandra's which smudged to panda eyes with one blink. The Duchess had class, sitting bolt upright, thin legs crossed at the ankles. Sandra thought she wore ten denier stockings until she managed to nick a pair. And realized they were silk. She had told Paolo they were missing because they had laddered in the laundry and she had thrown them out. That had been a difficult moment. The memory distracted Sandra and she nearly bumped the Corsa in front. Paolo had looked confused as he explained that he did all the Duchess's washing for precisely that reason; her clothes were too delicate to go anywhere near the care home laundry.

Being the excellent liar she was, Sandra had acted upset and said that she would replace them out of her own pocket, knowing well that Paolo would refuse.

Sitting here, looking around Lidl car park, she wondered if that was the start of it. Plan A becoming plan B with plan C slowly cooking in the back of her mind. God, Paolo was never far from her mind nowadays. He was becoming her work in progress. She had even wheedled this car out of him, hinting that she could look after the Duchess better if she could get through the traffic quicker. He had agreed, quickly. Paolo was a nice bloke, and that was a first for her. A nice man was so rare, she was considering having him stuffed and stuck in an exhibition.

She pulled out on to Moss Road, thinking through her route

to the care home, via the back streets. The screaming and screeching of the opera continued, reminding her of the Duchess, sitting in her wheelchair like a queen on her throne, looking down on to Athole Gardens from the big bay window with Piero the cat sitting on the window ledge. Both looking very smug as if they deserved nothing less than the most expensive room in the care home.

The old dear never said very much. Occasionally she spoke a small smattering of Italian; an odd *vita mia*, a hello or a goodbye to Paolo, a thank you when Sandra fixed a hair that had come loose, when she handed her a cup of tea or a piece of Battenberg cake. Generally there was very little response, maybe a wave of the hand like she was dismissing a servant. That and a slow blink of individual false eyelashes – not the long thick tarty sort; nothing was tarty about the Duchess.

She was shrouded in mystique. It was rumoured she had been a famous opera singer in Italy. The home was only for actors and singers, so she had been a 'somebody'. She had been there longer than any of the staff, always the big room with its en suite. The young man who introduced himself to Sandra said he was Paolo, just Paolo, and 'this was the Duchess'. Sandra had choked back a snigger when she realized he was serious. He didn't say, 'I'm Ilaria's son', or 'this is my mother', or 'my mum'. Just, 'this is the Duchess'.

It must be nice to have a man to adore, Sandra thought and there was no doubt how much the Duchess adored Paolo. She would caress the side of his cheek, as he did up her shoes. He came in every day to help her dress, usually before the morning staff had started serving breakfast. He came again at night, to undress her and put her to bed. Sandra had thought that a bit odd at first, but devotion was devotion and she now ignored the jokes from the other carers about Paolo, Bates Motel and mothers.

Sandra knew that to get to Paolo, she needed to get the Duchess onside. Or get rid of her. Either would do.

The Panda got caught, of course, at the mouth of the Clyde Tunnel. Not the shady bit, but right in the suntrap. She felt her eyes burn. Sandra turned her attention to the CD, trying to listen and learn. She had asked Paolo about this opera and he had sat her down on the Duchess's big wide bed with its ocean of Italian linen and lace to explain. 'It's about a young poor boy who falls in love with a girl, but the girl has already fallen in love with the rich, handsome soldier.'

Sandra had looked back into Paolo's huge blue eyes but couldn't pluck up the courage to ask how the story ended. Did he get the girl in the end? Try as she might, she had no bloody idea what was going on in the opera. They could be at a summer picnic or dying of consumption. It all sounded the same to her.

Paolo had given her the CD so now she felt compelled to listen in case he asked. She had Googled but couldn't find any opera singer called Ilaria Girasole on the computer at the care home, but she must have been somebody. And must have been successful to afford to stay at Athole House.

One day, when she had first returned to work, she had plucked up courage to ask Paolo, 'So what did the Duchess do?' and his answer was 'You mean you don't recognize her?' He had smiled as he said it. He was speaking in true wonderment, not arrogance.

Sandra smiled and stayed quiet, hoping she seemed enigmatic rather than secretive. So, Sandra deduced, the Duchess must have been really famous in her day. She was now maybe in her late seventies, or early eighties but if she was an opera singer, which looked the case with her hair and make-up, that would explain why nobody at the home had heard of her. They were all skanks who worked there; no taste, no culture.

The traffic queue moved and Sandra pulled forward into the welcome darkness of the tunnel. Sandra liked the dark. She could always hide in the dark.

'So you finally decided.' DI Costello looked out the window of Archie's Mercedes to admire the ornate front door of Athole House. She knew it was some kind of old folk's home, having driven past it a hundred times, but she had never had cause to notice the nameplate. Or the huge bay windows that must have such magnificent views over the manicured lawns of Athole Gardens. It was certainly a beautiful setting, high on the hill for those no longer able to look after themselves or a husband getting to the end of his tether.

Like Archie Walker, Chief Procurator Fiscal.

'She's in there.' Walker nodded his head in the direction of the curved sandstone facade. 'One of the most difficult decisions I have ever had to make.'

'But in the end, it wasn't your decision, was it? I mean, not after she escaped, running down the road in her nightdress at three in the morning. Anything could have happened to her. You couldn't watch her twenty-four-seven, could you?'

Walker snorted. 'Costello? What do you mean "she escaped"? I have been married to that woman for thirty years. She did not "escape".'

Costello opened the window, the glass dropping with a dignified hum as warm still air drifted into the car. She did not want to think about the wife confined to a home while she, the new relationship, was sitting outside in the car, enjoying the sunshine. Truth be told, it really didn't bother her. She had not given Pippa the Alzheimer's. She had not made the decision to put her in a home. Costello was a fatalist not an opportunist. What came around went around, nothing could change that. So she looked at the crescent moons worn on the sandstone steps that ascended to the deep green mat at the front door. Although a five star hotel would be proud of that, it was still a prison by another name. It was HM Prison Barlinnie, with nice carpets.

From the roadside, Costello could see the big brass button of the bell, worn down to dull steel with years of use. The whole place had the look of a tobacco baron's townhouse, a Downtown Abbey in the middle of Glasgow, each brick paid for by the blood of slaves. She read the wording on the frosted glass, Athole House, in solid, rather stern font. No mention of its current use, a secure living facility.

She looked up. The weather was beautiful, only one small cloud scurrying across the infinite blue sky. It was the first day of the West End Festival and it looked like the weather was going to hold up for them. She didn't look at Archie when she spoke to him, directing her words instead out into the warm air of a dry Scottish summer. 'Your wife went AWOL, Archie. She left your house without your knowledge and did a fair impression of Usain Bolt down the street in her Marks and Sparks PJs. And she wasn't for coming back, was she? She—'

'Costello . . .' warned Walker, turning off the engine and the air con now that Costello had opened the window.

'Oh no, you couldn't catch her. You had to call us in and she managed to bite one constable before they rugby tackled her and got her into the van.' She turned to face him, 'So yes, she did escape. And no, you had no choice but to put her somewhere secure. Her home is already lost to her, Archie. The woman you married has already drifted off to some other place and that is very sad. But that doesn't exclude you from making the tough decisions. Or excuse you making the wrong ones,' she added.

'I know. You don't need to be quite so blunt about it.' Walker glanced at his mobile, wishing that something might save him from this hard-nosed logic.

'Well, it's a subject that people pussyfoot around. And it's not a subject you can pussyfoot around. That helps nobody.'

'Most people are sensitive about it. *Most* people.'

'Archie, she's in here getting fed. Getting her medication on time with somebody making sure she swallows it. You don't need to worry about her every waking moment. She will be well cared for. So instead of going home knackered after a full day – as full a day as you fiscals ever do . . .' Costello paused, realizing she was deviating from an unpleasant subject to one of her favourites. 'You will now get a good sleep. And it's not as if you haven't tried every option before this. All those carers. If you can't trust them with your house keys, why would you trust them with your wife?'

Archie Walker winced at the memory, embarrassed. The last carer had taken a brooch here, a ring there. Nothing that he would miss and no witnesses as nobody believes anything a dementia sufferer says. The guilt still hurt. He had never before doubted Pippa in the thirty years they were married, not once. But he had taken the word of a thief and a liar over that of his wife.

In some ways, he felt more conflicted over that than he did about the fledgling relationship he was trying to have with the woman sitting next to him.

Archie put Costello's window back up and removed the key from the ignition. 'Well, do you want to come in and see her and be nice? If you are going to be yourself, you can stay in the car. I need to drop her clothes off. All neatly labelled, like being at school again.'

'I thought I was only here for a brunch and a wee swatch at the parade. In all these years I've never been at it except to arrest folk. Do you want me in there? Moral support?'

'If you want. I don't think anybody in a million years would ever think that you and I might be in some kind of supportive relationship. I mean you look exactly what you are.'

'Hungry?' she offered.

'A hard-nosed wee cow.'

'Still taller than you,' Costello retorted smoothly, getting out the car, walking across the pavement to the warm, worn steps.

'Athole House. Retirement home for stars of stage and screen,' she read off the highly polished brass plate, subtly placed on the wrought iron railing at the bottom of the steps and she recalled some station gossip about Pippa Walker being an actress in her younger days, but as she had never got her Equity card she was limited to speaking three words or nodding twice or whatever the bloody rules were. Costello wished there were such rules for interviewing suspects. 'At least the sign is at the bottom of the steps, saves you the bother of climbing up to read it. I wonder if any of them die on the ascent. A bit like carving steps on the north face of the Eiger.'

'There's a lift at the back.'

'So they don't have to bring the bodies down the stairs.' She looked up at the corner windows over four stories above them. Bevelled, arched, they looked right out over the gardens. High over the city. 'What a great view to have as you go slowly gaga and have no retentive memory to appreciate it. Enjoy the scenery as you fill up your incontinence pads and ring bells that nobody ever answers so you are left to rot and decay in some old stinking armchair, the TV left on, sound blaring and the same episode of *Deal or No Deal* playing over and over again. Noel Edmonds wearing a shirt with some God awful pattern on it and the smell of boiled cabbage creeping under the bolted security door. Boiled cabbage, death, urine and Noel Edmonds. I'm off to Switzerland.'

'Oh, you are so cynical.'

'Sorry, I didn't mean to say any of that out loud.' She sounded genuinely contrite. 'But that was the way it was when my mum went into a home. That was local authority, of course, not a posh place like this. In here, they probably watch the *Antiques Roadshow*. Probably see their own kids flogging off the family silver to spend the dosh on gin.'

'Please stop talking.' Archie leaned over and pushed the bell, it resonated deep and loud in the hall behind.

'You rang, milord,' said Costello in mock seriousness. 'Do you think a butler will open it, a Hammer Horror butler with parchment yellow skin, red-rimmed eyes and a dead man stare? Or do you think it will be opened by—'

'Your mum must have been young, when she went into care?' Archie interrupted, knowing the question would halt her babbling.

Costello looked the other way. Archie had to strain to hear her. 'Quite young, I suppose. Younger than I am now. She had totally fried her brain with alcohol. She didn't know the day of the week. She kept thinking she was Bonnie. Or Clyde, depending on her mood, and that ranged from psychotic to dangerous.' She bent down to look through the letterbox, removing herself from Archie's gaze, uncomfortable with the conversation. He knew about her family, of course. The whole team at Partickhill Major Investigation did. But knowing about it was one thing. Talking about it was another. Costello suspected her family might be behind the subtle but definitely sideways shift to the proposed cold case unit. She was only too aware that there were folk about who could, and would, use her family against her. In the modern Police Scotland, it wasn't enough to get the job done; they had to be squeaky clean as well. Politically clean. No mavericks in the force, they all put their pens down and went home at 5 p.m., shoes neatly polished, all 'i's dotted. It was all down to that bloody James Kirkton, the new police czar. And it was rumoured that Kirkton was the best pal and golfing buddy of ACC Mitchum. Kirkton had been on Walker's case, constantly interfering in his running of the Fiscal Service and Police Scotland. Every complaint made by every low life piece of shite had now to be investigated to the hilt. Costello was sick to the back teeth explaining that sometimes people had an agenda for complaining; like being guilty. But they were all conscious that Partickhill and West Central were coming under special scrutiny. Like a bad smell that everybody was aware of but nobody knew exactly what was causing it. They weren't paranoid. They knew something was rotten.

The door opened, silently, catching Costello by surprise. A slim middle-aged woman, with crimson thread lips set to disapproval, stood like a custodian in her navy blue uniform, white apron and a starched hat. Costello, who hadn't seen a hat like that since she had the flu and watched the entire 'Carry On' box set, smirked. The badge said Matron Nicholson.

Matron?

Matron Nicholson gave her a look that was as soft as slate and half as empathetic.

'Your letterbox is very clean,' said Costello with a hint of dangerous cheerfulness.

'So it should be,' answered Matron Nicholson, adjusting the white badge, in case Costello had missed it. Then she turned her attention to the small, immaculately dressed man on the step, taking in his neatly ironed Fred Perry top, the chinos with a blade for a crease. The change in her expression was instant, her voice suddenly welcoming. 'Mr Walker, do come in. How are you?'

'I'm fine, fine. Thank you. And yourself?'

'Oh busy. I do believe your wife is up in the day room.' The matron softened her small lips into a reluctant smile but her dark eyes stayed as hard as ebony. 'Visiting is a little inconvenient at the moment, we are still clearing after breakfast.'

Costello glanced at her watch. It was half ten.

'I am dropping these clothes off, labelled as requested.' Archie lifted the bag.

'Oh well, we could do you a coffee? Do you want one sent up for you and your . . . friend? You could take Pippa to her room?' The matron gestured to Costello, looking past the bad scar on her forehead to the good suit, the neat blouse and sensed something official.

Archie tried to interject but was a millisecond too slow.

'Oh, no thanks. I can see you are busy. We'll nip up and say hello to Pippa but we have to go straight to the mortuary for a post-mortem. Interesting one, the body had been lying in a bath for eight weeks before it was found.'

'Oh, that's terrible,' said the matron, a hand going up to her throat, a gut reaction to the horror.

'Yeah, poor soul, settling in for a soak and shrugged off her mortal coil. All alone. She had no friends, so nobody even noticed she was missing, until the smell got too strong, of course, then the neighbours called in Rentokil. Eight weeks. Terrible to have no friends to notice.' Costello allowed her face to fall into wistful reflection. 'She was a retired matron, I think.'

Another flicker of a smile. 'Well, I will leave you to it. Please sign the book on your way out.' The matron scribbled on the leatherbound book that rested on the highly polished table behind her, glanced at her fob watch and noted the time. As she looked up she caught a close glimpse of the arrangement of roses, looking rather bedraggled in their vase. 'They need a good water.'

'Can't get the staff these days,' empathized Costello, and took the heavily carpeted stairs two at a time.

DCI Colin Anderson looked at the picture of Paige Riley lying in its thin file, missing for a week now and wondered why they bothered. They didn't have a chance of identifying her with this photograph; it was years out of date, and the years involved were those when the features changed the most. She looked like a kid in this, she might look like Cara Delevingne now. But he doubted it. She'd be heroin thin, with bad skin, worse teeth and some chronic infection festering in her lungs. Nobody had noticed her go missing except for a woman who put a pound in her plastic cup every morning outside Hillhead Station. Nobody was waiting for her to come back. It had been seven years since somebody cared enough to take a photograph, and from the deadness behind those eyes, it was a fair time before that since somebody had made her smile.

For now, the case of Paige Riley was open but inactive. Left standing still until something came up and that might take so long she might drift into the thicker file on Anderson's desk; the proposed cases for review for a new cold case initiative, CCAT He was being touted as the cold case assessment coordinator, CACC.

Unfortunate initials, he thought.

He had a quick flick through the cases. All the likely suspects were there, a few unlikely. Some that nobody would ever prove and two that nobody in their right mind would touch with a bargepole. The words 'poison' and 'chalice' crossed his mind. He swore loudly. Another wee nudge that a career was now cruising in two directions: sideways and nowhere.

Did he care?

Not as much as he should have.

Maybe it was for the best. He felt like a cat running out of lives. The idea of sitting behind a desk and finishing at five p.m. was starting to appeal.

DCI Colin Anderson was now a very rich man. He had been the sole beneficiary of Helena McAlpine's will, give or take a few grand here and there.

Life was a lot easier. Everything was easier. Everybody had room to breathe and blossom. Colin and his wife Brenda were living apart. Anderson and his daughter Claire at the townhouse on the terrace while Brenda and Peter had chosen to remain at the family home on the south side. Ten minutes apart in quiet traffic. And, proving that family dynamics and women in general were a mystery to him, they were more of a family now than they had ever been. They might not be living as man and wife, but their friendship had strengthened. They could now laugh together.

Brenda had not wanted to move. Colin was not all that sure he had asked her. But they had more quality time, going out, the four of them for a meal had become a weekly occurrence – as it can when money is no object. Peter had been working hard at his National Fives and didn't want to change school. Claire had spent the last few months before the summer break at a private school with extra tuition to help her through the coursework that she had missed. She had not liked the school, had not fitted in, but it was the quickest route for her to achieve her dream and attend Glasgow School of Art.

Nesbit, the arthritic Staffie, floated between the two addresses, getting fed at both and exercised at neither. Which suited him just fine.

Colin had never been a particularly solitary person, maybe because he had never had much opportunity. But at the terrace he could lie down with a good book in peace, save the occasional rumble of traffic along the Great Western Road or the sudden sound bite from the TV as Claire opened the door of her bedroom and slipped up to the studio on the top floor. But the big advantage of the house on the terrace was never having to leave the room just to get some thinking space.

His brain had been calmed and charmed by the tranquillity of the big white house. It had absorbed them. Now they could all live with the drama of his life, but be no part of it. And he felt that he owed his family that.

Life was good.

Moving over to the window, he looked down at the small throng of journalists and photographers, feeling some relief that he would never be promoted into Mitchum's job. Poor sod, forced to be nice to fork-tongued scum like Kirkton.

He saw some movement in the crowd, a young woman snaking her way through them. Devoid of handbag, and phone, looking a little dishevelled. Two minutes later he heard the discordant ringing of phones downstairs, immediately followed by his own phone, and the rattle of DC Wyngate in the incident room next door scraping his chair back, footsteps coming to his own office door. Maybe not such a quiet day after all.

Philippa Walker was reading a book. She was sitting comfortably in a wing-armed easy chair in the corner of the day room, under a faded framed photograph of some aged Scottish actress in a tartan hat meeting the Queen. Pippa had her head down, legs crossed at the knee. A paperback sat on the blue flowered skirt that covered her lap. It was a Maeve Binchy book, a bit tattered showing it had been well read, well enjoyed. And it was upside down.

Costello crept into the room, the deep pile cream carpet silencing her footfall. She was impressed by the decor; the lush gold and marble, clean and fresh, no hint of boiled cabbage or stale urine. She stood in the middle, smiling vaguely at each of the six residents and hoping to God that none of them would react. Archie was struggling, hanging back at the door – too scared to come in. In case that made it real.

'Why don't you put her stuff up in her bedroom,' Costello said, pointing to the bag of unidentifiable, but properly labelled contents. He didn't need to be asked twice, he was off. His feet hitting the heavy carpet on the stairs, the old wood underneath squeaking and creaking with every step.

'Hello Pippa,' Costello said, inclining her head to catch the older lady's eyeline.

Pippa seemed totally unaware. Of who Costello was. Or if she was there. Then she raised her head, smiled her lovely smile and went back to the book balanced on her knees. Her fingers drifted up to the long single strand of pearls hanging from her neck. This was her thing, her obsession, her 'tell' when stressed. It was distressing to think that Pippa had enough awareness to know that there was something very wrong with her and the few functioning neurones that remained took solace with the familiar; her beads. She played with them, rattled them, jiggled them constantly. That was bad enough but Pippa looked so . . . normal. Her short blonde hair was neatly cut, she had a healthy pink blush in her cheeks and a lively sparkle in her blue eyes. There were no clues; no signposts to the horrific disease that had robbed her of herself.

Costello felt awkward, aware of the silent scrutiny of the others in the room, even the long-haired black and white cat was giving her the once over. She strolled over to the window to admire the view. The single pane of old glass let a refreshing draft of air through the room. The view of the gardens below was chocolate box pretty. She thought again of the obscene amount of money it must have cost to build this house here on the top of the hill. Was it worth it, just to look down on everybody else? She looked up at the sky, her cheek to the glass of the cold window pane. No sign of the heavy rains that had caused millions of pounds worth of damage earlier in the year. The good weather was holding for the parade. Down in the West End, the participants would be applying glitter and tuning instruments, having last-minute rehearsals, climbing onto coaches before strolling up towards the Botanic Gardens. Partickhill Station was taking on the role of community liaison for the event and West End Central was overseeing the security. The terrorist threat was omnipresent when crowds of people gathered. She hoped they had a quiet day.

She glanced at her watch. Ten thirty-five. All was calm and peaceful in the gardens. Green, lush, disturbed only by birdsong and the mildest of winds. The residents of Athole House, deep in their post-breakfast slumber. The cat purred softly.

Somebody growled behind her. She looked round, checking each resident in turn but nobody had moved. All were stalk still. Silent. Only the clickety click of pearl upon pearl. They could have been playing statues with her. If she turned round again, they would have swapped seats and returned to stone.

But no, Pippa was back in her own world with her pearls and Maeve Binchy upside down. On one side of the marble fireplace, a thin old man sat curled in a high-backed easy chair. His red tartan shirt matched the dried flowers arranged in the hearth. Costello caught herself staring at the scarred, puckered face with raw burned skin. The red shirt was pulled tight up to his neck, the sleeves well down over his wrists, a white glove on either hand. One eye, the right, darted round the day room like a crow's searching for a day old lamb. His vision was trying to settle on Costello. The left eye was a creased narrow slit, devoid of sight. As he saw Costello his head slumped slightly, his hands falling into his lap as one swollen foot escaped from its tartan slipper to rest on the carpet. She suspected he had adjusted his posture to get a better look at her.

The fat man on the other side of the fireplace coughed. A drinker, from the look of his ruddy complexion. They were like two ugly bookends. Or the couple that lived in the weather house, close without ever being together. One fat, one thin. She vaguely recognized the fat one. Take off five stone, forty years and stick him in a shiny suit with shoulder pads and he might be that comedian her granny had liked on the TV. Chic somebody? His wit had seemed unscripted, a surprise to his straight man. Or was that part of the act? Now he looked like he'd have trouble telling the time, never mind a joke. If this was what old age did for you, you could keep it. Chic and Chas. The Cheeky Chappies.

Behind the door, in the opposite corner, two old ladies born of seaside postcards were snoozing rhythmically; one fat-bellied with a red jumper and a round, steroid-swollen face that inclined at an angle giving her the appearance of a Christmas card Robin. The other was thin and frail, her legs so narrow at the ankles, they looked like they would snap. A canary of a woman, her fingers pecking at her yellow blanket in her sleep. They were both happy in their snoozing where they had chosen to see out their final days. But how they could sleep through the rattling of Pippa's pearls was anybody's guess. Probably had their hearing aids turned off.

Costello looked at her watch again, ten thirty-eight. The constant but irregular noise was getting on her nerves. God knew how Archie had put up with it. She could hear the background hum of a fan somewhere, buzzing on and off, no doubt helping the drafty window to circulate the air; old people and their bad digestion and public private habits. They would be better opening the window, but it was the old sash type and they were one floor up. Some health and safety boffin had no doubt drawn up a risk assessment in triplicate and nailed the window shut. Costello could imagine herself tying the curtains together to form a rope ladder and make her escape. The poor buggers must get desperate in here.

Costello turned round, tucking her blouse into her navy blue trousers, adjusting her handbag over her shoulder, flattening down the collar of her jacket and wishing that bloody Archie would reappear. She had come out for a Sunday brunch and to see the parade, her stomach was starting to protest loudly. She paced once up, once down, then moved towards the woman who sat in the bay of the other window, far back, as far away from the others as if any little solitude she could get was precious to her. The woman certainly smelled differently from

the others, of expensive perfume, lightly worn. Costello thought
she recognized the scent. Fracas? That was a hundred pounds
a throw. The styled ebony hair was dyed, her make-up was
immaculate and highlighted the contours of a face that must
have been beautiful once, but even now, was striking in its
presence. Her jewellery was minimal but genuine, quality. She
looked a formidable character. This might be the Duchess
Archie had mentioned once. She reminded Costello of some
grand old dame of the theatre. One with her best days behind
her but clinging onto the memories the best she could.

The jet eyes opened and stared at Costello. A faint smile
curled the bright red lips. The gnarled hand, ringed and decor-
ated, floated out like Nosferatu's. Bent, withered fingers
reached out for her, then stopped in mid-air. The fingers started
to dance. The lips worked, she took a deep breath and
fought to pull faint words from her throat: '*Pietrino, finalmente
sei venuto.*'

'Sorry?' said Costello smiling, trying to ignore the hand,
watching the door, and wishing that Archie would hurry up.
Then she heard rushing footsteps along the hall. Not from the
stairs though. A care assistant appeared at the door, a middle-
aged lady in a blue uniform hastily tying a plastic white apron
behind her back, hurrying across the thick pile carpet in light
blue crocs. Fake crocs, Costello noticed. She had seen the
notice from Trading Standards.

'Oh God, I am soo, sooo late. The bloody traffic is terrible
out there,' she said with the flashing smile of the professionally disinterested while pulling her fingers through her short
brown hair. 'Are you here to visit Pippa? I haven't seen you
before.'

'Just popped in to see how she was doing,' lied Costello.

'Thank God. I thought you were from the management for
a minute.' She relaxed, catching her breath. 'Couldn't even
stop for a fag.'

That was a lie, judging by the smell that hung round the
woman like a halo. 'Are you one of the nurses?'

'I wish. I'm Sandra, one of the carers. If you are looking
for Pippa's designated carer, that will be Lisa, wee dark girl.
Got a dolphin tattoo on her arm, you can't miss her.' Sandra

shuffled over to the lady in the wheelchair and flicked the brake with the toe of her croc. 'We are so short staffed.'

'Way of the world these days,' agreed Costello, standing to one side, as the wheelchair and its passenger glided past. The dark eyes cast a dismissive glance at Costello and the hand drifted through the air, playing its invisible piano andante.

She left a suggestion of Fracas behind her, and took something just as subtle with her. Maybe somebody less sensitive to human emotion would have missed it, but Costello sensed the tension had eased, the atmosphere relaxed, as if a suspect had realized that the difficult question had not been asked and the conversation had moved safely on. Chic and the robin woman were staring into space, canary lady was still worrying her blanket. Pippa was still head down in her Maeve Binchey, rattling her beads. Only Scarface was different, his posture had relaxed, his lips curled at one corner. He was looking at the spot where the wheelchair had been, amused, having driven her out by the power of his will.

His dark eye flickered. Costello wanted to walk out, but felt fixed in his stare. Threatening? Curious? Scared? She stared back, stony faced.

A loud screech made them jump.

Costello was at the window in an instant, hearing the slam of a car door; something was happening in Athole Gardens. Costello pulled out her phone, saying, 'Even for parade day, it's a bit early for a drunk and disorderly.' She could see two squad cars park up at the end of Athole Lane but she could see nothing more, not from here. She turned round. There was another change in Scarface's demeanour, the look in his eye. Pleading? Needy for an escape away from this life? 'I'll tell you all about it next time I am in,' Costello whispered conspiratorially as she passed him on her way out. Heading down the main stairs, she could see Archie's shadow coming down from above. Maybe he had heard the commotion too, but she hurried away before he could catch up and remind her she was off duty. The matron was still in the main hall, another one who had not appeared to have moved position. She gave Costello a thin-lipped little smirk before flicking a look at the clock high on the opposite wall. A silent accusation: You didn't stay long?

'Duty calls,' said Costello, lifting her mobile to her ear.

Matron tried not to cross her arms in disapproval.

'The Italian looking lady . . .?'

'The Duchess?' Matron Nicholson confirmed.

'Of where?'

'That would be confidential.'

'And the old gentleman, sits in the corner? Badly scarred face? Was he ever a cop, do you know? Or is that also confidential?'

'Mr Kilpatrick? No. To be in this establishment, he would need to be a member of the Theatre Trust or the Actors Guild.' She softened a little. 'Well, anything connected with the stage nowadays, if they have the money. So, not a cop. No . . .' But something in her attitude had altered, a flicker of respect.

'Maybe he was an actor who played a cop? Probably murdered in *Taggart*. I bet they all were at one time or another, eh?' Costello joked.

The matron's face cracked a little. 'Mr Kilpatrick is one of our characters.' She was going to add something, but the thought died before it grew to action. Her hand had lifted to her cheek, a comforting rub, subconsciously connecting his name with a sore face.

Costello said goodbye and was out the door, jogging down the hill following the curve of the railings at the north end of the garden, her footsteps quickening as she saw another unmarked car arrive. The tape was already up.

Here was a story she could tell Scarface all about. He might not be a cop. But that little look on the matron's face spoke volumes. Mr Kilpatrick was no stranger to criminality.

Going up in the lift, Sandra Ryme checked her make-up in the mirrored wall. She was, as her mum would have said, making some effort. The cake might be a bit bashed, hanging in its Lidl's bag round the handle of the wheelchair, but the old dear wouldn't notice.

Sandra had got a fright when she walked into the day room and clocked the spikey-haired blonde in the officious suit. She recognized those calculating eyes that flickered everywhere, checking this and assessing that, seeing everything and forgetting nothing. Sandra had thought she might have been from the Pearcy Kirkton senior management team, coming to invite her for a performance review to kick her arse for yet another misdemeanour. But as she got close Sandra had spotted the casual uneasiness of the unfamiliar visitor to the facility, the guest that did not want to be here, the reluctant, the guilty and the neglectful. It was logical to Sandra that if she was new, she must be here to visit Pippa Walker, as she was the facility's newest resident.

Sandra herself had only worked here for a couple of years, a lifetime as a carer with no real qualifications or monetary reward. She had worked in much worse places than Athole House, home for retired stars of stage and screen with prudent health insurance. Or were rich enough to be self-financing like the Duchess. She had class and money. And jewellery. Good jewellery. And she, Sandra Ryme, was her designated carer, which was a good start. She couldn't believe her luck when Lisa told her Paolo was the Duchess's only son. And was single. And best of all, the Duchess was gravely ill. And really old.

It was perfect.

Sandra looked at her watch. Paolo would be round to give his mother her lunch later. He never, ever, let the Duchess eat with the other residents with their slurpy, dribbly habits.

Sandra squared up her blue nylon tunic, dusting a few doughnut crumbs from the front. She checked her eyeliner in the mirrored panel in the lift, pulling faces to check that she didn't have bits of doughnut caught in her teeth. The lift jolted to a stop and the door rattled to the side, in need of oil. She might mention it to Paolo, saying she was concerned it might jar the Duchess's spine. That would get her Brownie points.

Sandra smoothed down her short brown hair and checked her lips again. She daydreamed what she could do next as she wheeled the Duchess slowly along the long hall to 'Tosca', her own room – the biggest, most expensive room, right at the front of the home and with best view over the gardens. There was money in that family. As she pushed her along, Sandra looked down the back of the Duchess's neck, at the red and black silk scarf and thought, with admiration and longing, of the solitaire diamond brooch that pinned it at the front.

As she unlocked the door of Tosca, the twinge in her wrist reminded her of that beautiful Wednesday when she came back to her work, six weeks after Deke Kilpatrick had broken her wrist with one swing of his good arm. Paolo had taken Sandra quietly to one side, and told her in his lovely soft voice that he was going to request that she became the Duchess's designated carer, to keep her safe from the likes of Kilpatrick. She went into nice mode and had replied that she was honoured but didn't think the management would allow it; she was not long enough in the job. He had then said that any attempt by the management to block the reassignment would be met with a few comments about the management's failure in their duty of care to keep their staff safe from a resident who had a history of violence. And he had held her gaze with those big blue eyes of his. Sandra didn't think she had taken a deep breath since. God knew she recognized blackmail when she heard it. She was a master.

She looked at the clock, ignoring the time while admiring the four silver spires. It was a fine example of a Gothic revival mantel clock. Two grand at least. According to an auctioneer's website. Two grand!

She parked the wheelchair in the curve of the bay window so the Duchess could enjoy the view, and switched the kettle on. The Duchess sat, stony faced, alone in her world, her right hand up, still playing its silent piano. Sandra then picked up her duster and looked round at the glass-topped dressing table, the bottles of Fracas perfume, the tubs of luxurious cream and the locked jewel boxes. She wiped underneath them, making sure she set them all down where they had been. Paolo would notice if it wasn't exactly right, just as he would notice if anything went missing. Which was a bit of an issue.

He noticed detail. He always dressed the Duchess in the style of the women she admired: Jackie Onassis, the Queen, Wallis Simpson. Today her ebony hair was pulled back into a whalebone clip, cottage loaf style and her make-up was pancake white, lips a deep ruby red, like a Disney queen. Her bright eyes were circled in blended kohl, the eyelids were painted bright azure, then blended to lend some colour to the faded cornflower blue of her eyes. And the eyelashes; each had been added separately and then mascaraed over, three times. Paolo had offered to teach Sandra how to do that. Sandra eagerly agreed, thinking he meant for herself, and then felt embarrassed when she realized Paolo had meant to show her how to do the Duchess's eyelashes.

Of course he had.

These were theatre people, and good make-up was part of that job. To be fair, he had then offered to teach her a few tricks of the trade but he hadn't mentioned it since. She needed to get some time alone with him. That one time when he had drawn his forefinger down the side of her cheek, saying something about her cheekbones, her spine had tingled. Funny how all those men, panting and puffing and stinking and sweating, Sandra had felt nothing. Well, not until they had fallen asleep and she had emptied their wallets. But one touch of one fingertip from an Italian bloke, and she felt as though her legs might give way.

Sandra draped the olive green cashmere pashmina round the old lady's thin shoulders, over the soft folds of her duck egg blue dress. Then she pinned it with the diamond brooch. The red scarf was discarded, it didn't match her room the way the pashmina did. Sandra loved the Duchess's clothes, and their muted colours. Even the rug under the wheelchair was the gentlest of green, marbled in white.

Sandra had a go at humming the tune from the opera, trying to better herself as she filled the china teapot from the kettle. The Duchess liked to have a cup of Earl Grey with her cake, a napkin across her lap or held gently to her chin.

The pashmina had slipped so Sandra straightened it up and gave the shoulders a little massage, thinking that the Duchess was getting thinner by the day. The old lady closed her eyes in gratitude, her right hand raised to clasp Sandra's fingers – a gentle squeeze, a little acknowledgement for how she looked after her, and Sandra surprised herself by the wee stab of guilt that pricked her conscience.

Sandra poured the tea into a porcelain cup; the cake sat on a doily on a matching side plate that was then placed on the

wooden carved table that was a bugger to dust. Sandra stood
it to the side of the Duchess's chair, then returned to her duties.
A little face powder had been spilled on the dresser, covering
the glass like a fall of fine snow. As she dusted, she heard a
car go past the home at speed, screech to a halt, then a door
slam. Of course it was parade day and the traffic was snarly
out there. There had probably been an accident.

She stopped dusting mid swipe, her eyes drawn to some
movement down in the lane, where the 4x4 families munched
on their artisan breads while moaning about their gluten intol-
erance. As she watched, a woman came out the back door of
a flat on Athole Lane, right at the extreme of her vision, a
police car, lights flashing blocked the entry into the lane.
Sandra looked round to ensure that the Duchess was safe in
her own wee world, then she cupped her hand against the glass
and pulled up her uniform so she could climb on the ledge to
get a better view. She saw the woman she had met downstairs,
the one with the short spikey hair and the official looking suit
walking quickly, mobile in hand, talking nineteen to the dozen
while looking back and forth. She looked like she would take
no shit from anybody.

One to be watched.

Sandra leaned her forehead on the glass, enjoying the coldness of it against the heat of the day. She watched a strip of
blue and white tape go up, the woman ducked under it and
vanished into a group of people. Sandra slid down. The
Duchess was staring right past her, out the window, her blue
eyes focused on an empty sky.

PC Graham sat on the front desk, settling down to a fresh
brew of tea and a full box of Jaffa Cakes for his break. It
was that kind of day; parade day and the madness had started
already. There was an incident kicking off down Athole Lane,
two units were attending. For now he was vaguely listening
to Amy Niven's story. He had been young once, he had been
there. Being a man, he couldn't help but notice how pretty
she was. Being a father he couldn't help but worry about
young students getting their drinks spiked. And of course, the
ACC had phoned from outside so he phoned Wingnut Wyngate

in the CID suite and he in turn had gone off to find DCI
Anderson who had last been heard, in his own office, swearing
loudly.

Amy Niven was voluble, enthusiastically describing the green
matchstick men hanging on the ceiling when the private door
of the outer office banged open. DCI Colin Anderson's handsome face did not look good when unhappy, and he was not
happy at being interrupted. He had grey patches under his eyes,
shadows of the sleepless. Graham put his hand up to stop Amy
Niven in mid-flow. She started giggling.

Anderson called Graham through, staying behind the
one-way glass. 'Who is she?'

'Amy Niven, she's nineteen. She seems to know you. And
Mitchum said—'

'Yeah, I heard what he said. Where does she know me
from?' asked Anderson, 'I don't recognize her.'

'She's not clear on that. She's very clear on the aliens
though. The Safer Society might need a new initiative for that,
you never know . . .' Graham's voice trailed off lamely, realizing that Anderson was muttering something about there being
a first for everything.

'And she hasn't got to the end of it yet. She says that she
was abducted by aliens and the aliens wanted her to tell you.
She is very insistent about that.'

As Anderson watched her, Amy slid off the seat and
recovered herself before she hit the floor.

'What is the exact protocol here, sir?' asked Graham, joining
the DCI at his viewpoint behind the window. 'Do I ask her if
she wants a coffee?'

'That would make sense if she was drunk. But God knows
what she might have taken, or been slipped. We need to get
a medic down to find out what it is and how it might affect
her.' He rubbed his face, tired. There was a lot to be said for
living alone with your teenage daughter, but the hours they
kept was not one of them. 'What do we know about her?'

Graham leaned across and turned round the computer screen
so that Anderson could see the Facebook page for Amy Niven,
age nineteen, a classics student at Glasgow University, who
had 567 friends and had been to secondary schools in Glasgow

and Fife. She wasn't in a relationship and she liked *Breaking
Bad*.

'God,' said Anderson, 'young people today. All life is a
goldfish bowl. Take her upstairs and I'll be with you in
a minute.'

DCI Colin Anderson looked at the girl opposite him, thinking
his own daughter Claire was not that much younger than Amy.
He had an A4 piece of paper. DC Gordon Wyngate had
compiled a very concise list of all that was known about Amy,
when and where she was last seen by her friends on the
Saturday night, her mother's opinion of her and that she had
a thyroid condition and had not had any of her medication.

Wyngate sat in his usual position, with his back at the
window, rubbing his jaw. Anderson knew he liked that seat
because his skin was still sensitive to strong sunlight after
suffering a chemical injury last year, and now the constable
was suffering a bad bout of toothache. Between him and
Mulholland's leg, they were turning into the walking wounded.

DCI Colin Anderson himself was sitting on the blue plastic
chair, comfortable, upending the piece of folded paper over
and over against his thigh, studying the girl opposite. She was
sitting with her eyes closed, unaware of his gaze, smiling
slightly to herself. He had tried to follow her story while
thinking how many ways he could kill Gordon Wyngate, Arran
Graham, ACC Mitchum and James Kirkton and in what order
he would do it in. Slowly. Painfully. With no mercy whatsoever.
Twisting their limbs and dicing them in a million tiny pieces
while playing Adele at full volume. That would hurt, they
would soon be begging for death.

Despite his benign demeanour, Colin Anderson could be
very vengeful when he wanted to be.

According to her friends, Amy had spent the previous afternoon watching them prep for their participation in the West
End parade. They were doing Zumba on a float for charity,
and had spent the day tweaking their costumes, then gone out
for a drink up on Ashton Lane, working their way up towards
Vinicombe Street. At some point, somebody had started a
drinking game and more people had joined in. Kate thought

Amy had gone off with Jo, Jo thought Amy was with Nick. Nick agreed that he and Amy were together until half ten when he called it a night. He had left with somebody called Russell and Russell had confirmed all stories. Wyngate was very good at this pedantic checking and cross-checking. From ten thirty onwards, nobody knew where Amy was. Least of all Amy.

Anderson considered green lighting a CCTV request but first he had to establish what exactly had gone on, and why she was so coherent in her story about aliens. And if a crime had been committed. Or had she just been spliffed out of her mind?

Now, a little over twelve hours after she was last seen, she was still insisting that she had been abducted by aliens and she needed to tell Colin Anderson all about it. Why him? The aliens had told her. Amy repeated this as earnestly as she repeated her name and address when requested.

Anderson couldn't place the girl; she was not in the Police Scotland system. Under observation she was calm, happy to wait, amusing herself with thoughts that made a broad smile drift across her face as she looked at the ceiling. Then she would frown as if some reality had penetrated whatever drug-induced state she was in. Occasionally her right heel tapped the lino, her knee pumping. She would look up again, her eyes to the heavens, her loose brown hair falling back over her ears revealing her small heart-shaped face, a young face; she could have been twelve years old. Dressed in typical festival boho student chic, she was wearing head to toe vintage lace, different layers, a vest top, a blouse, a cardigan, a longer skirt that dragged on the ground as she walked, a shorter skirt, with frayed scalloped edges, over the top of that. Nothing matched, all varying shades of cream: white, ivory, oyster, taupe. The overall effect made her resemble an overstuffed but pretty scarecrow. Round her wrists and neck were a tumble of fine chains and seed pearls over the slight swelling on the front of her neck that might be related to her thyroid problem. Anderson wondered if this had altered the rate she had metabolized whatever drug she had taken, or been slipped. Hopefully once her mind cleared, she would remember. When Wyngate had pressed her friends for details, they said categorically that Amy didn't touch drugs, and he was of the opinion that they would have said if she did, now that she had ended up a victim of something.

She was a bright girl, stable family, and her academic record showed no sign of physical or psychological stress. She seemed aware that she was in some state of altered consciousness but had no idea why. There was something in her memory that troubled her when she tried to focus on it, but it remained safely out of reach. He passed her a plastic cup of water. She took it, the shaking of her hand rippling the surface.

Anderson checked the clock, placed low on the wall so he could glance at it without the interviewee noticing and taking offence.

'So Amy, do I know you from somewhere?' Anderson leaned forward, trying to detect any scent on her breath. Garlic? Wine? He smiled at her, seeing that her cardigan was buttoned wrongly, the ruffling at the neck of her blouse suggested that might be wrong too. This could be a nothing rather than a something; she could have been sick down a toilet and not been coherent enough to tidy herself up afterwards. He looked at Wyngate, signalling him to pay attention. 'So where do you live? Where is home?'

'Carnoustie.'

'Don't think I've ever been to Carnoustie.' He gave her his beguiling smile that calmed dogs and stroppy pensioners.

'No point in going there unless you play golf. We lived here before.' She recalled that clearly, biting her lip in concentration.

'OK, so what did you want to talk to me about?'

She hesitated, blinking a few times, as if she was catching a glimpse of the memory, through an ever-changing mist. Then she shrugged, took a sip of water. 'What day is it today?'

'Sunday.'

'I can't remember.' She bit her lip again but this time she was really finding it difficult to concentrate. She frowned, then rubbed at her face with the palm of her hand.

'Were you with friends? Or family?' Anderson prompted, knowing the answer but keen to see if her memory was gaining any clarity.

Amy recognized solid ground now. 'Yes, I was with two pals from uni, we were hoping to stay at Jo's mum's. They were . . . Oh God, I can't remember.' She shook her head as if she was clearing her mind. 'Sunday? Does the parade go off today?' She glanced at a watch that was not there.

Anderson nodded.

'What happened to Saturday?'

'Well, you had a glass of wine, with some friends from uni. You were up Ashton Lane.'

'We were listening to a band. They weren't very good so we went outside. It was very warm.' Amy tilted her head on one side, eyes closed, confused. 'Then I walked away. I don't recall why. To the car park behind the lane, I do recall that, you know the one? Lilly something?'

He nodded, his arms unfolded, leaning in, the paper now folded up in one hand, inviting her confidence.

'But then . . .' She smiled, her mood changed immediately. 'I woke up and there was an alien standing over me. I was lying down. The sky was really blue, incredibly blue. There were little green aliens high above me that moved in the sky.' Her eyes opened wide. 'They were so quiet, so deathly quiet . . .' She shook her head a little, the memory making her shiver.

'And where was this?' asked Anderson, glancing at Wyngate, the same thought going through both their minds, wondering about the quality of whatever she had been smoking.

'I don't know. But I think, I think it was here?'

'Here?'

'Here on earth.'

'Well, the sky is red on Mars,' added Wyngate in all seriousness, getting a dirty look from his boss. 'A kind of reddy brown, if we are being accurate . . .'

'Have you been there? Mars?' Amy beamed at him, looking for a kindred spirit. 'Mars is beyond the stars.'

'Err no,' said Wyngate, shaking his head then stopping abruptly as a bolt of toothache shot through him.

'OK, so how did you know he was an alien?' asked Anderson trying to get the conversation on point, trying to get it over and done with.

Amy Niven shrugged. 'He had dark eyes, the alien. Black. Silver.' She pointed at her own face, outlining another shape of face with her podgy fingers. 'Huge dark eyes.'

'We can get a sketch artist?' suggested Wyngate.

'Where from, Roswell?' snapped Anderson.

But Amy was talking again. 'I had no idea what happened, one minute I was down here then I was up there with him and he was going to dissect me.' She nodded and tapped the palm of her hand on her chest. 'He was going to dissect me to see how humans worked. But it didn't hurt, it was lovely, it was warm and lovely.'

Anderson raised an eyebrow at Wyngate; 'dissect' was a very precise word.

'And he was all dressed in black, a silvery black.' Amy pulled out her own blouse, feeling the fabric.

'Makes a change from the little green men,' Anderson joked.

'No, I told you that the little green men were up, above me, in the blue sky. He was a big, silver, black alien. With a pointy face and . . . well, you know . . .'

'What?'

She bit her tongue, looking very young again. 'Sorry, I can't recall what I was going to say.'

'Was he good looking?'

'Kind of, yes, I suppose, if that's your type: aliens, silvery and hot and h . . .' She nodded smiling. 'He was still attached to something.' She looked up at the strip lights in the ceiling, checking if she herself was attached to something. 'Like pipes that ran from him to the sky and the sky was so, so blue, with the green men. I thought that maybe he couldn't breathe in our atmosphere or something.' She sighed.

'And why did he want you to talk to me?'

She shrugged. 'He said your name, Colin Anderson. He said you would be here.' She didn't elaborate.

'Amy, would you mind if we got a doctor to take some blood from you?'

'No, not at all. He already gave me something to take the pain away, so I am not feeling so bad at the moment.'

Anderson was holding his breath as he watched Amy's hand float down to her knee.

'OK,' said Anderson slowly, as Wyngate pulled out his phone. 'What pain, Amy? What pain are you feeling?' he asked gently, the whole tone of the interview had changed now.

'Well, like I said, he was going to dissect me and put me back together again.' She laughed a little, and drifted away, suddenly very sleepy. Her small fingers were ruffling up the fabric of her skirt.

Anderson's next question was interrupted by Wyngate's phone ringing. Amy snorted and succumbed to sleep. Anderson found himself humming a few bars of 'Life on Mars'.

Wyngate's call was quick. 'We need to go, sir. Now. I will get the doc to come over. That was Costello and we really do need to go. Incident, sir.'

'I thought Costello was off today, was she not going to watch the parade with Archie?'

'Something has come up.'

'That's fine, you two go and I can stay here until you get back,' Amy offered, now wide awake again. Whatever she was on was wearing off, she was wriggling uncomfortably and rubbing at her knee.

'OK, well, we are going to get you to the hospital to get you checked out. A police car will get you through the traffic OK. You mother will meet you there.'

Amy grimaced, pulling her foot up onto the chair and lifting up the longest of her skirts. Her knee was a swollen blue black ball, puffy and engorged, bright red blood under the surface of her skin outlined the position of her patella, and Anderson could see a bold black line snaking between the freckled skin. There was a deeper shade of violet on the muscle of her thigh, the imprint of fingers very clear.

It looked incredibly painful.

'So, Wyngate? A nutter running around pretending to be an alien or an alien running around pretending to be a nutter? Any ideas.'

The digital clock in the car showed eleven thirteen when Anderson got out the car after the five-minute journey. He slipped his dark jacket on over his white shirt, making sure that his tie was tucked in. This was a public location, and a smart Police Scotland was important PR; so he was told. The first thing that struck him was that Costello, supposedly on a day off, looked exactly the same as she did at work. His DI, dressed in a fine French navy trouser suit and a white blouse, was arguing with Archie Walker about something. They stopped when they saw his Beamer. The fiscal nodded in greeting then walked away, leaving Costello to march towards him, pulling her blonde hair into a small ponytail and securing it with an elastic band. Just as she would if she was at a crime scene. Her eyelids had the merest touch of blue colouring, but no amount of make-up could take the Arctic coldness away from her grey eyes. Anderson was never very observant about such things; it was Archie Walker who had pointed out Costello's thousand-mile death stare. Anderson would have thought that in itself was enough to stop the fledgling relationship dead in its tracks. Walker would find out to his cost that Costello's soul, like her mind, existed only in monochrome.

He stood at the end of the lane for a moment, the tenements on either side blocking out the sun. On the left they ran into an unending row of Victorian flats, those on the right broke to turn on to Bowmont Terrace. This was an old tree-lined lane, the termination of all the gardens. Now cars crept along to garages secreted in the long continuous wall that originally had only the garden doors. The doors themselves showed every type of security lock.

Costello's grey eyes sparkled black and silver when her expression was as grave as it was now. She looked otherworldly. Like one of Amy's bloody aliens. Anderson wondered what that girl had actually seen, in a city where a fancy dress parade was kicking off the next day. Maybe that question was academic now. The injury to her leg was real, that damage had been done by human hand: blood and flesh. She'd remember soon enough. He wondered what was happening to her at the hospital.

But that was not his case. DS Vik Mulholland was desk-bound for the moment. DC Gordon Wyngate had his head screwed on. Between the two of them they would get to the bottom of it. For the moment, Amy Niven was being cared for, and that was that.

Costello was doing her Nazi march towards him, pulling the sunglasses off her head, her jacket flapping in the breeze. He ducked under the tape, the uniform on it already recognizing him, greeting him by name.

'Why are you here, DI Costello?' he asked her, before she could get started.

'Here?' She pointed to the big, blonde sandstone block at the top of the gardens. 'Because that is the care home where Archie has put Philippa and down here we have this . . .'

'What?'

She stood to the side slightly to let him have a better view down the lane. 'There, next to that white building, is an old tea chest. You see that?'

He muttered that he might be getting old, but he wasn't blind yet.

Then Costello stopped, her eyes squinted shut to look at the sun, her face puckered slightly. 'Go and have a look for yourself.' And she stood to one side, her arm out, handing him a pair of shoe covers.

'Body?'

'Male. Late teens, early twenties. We can't get a good look at his face, he's kind of . . . folded up. He was found by a chap out with his dog, Stephen Pickering. He lives around here somewhere.' She swept her arm round vaguely. 'He was out at one o'clock this morning and the chest wasn't there. Just after ten, it was and the dog went nuts.' She shrugged. 'The chest was closed over, nailed shut.' And with that, she walked away.

Without a protective suit Anderson walked to within two feet or so of the chest, then found himself being drawn nearer, as he worked out he was looking at the back of a neck, the head tucked well down, the downy hair on the skin clearly visible. He could see the top of the boy's head, messy light brown hair, the curls the colour of dark honey. The deceased was curled into the wooden chest. The skin was Caucasian and even in death it shone with youthful vitality. The arms appeared to be folded across his chest, his knees pulled up tight under his chin, a red plastic wristband was tight to his left arm. There was no part of his face visible. Overall, it looked as though he had crouched into a box and ducked his head down, scared of something, or caught in a drunken game of hide and seek. Then somebody had nailed him in.

The tea chest was made of cheap wood in a simple tin frame, like the sort old packing companies used to use. Under the open lid, Anderson could see padding to cushion the contents in transit. It had writing down the side; it looked Italian.

O'Hare, the pathologist, appeared from the shadows, drifting out of nowhere. 'And so the funny season begins, DCI Anderson. Good morning to you.'

Anderson said hello. 'Who is here?' he asked, not able to take his eyes off the tousled blonde head, trying to work out what limb was where, registering it didn't look right.

'Well, I was on-call, came over on foot from the uni. Be careful as you go, we don't have any perimeters up yet, no crime scene guys. I think they are all stuck in traffic, so we had better behave ourselves.'

'I'll try not to offend their sensibilities.'

'Costello's saying it's already out on social media, hence the growing audience. This site is like an amphitheatre.'

'Do we have a likely cause of death? Any ideas about that?' asked Anderson, pulling on protective gloves.

O'Hare, the pathologist, looked at him, then at his watch and then at the sun and stepped out from the shadows. 'No obvious wounds that we can see, which isn't much. But no blood, just the usual body fluids.'

Anderson was looking at the back of a jumper, one forearm visible. Denim jeans covered the thighs but the toes were bare. The body was indeed folded up.

'It's as if he has curled up into a ball and gone to sleep. No smell of drink but I can smell vomit. You'll need to wait until the crime scene guys get here – whenever they get here. We still haven't got a photographer, nobody,' emphasized the pathologist, trying for some reaction.

'Do you think he crawled in here drunk and died? And somebody nailed him up?'

'Why would somebody do that? But he wouldn't be the first who has asphyxiated by vomiting. No rigor yet, so it would appear recent. That's all I can say.'

Anderson looked up at the sandstone wall of flats on either side, four stories high, windows everywhere, unseen eyes peering out. They needed the InciTent. They needed to get the body covered before the professor and the crime scene technicians could get to work. 'So, recent time of death?' asked Anderson hopefully. 'Any idea, anything at all?'

'Recent, no time for rigor,' repeated the pathologist, then added, 'weird,' as if that was more helpful.

'It's the West End Festival, of course it's weird. I've just interviewed a girl who was kidnapped by an alien yesterday. He drew marks on her so that he could dissect her body and I thought she was joking until I saw the mess on her leg. Looked like somebody had jumped on her knee with football boots on.' He was talking to himself, still looking in the chest; the forearms folded across the denim-covered knees, the bare feet beyond, turned slightly on their sides. The big toe was clearly visible on both feet, a blueish hue that might have been dye from the denim. He looked back at the contour of the shoulder. Too flat. The curve from the neck down to the waist was not peaked by the outward curve of the humeral head. The same blue was visible around the upper elbow where the long sleeve of the jumper had got caught on the rough edge of the chest.

He pointed round the elbow.

O'Hare answered his unasked question. 'The blue colour? I think that's blood. Bruising. It's the full length of the compartment. I think it's from the shoulder injury.'

'So he was beaten up?'

O'Hare gave him a grim smile. 'Don't know. But it means he had time to bruise, time alive, I mean. Which might be of interest.' The pathologist checked his watch again.

'Why has he got no shoes on?'

'No idea, I can't see anything but feet. I'll call Mathilda McQueen to see if we can get him into the morgue, crate and all.'

'They won't like that in their nice shiny new lab.'

'Well, I don't like dead bodies folded neatly into crates, so they will have to get over themselves.'

Ignoring O'Hare's remonstrations, Anderson leaned in again and gently pulled the puckered denim leg of the jeans up over the ankle with the tip of his pen, seeing the dark blue thicken to black bruising. The slim ankle was swollen and grotesque, and there, a couple of inches higher, was a black line. Very fine but definite.

'Shit.'

Anderson retreated from the body and snubbed the enquiring look from the pathologist as he walked back down the lane. Costello joined him, talking like she had never stopped. 'Stephen Pickering opened the chest and got the fright of his life. Him and his missus Jackie are in that flat now.' She nodded at the nearby tenement. 'They'll be taking their Prozac with their ground decaff. The crime scene team are stuck in traffic. I've cordoned off the lane, hopeful for tyre marks. It's been dry for a while but the surface is potholed all over and the deeper ones are earthy. Just in case we get something. A vehicle must have dropped that crate here and some neighbours have mentioned hearing a car in the small hours of the morning and a scrape like a garage door, or maybe a garden door, so I was . . . Bloody hell!' she said turning round at the screeching arrival of a blue Saab. It stopped inches away from the bumper of Anderson's 4 series BMW. A woman stumbled from the passenger door. A mass of limbs and screaming hysteria, she moved like a demon, pushing the officer at the tape to one side with the strength of a rugby forward. She bent under the tape, not breaking her stride. The Saab's driver's door opened. Another woman, darker and more in control, appeared. Her outstretched hand was too little, too late, so she started shouting. The words made no sense but her intention was obvious; she wanted the other woman to stop.

The cop on the police side of the tape didn't move quickly enough. Two female hands firmly on his chest pushed him off balance enough not to impede her progress further. She weaved round Anderson and then the professor. It was Costello, nifty in catching shoplifters in her uniform days, who caught the woman with a neat tackle at waist height that swung her round and was balletic in its choreography. Both women stayed on their feet, both now facing the opposite direction, but as Costello was straightening herself up, the other woman drew her elbow back and jabbed Costello right in the face. Costello recoiled but refused to let go.

The cop from outside the tape was running towards them as blood poured out of Costello's nose. Instinctively Costello swung round again, ready to defend herself. The banshee screamed louder. The darker haired woman was shouting, clearly now, 'Leave her,' and 'Irene, for God's sake.'

As Anderson and the prof both helped to secure the woman, restraining her as delicately as they could, Anderson repeated the name Irene and the phrase 'calm down,' while the prof kept well clear of her elbows and feet.

The darker haired woman had caught up by now. 'Irene, Irene, not here.' She took the sobbing woman and held her to her chest; 'Irene' was now all tears and snot, a trembling hand pointing down the lane. Anderson could not make out a word of what she was saying; it was a gabbling stream.

The smaller woman looked at Anderson with some desperation, then at a bloodstained Costello. Archie Walker had appeared with a handkerchief at the ready, appalled by the scene that met his eyes; two uniformed police officers rubbing injured parts of their anatomies, a bleeding inspector, a chief inspector and the senior pathologist made to look like fools. A member of the public assaulted in front of a crowd of onlookers who had their mobile phones ready to film. This would be on YouTube within the hour. Archie Walker sensed PR disaster.

The woman halted in the middle of the lane. Standing still. Totally alone in the small sea of people. Her eyes stared down the lane, past the police officers to the white building that sat at the dogleg, obscuring the path beyond. She didn't move her body as she turned her head to see the tea chest nestled against the wall, tucked into the shadows. Its top broken and open, looking as innocent as a child's blanket box. The scene fell silent, just the rustle of the faint breeze through the trees, the odd cough, the electric click of a phone camera.

They waited, holding their breath, for a reaction.

The calm woman spoke to Costello in the gentlest of whispers, a pleading in her eyes. 'Irene's son is missing. David. We heard that you had found—'

Irene began murmuring to herself, a tuneful little chant, 'He only went out this morning.' Tears streamed from her blue eyes, which were still focused on the tea chest, then absorbed the professor, his purple gloves, the plain clothes police, uniforms and tape, the cars. On cue the crime scene officer appeared through the crowd that parted in front of them. 'Just this morning,' Irene repeated.

Costello pulled out her notebook, ignoring the small spots of blood dripping onto it and the puzzled look that O'Hare had given Anderson. 'What time did you last see him? David is it, your son?'

A slow nod, but Irene was calmed by having to think. 'Half eight. He has a sick friend, he went to let his dog out.' She frowned, recalling the mundane start of the day. She took the offered tissue from her friend with an automatic 'Thanks, Maggie' and started dabbing at her eyes.

'What age is he?'

'Nineteen, he's nineteen.' She nodded, keen for information.

Costello nodded at Anderson, asking him to take over and get her out of here, so he took Irene by her elbow, guiding her over to the side of the road, away from the gaping onlookers of the rubberneck collective.

'I'm DCI Anderson. Can you tell me what your son was wearing when he left this morning?'

Irene shook her head, shrugged and wiped the snot from her face. Her eyes were wide, not really understanding what was going on. A door opened in the lower flat, next door to the flat where the Pickerings were being interviewed by the uniformed branch. Another woman, in her mid-fifties, wringing her hands out on a towel, motioned to them that they could come in if they wanted. She gave the rubberneckers a dirty look.

'It was a black sweatshirt? T-shirt?' suggested Maggie, the dark-haired friend, her silver dangling earrings zipping back and forth, nodding encouragingly.

'Hollister T-shirt, his Hollister T-shirt and his jeans. I ironed that top yesterday. He was going out to watch the parade and he didn't meet up his friends like he said he would and . . .'

As she began to recant the day, Anderson thought about the boy in the chest with his black long-sleeved jumper. 'We need to get you inside somewhere, away from these prying eyes.'

'You can come in here,' said the woman coming out of her doorway, 'please, you can come in here. I am, so, so sorry . . .' She handed Costello another dishtowel, this one with ice in it. 'Try and stop that bleeding,' she said, rather unnecessarily.

Vera Morrison's kitchen was large and would have looked more in fitting with a farm somewhere in southern France. Above the six-burner cooker was a wall clock with paintings of wildlife at each numeral. At the moment it was otter to fox, twenty to twelve. Anderson checked it with his watch, the clock was a little fast but not by much. The big pine table was full of the detritus of a fairy costume: lace, tinsel and fabric glue, glitter and sequins. On a large wooden board lay the remains of a loaf of homemade bread, knife sitting beside it. The back door was open on to the small garden and the lane beyond, letting the warm air drift through the flat. Anderson had seen the two crime scene officers pass the door. Archie Walker had reappeared with his phone glued to his ear, studiously avoiding looking at Costello, keeping their relationship covert. The photographer would be getting underway with his wide shots, as the scene was being videoed. Costello, who had refused to go to hospital, was on her mobile organizing a door-to-door and a grid search of the area, in-between sniffs and ignoring Walker. Anderson heard her specifically mention car tyres again. She was right, nobody could have carried that tea chest by hand, but it could have been dragged out of the boot of a car. She had the situation under control. He may as well stay in here with the scents of a summer day, fresh bread and Bostick. Four pictures drawn in bright crayons were pinned to the front of the fridge door by magnets. Pride of place in nice Granny's kitchen.

It was an incongruous place to have a meeting like this but in the circumstances, with the parade on, it made sense to sit here with the windows open and the gentle draught flowing from the back door. They could hear the rhythmic bang bang of a drum in the distance, and waited for it to go past. The tune was tantalizingly familiar, it made it difficult to concentrate on Irene Kerr.

She was sitting on a kitchen chair, a glass of ice-cold water in front of her and dabbing her face with a clean hanky from a pretty Incan inlaid box that covered the cardboard box of tissues. They were taking it in turns to take a tissue from the box; Irene Kerr, in-between sobs and DI Costello, in-between phone calls. One woman dabbing at her tearful eyes, the other dabbing at her bloody nose. An ugly jagged cut was swelling under Costello's eye, opening in a rugged red tick mark on her otherwise pale face. Wyngate had appeared in the flat, after sorting out the two uniforms on the tape, and then securing the crime scene, organizing staff as they appeared. He was now standing at the window in the shady side of the street, his notebook out ready. Even from here Anderson could see the sheen of the barrier cream on Wyngate's face, protecting him from the sun, more evidence of his skin's sensitivity. His face looked puffy on the cheek overlying the bad tooth, like he was chewing something. Wyngate then spoke to another short-sleeved uniform telling him to stand at the door of the flat with the further instruction that he was to look like he was committed to a safer society.

So far, through the tears and mild hysteria, they had found out that Irene Kerr's son, David, had missed meeting his pals that morning. They were supposed to be meeting at eleven for a fry-up. The boy had gone out earlier to visit another friend, known as Winston, who had been unwell with Crohn's disease. David had offered to go early, let his dog out and leave him some coursework Winston had missed. They were all students at Glasgow, doing pure mathematics. Not the sort to get into trouble, she added, a studious boy, a polite boy, never been an inch of worry to her. She had nodded and Anderson had nodded back, letting her speak trying to ignore the connections his mind was making about students at the university, black lines and teenagers folded up in tea chests. It fitted that if the body in the chest was that of her son, then the death, the murder, was very recent. And that echoed O'Hare's initial deductions. Costello was now back in the hall, speaking like she had a cold, but still doing all the right things, getting the CCTV, making sure the intelligence from the door-to-door was being collated. Picking up on details that Irene was providing, the boy known as Winston was now getting a phone call. She was commanding the troops.

Anderson was glad Costello had his back, with Kirkton around and the fracas at the end of the lane, all this scrutiny, the carrot of the cold case squad being dangled. This could turn into a media circus, a suspicious death on the day of the parade. Anderson's mind was whirring; if this was David Kerr, he was dead and folded into that chest. If it was not David Kerr, then . . . either way, there was the chilling prospect that a murderer had slipped away into the crowds of the West End Festival. The ever present chip of ice in Anderson's heart looked a little more closely at Irene Kerr, who seemed very sure that this was her son. She had reacted extremely quickly. Too quickly? He wondered about the boy's friends. Had any of them been late at the University Café, where they were supposed to be meeting? Arrived nervous and sweating? Then he remembered that his own daughter Claire was out on the parade route with her favourite camera.

Sometimes Anderson hated his job.

Maggie started to talk, filling in the gaps about Winston, the boy with Crohn's. She had popped in to see her neighbour, Irene, that morning and suddenly found herself caught up in the drama. Irene had phoned her son, no answer on his mobile, first voicemail then it had been turned off. They needed to know when it was turned off. Irene was vague. About eleven? Irene could not recall what Innes, one of the friends waiting at the University Café, had said when he phoned the house. She could only recall him asking if David had changed his plans, the middle-class version of 'where the hell was he?' That was when Irene got the phone numbers from Innes and started phoning around. Winston, so called because his surname was Churchill, had told her that David had been and gone, dog exercised, the notes left. All was well. Irene's memory cleared, the phone was ringing, then voicemail. Then, it had been switched off. Or the battery had died. There would be a precise timeline here. What teenager turned off their phone nowadays?

'Irene? Is that your son's number?' Anderson pointed to it on the sheet that Mulholland had given him.

She pulled her own phone out her cardigan pocket and checked, nodding. 'Yes it is. Can you trace his phone? Are you looking for the person that killed him?'

'We don't know what we are looking for yet,' said Anderson blandly, although she had voiced his plan exactly. He texted Mulholland in the MIT suite and told him to get the phone traced.

Anderson continued talking Irene through the sequence of events. She had phoned David's friends, asking if they had seen him. Then she had posted a message on Facebook, expecting him to be around, caught up with another group of friends somewhere. She had been quick off the mark. Anderson wondered how long he would have left it if Claire had failed to turn up at a date with a friend and disappeared from the electronic radar.

'You are friends with your own son on Facebook?' Anderson clarified.

She nodded. 'And with most of his friends.'

And that explained how she got here so soon, Anderson thought, smiling back in what he hoped was an engaging smile. The West End of Glasgow is a small village in a big city. The finding of a teenager's body had quickly got on to social media, probably from one of the neighbours whose property over-looked the deposition site. Social media spread news like the plague, people overheard titbits and made up the rest. Innes, one of the boys who was supposed to have met David, saw a tweet and had phoned Irene again as she saw it herself on Facebook. Nothing much, just that a body had been found, believed to be that of a young man. She had put two and two together and . . . well it looked like she had not been wrong.

The Kerrs lived only a few streets away in Sydenham Road, in a mews house very typical of the area. Maggie, caught up in the escalating panic, had driven Irene round to Athole Crescent.

It had only been a couple of hours, but nobody needed to

tell Anderson how quickly life could be taken. The Hollister long-sleeved T-shirt was common smart casual dress amongst young men, but the issue of 'last seen wearing' and the very recent time of death indicated by lack of rigor, made Anderson fear the worst.

He nodded and told them to stay where they were. Maggie got the undertone and placed her arm around Irene's shoulder, rubbing her across the back, but subtly keeping a hold on her. Anderson stood close enough to Wyngate to talk quietly without using a conspiratorial whisper and told him to phone Winston again to confirm what David was wearing when he had left. Anderson himself slipped out into the hall, out of earshot of Costello and phoned Claire. She had intended to spend the whole day at the parade, watching the fun roll by and photographing whatever took her fancy. On her own. His daughter sounded slightly panicked when she answered her mobile, then a bit annoyed when she realized he was only calling to see she was OK. He lied, saying that there were reports coming in of a pickpocket gang working the parade route and to take care of that expensive Canon. His daughter corrected him, it was a Nikon, and then asked him what age he thought she was.

Anderson stepped into the garden and the intense heat of the sun. The sky overhead was a brilliant blue, only a few grey clouds on the horizon. The music from the parade, some Bee Gees classic was slightly louder now. He had heard a more discordant version down the phone. Claire was in the middle of the ever-growing buzz. She had sounded happy. Be careful, he said, there are a lot of nutters out there. He ended the call and hoped Irene Kerr had not overheard.

One look down the lane told him that the prof had not yet disturbed the body. Anderson signalled to the pathologist, their own tic-tac developed over years of working together and a disinclination to shout sensitive information. He asked if any ID had been found. O'Hare noticed him signalling and picked out his mobile from his pocket. His call was short; there was no way he was going to compromise evidence because rumours on social media had accelerated normal procedure. Traffic congestion could hold up the identification even more. So that left Anderson to go back into the flat and explain to a mother that 'following procedure' meant she still wouldn't know if her only son was lying dead a hundred yards away, folded into a box. He ended the call and let out a long slow breath through pursed lips.

Sensing the need for moral support, Costello followed him in, one half of her face pale and gaunt. The other cut, red and swollen. She was starting to look like a deformed clown.

'I have to see him, I have to, please. Please,' pleaded Irene as soon as they entered the kitchen.

'Not yet. We could lose evidence. These things take time,' Costello sniffed, patting a handkerchief to her throat, her flatness, weirdly, seemed to dispel Irene's anxiety. Costello could have been talking about waiting for concrete to set.

'What happened to him?'

'We don't know who it is yet. All we know is that we have the body of a young man.' Costello knew that even if there was no ID, O'Hare's estimate of the time of death supported the theory that the body was David. And the evidence suggested that the boy had not been killed in the lane outside, merely dumped there, folded up and nailed into a tea chest.

'But the clothes? You can tell by his clothes?' Irene watched as the two cops deliberately did not look at each other. She sniffed loudly and pointed. 'You know, don't you. Oh my God, I don't believe this is happening to me.' Irene sank her head into her hands, her shoulders heaving. Her sobbing was painful to witness.

Costello met Maggie's eyes; the question was there. Costello gave a slight shrug; they had nothing to argue with.

Maggie went a shade paler and bit her lip, a tear gathering in her eye, but she wiped it away and embraced her friend's head a little closer.

Anderson sat back down at the table. 'There is no easy way out of this but to wait. I'm sorry but as my colleague said, if David has come to harm then we can't risk losing valuable evidence.'

'Oh my God.' Irene leaned forward, a long slow scream escaped from her soul somewhere, the cry that life would never be the same again. Anderson reached out and held her hand. Her friend cradled her head and let her cry, it was the best they could do.

And Anderson knew exactly how they felt.

At twelve twenty Mulholland was in the office watching the Twitter feed come in from the parade route, and monitoring it. He had been really bored until somebody uploaded to YouTube a video of two blonde women having a fight; one in a familiar dark suit getting an elbow in the face. Mulholland played the short clip over and over. He was enjoying it frame by frame when his phone rang. He was not really interested in Costello's update that the DCI was trying to get back from the locus, no mere feat in the throes of the parade, but the appearance of a concerned individual, maybe the deceased's mother, meant that the DCI really needed to stay at the scene.

'His mother?'

'Sorry, I'll explain. That's the creature that gives birth to humans, a bit like a dad but more intelligent. But Colin's instructions are perfectly clear, treat David Kerr as a missing person for now.'

He heard her sniff on the end of the phone. 'Is that the ID of the deceased,' he began typing, 'David Kerr?'

'If he was I would have used the word victim, wouldn't I? He is not the deceased, we have a body and we have a missing person. Two different things. For now you are treating David Kerr as a missing person. There is no identification on the dead body.'

'He's only been missing for what an hour? On the biggest drinking day on the West End? The boy will be pissed some-where. What is Colin thinking?'

'David Kerr does not drink. He doesn't seem to do anything except study. He's a very low-risk victim. But the body type, age and clothes all match.'

'Well, there you go then, it's him. What's the palaver?' muttered Mulholland, bored at the mind-numbing Twitter feed scrolling in front of him, stuck in the office when the weather was so sunny outside and the dull pain in his leg, throbbing away to remind him why. Even attending a murder scene would be preferable to this.

Costello's voice was as soft as diamond. 'I am telling you, for now and the foreseeable future, the body is unidentified and you are treating David Kerr as a missing person. If this all goes tits up and he is the victim, we will be ahead of the game in tracing his last movements. We don't want to miss out on valuable intelligence with regards to his "last seen" and we have already gone a fair way to narrowing that down.'

'So it was the mum who nearly beat you to the crime scene. Is that true?'

There was a slight delay while Costello weighed up gossip against authority. 'Indeed, bloody traffic. It put us all in a delicate situation. Look, can you trace his dad, Duncan Kerr? I think he might be away in Dubai but I don't know if that is hardworking father away or shagging the mistress in Dubai type of away. The mother is not for leaving the scene, but Colin is keen to get her away.'

'Why are you talking like that?' mocked Mulholland. 'You got a cold?'

'Hay fever.'

'Nothing to do with being elbowed in the face then?'

A pause. 'Injured in the line of duty.'

'I'm so sorry. I saw it on YouTube and I thought it was awful that your humiliation was filmed for the amusement of the general public. Bloody funny though. I've shared it on my Facebook page.'

'Well, thank you for that. If you weren't a complete girlie with brittle bones, you would be out here with us. So you get on the little bit of your job you can still do: the typing.'

'You can't say that, I am a disabled person.'

'And I'm haemorrhaging blood, so piss off.'

And she cut the call.

Costello left Anderson with the two women and a strong brew of tea, then walked back into the warmth of the sun. The crowd at the end of the lane was steadily growing, a few more casual passers-by on the way to the parade had stopped, thinking that this real life CSI might be more entertaining. And the usual pack of journalists, cameras out, interviewing people in the crowd with tape recorders had arrived. She was thankful that a tent had now been erected over the tea chest. The sensitive part of the job could now get underway. Costello pulled on a protective suit and negotiated her way through the crime scene team to get to the body, ignoring the shouts of the journalists from behind her.

'How do they know stuff before we do?' she asked vaguely, once in the safety of the InciTent.

'The collective consciousness of Facebook, Twitter and every other thing that will cause the next generation of humanity to have extra-long thumbs, no fingers and only three functioning brain cells. You have no idea how many deaths mobile phones cause. Still, I suppose if you watch a screen rather than where you are putting your feet, then eventually you will fall down a manhole or off a cliff and that is Darwinism in a nutshell.' The old pathologist flashed her a crinkly smile. 'You should see a doctor about that.' He pointed a gloved finger to her face.

'Irene has sharp elbows.' She nodded at the body; all she could see was gently curled, honey brown hair. 'Is this her son?' She handed O'Hare her mobile with a picture of David Kerr, a very recent picture, Irene's background picture. David had a broad smile, a sensuous thickness round his lips, his hair was light brown in the picture but spiked with wax, tiny needles covering his scalp. It was a casual photograph, not posed or prepared. She could draw the conclusion that David liked to wax his hair. The boy in the box had not waxed his hair on the day he died.

'There is no ID on the body. We've been through his pockets, well his obvious pockets. No wallet, nothing.'

'Mugged?'

The pathologist shrugged. 'Maybe.' He shook his head. 'He looks untouched, asleep. Only the merest smell of vomit round his face.'

'He would have been stone cold sober.'

'And now he is stone cold.' O'Hare looked at her, then back at the body. 'Stone cold with no rigor at all. That's odd.' He shrugged. 'It's an anomaly but I refuse to second guess.'

'Oh I know. Put two pathologists in a room and get three different opinions.'

O'Hare ignored the old joke. 'Has he had any fits? Epilepsy? Drug abuse?'

'Not that the mum said. I think she would say if she knew. Nice boy from all accounts.' Then Costello added at the sight of O'Hare's disbelieving eyebrow and retold the verified story of the sick friend. 'He's not the type to think "Oh I have a spare five minutes so I'll knock back a quarter bottle of Thunderbird".' Costello sniffed, and winced, holding a fresh paper tissue to her nose then pulling it away to examine the crimson rosette pattern. 'How much blood can I lose before I die?'

'The same as everybody else, Costello.'

By the time Anderson brought Irene Kerr back to Partickhill Police Station, Mulholland had managed to get a whole page of typing on David Andrew Kerr. The boy had not been admitted to any hospital in the Glasgow area. David was a nice looking boy, orthodontically straight teeth, fair hair usually waxed into spikes, a good student, and a good friend. He was bright; he walked a very specific path in life. The safe path. And that did not make him an easy target.

He looked at the E-bulletin about Paige Riley. She was there, on the missing persons list. She had enjoyed none of the advantages that David Kerr had enjoyed in her short, and probably now ended, life. It was sad to say but that was a surprise to nobody. She ticked every box; the perfect target. Homeless, street living, addiction; born to fail, some would say. The only person who noticed she was missing was a commuter who walked past her begging every day and had got concerned. Nobody else. This boy, David Kerr, was a different animal altogether. That's not to say he hadn't been complicit in some way, he might have found his life too stuffy and too controlled, looked for a little secret release from being the perfect child. Mulholland could relate to that. Being perfect was a lot of pressure. David might have bought drugs, got into somebody's car and got a whack over the back of the head before being driven round the block. He might have been flashing his money about. His posh boy accent might have been noticed by some of the incomers into the West End,

hiding in the crowds for the parade. He might have been ripe
for the organized gangs of pickpockets. Mulholland thought
what a field day James Kirkton would have with this. More
fodder for his hobby horse of illegal immigrants, the Romas,
the gypsies. They would all be blamed. *These people flooding
into our country.* God, he would go to town on this.

Mulholland scanned through the missing persons. Plenty of
young men, too many of them. None yet matched the very
precise timeline they had with David, they couldn't argue with
that. If he was the victim, this had been meticulously planned.

Mulholland scanned over his notes about David Kerr. The
complicity didn't fit well with his knowledge of psychology;
David Kerr fitted more the 'Bundy MO'. The killer would
appeal to their victim's good nature. Maybe struggling with
something – a baby, a pram, a bit of furniture. A tea chest?
That fitted better. 'You couldn't give me a hand with this, son,
could you?' A broken arm, or a wrist support and a tea chest
sitting at the back of a 4x4 with the tailgate open. 'The kids
need it for the parade.' And then the blow on the head, the
'disabling insult' as pathologists liked to put it. The body
pushed into the back of the vehicle. But according to early
reports, there was no injury to the head of the body on the
tea chest, nothing obvious at least.

He put David's appeal out to every police officer on the parade
route. Even as he looked, Mulholland's screen bleeped. The
picture of Paige Riley reappeared. It was also going out to all
officers, a special appeal today for those round and about the
parade. The public being requested to keep their eyes out for
her. They knew the photo was years out of date now, but it was
the only one they had. She was typical of every teenager; long
brown hair àla Kate Middleton, eyebrows like two black caterpil-
lars lying dead across her forehead. She'd turn up dead in a
ditch. Mulholland was thirty-seven now. How many of those
had he seen in his professional life? Way, way too many. He
decided to have a coffee and a painkiller.

Mulholland was on his second cup when his phone went.
Frank Wyse, a young cop, had been chatting up the waitress
in the Zeitgeist Café on the corner of Byres Road and

Vinicombe Street when David's picture came through and showed it to the staff. The girl behind the counter called over her colleague and the result of the conversation was that the boy in the picture had been sitting at one of the outside tables before the parade. He had been there about nine, one of their first customers. Described him as a good-looking, polite young man, which fitted what they knew of him. And he was on his own. He had ordered an Appletiser and one of their granola bars. He had told her to keep the change, and there had been some commotion outside but she didn't know what exactly. They had been busy.

Mulholland jumped on the information, perfect time, perfect place. Because of the parade in the city all the CCTV was active. He phoned Anderson to tell him he was ordering the footage as he had a definite sighting. The boss had been curt in acknowledgement, no doubt the boy's mother was a few feet away and he was trying to prevent her from finding out that they were on the track of what was probably the last piece of footage of her son alive.

Anderson asked the precise location of the camera. It was positioned high on the second floor of the hotel on the opposite corner of Byres Road, and looked across the street. It should show, at least on the south sweep, the corner where David had drank his Appletiser, and a little of the side street, Vinicombe Street. If something had happened to him then it would have been in that hour and up Vinicombe Street. He must have been enticed up there. The lanes off Vinicombe Street ran parallel to Byres Road on the east side. The tea chest and the body had been found on the west side. And Byres Road, in-between, would have been busy, even at that time. Somebody would have seen something. Hundreds of people had been milling about and Mulholland found it hard to believe that nobody had witnessed any foul play.

So there might be another explanation for his absence, maybe one with no foul play. Maybe the boy did have another life, something that his mother and friends knew nothing about. A girl he was meeting? Or a boy? That might be more like it if he wanted to keep it a bit quiet. It struck Mulholland that the boy might have deliberately arranged to see his friend with the Crohn's early and so he could be 'at a loose end' for an hour before meeting his friends at eleven. He could have stayed with his friend but he didn't. He walked down to Byres Road and waited, sitting at an outside table on one of the busiest corners in the whole street, waiting for somebody. Or something.

He gave a quick call to Winston. The student was panicky on the phone, had they found David yet?

'No, not yet but don't worry.'

'But it's going round Twitter that you've found a body.'

'We find bodies in Glasgow every day of the week,' said Mulholland in a voice fused with humour. 'I'm sure it will be fine. What I want to know is, did he seem in a hurry to go?'

'David? No, not really. I asked him to go. I was tired and wanted a lie in.'

'OK, so he didn't mention he was going anywhere?'

'Yes, to meet Innes and the gang at the University Café. I've already told you that. He was taunting me with his breakfast ideas: fried egg, potato scone. All that stuff I can't eat. He said he would treat me when I was better, to cheer me up, you know. But he never made it, did he?' The boy's voice choked a little.

Mulholland promised to phone back as soon as they had any news, then put down the phone and looked at David's picture with his wide honest smile and spikey hair. 'So where the hell did you get to?'

Sandra hummed along to the opera as she worked, the one she had been listening to in the car. She knew this bit. The Duchess didn't seem to mind her joining in. Although previously, Sandra had caught the Duchess glaring at her, and she had realized that she was making up words that sounded like the Italian. The libretto, the libretti – something like that. Paolo had told her where to find the right words, but in that glare from the Duchess had been a smirk of humour and Sandra found herself warming to her charge.

There was beauty up here, in Tosca. It was a pleasure to work with so many beautiful things, doilies and fine china, when the world outside was so ugly. And Sandra knew that her great weakness was beautiful things, usually somebody else's.

With some shame, she recalled the first time she had ever been alone in the room. She had tried the jewel boxes. All locked. So she then started looking through the Duchess's photographs; her memory box. It might be of no intrinsic financial value but Sandra believed knowledge was power. Secrets were currency.

Instead Sandra had studied the old photographs and romanticized about the old lady. Filling in a backstory; imagining her walking round the back streets of Naples, performing, reciting, and being a somebody in her neighbourhood. Hanging around the Piazza del Plebiscito, drinking red wine and being chatted up by gorgeous men. Sandra had never been to Italy, she had barely made it out of Springburn, but she imagined the Duchess transported back into the sepia world of her memory book. In the room was a whole pile of music scores and other tattered books that had drawings of stage designs, forests, sunflowers, toadstools plus lighting rigs and all sorts. Standing on its end next to the books was a wooden and leather case, and in that was a huge tome. The title of the story was *The Enchantress*. It was a story the Duchess never got tired of hearing, indeed the old woman had caught Sandra looking at the pictures, hand drawn pictures and had gestured sharply. At first Sandra thought she was to put the book back, but no, the Duchess wanted to see it. She always wanted to look at it. It was heavy so Sandra held it as the Duchess ran her fingers over the beautiful illustrations, gold leafed and colours so vibrant, they almost hurt the eyes.

Sandra had tried to get the Duchess to speak about it, but no. In reality, the old lady had not really spoken for fifteen or sixteen years. She muttered in Italian every now and again, the odd word in English. It was rumoured by the B shift care team that she had been struck dumb by some terrible incident that was referred to but never actually clarified. And it wasn't the sort of thing that she could ask Paolo; well, not yet anyway. She was working on that. She would wait until the Duchess had eaten Cranachan, the cream always made her feel a little poorly. So Sandra had a plan to wait until it was on the menu

again and she'd make sure the Duchess got a good portion.
Then later when she was quiet and a little hangy, Sandra would
ask Paolo while his mother, sorry 'the Duchess', was feeling
so bad, why she looked so sad at times. And she'd let the
question linger a little.

Keen to improve her loveliness quota, she had sought Paolo's
permission to sit with the Duchess and go through her memory
book with her, flicking through the pages pointing out snap-
shots of her and her husband. Sandra had read that this kind
of stimulation could be good for the mind of the elderly,
revisiting moments in their life. Paolo had thought it a good
idea. The Duchess would look at the photographs, occasionally
pushing the book away as if the sight of something made her
angry. When she looked at the illustrations in *The Enchantress*,
the tears would start rolling down the Duchess's face, a thick
bony finger with a ridged bright red talon moving along under
the scrolled lettering which might have been Italian or Latin,
could have even been Serbo Croat for all Sandra knew.
Handwritten alongside on some pages were little numbers in
a Greek script, in a little column of four digits ready to be
totalled. But she thought, suspected, that the gold leaf might
be real, and that the book was worth plenty but too individual
to be sold at auction, too recognizable.

Now, Sandra was concerned about the location of the money.
She turned to look at the silly old cow, sitting, eyes closed,
her head lolling to one side as her right hand played its invisible piano. Sandra thought those guys in Switzerland had it
right. The planet was busy enough.

'I haven't been up here for years,' said Costello, looking around
her at the huge tenements to the left and the right, sandstone
fortifications that lined Athole Lane. They could have held
back marauding hordes from anywhere. 'All this a couple of
hundred yards from Byres Road, the hidden face of Glasgow.'

O'Hare replied, 'That's what I like about this city, turn a
different corner and it changes character. I haven't been up
here since that cold snap at the end of February. They found
a homeless person, hypothermic, right over there. Stiff as a
board. At least five cars had driven round that body and nobody

noticed. I can't think what is worse, seeing a dying person and ignoring them or being so blasé and locked up in your own Volvo and Waitrose world that you don't even notice. At least this tea chest here was spotted.'

'Only because the dog was having a benny and I bet Mr Pickering thought there was something valuable in it. He saw that padded lining and thought hey ho, we are onto something here. Car boot sale or a reward. He might have thought it really did fall off the back of a lorry. I mean look at them all, over-privileged arseholes.' Costello kicked a stone around with her toe, watching it rattle across the cobblestones of the lane, then winced at the pain in her face. 'I suppose the homeless are not sexy, they are not vote catchers, and probably don't vote themselves so why should Klingon Kirkton and his golf club pals care about them. But somebody has to.' She looked round her, seeing the white extension that was so at odds with the lane and the old walls, the aged trees. The backs of the tenements were far apart, built in the days when the rear lane was access to the bin area and the huge back garden each tenement had. There would have been washing sheds, and toilets and all sorts down here. A few of the houses swallowed up the entire rear garden, extending back to the lane, which would afford a square footage to rival that of a football pitch. These houses may have been tenements but they were huge. Some of them had eight or nine bedrooms, with spiralling wooden staircases and stained glass windows that ran over two or three floors. Athole House, the secure living facility, was two such properties knocked through. In this part of Glasgow, there were still some that remained complete. A few streets further back they had been knocked into tiny flats with a jigsaw of a floor plan. Further back they spawned the student bedsit. The bigger flats around here were occupied by rich artists, architects, a few TV personalities and some literary writers. It was a clever piece of marketing to open the secure living facility and an even better bit of marketing not to call it an old folk's home. Secure living facility sounded so much nicer, so less elderly. She looked at her watch and wondered if Pippa had managed to eat any lunch without spilling it down her.

She backed up a few steps to get a better look at the building extended back to the lane, the white single-storey extension; new and architect designed. It looked so odd among the Victorian tenement splendour, minimalism among much loved bric-a-brac. She was pretty sure that was on the site of the house that had burned down. It too had been an ugly architect's conversion in the row of fine Victorian tenements and it had been somewhere round here, Marchmont Terrace if her memory served her right. There had been outrage it had ever got planning permission in the first place. If it had not been for the tragedy, where three people and a firefighter had lost their lives, there would have been a collective sigh of relief that the bloody eyesore had gone up in flames. Unfortunately it had been replaced by a building even uglier, if that was possible. Costello was sure she was looking at the back of it right now.

O'Hare stood up, his back making its usual crack. He swore quietly.

'Why here? Why right at this bit? Where this eyesore is?'

'It's not easily visible from either end, I noticed that when I came through. It doglegs a little, so there was some aspect of the tea chest being concealed.'

'By why next to this white outbuilding? To stop a vehicle getting through here?'

'Costello, a double decker bus could get through there.'

They both looked up at the roofline, the gap of the new build.

Costello asked, 'But this is the rebuild after the Marchmont Terrace fire?'

The pathologist walked a few steps backwards, lifting his hands to protect his eyes from the sun as he looked up. He pointed his finger, charting the roofline of the building. 'Yes. It was brought down the first time by subsidence, and then the house that burned down was built. This is the third one on that site. Lucky white heather.' He ran a bony hand through his unruly grey hair. 'I did the post on the Marchmont Terrace firefighter; McGuigan. David? Derek? Drew? God, my memory is terrible these days.'

Costello turned round to look. 'Roof fall?'

'In the end, yes. They thought there was a child in the

building. He was told not to go back in, he did. He got caught.
The couple who owned the house were killed. There was
another death . . .' He paused to think.

'The woman who jumped. She died later in the hospital. I
know that much,' Costello murmured, the wind in the lane
chilling them a little. She was thinking if that had happened
nowadays, everybody and his dog would have filmed that
woman's fall. Death was now in the public domain.

'Deke Kilpatrick survived the fire, he was a wee bit famous
back then, back in the nineties round here on the jazz circuit.
He played a mean sax. I used to go and listen to him,
sometimes.'

Costello looked at the pathologist, tall, getting a little
stooped, his tie always done tight to the neck, his grey crinkly
hair, and found it impossible to think of him in a nightclub,
listening to jazz, describing anything as a 'mean sax'.

O'Hare searched his brain for the name. 'McEwan. That was
the dead couple's name, the boy's name. Ally McGuigan
was the firefighter who died. Knew it would come back to me
eventually. It normally does, at three in the morning when I
am trying to get to sleep.'

Costello nodded, the name made it real. A round-faced man
with an Oliver Hardy moustache. She could see the headlines,
he had died a hero. But he had died for nothing. The boy
hadn't been found. As she stood there, she could hear the
sudden cracking and burning of flames, the crashing of wood
caught by fire and breaking, burning, that acrid smell of
burning. She opened her eyes. O'Hare was standing looking
at her. The air was clear, it was a bright sunny day, the only
noise was the distant drumming of the parade. The auditory
hallucination of a memory disturbed, a memory that came too
close. She shivered.

'Are you OK?'

'Yes. I was thinking what a terrible way to die, like that.
When we were up at the loch side, you know.'

'You don't need to . . .'

'But when that fire was behind me and the deep, ice-cold
water in front of me. It was an easy decision to walk forward.
Anything to get away from those flames.' Costello's eyes

closed and she shook her head. Two years on but that memory came back as quick and fresh as the summer breeze. 'And the survivor?' The words tumbled out her mouth. Costello was thinking about the home for the elderly she had just visited. She knew a burn victim when she saw one. Scarface. 'Kilpatrick?'

'Kilpatrick. Deke Kilpatrick. The cool sax, the very man,' agreed O'Hare.

'Well, he's up there at Athole House, where Pippa is. I met him this morning.'

O'Hare looked at her in disbelief. 'You're kidding? Well . . .' He thought for a bit. 'Maybe not so odd. He would be a member of some musical union so it's the obvious place for him to be.' O'Hare looked at the floor of the InciTent, a narrow strip of worn concrete, dried mud and the odd weed poking through.

They both looked about in the quiet, chemical air of the tent. Both thinking the same thought.

'Do you think it relates to the deposition site?' mused Costello. 'At the back of that building, where his wife jumped to her death, and he lives over there. He can look out the window and see this corner any time he wants. But he's not fit to do anything, not this. Is there a message here? It's very odd.'

'Yeah, that's a little odd, Costello. But since when was killing somebody and folding them up into a box perfectly normal?'

A strong gust of wind down the lane carried a slight chill. The sides of the InciTent flapped as if the body was reminding them of its presence and their business. The boy in the tea chest was waiting.

By three p.m., Irene Kerr was pacing the floor, her navy blue trousers now creased like crepe paper, her woollen cardigan stained with tears and coffee. Maggie had placed her own blue cardigan, bobbled and worn, round her shoulders. The neat cut of Irene's blonde hair, the careful polished colour in her toes exposed by her leather sandals, testified to somebody who normally took greater care over their appearance but now

Irene's eyes were red and swollen from crying and her white top under her cardigan was stained with the reddish brown of Costello's drying blood.

Anderson introduced himself again, clearly. She had not been in a fit state to take anything on board when they had met the first time.

She shook his hand warmly, a dry, firm handshake. 'I knew there was something wrong; I could feel it in my bones.'

Anderson smiled, pulling out an easy chair so they were more side by side rather than a confrontational head to head. They were in exactly the same room, exactly the same chairs, as when he had interviewed Amy that morning, although it felt a very long time ago. She had been admitted to hospital. Her mother was with her. A doctor had phoned Wyngate to say that he thought the student had been drugged and that they had taken blood samples, as they had no real idea what with. And that she had nearly dislocated her knee, but they didn't think from a fall as there was no abrasion or laceration of the skin. More like she had been hit with something. It could still be accidental. Then he had added the anaesthetic effect of whatever she had taken was wearing off. She was in a lot of pain.

Wyngate had to ask about the strange black lines Amy had on her body. The same lines Anderson thought he saw on the ankles of the boy in the tea chest. Black lines drawn round a joint? The doctor was a little off-hand; 'Oh, we had thought they were tattoos but they washed off OK. She had them on both knees.'

'And you didn't think that was strange?' Wyngate had asked the doctor.

'It's parade day. You have no idea what comes through A and E on parade day. We have a Munchkin here who choked on a fox's tail.' With that he hung up, not in bad grace, just very busy.

But those black lines on both knees and on the ankle of the dead boy. It made Wyngate feel more than a little uneasy.

Anderson waved a hand, indicating that Irene should sit.

'Do you know how long it will be? I mean, I know you

have to do all these tests and things but if I could see him – have a look at him then I would know. And until I know, I really don't know what else to do.' She looked at Anderson, deep into his eyes. 'Please.'

'I am so sorry. As soon as I can, I will let you see him, of course, but at this stage I am not in charge. It's the pathologist's call and he knows you are here waiting. As soon as he can involve you, he will.' He moved slightly in his chair, leaning forwards. He needed her to concentrate, and he couldn't say that the boy's face was hidden, tipped down between his own knees.

'Irene, do you know anywhere that David might have been? I know he is your son but a lot of sons do things that they don't want their mother to know anything about. He is an adult.' He was careful to use the present tense.

Irene clasped her hands and looked at the ceiling, tears still pouring down her face, leaving wet runs on her cheeks. 'You have no idea how much I want him to be somewhere right now; somewhere that I would totally disapprove of. Anywhere except lying in a morgue, anywhere but that. But no, that would not be like him. I know him.'

'Do you think he might have gone somewhere and not noticed, not realized that time has passed, switched his phone off? He might not be aware that we are looking for him? There's a lot of street entertainment on, something might have caught his eye?'

'He would have let his friends know. You have asked at the hospital?' She pointed, half-heartedly, over her shoulder towards the Western by force of habit. It had been closed for a year now.

'Yes, we have.'

'So what happened to him?'

Anderson had the permutations of a thousand scenarios tumbling through his mind, only a few of them had a happy ending. If the body was David then this healthy young man was killed and dumped within a sixty-minute time frame, in broad daylight, in front of a lot of people on a busy street corner on the busiest day of the year. That suggested that something very planned, very deliberate and probably very awful had happened to him. 'There is one question that I do have to ask?'

'Ask away.'

'Is everything OK at home?'

She blinked once. 'Fine.'

But Anderson had noticed. Hesitation. 'Totally fine?' he asked, giving her that small smile that bred confidence, the expression that worked on everybody as long as they were innocent.

'My husband works in Dubai. I have ulcerative colitis. I am not sure that those two facts are entirely unrelated. My illness is one of the reasons David phones me so much. And I had a bad attack a few weeks ago, small hours of the morning. David phoned his father. A woman answered.' She couldn't keep the disdain from her voice. 'She was in my husband's house at an unsuitable hour and . . .' She stopped. 'Maybe his dad isn't the man that he thought his dad was. I think he has learned that lesson.'

'And there is no way David could have done something on impulse, like flown out to have it out with his dad?'

'No,' she sighed. 'I have his passport.'

Another thing. Too close.

'Does he spend a lot of time online?'

'What boy doesn't? But he's chatting to his friends. He's not the type to be groomed or anything. He's not a child.'

'We need to check his computer.'

'Please do. I want him found.'

'Irene, your son was last seen sitting outside a café, as if he was waiting for somebody. It does happen that trusting young men can be exactly that, too trusting. Did you see any change in him over the last few weeks?'

'No. Maybe a bit off with his dad. But not me. I suspect that you don't believe me, but I would know if there was something going on. I am his mother.'

'Well, one of my colleagues is talking to his friends, getting a picture of what they were doing.'

'Mr Anderson, he is studying pure mathematics at university. He is going into his second year. He was top of his class.' Her mouth pursed in determination. 'He doesn't drink. He does not have friends that I don't know about.'

Maggie raised her eyebrows.

Irene smiled, sniffing back tears. 'I know you think that I am an overprotective mother who won't let her boy grow up, but David is a nice lad. Winston is a nice lad. He has missed a lot this year so David was trying to make sure that he was keeping up. He looks out for people, does David. He has been friends with Innes since primary one. He has never been late for anything. So you see what I mean when I say that I know that something awful has happened to him. I am his mother.' She was on her feet, angry and shouting. Then she placed her crooked finger at her lips, took a deep breath, trying to stop the tears.

Anderson nodded and wondered how many times he had heard those words from a parent, only for them to find out that they did not know their child at all. A bit unworldly? He'd go out of his way to help anybody. He was ripe to be the victim of a groomer, if a bit old. Anderson's phone bleeped. He read the text message. Irene Kerr studied his face.

'What's happened?' She put her hand out on his knee, clamping her fingers in hard.

'I'll get Caroline, our liaison officer, to make you a cup of tea. There's something come in that I must attend to.' And Anderson left the room, leaving the two women watching the door close behind him.

By three thirty p.m. the Duchess was back in her usual place, at the window of Tosca with a lilac quilt over her bony knees, looking out over the gardens that were resplendent in the summer sunshine. The meticulously cut grass was so green it looked as though it had been dyed by a student of Chagall.

Her patent, black, kitten-heeled shoes sat neatly on the footplates of the wheelchair. The olive green pashmina was wound round her shoulders and pinned with a single diamond and the duck-egg blue dress draped neatly round the front of the wheelchair. Her gaze rested on a spot somewhere over the skyline of the city, her crimson lips pursed tight with concentration as her mind tried to make sense of it all. Her imagination was playing out another scene that she knew well but could not immediately recognize. Her right hand knew what it was doing, held out horizontally, fingers twisting slightly. Her head rested to one side listening to a melody only she could hear.

'Pietro?' she whispered. '*Pietrino mio, sei tu?*' Her hand fell, a self-conscious wipe of her palm on the blanket. Thin, arthritic fingers clasped the arms of the chair and she pulled herself into a more upright position, smartening her posture. 'Pietro?' She asked again, little more than a whisper, barely audible, thinking that he was right behind her.

'Pietro? No Paolo. It's Paolo and he's not here yet,' the carer said. 'It's Sandra ready to take you through for your afternoon tea, time you had something to eat. Come on, sweetheart.'

'*O, Pietrino mio! Perche non vieni a trovarme?*'

'No Paolo, now come on, pet.'

The old lady spat out something in Italian, the finger jabbed at Sandra.

'Sorry, Duchess,' corrected Sandra with automatic false diffidence. They were all the same these old dears. Sandra had found it quite funny at first but then Paolo cornered Sandra and asked her to apologize for the 'sweetheart', explaining that he had hoped their relationship had gone beyond client and carer and that the Duchess was very old, very Italian and should be treated with respect. Sandra pretended to be mortified, when in reality she couldn't give a stuff and resorted to calling the Duchess all kinds of names under her breath. The old woman couldn't live forever so all Sandra had to do was keep Paolo onside. When Paolo was around, Sandra always appeared to go that extra mile. And she made sure he noticed. Today, as well as the Italian cake, she had made a bit of an effort on herself, mascara, eyeshadow lifted from Superdrug.

If there was one thing Sandra was done with, that was living in her tiny council flat alone in Govan and being skint. Well that was two things. Two things at the start of a long list.

She wouldn't be left here, not like this lot. The residents here now lived a life of bottoms needing to be wiped, false teeth needing to be scrubbed. Their past might have been that of film stars, singers, actors, comedians; on stage receiving applause after applause, bowing for the curtain call. Well, it was all over for them now. And they'd never had to wait until seven thirty to buy the groceries at their sell-by date for half price. They were waiting for their big final curtain, their swan song. They were all standing still. Waiting for death.

'Paolo's not here, not yet,' Sandra whispered to the old lady for the third time, a harsh whispering that might have sounded threatening. But then she relented, a little. At the end of the day the Duchess was an old rich woman with a single son. 'Come on now, Paolo has his own life. He can't be running around after you every two minutes.' She smiled at the creased, painted face. 'Not that he wouldn't want to.' She held the smile, feeling like a children's TV presenter. The Duchess looked right through her to the door, looking for Paolo.

Sandra glanced at the big silver clock. 'He'll be along later.' She checked the Duchess's dress was clean, no crumbs, no stains. The Duchess hated her clothes to get soiled. Funny how some residents were so perjink when others took great delight in smearing egg yolk all over their faces. Bloody Kilpatrick always had a dribble of something escaping from the side of his mouth.

The Duchess however, wasn't for settling. She was pointing, her eyes scanning the room as her red lips pursed and loosened.

Sometimes it was easier to do what the old bird wanted. 'Do you want some photographs?' Sandra said, picking up the memory book.

The Duchess shook her head violently, her lips muttering something in Italian that sounded very rude.

Sandra lifted the wooden case with the big storybook in it. The fracture site in her wrist gave a sharp twinge. 'Would you like to hear the story again? *The Enchantress*?'

The Duchess held her head still, and blinked, nodded slightly. The thin crimson lips bent into a sad smile, down-turned, the creases in the old face deepened. She pointed a bent arthritic finger, reaching out to the back of Sandra's sore wrist and gave it a gentle scrape with her taloned nail, as if the pain had registered in her subconscious. The book was heavy, Sandra was slim built. For a moment they looked at each other. Just because Sandra never got the big breaks, it was no reason to hate those who did. She smiled at the old lady, her eyes drifting off to the pearl earrings. There was a choker to match them somewhere.

'I'll read it,' she said loudly, adding under her breath, 'as if there was any other poor sod here.'

Sandra settled herself on the fluffy stool that normally sat under the dressing table. She slid her feet out her Crocs, the sweaty stink drifted up. She had been in a bit of a hurry that morning and hadn't showered. It was very hot. She wiped the sticky soles of her feet on the woollen rug. If part of her job was reading out loud in bad Italian, then so be it, it wasn't difficult and there were loads of pictures to help. And she had no difficulty in imagining herself as a princess.

Despite herself, Sandra enjoyed the story. Page after thick page of beautiful hand-drawn pictures, separated by fine white tissue, each page rimmed in gold like a religious parchment. The italic writing was in indigo ink, complete with the odd mistake blotted out. It transported her to another world where she was a princess wandering through the enchanted wood, looking for her one true love and finding her prince. She liked to run her fingertips over the words, mouthing them if it got difficult. She envied those women with long pink and white fingernails and soft hands. In fact she'd like to have straight teeth, like the princess in the book. Teeth that only money could buy. The long, flowing, caped dresses, she had no idea what style they were? Pre-Raphaelite? She didn't know what that really meant but she had once seen a dress like the princess's. It was on Rapunzel in a toy shop window when she was young, so young she was still in her pram and her mum was pushing her down Sauchiehall Street, going out to meet a friend for a cuppa. She wondered what had happened to those years, all the people her mum seemed to know. All gone now. Every one of them. There was nobody left.

Nobody left for Sandra.

That loneliness had eaten away at her soul and led her to make some very bad choices about her life; choices people who bought their teeth, wore silk stockings and bought their biscuits at full price never have to make.

The Duchess placed her cold, bony hand on top of Sandra. It was a gentle minding to get on with the story.

Sandra opened the book, heaving the heavy cover over and letting it rest on her thigh. She knew the story off by heart. The poor boy got lost in the forest and the princess found him and saved him. They fall in love and go back to the castle.

Or something like that.

Sandra got the names confused sometimes, the boys and the girls mixed up. Sometimes it looked like the prince who was lost in the forest, asleep under the tree, and a pauper boy came along and saved him from . . . well Sandra didn't know what, but it all turned out well in the end. Sometimes, the blonde princess saved the pauper boy. Sandra was sure she was reading it and that the writer had changed his mind. However, at the end, the princess ended up with the dark-haired, good-looking bloke and she got lots of fab clothes to wear, a nice horse to ride about on and a shitload of pasta to eat. Sandra couldn't actually read the Italian, but she talked about the pictures, showing them to the Duchess. The Duchess liked the character of the queen. The queen, in her deep pink evening gown and her rolled-up black hair with her tiara – or was it a crown – did bear a resemblance to the Duchess. Sandra wondered idly if there was some truth in the old bint being a duchess, a real life duchess? She had seen a programme on Channel 4 when she'd been too rat-arsed to reach the remote. There had been loads of minor royalty displaced during the war, maybe there was something in it. So there might be a duke somewhere, but the old photographs looked like a normal family. Sandra traced her nicotine stained fingertip over her favourite picture of the princess. Either dressed for bed or dressed like a slave or a Roman goddess, she was standing at the narrow arched window of the castle, looking out into a fairy-tale woodland beyond as if she knew that her true love was out there somewhere. She cleared her throat and made herself comfortable, imagining that she was reading this out loud in front of an open log fire and Paolo had gone out to chop logs. There was a nice meal in the oven, a bottle of good wine in the fridge for them to enjoy once the old dear had gone to bed. Well, the old dear would already be in bed and

. . . Sandra allowed her imagination to run riot, feeling the base of her third finger. Empty. She wished she could feel a band of gold on there. The Duchess could be on her death bed, and it would be a matter of hours. Sandra would be caring and lovely, staying up to nurse her while thinking about what holidays to go on with the money. Getting out of Scotland, going somewhere hot. She looked at the picture, wondering if that was an idea of what Italy was like. Beautiful Disney castles on the top of green pastured mountains? She could suggest to Paolo sensitively that they could go back to the Duchess's homeland, to bury her. Even if she wasn't dead.

She cleared her throat to begin the story, her stubby finger pointing at the words under the picture. 'One fine day, Paolo . . .'

The old lady hit her on the knee, deep angry furrows on her forehead.

'Sorry.' Sandra put her hand over her mouth and felt herself redden at the Freudian slip. She wanted the ground to open up and swallow her. But then she heard a polite little snort, and the Duchess was laughing. The old lady reached out. A curved hand, cold dry fingers touched the side of Sandra's face, the Duchess's eyes travelled over her face, finding some pleasure in it. Then she sat back in her chair and clicked her fingers, wanting the story to go on.

Irene Kerr was brought into the small section of the interview room, her crooked elbow cupped in the hand of the faithful Maggie. She was a ghost of the feisty woman who had struggled with Costello only a few hours before. Maggie guided her to a seat and she collapsed into it.

'Do you recognize this man?' Anderson held out a print of the screen shot.

She nodded again, enthusiastically. 'That's David,' she said.

'We have found some CCTV footage. I want you to be prepared for it.'

She nodded. A long deep breath of control.

'He's sitting at the Zeitgeist Café.'

'Yes, I know that place.'

'We'd like you to watch the film, and tell us anything you think might help us. Anything at all. Are you OK with that?'

She nodded keenly. They pulled her chair in front of the screen. Maggie sat behind her, to help if it all got a bit unpleasant.

DC Wyngate was at the mouse, his fingers flicking back and forward. 'Watch this.'

Anderson was going to watch the film. Mulholland, who had sourced the tape, was on the opposite side, watching Irene's reaction.

Anderson sat down.

The film itself was quite clear, occasionally they had a good view of the boy sitting at the corner of Byres Road and Vinicombe Street, outside the Zeitgeist Café on a wrought iron chair enjoying the sunshine. One foot parked up on the other thigh, his head back, taking the occasional sip at a can that they knew was Appletiser, and the occasional bite of his granola bar.

'That's him, that's him.' Irene's fingers flew to the screen, her son's slightly fuzzy image smiled at something. His mother smiled back, entranced.

The camera swung slowly away, catching images elsewhere. Untidy rows of a marching pipe band that were heading towards an assembly point. Among the black and white shades of grey images, it was only really strong colour which stood out, making it a weird one-point colour world. Wyngate moved the tracker ball to get the best picture, then enlarged it to fill the screen without distorting the image. The view was hindered constantly by the crowd on the pavement passing, making their way up to the start of the parade. The movement of people from right to left and the camera occasionally moving up and down, gave the impression of a boat on a heavy swell. It wasn't easy to get a good full view of David. Every time he appeared on the screen Wyngate halted the video.

'People watching? Or is he waiting for somebody? He wasn't meant to be meeting his friends until eleven,' said Irene.

'Maybe he's waiting for somebody else,' hinted Anderson.

'So what happened to him?' Irene looked round at the faces of Wyngate and Mulholland, knowing they had seen it. Her eyes searched Anderson's face for answers. She got nothing back.

'Watch please, we need you to keep your eyes on the screen.' Anderson was polite, then added, 'It's the best thing you can do. Give us any answers you can.'

She nodded, turning her eyes to an image both hypnotic and repellent.

Wyngate moved the CCTV film on, the pipes passed, the drums passed, there was a space about 09.08 where David was clearly visible doing nothing much of interest. A teenage boy taking time out, relaxing, drinking his Appletiser, casually checking his phone. Wyngate slowed the tape down as a waitress went past carrying a bin bag. She held it open for him to put something in it, the empty granola wrapper. A laugh and a few flirtatious words passed between them before the waitress walked round the corner to take the bag to the bins.

David lifted his phone again.

'He's not texting or taking a call, he's checking it,' Mulholland said, transfixed by the footage.

'All kids do that, Vik, they look at their phone a hundred times a day. He puts the phone back down on the table beside him,' Anderson said.

David was sitting with his back leaning against the wall of the café, then lifted his head as if somebody had caught his attention.

Irene was sitting up, energized suddenly, full of hope, an excited expression on her face.

A woman moved into view, her back to the camera but she was close to David. Her white trousers stood out on the film. She wore a bright silky top so beautifully cut it drifted as she moved. Her striking figure glowed in this monochrome world. She was pulling something behind her, like a shopping trolley or a case but the body of it was obscured by others passing by and she herself obscured the view of David as she passed in front of him. Then she hesitated, stopped. His arm was seen, outstretched so his hand appeared from the other side of her body. The universal language of giving directions. The woman seemed to lean over towards him, one hand cupped to her ear to hear better over the noise of the street. Then she raised her hand in thanks and walked away, crossing Vinicombe Street to carry on to the bottom of Byres Road.

She strode out of view with confidence, now she was sure where she was going.

'In the direction of the University Café,' muttered Irene.

They watched as David turned his head to watch her go, a handsome young man, caught in profile, rubbing his upper arm against an unseen chill. The look on his face was slightly puzzled, querulous.

'Do you know that woman? Difficult to tell seeing her from the back, but do you know her?' Wyngate stopped the film, Irene's son's face was frozen on profile. The quizzical look etched on his features. 'It looks as though he might, or he thought he might.'

'But she was only asking directions, wasn't she? And I couldn't even see her face. Is that it? Please tell me that you have more than that?' Irene looked at Anderson, hands out, pleading.

Wyngate looked at Anderson.

'No, there's plenty more. Are you OK to go on?'

She nodded. The film restarted.

'It goes on for about five minutes. David is just sitting. The Irish dancers walk past with their band following and then the characters from the Woodland Theatre. You'll see a few mice, rabbits and squirrels walk up, plus a very convincing Mr Fox. David is watching, not paying much attention to anything or anyone. We see glimpses of him here and there. Then there's this. Nine thirteen.' Wyngate slowed the film down, another figure appeared at the edge of the shot. They appeared to be standing in the doorway of the Zeitgeist Café. A female in jeans, long hair twisted into a clip, thin, vest T-shirt, bracelets round her wrist. There was a large camera hanging round her neck. A can of Diet Coke came into view as she lowered her arm. She leaned over to him, her back to the street-mounted camera. A can of Diet Coke was placed on the table. They saw it wobble as the table was then pulled jerkily to one side. Anderson moved his seat forward, transfixed by what was now unwinding on the screen.

'Can we get a better view on that, Gordon?'

Wyngate looked round at the use of his first name, 'We can once we send it to be enhanced, but I thought that we needed to see this straightaway.'

Wyngate pointed at the screen with the tip of his pen, 'David seems to slump here, in front of this girl. Then the woman from earlier, the lady with the white trousers, comes back again. Her back still to the camera. She says something to the younger woman, then this passer-by seems to stop and ask if they need any help. The view is blocked. Then the passer-by moves away, the view clears to both the women bending over David. He's now on the ground.'

Wyngate paused the film. David was sitting on the pavement, eyes open, almost laughing as if he had fallen off his seat.

'Oh my God, what has happened to him? What did they do to him?' Irene's hand was at her mouth, her voice trembling. Maggie was staring at the screen this time as well, fixated by the drama.

Anderson nodded to Wyngate; move it on.

As they lifted him up, a glimpse of the side of their faces came into view. The older woman helped David up and onto the chair and then onto his feet. She began to walk him away. Her arm through his, giving him some assistance. The second woman, much younger, called after them, skinny arm outstretched as she takes two steps to catch them up, holding out the phone that he had left on the table. For a moment their hands meet, and grip. The time on the film was 09.17 a.m.

'It looks as though he knows that girl, the one with the bare arm and the bracelets . . .' *And the camera round her neck.*

'Do you know her?' asked Wyngate. 'He seems to know her.'

'And the blonde woman was pulling something the first time she passed. She's not now.' Maggie pointed out, clearly puzzled.

'I don't know her. Oh my God. What happened to him? Who are these people?'

Anderson ignored her. 'Stop the film.'

Wyngate jumped.

'Right there, stop it,' said Anderson, pulling out his own mobile phone, and swiping the screen once. He left the room, leaving the door to close slowly.

Wyngate looked back at the film, and then Mulholland

looked at the T-shirt, the camera swinging free. Older. Curvier. Long dark hair pulled back in a ponytail. Now they knew.

'What's going on?' asked Irene. 'Do you know that girl?'

'Yes, I think we do,' said Wyngate. 'We need to wait until the boss comes back.'

Anderson walked to the window in the corridor and said, 'Claire, we need your help. Did you come across a young man, light brown hair, long sleeved black T-shirt at the—'

'Zeitgeist Café,' offered Claire, struggling to be heard over the rabble of the crowd. She talked on. He couldn't hear it all, but he caught enough.

'OK, look, Claire, this is important. I want you to stop what you are doing and go to the nearest police officer you can see. He'll get you in a car . . . yes I know it will look as though you are being arrested . . .' Her voice interrupted. 'Yes, I know you can walk it in ten minutes but I want you here in two. Buzz when you get to the door. I'll let Graham know to bring you up here.'

He cut the call and phoned Graham downstairs to get a car out to her ignoring his protests that nobody was going anywhere at the moment.

'Who is that girl?' asked Irene, on her feet the minute he walked into the room, her face right up at his.

'Her name is Claire. It would seem that your son ran into my daughter. Twice.' He carefully sat Irene back down. 'Can I have a word?' He gestured at Wyngate. 'Outside.'

Once in the quiet of the corridor, Anderson spoke in muted tones. 'Claire thought the boy had some kind of fit and presumed the other woman was his mother. The woman took him away. Can you phone the QE, ask them to check again if a teenager was admitted? If he had a fit, he might have no memory. The woman might have given her details and they also might have presumed that they were related. These things happen. We will look bloody stupid if he has been in the hospital all along.'

'And what do we tell Irene?'

'As little as possible,' was all Anderson said.

*　　*　　*

'OK, so the boy walks in the forest. He is sad and alone. The sun goes down and he gets lost. He climbs a tree to eat the single apple. He leans on a branch to reach the apple and he falls. He can't walk and lies down among the leaves on the forest floor.' At this point Sandra turned the book to let the Duchess see the stunning drawings of the stylized woodland animals that turned up to watch over the boy as he lay, dying. The animals were not Disney beautiful, not cute. More realistic than that, but somehow not real. Hyper real. The last picture was a magnificent stag leading the princess to the little boy; the princess to the pauper. She plucked an apple from a tree and gave it to him. They fell asleep in each other's arms, cuddling into each other against the deep, cold snow. The boy perished from cold, but the princess survived. At this point the Duchess started to cry and Sandra began turning over the pages until she got to the bit where the Enchantress appeared, a weird goblin-like fairy with gold gossamer wings who flew through the air and brought the boy back to life. They stumbled together through the forest, through the snow, following the lead of the Enchantress. As they walked, the forest became green and the snow was replaced by beautiful flowers. Sandra presumed the deep part of the forest was under some spell to make it dangerous and inhabitable. She knew bits of Glasgow like that.

In this version, the king and the queen were waiting on the return of the princess and they make the poor boy a prince, marrying him off to the princess who spent the last few pages looking out the window, combing her hair. She was gazing beyond the forest, to billows of smoke on the horizon.

'And so the princess married the poor boy and they lived in the castle. Look there, look at her beautiful wedding dress.' Sandra turned the book again for the Duchess to see. It was a stunning dress, the drawing detailed to the extreme; a golden gown, layered in diamonds and silver thread. The pauper stood by in his shining armour. The Duchess pointed a quivering single finger out to the picture of the Enchantress, ethereal looking now, high in the dark cloudy sky above the wedding feast, soaring on her gossamer wings. The finger moved from the princess to the Enchantress and back again.

'So the Enchantress is the princess?' Sandra asked, totally confused.

The Duchess's eyes watered up a little. Then she moved her wrist, her shoulders too stiff to move, and lifted her hand to the window. For a moment Sandra saw her in profile, thinking that she must have been truly beautiful once. The old lady's eyes stared into the cloudless blue sky, looking for an Enchantress of her own.

And she cried.

Despite herself, Sandra put her hand on the thin, bony shoulder and gave it a little squeeze. The Duchess might be a right old cow, but she was a human being and she was hurting.

'So the Enchantress makes everything OK?'

The old lady gave a tearful nod.

'That was very charming,' said a voice from the door. It was Paolo.

Sandra reddened. 'Sorry, I never saw you there.'

The Duchess turned immediately at Paolo's voice. She cried tears of joy and shook her head in thanks. There was a lot of Italian hugging and kissing, they were worse than the Irish for that.

'You did fine. Do you want to go home now, get some rest? It's nearly tea time. Oh, do you know who this belongs to?' He showed her a brand new Samsung phone, holding it out, his forearm nicely tanned, the old watch round his slim wrist.

She looked at the phone he held in his hand, then at the watch. She knew it was an eighteen carat gold, Patek Philippe watch, probably from the 1950s. So it said on the auctioneer's website, worth five grand if it was worth a penny.

Sandra looked again at the phone, her mouth intervened. 'No, have you been treating yourself?'

'I found it out there.' He looked at her. 'There were a lot of people out there earlier, at the incident. Somebody dropped this.'

Sandra looked wistfully at the watch, and then went into nice mode. He had to learn to trust her. 'Maybe you should take it to the police, I can stay with the Duchess if you want, you know, until you get back.'

'No. No, I will sit with her and take this round later, when she has fallen asleep.'

He looked at his watch again and Sandra wondered how anything that old could be so valuable. Then she thought of the Duchess, she was worth a bob or two. She tried to think what a nice person would say. 'Somebody will be missing that. Kids have their whole life on their phones these days.'

'I'll walk round later. Take me fifteen minutes max.'

'Oh.' Sandra seized the opportunity. 'But you gave me that car as a little run-around so I could be here for your mum. I could drive you to Partickhill Station, or you take the car,' she added, hoping to be in his company for a little longer, then regretted it when she recalled what was in the boot.

Paolo smiled at her, a genuine smile that crinkled his Paul Newman eyes. 'In that traffic, I don't think so.'

And she felt stupid.

'Thank you but no. I'll enjoy the walk. I'll get her dinner brought up here.' He pulled a tissue from the mother of pearl box on the dressing table and dabbed the tears from the Duchess's cheek. 'You know, Sandra, you do so much for us, here at all hours. And I know you work much more than you get paid for.'

'I like her. I like my job,' she lied.

'But you should go out, enjoy the weather, go to the festival. There's a great atmosphere out there. Meet some friends.'

Sandra smiled what she hoped was her best smile. Was that a hint, a wee fish for information? 'I haven't any friends here at the moment. And I have something to get finished.' She added, trying not to sound like Sandra No Mates.

He nodded, that dismissive way he had. And she left.

Once alone, Paolo started to undress the Duchess, putting his arm round the back of her shoulders, helping her to her feet on her wheelchair and then he wheeled her to the wet room. They were listening to *Carmen*, one of the Duchess's favourite operas. She would smile and nod her head slightly in time with the 'March of the Toreadors', then close her eyes at the aria, 'Habanera', enjoying it, losing herself in it. He knew that the hearing was one of the last senses to go, and that she was fully aware of the music. Every day, another bit of her slipped from him. He would do all he could to keep her with him for as long as possible.

He helped her into her wet chair and turned on the shower. He used oil on her. She held out her limbs for him, lifting her feet so he could wash, cream and powder them. Then he rubbed cream into her hands and arms, massaging her stringy muscles as he did so. Not caring about the time it took. He did this every day.

Then he would do her hair. In her wheelchair, she was aware that people looked down at the top of her head and she saw no reason why that should not be as immaculately groomed as the rest of her, so every month he dyed what little there was left black, and then painted it with a thickening agent so it looked bountiful as it sat on the top of her head, in the style of an opera diva. Paolo would not have people seeing her scalp. After doing her hair, he would wrap her in a pure silk dressing gown with a feathered border, placing it carefully around her as if she was fragile and valuable, lifting up each arm and slipping them into the sleeves as if they were beyond value. He then sat her in the wheelchair and took her out of the wet room and into the bedroom, sitting her in the warmth of the sun so she wouldn't catch a chill. She looked into his eyes, her hand resting on his head as he knelt in front of her and slipped each foot into her slippers, then lifted them onto the footrests.

By this time he was always very wet so he took a shower himself. He then changed into his clean dry clothes and packed the old wet stuff away in the laundry basket with the Duchess's old nightdress and her clothes from the day before.

He tried to ignore the slight hesitancy in her breathing, that wheeze with every breath in, louder with every breath out. She was in the early stages of her illness. The doctor kept mentioning it as if trying to prepare him for something that he could never accept; one day the Duchess might not be here.

'David Kerr's phone has been switched on.' Wyngate pointed at the blue dot on the computer screen. 'Wait a minute. Yes, yes, it is very close to here.'

'Close as in we can get there?'

'Are you wanting to send out uniform? Because I can do this by phone,' said Wyngate, matter of factly.

'Then why the hell are we still sitting here? Anderson can get Costello to sit in on the interview with Claire. Protocol dictates that somebody needs to be there when he speaks to his daughter, and with Kirkton taking such an interest he needs to be squeaky clean, so Archie Walker can do that. He's been hanging around all day like a bad smell. Come on, let's get out of here.' Mulholland already had his jacket on. He scribbled a quick note for Anderson and grabbed his car keys.

'But Claire will be here in a minute, we might be better to wait,' argued Wyngate, knowing where his allegiance was best placed.

'But she's not here yet is she? And that phone is on the move right now.'

Wyngate walked, head down, eyes constantly on his phone as he navigated the crowds by keeping very close to Mulholland's shoulder. He noticed the rhythm of the limp of his colleague, the hurl of some pipes in the distance and the smell of hotdogs in the air, but he was concentrating on his phone.

Once they were in the car, Wyngate changed the screen to show the street map location. 'It's on Prince Albert Road.'

'We can't get down there.' Mulholland drove forward keeping one eye on the phone that was now fixed on the dashboard. The blue dot moved, making its swirly way through the West End, but moving very slowly.

'Is he driving or walking?'

'Difficult to say in this traffic.' Mulholland swung the Audi round in a sharp U-turn.

'Slow down a bit. He's coming towards us, he's on Hyndland Road.'

Mulholland pulled in.

'He's going past us right now, he's driving.' Wyngate looked out the window. The traffic was snarled to a standstill but the dot was still moving. 'No, he's on foot.'

They watched the crowds go past, he could be in there anywhere. The blue dot on Wyngate's phone turned up the street they had just turned out of. Wyngate was watching a slim young man, jeans and suit jacket, stride out across the road with a worn leather satchel swinging round his shoulders. Mulholland pointed at a slightly older man, walking more sedately, but with determination, a plain shirt, jacket held in his hand, sleeves rolled up, going about his business.

'I have a dreadful feeling that I know exactly where he is going,' murmured Mulholland.

'Where?' asked Wyngate.

'Up to the station to hand the bloody thing in.'

Anderson and Costello waited for Claire and watched the CCTV film, frame by frame, time and time again. Anderson was watching David, Costello was watching anything that went past, anything she thought was a little odd. Graham had been called up from downstairs, he was at the controls, stopping to take a screen shot every time they thought they saw something that might warrant closer attention. Archie Walker was sitting beside them, notebook in hand, thinking of the media fallout that this might precipitate. Be prepared was the law of the fiscal.

Anderson had asked Graham to wind the film right back to where Claire had said she had bumped into David, before he made it to the Zeitgeist Café.

They had viewed the second half many times. David sitting with his Appletiser. The image being blocked by the passage of a high-sided vehicle going up to the start of the parade. They had scrutinized the early morning crowds, watching as they meandered around, looking for a nice place to have breakfast, enjoying the sun and the aperitif of the street entertainers. They had noted and traced who David had spoken to: the waitress with the bin bag, a man who asked directions before he and his wife went off on their way, a younger man texting as he walked and tripped over David's legs; there was a charismatic smile, an apology, a bit of a laugh between them. David had waved his hand; *Oh don't bother about it.* Heads turned, listening to something coming down Byres Road. The Glasgow Gospel Choir singing 'Proud Mary', a straggly bunch; singing and dancing with no real cohesion, just enjoying themselves.

A few people gathered in front of David, a dark-haired girl came into view. Colin thought he recognized one of Claire's school friends. Well, maybe not a friend. Definitely not a friend. Costello kept her head down, making notes. Archie Walker was looking at the screen, frowning slightly, some vague recognition trying to come to the front of his mind.

Anderson fell very quiet as the stilt walkers, stilts over their arm, came into view. They carried some rolled-up banners high, others scattered red paper high into the air.

'They were promoting that new nightclub. Kenny Fraser had trouble getting planning for it so they are six months behind. It's still being refurbed. Insanity,' said Walker.

'What? Advertising it now when it's not opening until Christmas?'

'No, the name of the nightclub is Insanity.'

'Kenny Fraser, not exactly a pillar of the community, is he?'

'I couldn't possibly comment,' said Walker, which was fiscal speak for yes.

Anderson asked for the tape to be wound further back.

From the distance of the camera, it looked as though they were scattering thick confetti but the close up showed they were casting red paper flowers that soared like birds into the sky. They floated down to the empty street, pattering the road with red petals. The small crowd were clapping. They couldn't tell from watching if the tune had changed but the dancing was different, a bit less Motown and a bit jazzier. Two girls were caught in the upper right of the screen Charlestoning in the gutter, falling over and laughing.

Claire came into view, a small figure in the upper left of the screen. She reached out and caught a rose in her palm with balletic grace.

'Where is she?' asked Anderson, looking at his watch.

'She's in the doorway of Papyrus, I think.'

Claire retreated out of view and three girls immediately obscured the picture. Her 'friends' from school, including the one with the purple streaks. Anderson watched closely and the room fell silent. There was a bit of horseplay. Claire appeared, words exchanged. She took a few steps back, one hand behind her to steady her against the wall of the shop as she gripped the camera. Then Claire retreated further into the doorway.

They could see the dark-haired girl turn and say something to Claire, now visible again. Claire's head whiplashed as if she had been slapped, pulling the camera up a little to help cover her face, creating a barrier between them.

The other girl was quite clear. She didn't spit at Claire but words shot out her mouth, insulting and demeaning. There was a gang with the bully, one against three. Her two accomplices walked away. The dark-haired one hung back, grinding her shoe into the pavement, made a final parting comment and swaggered away. Claire stood quite still, chin up, poised, dignified in her defeat. The others walked out of the upper corner of the screen and Claire gave a little look of relief over her left shoulder, making sure that they were gone. Anderson twitched slightly in his seat, wishing that he had been there, that he could have done something.

The room was quiet.

Walker glanced at Costello, telling her to keep quiet.

Anderson sat back on his seat, his eyes narrowed. He was very angry. He recalled Claire coming in from school, month after month, just going straight up to her room, sneaking upstairs. Unseen, like she didn't exist. The psychologist had told them to watch out for a return to this destructive pattern of behaviour, a pattern that had its roots on the banks of Loch Lomond, when she had got caught up in a horror that nobody could fully explain. His daughter was a happy person by default, she had good parenting behind her. Maybe not the most conventional of family set-ups, but she had never been hurt by them. Everything that hurt her had been external. If she was starting to veer down that path of self-destruction again then something definitive had triggered it. And he had picked up that signal in the spring. He had the strangest feeling he had just witnessed the reason.

'Can we take a look at that girl?' he heard himself say, his voice sounded odd, too calm, too controlled. 'I think she goes to the same school that Claire does. Did,' he corrected himself.

'Does that posh school produce a better class of hooligan?'

asked Costello. 'If Claire knows her then why don't we ask Claire.'

'I like to keep my private life and my work separate.'

'And is this some new kind of arrangement?'

'I have my reasons.'

'And they are?'

'Because,' snapped Anderson. 'Sorry Costello, it's just that there had been some issues at the school.'

'Why didn't you say so? Can we get a close-up on that lassie?' Costello asked. 'It's not nine o'clock yet, those girls look like they have been out all night.'

'It's not easy for her, being my daughter. Look at that body language.'

'It's that skinny one with the streaks who is the ring leader. What does she do with her foot? That looks like Vik doing the twist at the Christmas party.'

Graham rewound the footage and scrolled the picture in tighter. There was something under the skinny girl's foot, scrunched up on the pavement. It looked like a little bird. 'She has stepped on the flower that Claire had caught.'

'What a lovely girl she is. If you want them leaned on let me know.' Costello's voice had that steely quality, something had hurt. And it was hurting still. 'Has Claire mentioned this situation?'

'She did. Said it was such unsophisticated bullying. That was the word Claire used, "unsophisticated". She was criticizing her bullies. She trivialized it.'

'Still hurts though, I wonder what was said to her.'

'A lip reader would be able to tell you,' suggested Walker, leaning closer to the screen.

'Or you could ask her,' suggested Costello again.

Walker pointed. 'Well, I can tell you who the dark-haired one is, the one with the streaky hair. That young lady is Tania Kirkton. James Kirkton's daughter.'

Paolo Girasole was as nondescript as anybody could be, anything from early thirties to late forties. Brown hair that was only brown, no red undertones, no copper highlights. It was brown. He was lightly tanned, wearing jeans and a faded denim shirt with his sleeves rolled up. Everything was neatly ironed but had seen better days. His shoes were old but well-polished leather, the watch a treasured classic and his leather satchel shiny and curled with age. And he looked worried, the worn-down weary fatigue of middle management, Wyngate guessed. He was worn out by the system and clinging on to a boring desk job by his fingertips, trying to smile as the bright young things were promoted over him. His job would be drifting sideways into mediocrity. He glanced at his watch and then the clock on the wall.

'Do you have to be somewhere?' asked Mulholland.

'No, I was visiting Athole House, and I needed to be back there before too long. I only nipped out to hand this in. Wasn't expecting to be detained.' But his manner didn't show any annoyance, he was stating fact.

They asked his name and address. Paolo Girasole lived in Manchester Avenue and he worked for the council in refuse collection, in the office not in the bins. He was born in 1980 on the 4th July.

'Girasole? That's a bit of a famous name in these parts? Fish and chips shop?' said Wyngate, who had grown up not three streets from the station.

'No alas, I wish. Then I might not be skint.' He smiled. An easy smile.

'Oh, so where did you find the phone?'

'At the bins at Athole Square, on the main road. So I picked it up and it didn't look that damaged.' He pointed out the little dent on the corner. 'I turned it on to see if I could find a number, but it's locked, so I stuck it in my pocket and went to visit the care home as planned, then thought I'd better hand it in. You know, when I heard about the incident at the bottom of the road. The boy?'

'Very public spirited of you.'

'It's a brand new Samsung Galaxy 7 edge. It's worth a few bob. So somebody must have dropped it.'

'Can you confirm where you found it?' They handed him a map and he put an X on the spot, an italic X in dark blue ink.

* * *

Wyngate filled out the paperwork, asking Graham to take Paolo's fingerprints for exclusion purposes while Mulholland listened to the voicemails on the phone, now confirmed as being David's, his mother knew the code to unlock it. All it contained were increasingly worried voicemails from David's mother, from the friends he was due to meet, and from Winston who he had just left. His calendar had gym, study periods for each subject and a few visits to the cinema planned. Nobody else had either texted, Facebooked or emailed him. Nobody that they hadn't already spoken to.

All that happened was that somebody had dropped David's phone. It was another lead taking them nowhere.

As Costello, Walker and Graham scrutinized the film at the moment David appeared at the Zeitgeist Café, Anderson's mind kept drifting. This was looking more like a murder enquiry and his daughter was right in the middle of it. Yet he kept thinking about the bullying, and the 'whatever'. He was looking for whatever it was that labelled David a victim. Maybe it was his location, sitting alone on the end of the row right on a corner. A corner that was only a few minutes' walk down Byres Road from Papyrus where the three girls had confronted Claire. As they watched, Graham's hands on the control, both Costello and Anderson said 'stop' at once. It was David, walking into shot, then stopping and bending down to pick something up. He held it out to Claire, a smile. Maybe their hands touched.

'Well, well,' said Costello. 'Chivalry indeed.'

'She did say she had bumped into him before, now we know. He picked up the squashed paper rose and gave it to her.'

They watched David slowly walk down Byres Road, to the camera that covered the Vinicombe Street/Byres Road junction. Once he sat down, he looked at his phone, then he leaned back in the seat, his can of Appletiser on the table beside him. He closed his eyes, slightly turned to his left to face the sun. He looked relaxed and happy, he was not expecting whatever befell him.

They all jumped when the phone rang. It was the desk

downstairs. Claire had arrived. The car had driven a huge detour to get through the crowd.

Anderson put the phone down. 'Just to make it quite clear, there's no way that I am not sitting in on this interview.' For a moment he stared at Costello, who shrugged and said it was no skin off her nose.

'I don't get paid enough to babysit a DCI flaunting the rules. Again. But Archie here does.' She smiled sweetly at the fiscal.

They had put her in the family room, where they had sat with Irene Kerr an hour earlier, their dirty coffee cups were still on the small table.

Claire was sitting a little nervous, a little in awe of her father. 'So, like, this is where you work?'

'Yes. Where did you think I worked?'

'And are you in charge of all these people?' She waved her finger at Costello and Walker. People she knew, but it had never dawned on her that there was such a strict hierarchy in the force and that her dad was at the top of it. 'And those blokes downstairs?'

'No, not really,' said Anderson, aware of Walker's bristle.

'If he was in charge there'd be a danger of us doing as we were told,' said Costello, making Claire laugh.

Claire began playing with the bracelets on her wrist as she looked around the blue-painted room, for a moment her teenage cool giving way to the child that was still in there somewhere. She was trying to conceal her excitement about the situation.

'So Claire, you were photographing the parade preparations this morning?'

'You know I was.'

'And something happened, we caught it on CCTV. The young man . . .'

'Yeah, the guy who had the fit, like I told you.' She shrugged as if to say, *So what?*

'OK, can you describe for us what happened?'

'It was like I said.'

'Again,' said Anderson, so Costello didn't have to. 'My DI

here has not heard any of it and she needs to record what you saw.'

Claire looked at Costello. 'I was watching the set-up for the parade, I wanted to do whole montage of the day . . . I was a bit thirsty . . .'

'Where were you at this point?'

'Up at Papyrus, they have a recessed doorway.'

'What time was this?'

'I was there from half eight.'

They knew the exact time from the CCTV.

'OK, so you were there for a wee while then . . .'

'Well, the Zeitgeist Café was the nearest place open that early so I went there for a Diet Coke. I took it outside and I heard something behind me, like a clatter.' She gestured over her left shoulder. 'And I turned and he was there, coughing like he was gagging. He was holding his neck and I went over and helped him up. Then his mum came and took him away, that was all it was.'

They all knew that the woman was not his mother. David had not put his hand on his throat. It was not on the CCTV. Claire's brain was making sense of what she had seen. But he continued with the questioning, somewhere in her memory there would be nuggets of the truth.

'His mum?' he asked.

'Yeah,' she said with a shrug, 'I presumed so, and she was kinda old. She knew him.'

'Did he say anything?'

Claire shook her head.

'Did he seem to recognize her?'

'No, he was . . . well . . .' Her eyes dropped. 'He was finding it difficult to breathe, but she knew what to do, so I thought she was his mum. Maybe a nurse, she knew her stuff. Competent.'

'So he didn't say anything?'

'No.'

'Why did you think she knew him?'

'Because she . . . knew him. She lifted him up a wee bit, you know, to help him away.'

'Away where?'

'Into a car, I think.'

'What car? Did you see it?'

Claire shrugged. 'No, she said that her car was parked round the corner. I don't know what make of car. I never saw it.'

'She called him by his name?'

'Yes . . . No . . . I don't know, I think she called him pet or something.'

'Would you recognize her again?'

'I don't know. Her face was turned away from mine most of the time. She had sunglasses on, blonde hair, well dressed.' Her hands mimicked a bob cut. 'Classy.'

Anderson nodded. That was something.

'Accent?'

'Scottish. Normal, not like posh or Edinburgh or anything. But not a ned. Nothing like that.'

'Smell?'

'Of what?'

'What do they smell of? Perfume? Drink? Smoke? Anything?'

'She had nice perfume on. Not a smoker. Very clean.'

'Clean?'

'Clean hands.'

'Could you draw an impression of her for us?'

She snorted. 'Draw her? I can do better than that.' She pulled her camera towards her, looking closely at it. 'I'll have a picture of her.'

The Nikon D750 had taken a perfectly clear image that was blown up by Wyngate. Technically it was a good photograph, but as the subject had kept her head turned, the slightly side view didn't show them any more than they already knew. What they had was a partial outline of the left side of her face, a few hairs blowing across her cheek. She looked very alive, something about the set of her jaw, she looked determined, on a mission.

They rewound the film with Claire's commentary. The boy in the Hollister top had stopped to pick up the paper rose from the ground – well, what was left of the rose. It proved that David Kerr had been walking down Byres Road, north to south, en route to the University Café. He never got there.

Why? It was early on Parade Day, Byres Road was already extremely busy. The one thing that did stand testament was that David Kerr seemed a very polite young man, he was gracious when people walked into him. He had been there when Claire got upset and had let himself be known to her, the rose was a ruse. He was saying, 'I saw that' and it had given her some comfort, restored her faith in humanity a little.

Wyngate was busy finding the section where David was, sitting outside the Zeitgeist Café about ten minutes later. That timing would be about right, slow walking against the direction of the pedestrians walking up to the Botanics. The film moved on, the time ticked slowly by. The blonde woman asking for directions, then a few minutes later David slumped forward, Claire stepped into the picture. The chair was pulled to one side. The other chair was kicked out the way. David was on the ground, his back against the wall, eyes opening and closing, feeling the ground with his fingers as though he was dizzy. Fear etched deep into his face. Then the blonde woman reappeared on the scene, bent over him and brushed his hair back from his face. The film went on as before. The woman lifted him from the ground, then hesitated, dropped her head for a moment, then with the skill of a nurse, or a carer, walked him round the corner, him unsteady on his feet, her as solid as a rock, to Vinicombe Street and out of the sight of the CCTV camera. She wasn't carrying or pulling anything with her, as she had been when she had asked for directions. Had she delivered it somewhere?

The camera on Byres Road looked right up the street, it wasn't well placed for them to see anything once they turned the corner.

'Go back a bit, what does she do there?' asked Costello.

Wyngate reversed the tape, they watched in silence as the blonde dipped her head.

'What is she doing?' Costello mimicked her movement.

'She's looking at her watch. What could be time critical? Somebody waiting with transport round the corner?'

They all viewed the tape. 'When she checked her watch, she is carrying most of the weight of David. So why does she look at her watch exactly then? Why?'

Anderson said, 'OK, I know we have watched it twenty times but go back to the scene on the corner. Wind it back to where David first appears on the street. Is that the only time that woman gets close to him? Where did she go, what happened to the thing she was pulling? Where did she go with that, where did she go with him? Claire said that she had car keys with her. How many hands did she have? How did she manage that?'

'She takes him up to the corner, then up Vinicombe Street. She's a relatively tall but slim woman. He is a slim built man. Costello how far could you carry Mulholland here?'

Costello looked Mulholland up and down, considering. 'As far as the nearest cliff, drop him over.' She looked at his bad leg. 'She must have had transport, maybe it was waiting for her. We could put a call out for any photos, any videos filmed around there. The parade was on later but there'll be hundreds of versions of that, all those mums and dads, and aunts and uncles. We might be able to get a good image of her. Claire got a good look at him, but not at her, not with those bloody glasses. I bet she never took them off. She has them on for a reason, she is careful not to show her face.'

'I don't think the finance office would accept the expense to trawl through all that lot, for so little evidential value. Do you want to argue with them? We have a budget to stick to.'

'So we need to work with the film that we have, for now at least. Anything else will take too long.'

'Talking of taking too long, is there any word from O'Hare yet?' asked Costello. 'This is incredibly cruel.'

Anderson shook his head. 'It's like a fair out there. And Irene would be none the wiser if it had been kept off social media. We will work with the film.'

'OK, so on the film, there is a bit where they touch, she puts her hand on David's jumper to steady him, a brief contact but it might be enough. Mathilda McQueen could get some DNA off the Hollister jumper. If it is the same jumper,' she added. 'Can you go back to the bit where she asks him for directions? Just look at his face as she leaves, he looks after her. A little concerned? A little puzzled? About eight or nine minutes past nine?'

'Why?'

'Watch, he falls off the seat. Then she comes back having walked away, picks him up and checks the time. Why? Then he allows himself to be carried away to . . . well, to be nailed into a tea chest.'

'If it is him,' cautioned Walker.

Costello pointed her pen at the screen. 'I wonder if she slipped him a drug or injected him with something like an epi pen, a powered syringe? A "disabling insult" as a pathologist would say. Colin, you said Amy had black lines, like the body in the tea chest? Was Amy limping when she came up the steps? That knee was very badly damaged yet she wasn't complaining?'

'She said that she had been given something for the pain.'

'Something that paralyses them and takes the pain away? Blondie was checking her watch to make sure it has had time to work. So how is it administered? Where is she getting it from? We need to know if they both have an injection site.'

Anderson picked up his phone and asked to be put through to the Queen Elizabeth Hospital.

Archie Walker picked up his phone and called exactly the same number.

Mulholland and Wyngate found Matron Nicholson as welcoming as Costello had warned them.

'This is really very inconvenient. If you want to speak to Mr Girasole then why can't you do it at his home or his work?' She studied their warrant cards very closely.

'Because, he said he was coming back here,' said Mulholland giving her the full benefit of his disarming smile. 'We will be very quick.'

They both got the impression that she was keeping them at the door for some internal argument to be settled, then she relented and opened the door wider. 'He'll be in Tosca, first floor, turn right out of the lift. It's the door on the corner.'

They climbed the stairs, Mulholland groaning about his leg and thinking that if he had been on his own he would have taken the lift.

On the top landing Wyngate noticed a big blue bin sitting

in an alcove with a computerized lock. 'What is that?' he asked.

'I suspect it's a drugs bin. Elvie was talking about them.' He went to walk away, seeing the corridor turn at the far end of the lift doors. 'Computerized drug distribution. Each nurse has a card, each patient a number. It's a big computerized dosette box.'

'With all kinds of drugs in there?'

Mulholland walked back and tapped his colleague on the upper arm. 'Only the everyday stuff. Nothing that might paralyse you. It'll be full of laxatives, beta blockers and diuretics. Not anabolic steroids. Or strychnine. Now, come on.'

They heard the sweet strains of an operatic aria from outside the door marked Tosca.

'*La Bohème*,' said Mulholland.

'Really,' replied Wyngate, knocking the door.

Paolo answered, showing less annoyance than the matron had. He glanced back into the room. 'Come in, she's sleeping.'

They crept into the room, large and full of the warm breeze drifting on through the open windows, wafting around an expensive perfume of musk. The old lady sat in a wheelchair, her head tilted at an angle, a scarf round her shoulders. The view was superb.

Wyngate commented on it.

'She deserves it. She still has good sight, something she can enjoy.'

'Just one question.' Mulholland pulled a photograph from the file he was carrying.

'Do you recognize this woman, just on the off chance? She might be from round these parts.' Mulholland handed over the colour copy of Claire's photograph of the blonde woman.

Paolo's blue eyes stared at the photograph and the atmosphere in the room tightened. His bottom lip started to quiver a little, a hand went up to his mouth, a sleeve rub over his chin. He turned to check that the old lady was still asleep.

Wyngate and Mulholland looked at each other.

'So you do recognize her?'

'No, I don't.' He looked from one detective to the other, but his mouth was curled a little in confusion. He walked towards the door, guiding them out the room and closing the door behind them to continue the conversation in the corridor.

'So you know who she is?'

'No, do you?' He recovered himself. 'I mean, she has the look of somebody I used to know but she'd be about, God, sixty by now.' He peered at the photograph again. 'Looking closer, there's a little resemblance but not much. She was a pal of mine, well, more a friend of a friend. So sorry, don't know her. This woman is far too young.' He shrugged and tried to hand the photograph back.

Neither police officer took it.

'Can you tell me her name? The name of the woman she looks like.'

Paolo breathed out slowly. 'Not really, Paula? Pauline? Something like that. She hung around with a guy I used to know.' He creased his face up and tapped the photograph with his forefinger. 'It's the haircut, same haircut. That's all.' He smiled. 'And the Duchess is the only woman I know who has had the same do for twenty years.'

They walked slowly down the stone steps of the care home, Wyngate phoning in the info for the board. Mulholland phoning home to ask his girlfriend Elvie McCulloch, who was a medic, if she knew of any drug that would have the effect they were looking for.

Costello was telling Wyngate that the picture of the blonde woman provoked no response from David's mother either. She had no idea who she was.

'Well, that is interesting,' said Wyngate, 'because Paolo Girasole definitely knew who she was. He just wasn't for telling us.'

By midnight Anderson was sitting at his desk at home, Nesbit snoring gently at his feet. He was watching the tape back and forward on his iPad, playing around with it, using the computer's ability to focus in on an area. They were looking around David for the woman they had called Blondie, no matter what Paolo Girasole said.

Every time he heard that name, Anderson couldn't think

why it meant something to him. Something more than chips and ice cream. Girasole? He had come across the name recently, written down in black type; he could see it in his mind's eye. But he couldn't think where.

He was watching the CCTV half paying attention, thankful for the fact that the average Glaswegian is filmed over three hundred times a day while on a city centre walkabout. He had found a section, around half eight where David had his initial encounter with Blondie; it looked like a stumble in a bottleneck on a narrow pavement. He was strolling, in no hurry at a point north of Papyrus, when she was about a foot behind him. There was a slight bump, an apology. Had she picked him out already?

Anderson was looking for faces that might appear more than once. He had accepted Costello's point that one woman would find it difficult to abduct a boy like David on her own. He was looking for an accomplice. But everybody seemed to be facing the other way, going about their business. Anderson followed Blondie out of the range of that camera, then up a side street where she disappeared. He picked her up again on the original piece of video Mulholland had put on the disc from the camera on the Vinicombe Street/Byres Road junction. He scanned the pictures, his fingers on the screen honing in on images of faces and enlarging them. His eyes settled on a woman standing in a dark spot, easily missed but doing exactly what he was looking for somebody doing; walking up and down a little.

Anderson focused in on her. She looked at her watch a few times then back up Byres Road, up Vinicombe Street, waiting for somebody. The woman continued her casual stroll back and forth. A few times the view of the street was obscured by the camera angle being blocked out by a high-sided vehicle stopping, probably for a delivery. The screen went black.

He waited and took a sip of the now cold, black coffee, watching the time roll on past nine o'clock. Was she waiting to meet David? Why? Why not at the café where David had been waiting? Or was this the accomplice? That didn't make sense, she was too weak, too small, slim, well dressed. Formally dressed even. In a skirt, black tights on a bright summer morning. Black shoes, a jacket. She looked as if she was going to her work. Early on a Sunday morning, on parade day? Waiting for a lift? In a dead end? It was the most stupid place in the world to wait for a vehicle. So there was another reason for her to be there. He put his fingers to the laptop screen, opening them up to enlarge the image, trying for the optimum of details before the loss of fine details of pixilation. He got her as close as he could get but the features of her face began to blur. He could see dark hair swept back and a scarf of some kind round her neck, like cabin crew. All he could see was dark. The collar of her jacket was open at the front with something hanging there. As she turned her head, the screen blacked out again and Anderson swore gently. This case was like that, see something, then it's gone. He was so tired, a dull insistent headache was pulsing quietly behind one eye. He didn't know if more coffee was a good or bad idea. He took another sip. Nesbitt stretched, sticking his claws into Anderson's ankle. Instead of winding the film on, he waited for the vehicle to move, to wait for the lights to change or the cop on duty to wave him through. Anderson looked at the clock, it was moving on but he was getting the sneaking feeling that Blondie wasn't going to get caught out. Where Blondie had walked, she had been in the crowd, obliterated almost as if she had known. Even his eagle-eyed daughter had not caught a good likeness of her. Was that intentional? Or was she lucky? Maybe her companion might draw her out, standing in the street, easily seen.

But so far, all they had was that bane of good police work, stinking bad luck. He was getting ahead of himself, they had no real evidence of anything really. Blondie might have nothing to do with any of it. She might have known him, taken him round the corner out of the sun, away from the buzz of the street corner. Maybe she had no connection with him at all but was a nurse or some kind of care worker who genuinely thought she was witnessing the start of an epileptic fit and had taken him out of the busy street, somewhere quiet in case he went into grand mal. And he had come to harm at some later point. But David was not epileptic. Maybe there was something else storming his brain? Drugs? A tumour?

But then how did he end up dead, folded up in a tea chest three streets away, on the opposite side of a busy road. If it was him, but deep down he thought, how could it not be? The timeline was tight, but the clothes? It was hard to argue with the identical clothes. He checked his mobile again, still no word from O'Hare; their last conversation had been a little blunt, 'Don't call me, I'll call you.' Anderson had worked with the hoary old git for a long time and knew there was something that the pathologist was not telling him. He could sniff it. Irene Kerr had been on the phone every hour on the hour. Anderson wished O'Hare would, or could, say yes or no, was it her son or not? It couldn't be that bloody difficult, but O'Hare was not going to be rushed. The face was curled into the body, and any attempt to unwind it could lose evidence and there was no second chance at that.

Amy was doing OK. He was getting updates on her. She was in for twenty-four-hour observation and they had found an injection site on her upper arm. Anderson looked at the time on the laptop; it was going on for midnight. For now David Kerr was a missing person. And there had been a suspicious death. There still had to be a direct and provable connection between those two facts.

The black van had moved away from the screen. He watched. The woman had turned her head and pinned her black hair back against her ears, and as she did so the pattern on the front of her jacket moved. It was a lanyard, with an ID on it? He couldn't make out the words, or the logo, but it was faint, light coloured. A bank? The council? Open on a Sunday? He didn't think so. It was a street collector's badge, no doubt to accompany one of the floats. He needed to find out which one.

The door of the room opened, it was Claire, dressed in leggings and a sweatshirt that reached her knees. She had her big sloggy socks on, a smoothie in her hand.

'You not going to bed?' he asked.

'I could ask you the same thing,' she replied.

'I'm the parent, you are the child.'

'Have you found David yet?'

He shook his head.

She leaned against the doorpost, and pointed to his laptop.
'Are you still looking for him?'

'Course we are, Claire, of course we are.'

'So he is not the body then?'

'We don't know one way or the other.'

She pulled a bit of a face. 'Shame if it was, shame for
somebody else if it isn't him.' Her face creased up, she had
seen too much random tragedy for such a short life.

He indicated the woman with the dark hair in the suit, and
Claire gave her a good look, but didn't recall her, amongst all
those collecting for charity on the parade route.

Claire slopped off, either back upstairs to bed or to the
kitchen.

He forwarded the film to watch the parade, making notes
of the organizations and noticed that most of them seemed to
have bold colours and strong images. Whoever this lady was,
if she was waiting to collect for a charity then it was charity
with a low profile and that in itself did not make sense.

He was jotting down the name of a school band that had
marched past when a float drove by, moving slowly, not a lot
going on. There was a hospital bed aboard, people waving,
cogs and wheels on the float and above the cab at the front
was a logo of white with writing, fine writing in light and
dark blue. The same as the image on the badge. So who were
they? He looked at the time, the float had been at the top end
of parade, easy to track them down and find out who she was.
Then he had an idea. He was about to pick up the phone and
ruin somebody's sleep. Then the phone went as he held it in
his palm; it was O'Hare.

The pathologist was curt. 'I think you should bring her
down. Now.'

'Who, Irene?'

'Who else?'

'Now?'

'Colin, you asked me to you call you "as soon as". This is
"as soon as". Trust me on this. Can you confirm that David
Kerr had drunk a can of Appletiser and eaten a nut bar or
something before he was abducted?'

'Yes. He's on the CCTV doing it. Why?'

'OK, I don't mind following protocol, Colin, but not when it is cruel. So go and get Irene Kerr and bring her here. To the mortuary. Now.'

In the end it was the faithful Maggie who brought a snivelling and white-faced Irene to the mortuary. They both looked dead eyed, ghosting around the seated area.

Anderson joined them. 'I confess that this is news to me.'

They went in; he held open the doors for them.

'Did he suffer?' was the first thing she asked.

'We don't know if it is your son yet, Mrs Kerr, I am not hiding anything from you. I know as much as you do. I am sorry.'

'I don't know how he came to this. How did this happen, why did it happen to him?' She was setting off on her well-trodden story. Her son was a lovely boy. Reminding herself more than anybody else, as she really believed that bad things don't happen to good people.

She stopped walking along the corridor, turning to face Anderson. She placed the palm of her hand on his jacket. 'You know, I always thought I would have time. I can't believe he has gone. The plans we made, the things we had planned to do. I was going to watch him grow into a man, meet a girl, get married. He would have been a good dad. He was going camping later in the year to France, with Innes and Winston, if he was well enough, have a gap year. You have no idea what his dad said to me when I told him he was missing.'

'Caroline, the policewoman, took the phone and explained,' added Maggie, 'when you phoned him the first time he said that he thought David was OK, you can't—'

'He kept saying that he knew David would be OK and that he would turn up somewhere safe and sound. So clinical, but you know I am still his wife. He is David's father. But there was no poor, poor David. What I am going to do without him, without my boy?'

Anderson opened another door, into a waiting room. 'Do you have other children, Mr Anderson, other than Claire, I mean?'

'I have a son, a little younger than David.'

'Do you think Claire was the last person who talked to David? I wonder if that was the last nice thing that happened to him.' She stared at Anderson, she looked older, creased, pathetic.

Anderson was incredibly grateful when the door opened and O'Hare came in, looking a little flustered.

'Mrs Kerr, I am the forensic pathologist.' He shoved his steel-rimmed glasses further up his nose, not really paying any attention to her at all.

The woman looked at him tearfully, somehow comforted that a scientist was now on the scene. O'Hare pulled the waistband of his trousers up and tucked the tip of his tie back into his belt.

'Mrs Kerr, I am going to ask you to do something that breaks all the rules. I want you to look at the body, see if you can identify him. Tell me if this young man is your son?'

Colin Anderson stared at his old friend. 'Can I have a word, Prof, outside please?'

'No, I want to,' intervened Irene.

'Of course you want to, anything is better than not knowing. We could be ages waiting for the DNA to come back,' said O'Hare giving Anderson a hard look as he headed towards the door. Irene Kerr was energized and followed him. Anderson followed them both out of the room, O'Hare wafting away Anderson's protests that this really was against procedure.

In the morgue, they stood behind the glass wall. Anderson continued his protests getting quieter as he realized that any noises he made were going to make a bad situation worse. It was quiet apart from the hum and breath of the air system. The body lay in front of them, covered in a white sheet.

Anderson had seen enough bodies to know this one was odd. Not with the usual contour of a supine form. The knees stuck up a little, too much of a peak, and his shoulder created another little mound of white sheet lower than it should have been.

'Are you OK,' asked O'Hare, looking directly at Irene for the first time.

'I want to see him.' Her chin came up, calm, resolute. Anderson stepped back, O'Hare was right, the worst thing was not knowing.

Anderson turned away, cupping his hands to his eyes and waited for the screaming, the cries, the outpouring of human grief of the worst kind; a mother for her only son.

But all he heard was the gentle thump of Irene Kerr hitting the floor.

David Kerr was groggy. He lay, trying to wake up, knowing that something very wrong had happened. His head hurt and his body felt weird, like he had recovered from a very bad dose of the flu. His right shoulder ached with a deep warmth that might have felt comforting – if he could move himself away from it. But he couldn't. He opened his eyes but the mere act of lifting an eyelid took a lot of effort. So he stopped trying.

He thought he might have died, but he was wrong. He had been asleep. He might have been unconscious but he did know, definitely, that there was a little light filtering through his eyelids, so he tried to open them again to try to make sense of it all. Rafters. A ceiling high above him. Not the sunken lights of his bedroom ceiling, not the pale blue paint he had picked with . . .

With? And there his memory stopped. And there was the scent of polish, and wood glue. The dead have no sense of smell so he made the effort to keep his eyes open.

The skylight he could see was so filthy, cracked and cobwebbed it allowed very little light in, but he got the impression that there was sunlight outside somewhere. There were bars across the skylight, and he could see trees on the inside. So he was outside but inside?

So he lay, glimpsing the skylight, thinking that if he snuck up on it, he might see it properly before his brain intervened and distorted it.

What was going on up there? In the trees? And why was he not out there? He had the vague taste of apples in his mouth? He had an image of red scarves and red petals. The words rolling down the river swam in his head. He had no idea why.

He felt light, floaty. He could see the sky, feel the mattress under him, and smell the glue. He could taste apple and hear traffic from somewhere and quiet clattering, as if his mum was downstairs filling the dishwater. He had no idea where he was or what had happened to him.

Out of the corner of his eye he could see something to his left, a plastic bag. And a pipe that curled in and out of his eyeline before disappearing down below his waist. He tried to follow it with his eyes, lifting his head to see further, to discover what it was and where it went.

That was when he realized that he couldn't move.

Not at all.

TWO

Monday 6 June

Anderson had phoned in to say he would be late in the office. He had been up most of the night, not just the heat keeping him awake. The relief at the body in the box not being that of Irene's son was heartfelt but fleeting. They had no knowledge as to where David was. Or if he was about to suffer the same fate as the unknown boy.

The unknown boy. It was too lacking in respect to call the body 'Jack In The Box', and the name Jack would only add to the confusion, seeing as O'Hare's first name was Jack. O'Hare hated referring to unidentified bodies by a number, it was one of the few things that really riled the old pathologist, so he had addressed the body as 'Mr Hollister, here,' and that had stuck in Anderson's mind, so Mr Hollister he was until they knew otherwise.

Since he got home from the morgue at three a.m., Anderson had been thinking about the dead boy. Somebody, somewhere, was waiting for that boy to walk in their door. They were still waiting. The technical cause of death was asphyxiation, caused by vomit blocking his airway. Some drug had retarded the onset of rigor; the stomach was empty. So the pathologist could offer no timeline as yet. He was waiting for the queue of work at the lab to be processed.

Claire had been sitting on the stairs waiting for him, asking about David, the boy who had given her the flower. He told her that the body was not that of the boy who had been sitting outside the Zeitgeist Café. She had pursed her lips and pulled her long hair back behind her ears. Her eyes filled up as she asked what had happened to the boy in the crate. Anderson had given one of his stock answers; they would get on to that tomorrow. He had tried to pass her, get up the stairs and into his bed but she asked her next question as he stepped over her long legs. So who was the boy in the lane? Surely somebody would be missing him. In today's society, the answer was 'sadly not'. Nobody had noticed Paige Riley had gone, or knew what had happened to her. Nobody noticed because nobody cared.

And then Anderson had sat down on the stair above her, looking down at the stained glass of the front door. Ceres was sowing the seeds of knowledge from a woven basket that sat on her hip. Anderson wished she would fling some his way.

He didn't need to remind Claire how lucky they were that they would be missed and that there was always somebody waiting for them somewhere. He looked at her, thinking how beautiful she was, how delicate her soul might be. She had a caring nature and that meant she was hurting; for the boy who had handed her the flower, and for the boy who been folded into a box and left down a lane. Two people who may never have met in life, yet their existences had collided so tragically.

As the clock wound round, he thought he may as well get to work. He took his shoes off and chatted to his teenage daughter, trying not to make it too obvious that he was subtly interviewing her. Going back over the meeting at the parade, what she could and couldn't recall about David, every single detail. Her thoughts and impressions. It took them a whole hour and they both crept up to bed somewhere at the back of four that morning.

The whole exercise got them nowhere. To the trained and untrained eye, David Kerr was exactly what his mother thought he was. And in that was a greater tragedy.

*　　*　　*

When Anderson walked gingerly into the investigation room, nursing a tired muzzy head, he was glad to see the windows wide open. The draught might be warm, but at least it was fresh. Archie Walker and Costello were already there, and looked settled as if they had been there for a while. Her face was still swollen on the right side. The cut now had small pieces of white tape holding the edges together. Her right eye was almost closed by swelling, giving her the appearance of being slightly lascivious, which was ironic to anybody who knew her. He wondered if they had spent the night together. There was never any sign of intimacy between them, if anything all he had witnessed was mild acrimony.

Costello had already split the board; a missing person on one side and a murder victim on the other: David Kerr still missing; Mr Hollister still awaiting his identification. The body's DNA had no match in the system. They were still examining his clothes. His list of injuries was horrific. Both shoulders and elbows had been dislocated. There had been an injection site on his left buttock. And he had not eaten for at least three or four days. The photograph of his face; eyes closed, restful, was on the board. He looked at peace.

'So we have no idea at all who Mr Hollister is, or what he has been through. Are we agreed that we are looking for the same perpetrator?' asked Walker. 'The Blonde.'

'I have that picture and description circulated. She knows this area, that's for sure,' said Costello.

Anderson said, 'And we need to find David before he turns up in a box somewhere. We need to dig a bit deeper. David is a low-risk victim. He isn't stupid. He is young, strong but they still took him.' He dropped his head into his hands. 'For somebody who has a medical degree, O'Hare may be good with the dead but he is shite with the living. In the end Irene ended up in A & E, she split her lip open.'

'Serves her right, she bloody nearly broke my cheekbone,' said Costello. 'But O'Hare knew that it wasn't David, so he wasn't going to let her suffer a minute longer than she had to. His stomach was empty.' She looked round. 'I asked somebody to get an updated list of missing persons. Why is it not on my desk?'

'The updated one doesn't seem to have arrived yet,' Archie Walker said automatically, staring at the board.

'Quite a few things dislocated? Like Amy's knee?' Anderson said and asked for a third column to add to the murder board. 'Amy survived, her memory is precise. It must mean something. The more facts, the higher the probability that the connection will become obvious.'

Costello wiped some text off the whiteboard to rewrite it smaller, then wrote Amy's name up in big letters. 'I've been on the phone to the hospital. Her mum says she doesn't recall anything else but is perfectly lucid in every other way. No illicit drugs in her system, her tox screen was clear bar a small amount of alcohol. Brain scan is clear, no physical or pathological cause for her memory loss. But the damage to her knee is severe. She will need an operation. Probably more than one.' She dabbed the top of the whiteboard pen onto the girl's picture. 'So she believes that she saw what she says she saw.'

Anderson said, 'And I saw the lines on Mr Hollister's legs. Black lines where the joint could be bent enough to dislocate it? We should get Dr Batten in on this. Serial attackers have their root in fantasy and all that. What is this guy fantasizing about? Being a surgeon?'

'Not my guess to make? How do you want to play it?'

'I'll take David Kerr. You take the dead boy, Mr Hollister. No doubt our paths will cross and cross. You happy with that, Archie?'

'Absolutely, we will support you in any way you see fit to run the case but I think there might be another victim who got away.'

Both cops looked at him.

'Why did you not say anything before now?' asked Anderson, hands out in wonderment.

'You need a few reps to recognize a pattern. The name is Jeffries. DCI Alistair Jeffries. I'll arrange an interview.' And that was all Archie Walker would say on the subject and left, his shoes squeaking and leaving a trail of Penhaligon's Sartorial behind him.

'Can you shed any light on that?' asked Anderson.

Costello shook her head. 'Nope. I don't think so.'

Anderson slid lower in his seat, started twiddling with a pen which was a sign he was thinking. 'Jeffries, eh? I heard he had been hurt in an incident. Lost interest when I heard it wasn't fatal.'

Costello climbed off the desk, the conversation over.

'So how is Archie doing?' asked Colin, trying to sound polite rather than nosey.

'You should have asked him yourself, he was here a minute ago,' she replied sarcastically.

He tried another tack. 'How's his missus up at the care home.'

'It's like one of our middle management meetings; everybody sitting around staring at each other, open mouthed and looking stupid. But he seems worse than her. She has taken it in her stride, much calmer than she ever was at home. I think that might be the effect of a drug regime given out on time.' She turned her grey eyes on him, 'Does the name Kilpatrick mean anything to you? No big career criminal that jumps to mind.'

'No, they are all Russians these days, or your young friend, Miss Hamilton.'

'Libby? She can't help the family she was born into.'

'She seems to be making a name for herself, right enough. Somebody was hacked to death in Castlemilk in the small hours of this morning.'

'Yes, I saw that. The drugs war continues. Not our case though. I'd let Kirkton deal with that particular aspect of the Safer Society.'

The phone went. Anderson lifted up his mobile, his eyes darting towards the ceiling when he saw who it was. 'Oh God, bloody O'Hare again, I wonder what he wants now.'

Anderson listened, Costello strained to hear and tried to make out the odd word. She didn't think she had heard right. Anderson swiped his phone off and looked at it, as if the phone had just lied to him.

'And?' asked Costello.

'Mathilda McQueen showed Irene Kerr the clothes that were taken off the dead body. And Irene confirmed that they were the clothes her son was wearing. Mathilda said she was very sure.'

'And Mathilda tested the DNA to prove her wrong . . .'

'And they proved her right. The dead body was wearing David's clothes.'

'The dead boy was dressed in the clothes from the missing boy?' She repeated slowly to be sure that she had got it right. She went over to the whiteboard and drew a big plus sign linking the two cases, her mind wondering what horrors David Kerr was going through now. So she underlined it, they needed to find him. Soon.

'So was Mulholland on the ball with tracing this woman then?' asked Costello, walking through the car park of the block of very nice flats in Jordanhill.

'Nope, he asked Elvie,' replied Anderson. 'Very useful having a logically minded girlfriend who's a medic. It's MindSafe, a brain injury charity. Elvie recognized the logo straight away so he phoned and asked them if they had anybody out doing collections yesterday. They didn't, but they knew who I was talking about. Happens she was meeting the person I spoke to on the phone, going out for breakfast before going collecting in the city. I'll be good cop, you be yourself. She might be a player in all this, she can hang around as if she's invisible,' He read the names by the buzzer. 'Flat three. Second floor.'

Wendy Gibson was a little wary when she opened the front door of her flat to two police officers in plain clothes. She looked carefully at their ID then let them in. Her suspicion changed to pleasure. Anderson got halfway down her hall before he stopped and pointed to the framed photograph on her wall, an assistant chief commissioner. The colours around the edges were going a little green, but the face was instantly recognisable. 'Is that your dad,' he asked, 'Billy Gibson?'

'It is indeed,' she said, delighted that her visitor had recognized him.

'Oh, that takes me back, he was . . .?'

'Greenock.'

'Yeah Greenock, I never worked under him directly but he was a great bloke, very well thought of.' Anderson nodded at the memory. 'Firm but fair was a phrase always banded around about him.'

'"Firm but fair bastard" was the term he used for himself, I believe.' She took the compliment graciously and opened the door for them to go into her living room. Very clean with a pale wood floor, the whole room kitted out from Ikea.

Anderson gave Costello a look, telling her that Wendy was off the suspect list. She gave him a raised eyebrow back. According to her, Wendy was not.

'Do sit down, and how can I help you?' She pulled her skirt down over her knees. She was very classily dressed, a long silky jumper over her skirt and a scarf loosely draped round her neck in a way that Anderson's wife complained she could never manage. 'Do you want a coffee or something?' An elegant finger pointed to the kitchen, curled in questioning.

Anderson shook his head, wishing that Costello would sit down behind him but his DI was taking her time, as if David Kerr might be stuffed down the back of a sofa. She was stalking the joint.

'I presume it is about that boy who went missing at the parade.'

'Yes, it is. We think that you might have seen him before he was abducted.'

'I'm sorry, I didn't see anything.'

'Meaning you saw something.'

Her eyes looked from one to the other. 'Well, I called the helpline number to say that I had been on that corner. Is that not why you are here?' She looked puzzled now.

'We found you on the CCTV.'

'And nobody told you about the phone call? Well, times don't change.' Wendy smiled, recalling her dad moaning about exactly the same thing; one hand having no idea what the other hand was up to.

'Can you tell us your movements on Sunday?' asked Costello, sharply.

'Well, we had a small reception breakfast for the charity volunteers. I'm with MindSafe Brain Tumour Trust, so I was going to meet Elspeth. We knew it would be busy so we decided to meet on Vinicombe Street. So that's how I came to be standing on the corner where the boy went missing, across Vinicombe Street but on the same side of Byres Road.'

Anderson smiled encouragingly and asked her to go on.

'Well, I texted Elspeth and told her that I was going to wait further up Vinicombe Street. That would have been about twenty past nine, half nine. I was early, but it was getting busy. We could have missed each other easily.'

'So it was the preamble of the parade?'

'The best part I always think, folk walking up to the start. More fun than the parade itself, no neds, no drunkenness. It's good to see the costume malfunctions, the dads dragging their kids along, screaming. However, Elspeth texted back. She was caught in traffic so I had a wee wander and ended up at the corner of Vinicombe Street, right at Vinicombe Lane.'

Which was exactly the place where the second camera had picked her up.

'Did you notice anything strange?' asked Anderson.

'On parade day? Everything!' she laughed.

She had a point.

'Did anybody speak to you?'

'A few people. I collect around the area so there are people I bump into, they stop and pass the time of day, but . . .' She stopped to think. 'Nobody of interest really.'

'Do you remember anybody supporting a young man, helping him as if he was injured? You might have thought they were drunk?'

'No, not really. There was a boy in a wheelchair. I held the car door open for him, so his mum could get him in properly. The wheelchair went into the hatchback.'

Anderson didn't look at Costello.

'Can you describe the boy?' asked Costello, sitting on the arm of the chair looking straight at Wendy. It was intimidating but Wendy didn't seem to notice.

'Well, a teenager, youngish teenager though.'

'And you didn't think to come forward when you heard we were looking for a teenager who had gone missing.'

'No, like I said I did phone the helpline, all the charity people did,' said Wendy, looking a bit embarrassed, 'but this boy was disabled. He was wrapped in a blanket, with his mother. The wheelchair folded into the hatchback. She lifted him well, like an expert. He had something wrong with him,

cerebral palsy, I think. He was rolling a little the way they
do and he was dribbling. He wasn't that boy on the news,
and . . .' She looked up trying to recall something.

'What?' prompted Costello.

'Well, just that I have met that woman before. She must
live or work around here and she's interested in the work that
the charity does. I've said hello to her before that incident,
nodding terms, you know? I feel I know her.'

'Do you know her name? Where she works?'

Wendy shook her head. 'Sorry.'

'And you presumed he was disabled because he was in a
chair? Or was there something else?'

'I presumed he was disabled because he was – well – unre-
sponsive. And I presumed that she was interested in the charity
because she nursed or knew somebody who had such an injury,
and so when I saw her with him I put two and two together.
I don't think that I was wrong.' She shook her head, lips
pursed, quite definite. 'No, I wasn't wrong. That woman knew
that boy and was used to handling him. It's not an easy thing
for a woman to do, moving somebody like that from a wheelchair into a car seat.'

Costello opened up the file she was holding. 'Was this him?'
It was Innes's picture of David Kerr.

Wendy looked at it carefully. 'No, I really don't think so.'
She got up and walked over to the sideboard, lifting up a pair
of glasses. She put them on, looked at the picture again. 'There
is a resemblance, though, but no, I don't think it was him.
The boy in the wheelchair was younger, smaller. His hair was
slightly darker, shorter. Maybe not shorter, but swept back,
different style.'

'So, not him.'

'You are making me doubt myself now. Do you think that
was him?' She went back to the settee handing Anderson the
photograph as she passed.

'What about the woman?'

'Oh her? Beautiful clothes. She always wears beautiful
clothes. A light blue silk top, beautifully cut, cream linen
trousers, French style.'

'Hair colour?'

'Blonde. Big dark glasses. Thought she was brave being so well dressed looking after a teenager like that. But I guess she's used to it.'

Costello was now frowning. 'Well, a woman managed to get a teenage boy off Byres Road without anybody noticing. We are wondering how she did that. She being female, he was a healthy teenage boy. So where was the wheelchair?' asked Costello. 'Did you see her with the chair empty? Or collapsed?'

Wendy raised an eyebrow. 'Sorry, I don't know what you mean?'

'She didn't have it ten minutes earlier on the CCTV. So what did she do with it in the meantime – the blonde woman?'

Wendy thought. 'Sorry, when I saw her, she had the chair.'

'Could you recognize the woman if you saw her again?'

'Oh, yes.'

'And the car? If we put some pictures in front of you, would you be able to identify it?'

'Yes, I think so, and it had a disabled sticker.'

'Did you see the car drive off?'

Wendy looked a little embarrassed. 'Well, it was parade day so she did a U-turn, and went straight across Byres Road. It was behind one of the sound units.' She smiled. 'I held up the cars on Vinicombe Street to let her get round. It was so busy.'

And there it was; how the body got across the busy street. Costello made a mental note to look at the CCTV again, find the car.

'How did she seem, the woman? Her demeanour? Anything odd about her?'

'Not at all, just as she always seemed. A little harassed maybe but that was because it was busy and she was pushing the chair through all those people. There was nothing odd about her.'

'But?' asked Anderson picking up on her verbal cue.

'The boot of the car had a jewellery box in it.' Wendy laughed. 'I thought it was odd. It was lying there. I thought, I bet her daughter borrows her jewellery so she keeps it in the

boot. I had a friend who used to do that. Strange but true.'
Wendy gave another little laugh.

Costello asked, 'Can you describe the car for me?'

'Yes, it was white.'

Sandra looked round the day room, all was well. The residents
were children, they had to be settled and kept amused but once
they had fallen asleep, they could be left alone. They fell
asleep quickly in this place, quicker than they had in any of
the other homes. There was no pacing up and down, anxiously
wringing their hands, stuttering on the same word over and
over again or shouting obscenities at each other like the bar
at a Tourette's convention.

They were better behaved at Athole House, compared to
the other homes Sandra had worked in. They turned to jelly
after a while. The place was tranquil, beautiful but soulless
and deathly quiet. Maybe the torpor ate into their bodies until
there was no way out but to capitulate.

Sandra ghosted up the stairs and slid into Tosca. She checked
the time on the Gothic clock on the mantelpiece. It was her
break now. Lynda had taken over downstairs, sitting in the
centre of the day room and listening to the snoring of the other
two, deep in post prandial sleep. Lynda could give Kilpatrick
his cup of tea and his digestive biscuit. They had to be dunked
for him since the old scrote had lost the use of his hands in
the fire. He'd also lost his wife so the rumour went. The fire
had been in a friend's house, round the corner from here. Just
behind the building where they found the body yesterday,
according to the care home gossip. The police had been three
times so far. Twice by normal uniform and the plain clothes
police had been in to see Paolo about the phone. Sandra knew
she had to stay calm and keep below the radar.

She was aware Kilpatrick had items of value in his room,
and he had no eagle-eyed visitors to keep tabs on his stuff.
He must have money as he had been here for years and, so
far, there had been no talk of him being transferred. One of
the owners, a nasty little doctor called Pearcy, was very
quick to claim the resident would be better transferring to
a nursing home as the secure living facility did not cater for

those who needed nursing. Or couldn't pay for it any longer. There was a joke about absent relatives paying extra to have their relatives taken downstairs to where the bins were, never to be seen again.

Although Sandra knew how keen people were to get on with their lives and jettison the baggage of the elderly, the dribbly and the incontinent, she had been attentive when she had witnessed some covert behaviour going on downstairs; Matron Nicholson and Pearcy were either having an affair or being enthusiastic about counting their money.

It was Philippa Walker Sandra was wary of; her husband was a cop or a lawyer or something. Pippa had more pearls than functioning brain cells. Too many to notice if any went missing, but her husband just might. Her man was the law so Sandra was steering clear of her. In fact, Pippa Walker being here bothered Sandra more than she cared to admit. What if he wanted a look at the employment history of the staff? That would be the first port of call if anything happened. Even something that Sandra had not actually done; one of the oldies could genuinely flush a valuable piece of jewellery down the loo or swallow an earring. Or die in their sleep unexpectedly. Pippa's man might think it was odd and get it investigated, he had that power. For Sandra that would be bad news.

It didn't stop her planning though. Last week she had wandered into Deke Kilpatrick's room while he was lying in the bed, covered in a single sheet. She had wedged the door open as she looked around, knowing he was watching her through his good eye but was unable to do much about it. He could only move his right arm, so she was fine if she kept clear of that. He had a record player in here, a pile of LPs stacked in exactly the same order they were on her previous visit. They were all by singers she had never heard of. She had moved on to the brass tray on his dressing table. Nice cufflinks and a signet ring that felt heavy and therefore valuable; marked and monogrammed so no value to her. The emerald ring with the diamonds had attracted her the most. Deke grunted if she touched it, the only response that ever came from him.

Did this belong to the wife who had burned in the fire? Was she wearing it when she jumped? There was a whole arc of photographs arranged so he could see them, neatly framed on the chest of drawers, all beautifully shot. The sort of thing that Sandra would have liked for herself, the pictures of a life lived. Sandra leaned against the dresser and slid the ring up and down her finger so that Deke could see. Then she returned it to the box, she always would but he didn't know that. Her favourite taunt was to walk round his room slowly, holding a pillow. Looking at him and looking at the pillow. As if checking that it would fit over his face.

Now she had bigger fish to fry.

Alone up in Tosca, she opened the wardrobe and began to finger the silks and the linens and the pure cashmere wools. She had her eye on a fuchsia jacket. That would look marvellous against her skin. She held it up to her, letting it slither off the hanger, then ruffled the wool sleeve under her chin seeing how it clashed with her face. The Duchess had a typical Italian complexion, Sandra's was more Ruchill than Rome; grey, flecked with skin tone, and pale blue eyes. She looked anaemic even when she was perfectly healthy.

Paolo didn't look much like the Duchess though. But he had said that people from Northern Italy looked more northern. That was how he had put it. And of course Italians had moved about a lot, goodness knew what was deep inside his DNA. Sandra pulled the woollen jacket over her navy blue uniform. She slipped her bare feet out of the fake Crocs she had bought down the market for a few quid, standard wear in the home as they were so comfortable and so quiet. Not that it mattered here as this lot slept through anything, the result of good soundproofing, she reckoned.

Sandra looked at the bottom of the wardrobe; boxes. Of course the Duchess's shoes would be kept in those yellowed boxes, aged but not dusty. Paolo hated dust and Sandra always made sure that Elsa, the young Polish cleaner who cleaned the four biggest rooms, always vacuumed inside the wardrobe as well as outside. Paolo approved of that.

He was too observant though. He'd notice immediately if

anything went missing, so Sandra had changed her plans, now a bigger prize was in sight.

Sandra's heart was thumping, her fingers trembling, reaching out towards the top box, lifting it slightly to look at the picture on the front. A little drawing of the shoes it contained with the word 'blu'. Well that didn't need a lot of translation. She was looking for the shoes that matched this jacket; everything the Duchess owned matched something else. 'Rosa'. She took them out. The shoes had been wound in fine tissue paper, each wrapped separately, then together. That would be Paolo. She wondered what he would do when his mother died. Sandra was going to work here until that day happened, and be so nice to Paolo that he would see her for what she was, what she was pretending to be. She sat down on the double bed with its huge amount of cushions, all in the best linen, Italian cotton or Belgian lace. She sat carefully on the end, her arms now in the jacket sleeves and her feet slipped into each shoe. They were made of fine leather, handmade and so soft, so incredibly supple they wrapped round the curves of her feet. As she stood up, the slight cushioning on the sole eased her feet onto the carpet. They had a nice heel, slim and elegant but not so high as to be tarty. The kind of heel Queen Elizabeth would have worn in her young days.

Sandra stood tall. The shoes made her feel slimmer, stream-lined, not that she carried much weight. She thought that she and the Duchess had a very similar build although Sandra was a bit taller, more Paolo's height. She turned to the mirror, pulling up her short hair into a small bun at the back of her head, pouting, then looking demur, then smiling, imagining going to a Christmas party. No, somebody's engagement. No, a wedding. Yes, an Italian society wedding and saying, 'Oh me? I am with Paolo, yes one of those Girasoles. The opera people.'

She heard the buzzer go at the front door. Matron would be expecting a member of staff to appear in case somebody needed showing round or taken somewhere, even keeping an eye on in case they wanted to see something that the guests of the residents were never, ever allowed to see. Like the bins. Or the basement. Guests were invited to look at the kitchens, the wet rooms, the infection control protocols and the state-of-the-art automatic drug dispensers that were housed on each floor, too secure for Sandra to get into.

She slid off the shoes and then carefully wrapped the shoes back in the tissue paper as well as she could, but it was like folding a map. She could hear footfall coming up the carpeted stairs. That was somebody who did not know the building well. They were walking up the middle of each stair, the squeaks heralding their arrival. Sandra knew better, she was skilled at ghosting around this building.

She replaced the box containing the pink shoes under the box containing the blue shoes and squared up the stack. Her heart raced a little with the thought that she could work her way through the whole pile. She put the jacket back on the hanger and placed in its original position on the rack. Paolo would notice immediately if it had been replaced wrongly. She checked the room before she left it, noticing the flattened area on the bedspread where her weight had been settled. She smoothed it out.

She opened the door of Tosca again, closing it quickly behind her.

The grey-haired man in the smart suit on the stairs said hello, stepping sideways slightly to block her path.

'Hello, Mr Walker, isn't it?'

He was a handsome man, lightly tanned faced with friendly bushy eyebrows and steely blue eyes. A bit too old, a bit too small for her, too well dressed. He was the fiscal or the cop. She hoped the alarm didn't show on her face.

'Yes, Sandra?'

'Yes.'

'I was wondering how you thought Philippa was settling in? She seems to have been asleep since she came here. Is she OK?'

'She is fine.' Sandra turned to walk along the hall, passing over the top of the sweeping staircase. 'Let me reassure you, I am not an expert but I have noticed in my time working with Alzheimer's, especially those with "unsettled torpor", you know, where they are still aware of the . . . well, you know, reality?'

'Ones who are aware that they don't recall all they should?'

'Yes. It keeps them awake. I heard Dr Pearcy say that by the time they get here, the patient and the family are totally exhausted. I'm sure you have been catching up on sleep, and so is she.'

'Obvious when you think about it,' agreed Archie Walker, thinking how great, and how guilty, he had felt on that first morning; a full, unbroken sleep through the night when Philippa was at the care home. He had no concept of how exhausted he had been. It had become such a way of life; her illness had become his way of life.

'So when they get here, I think they feel safe and they sleep.' She smiled, she had a nice smile, what his mother would have called homely. 'And that can only be good for them.'

'She's asleep now, should I wake her up or . . .?'

Sandra consulted the watch hung upside down from her breast pocket. She had wanted that ever since she was a wee girl, and an absent-minded theatre nurse had later obliged. 'Well, she has just had something to eat and they like to have a little sleep after that.'

'Maybe I'll pop in and see that she is OK.'

'OK, but they do get into the routine in here very quickly, don't be surprised if she is deep in snooze land. I'll be about on the landing if you need anything. In fact, I could rustle you up a cup of tea or coffee?'

'That would be lovely, Sandra, thank you. It is Sandra, isn't it?' he confirmed.

'Yes,' she said, 'Sandra Ryme.'

But he did look at her for an extra beat, a quizzical narrowing of the eye, a crinkling of his forehead. As if he knew.

Archie Walker had a good game plan. An hour after he left the care home, he was walking through the vast atrium of the Queen Elizabeth II University Hospital with zero enthusiasm for life and the frailty of the human condition. He felt better now, fuelled by black coffee and a pain au chocolate. He got on OK with most of the cops he had worked with. He might not have liked them, but they could rub along together and get the job done.

Then there was Alistair Jeffries, a man Walker would cross the road to run over.

Walker picked up a copy of *Classic Hi Fi* magazine, then thought again and put it down to choose the *Top Gear* one instead. He could recall Jeffries having a souped-up car with an exhaust that announced his arrival at a crime scene from about a mile away. Then he bought a packet of shortbread and a bottle of Lucozade at the shop and checked that the envelope of photographs was still tucked underneath his suit jacket before setting off again across the vast concourse that looked like an aircraft hangar designed by a Lego fan.

All very trendy.

All very pretty.

All very noisy.

While being built it was known locally as the Death Star but the news that the super hospital was to be named the Queen Elizabeth II University Hospital, had it immediately rechristened 'Sweaty Bettys'. No matter what they called it, the towers with the wards still smelled of hospital: of antibiotic spray, stewed apples and death. The atrium, though, smelled more like an airport: coffee beans and pesto. Walker made his way to the lifts. He had been here with Pippa often enough. He knew where he was going, he didn't need the map. He checked ward and bed number, showing his ID when he was half challenged by a bored nurse. She lifted her head from her computer screen at the nursing station and tilted her head down the long corridor.

All he could see was white wall and more white wall.

The new hospital was all single-room occupancy, which, as Walker strode past window after window, reminded him of a zoo. He looked into each room to see if there was anything interesting going on. Some inhabitants looked vacantly at the screen hanging on a metal arm over the bed. He heard snatches of a pointless TV quiz through open doors. Others were asleep. Or dead and nobody had noticed yet. The young chap in room 10 looked as though he could beat the fiscal in a hundred-meter sprint. The old man in room 12 looked hopefully at

Walker as if he might be the Grim Reaper, before turning his head away in disappointment.

In room 14 a plump man, chin grizzled with dull stubble, lay on his back, propped up on a mountain of pillows, reading a western. He was still attached to the drip, an oxygen tube taped onto his top lip like a comedy white moustache. Walker stayed at the door, to make sure before raising his hand and knuckling the door. The occupant of the bed responded with a slow head turn.

Alistair Jeffries smiled, a sore bitter grin, eyes narrowed with the pain. He curled his fingers at the door, *Come in, come in.* 'Archie Walker? Christ – have I died and gone to hell?'

'Not yet. But we live in hope. How are you feeling?' Walker tried to be friendly; well, not friendly, more concerned and professionally polite. He was banking on the fact that Jeffries would be up for some fiscal baiting.

'I am bored out my tiny skull. My tiny fractured skull.' He pointed to his bandaged head. 'I am going to be pensioned off after this. Years on the beat chasing nutters up blind allies, kicking Dobermans in the balls and never got a scratch. And now this, career over. Good bye and thank you.'

'No problem with your speech then, Alistair.'

'I've been in the force twenty-five years and the only injury I have ever suffered was a sore face when I chatted up Costello at the Christmas party.'

'You got away lightly.'

'She's a cow. I heard the rumour that you were shagging her?' Jeffries sucked at his lips, making a noise like the aspirator at the dentist. Walker made a show of giving that some thought.

'I heard that rumour too, but as I still have my testicles intact, we were obviously misinformed.' Walker handed over the Lucozade.

'No vodka then?'

'No.' Walker pulled up a seat. 'We need to talk.'

'No, we don't. You are not the boss of me.'

'Correct.'

'I was jumped. I banged my head. Unlucky, that's all.'

'It was a nasty injury.'

'Consistent with my head hitting the corner of the pavement, that's all.' Jeffries pulled a face, like he was sucking something that had been caught in his teeth. 'Why are you here?'

'Following up some vague thoughts,' he answered, opening the shortbread and offering some to Jeffries in an attempt to stop that awful noise. He put the magazine on the bedside table. 'Alistair. I don't like you. You don't like me. Neither of us have an issue with that.' He placed the picture of Mr Hollister, lying in the mortuary, on top of the magazine. The lack of colour in the skin, the wet hair swept off his face, made him look about ten years old. Walker wasn't going to tell him otherwise. 'But you have done the job a long time. Look at that and then tell me what happened to you. It was a mugging but nobody touched your wallet? You were not hit on the head, you fell. The admission officer at A & E noted that you had a red mark on your left buttock, like an injection site. But your GP said that you are not on any injectable medication.'

Jeffries shook his head. 'They keep asking me about that, like I am some arsehole junkie. They were in here, you know, looking between my toes and bloody everywhere.'

'I think if you were injecting yourself with something you would find an easier place to do it than your own backside. It was done to you.'

Jeffries looked at Walker with something as close to respect as he could manage.

'I've been watching some CCTV of another incident. A young man was abducted off the street. Somebody bumped into him. He is then seen rubbing his arm. He then becomes very compliant but not unconscious. So I am wondering about you?'

Jeffries shrugged.

Walker pointed to the picture. 'It might have happened to him. It might have happened to her.' He pulled out a photograph of Amy's bloodied knee, with its dark line drawn round the joint.

Jeffries placed a finger on the skin of his own knee. His hand tremored a little, and he paled, suddenly looking every day of his fifty-eight years. 'I can't help you.'

'For Christ's sake, look at the mess of him. This boy—'

Jeffries shook his head. 'I don't remember. I can't help you. Not that I won't.'

'Really?' Walker pulled his chair closer, he was going to stay until he got an answer.

'It's fucking embarrassing.' Jeffries ruffled the blue blanket, the heat beamed in through the window. He looked close to tears.

'Not the first embarrassing thing that has happened in your career.' Walker tried for levity.

Jeffries winced and pushed the photographs away. He tried to move up the bed a little. Walker didn't help him.

'I have no memory of it. Nothing at all. So there is no point in you being here or talking to me.'

'You know I am a tenacious wee git so I'm not leaving here with that crap. What do you remember? Waking up in here? You must recall something.' He braced himself for a story about aliens.

'I recall picking up my jacket at the station. Then wakening up in here. And that's all.' He looked out the window, tasting the fear on his lips. 'Feeling helpless and I don't know why.'

'You were found on the pavement up Foremount Lane just behind the Rock. You were drinking there. How did they know you were there?'

He told the same story Walker had read on the initial report.

'My mates say I was having a drink, went to the loo and didn't come back.' He shrugged. 'They thought I had met somebody I know. They texted me. I texted them back, seemingly. I mean I don't remember doing it. I told them to go on without me. I have no memory of that at all. Now I think that . . . well, I don't know what I think . . .'

'The perpetrator did that so nobody came looking for you. Somebody targeted you.'

Jeffries dismissed it with a sharp shake of the head. 'Didn't happen, just a mugging. So there you go, you can take that back to your hot shot team and see what they make of it.' He made his aspirator noise again.

Walker looked at the picture of Amy. 'She can't recall it

either.' He tapped the picture of the dead boy. 'I'm sure his mother wishes all he had was loss of memory. There's another young man missing and we need to get to him before he becomes a victim; dead, I mean, not just embarrassed. So what happened to you? How did you get from inside the pub to outside up the lane?'

'Anderson is smart. He'll get on with it without my help.' But he didn't look Walker in the eye, his hand reached out again to the photograph. The eyes swept the picture, instinct, alive through the drugs.

'Come on, tell me. Anything.'

Jeffries' expression changed.

Walker pulled his seat further forward and looked round, making sure the door was closed. He placed the photograph of Amy right under his nose. 'Amy Niven, nineteen years old. Like you, she got away, the next one wasn't so lucky.'

Jeffries lifted a hand, pale, paper-thin skin stretched and wrinkled over his fingers as he took hold of the picture. The photograph shivered with his tremor. He shook his head, then pointed at the table and Walker got up to pull it over to the bed. 'My glasses, hand me my glasses?' The pallor seemed to have slipped from his face, a more natural colour, something had his interest now. 'Should I know her?'

'She is a classics student from Glasgow University,'

'No, sorry.' He handed the picture back, looking questioningly at Walker.

'You know what criminologists say about the mechanics of this crime. The killer separated her from the crowd, like a lion taking a gazelle. Just as you were separated from your friends.' He went on as Jeffries failed to respond. 'Somebody sent them a text from your phone to keep them away. You were found a street away, lying in the bottom of a lane bleeding from a serious head injury.'

Jeffries moved slightly on the bed, still sore from the surgery. Walker saw it. People were people. Fear was fear.

'Alistair, I can get Costello to go over old cases, talk to your old colleagues and pull out some files of those who might bear a grudge that strong. See anything that might not be quite as it should be. I am the chief fiscal. I can do anything I want.

You know that. You have a reputation of not being the cleanest of cops. And you know Costello, she will not let it go. And if Anderson starts to head up a cold case initiative—'

That hit home, a flash of a more feral fear crossed his face. 'Fuck off.' But his resolve was diminishing.

Walker smiled. So there was something there. Funny how the guilty saw a vague accusation as a direct threat; the guilty mind saw proof of knowledge where there was none. 'So if you tell us what happened, I don't need to get Costello to trawl. I have no interest in what dirty little shite you had going on. You aren't coming back to work, but you might be able to save this guy's life, so tell me what happened that night at the Rock.'

'Nothing. I don't recall anything.' He opened his palms, the fight seemed to have gone out of him. 'Honest.'

Walker nodded. 'OK, so if we could get you hypnotized, would you agree to that?'

'What?'

'Hypnotized. You know, dangling a watch in front of your eyes and all that. Force you to tell the truth.'

He saw Jeffries wince, his mind whirring to think of a reason to refuse.

Walker backpeddled. 'Limited to this crime only. I can get Dr Batten to do it, you know him. He's one of the guys.'

Jeffries looked out the window, his thumb shaking on the photograph, flicking the corner making a faint clicking noise.

'The last time you were in the public eye was not good. You were on the front page of the *Daily Record*.'

'Bloody awful picture, made me look like Peter Stringfellow's pervy older brother.'

'There is a resemblance, from a certain angle. What about this woman, do you recall seeing her?' He put the picture of Blondie on the table in front of Jeffries.

'Not a very good picture, is it? I wouldn't be able to recognize my own granny from that. I can only see the side of her face.' He screwed his eyes a bit. 'No, I don't know her.'

He looked out the window seeing the blank white wall of the other side of the atrium, catching sight of an admin worker in her glass box, sneaking a coffee. 'The wife hasn't been in to see me.' A tear ran down his face. 'It's so embarrassing. He must have been so close, right up, personal. His hand was in my pocket to get my phone. And I don't recall anything about him, not one thing. The one lead we might have and I don't recall one damn thing.' He had spent his time in hospital reflecting a life that was not well lived. A man who was not well loved. And now he was feeling it.

'So are you going to let us hypnotize you? Or do I tell James Kirkton that you are refusing to contribute to our safer society.'

'He wouldn't care.' He snapped. The instancy tinged with something. Disappointment?

Their eyes met. Jeffries looked away first.

'Aye, whatever.'

Sandra was early finishing her duties. The linen cupboard on the first floor was so clean, it could have been a House Of Fraser window display. She had taken her time, waiting for Paolo to pass, so she could be here, casually being helpful.

That had been her plan but then that bloody woman Nicholson had started talking to her in the walk-in cupboard, blocking her vision. She thought she had heard Paolo on the stairs going into the Duchess's room. He was light on his feet. She wondered what he did for a living. He was in and out here at all hours. She thought he might be a doctor. He spoke like a doctor. He knew medical terms and he had those nice strong white, very clean hands, just like a doctor.

It was late, nearly eight o'clock before she got rid of the matron. She needed a ploy to get to Paolo. She could say that she was popping in to make sure his mother was OK. Get more brownie points. She stopped outside Tosca and tried to remember how she would usually approach the door. She reversed a few steps and approached again, grasping the handle. No, she didn't do that. She reversed again and lifted her hand ready to knock. No, she didn't do that either. She only knocked if she knew Paolo was there and she was pretending that she did not know that. Anybody who knocked on that door would wait all day. The woman had dementia. Paolo was in there, and she didn't want him to think that she was disturbing him, but then she wasn't supposed to know that he was in there. She was over-thinking this. He would presume that somebody had told her he was there. And she was supposed to be at home. But he must not think that she had been waiting for him. She had been, but he needn't know that. She went all the way back to the top of the stairs; *just don't think about it*. It was a walk up to the door, a quiet, perfunctory tap with the knuckle of the forefinger and then immediately she would open the door. It was an unconscious, habitual thing.

She entered the room. The Duchess was sitting on her wheelchair, her throne in the middle of the room, dressed in beige swathes of towelling like a sculpture waiting to be unveiled. She was playing with a white flute of handkerchief, waving it in the air as she conducted the imaginary orchestra in her mind. Paolo was nowhere to be seen but Sandra could hear the shower running. He must be swishing out the wet room after showering his mother. She looked like Joan Crawford, or Jane Russell in her long nightdress with its feathered collar, those days when stars were real stars. She turned to look right through Sandra, the handkerchief of material now furled into the palm of her hand. Sandra noticed that her nails had been repainted, bright red and newly shaped. The air in the room had the scent of acetone.

Sandra checked the door was closed, then went to the mirror and sorted her short brown hair, newly highlighted. Paolo commented that he liked the colour of her hair. Funny how he should think that. Her hair had been every colour under the sun but nobody had ever commented on it before. She liked how he had noticed, how he had a good eye for that sort of thing.

The Duchess's make-up bag was on her dressing table. Keeping one eye on the door to the wet room, she took out some lipstick and put it on. It was a deep red, she recognized it as the shade that matched the nail varnish. It was too dark for Sandra but she really didn't want to be bare faced in front of Paolo, not after all her hard work and effort. She had a quick squirt of Fracas perfume behind the ears then wafted the air around her head with her hands to disperse the smell. Then she felt guilty. Paolo would spot that. She panicked, and turned round, bottle still in her hand as if offering it to the

Duchess. The old woman's ebony dark eyes were watching her, watching her every move. Sandra saw the silk-covered pillows on the bed, one of those and that would be all it took. When the time came.

What was she thinking? Where had that got her before? Absolutely nowhere. Slowly, slowly. Nobody ever got rich overnight. She was working the long game on this one.

And Paolo was a rich, handsome, young man.

He was lovely, attentive to his mum. Not like the tossers she had met in her life. One had put her in Casualty twice. One had left her pregnant. One had moved in, started up his own business and then did a moonlight flit with all her money. It was only when the letters came from the mortgage company that she realized that the money he had raised on her house was gone. And the home her mum had left her was no longer hers. And she was now in a council flat. And with her change of address came a change of attitude towards men.

It was on her terms now. Take. Take. Take.

She flattened her navy blue tunic and walked over to the en suite, leaning her ear against the door. Behind the noise of the water running was the soaring melody of an opera. The sad bit from *Madam Butterfly*, where the woman is crying her eyes out. She opened the door, quietly but not slowly so that if he caught her she would say that she thought somebody had left the water running and apologize.

He didn't hear her, he didn't notice.

Paolo was in the shower, naked. His back was towards her. He had turned his face up towards the jets of water as if he was facing the sun, his eyes closed. He was slim and lightly muscled, a little taller than Sandra. She watched for a moment, transfixed by him and his beauty, then pulled herself away. As she closed the door behind her she knew the Duchess had been watching her, watching him.

The old woman's eyes were alive with wicked light.

THREE

D avid could recognize the taste of apple that covered his tongue. The tune of 'Proud Mary' still ran through his mind, a song he didn't really like. But it was all coming back to him slowly. Pieces of the jigsaw falling into place but not yet in the right order. He had been walking along the street, leaning on somebody he didn't know but she was a nice lady. He recalled feeling dizzy, holding on to a metal table that slid away from him and he fell. There was a girl, with a paper rose and a camera. Then the power had gone from his legs and the lady had picked him up, and ran her fingers through his hair. There was a wheelchair tucked behind the bins of the Zeitgeist Café. He had been impressed by that, by the organization. He had felt so grateful, being pushed along, up Vinicombe Street and he thought he would be going to the hospital. Then his memory ran out.

Or did it? He could recall the rose petal, a paper rose petal curled in his hand, and a hand that had outstretched to hold his.

Now he was in a place with no fresh air and a mild dancing light. There were some trees overhead, but he was indoors. That was all he could remember, nothing more. He did know that he could not move. He could see, but it was so tiring to blink, it was better to keep his eyes closed. He felt a tear roll down his face but could do nothing to remove it.

The briefing kicked off at nine a.m. Everybody was updated with the events so far. It was Costello who took the meeting; despite the heat building outside she still had on her navy blue suit, it was becoming her second skin.

Walker had put something up on the board about the thunder and the downpour that was expected, like they couldn't tell by the pressure in the air. There were storm warnings of lightning flash floods and extreme rain for the next twenty-four hours. But so far, the sky was clear.

Anderson was there in body but not in mind, sitting with his chin cupped in his hands, as if in deep concentration, but in reality, he was a hundred miles away. Twice he had to be prompted by Costello to fill in the details about the injection sites that had been found on Amy, Jeffries and Mr Hollister. It was the big connection. An incidental finding was some cat hair Mathilda McQueen had found on the black jumper; a long-haired black and white cat hair. The Kerrs did not have a cat.

Mulholland reported that both O'Hare and Elvie McCulloch were researching injectable drugs that metabolized so quickly nothing would be left in the system of the victims. He had heard a few generic names which he promptly forgot, the more important aspect was that whoever Blondie was, she had access to serious pharmaceuticals and knew how to use them.

Anderson was deep in thought about the hypnotherapy that Professor Batten was doing with Amy at that exact moment. He would rather have been there but her mother was present instead. The girl could obviously remember something but had got it confused in her mind, with the injected drug, the stress and the drink. Anderson had high hopes that Batten could find out exactly what Amy saw and that they, in the cold light of day and perfectly sober, could make sense of the aliens and give them the lead they needed.

Unfortunately, as James Kirkton had witnessed the girl stagger up the steps himself, he had taken a keen interest in the case and that fact alone made Anderson very wary. Not only would they have to investigate it, they would have to be visibly busy investigating it. It afforded them little chance of keeping their progress in-house.

Amy was young and pretty. She possessed that increasingly rare quality of 'every girl' that the press in general, and James Kirkton in particular, so loved in a victim. Amy Niven had nothing anybody could object to: youth, class, intelligence. If such an assault happened to her, there was no hope for the rest of us. Her looks, and her injuries meant she was in danger of being drawn into being a poster girl for the Safer Society campaign. James Kirkton had already been dropping hints to the media about the scuffle at the end of the lane and why six police offers could not save Irene Kerr from the trauma of seeing her 'son's' body. Anderson refused to be drawn into a tit for tat correction of the facts and be caught between Klingon Kirkton and ACC Mitchum, which was about as unpleasant as being between a urine-stained pavement and a dog turd. Anderson wondered how close the friendship was between the two men. Did they play golf together because they liked each other's company? Or because it was good for their careers. Anderson knew that Mitchum was nobody's fool. Anderson could see him as a man who would keep Kirkton close on the 'keep friends close and enemies closer' theory.

Anderson had planned his day. They had solid leads to work and he felt that something would break today. He was letting Mulholland field all his calls, saying that he was at the hospital interviewing two vulnerable witnesses and wasn't available for comment. The fact that Kirkton had previously availed himself of Alistair Jeffries' professional expertise as part of his Safer Society campaign meant he would have to tread carefully. Any mistakes on his part would be fodder for the incompetent police argument and his cold case role could go down the drain. Amy was a victim and he could argue well to keep her out of the limelight. Batten was medically qualified and he could lend a lot of weight to that. Amy's mum was very sensible and Anderson didn't see her pushing to get her daughter splashed all over the papers. It was Jeffries, Kirkton and Police Scotland who were the weak links in the chain. If he was not careful Jeffries would be the way for Kirkton to get in to the investigation. He wondered what Walker had said to him, or promised him.

As usual Anderson found a parking space at the Queen Elizabeth II University Hospital that was about four miles from where he wanted to be. In fact he was now nearer his own family home than he was to the coffee shop in the atrium where he had agreed to meet Batten.

But the walk in the sunshine was pleasant, despite the noise of the constant digging and earth-moving that was going on. They were still building offices and wards and treatment rooms for the ever-expanding super hospital. More and more patients but still nowhere for them to park.

Batten was sitting with an espresso, his pen in his hand held like a cigarette. He sported a filthy looking suede jacket and Iron Maiden T-shirt. He looked like he could be a Care in the Community patient waiting for his discharge papers. Anderson was wondering if his friend was on or off the fags. You could never tell with Mick. And his friend was starting to look old, much older than his years. Which again begged the question: was he on or off the drink? They shook hands warmly, both men gripping the other in a half embrace that was reciprocated. A true mutual friendship that had occasion-ally gone beyond the bounds of their respective work.

'You compartmentalize your life,' he recalled Brenda saying to him, or had he said it to Costello? Probably both. Maybe that's the only reason their friendship had lasted so long, it tended to stay well within its own boundaries. Adjustable, flexible boundaries.

'How is the coffee? Worth having?'

'Passable, definitely passable.' Batten pointed. 'Over there, coffee's good and she doesn't try to sell you anything exotic with salted caramel.'

Anderson got his coffee and started to walk towards the lift, making their way up to Alistair Jeffries' single room.

'So how did it go with Amy? Anything useful?'

'Very interesting. Little Amy under hypnosis. Her version under hypnosis was exactly the same as her recall when not under hypnosis.'

'So what does that mean?' Anderson asked.

'It means she was abducted by a load of aliens and a man walking around in a space suit.'

'Really?'

'Yes, everything points to the fact that she believes it. What that actually means is up to us to find out. No pressure.' The lift doors opened with a slightly disapproving hiss. 'Somebody whose memory under hypnosis is the same as their recalled memory is very rare, very rare indeed. So rare it's bloody odd.'

'But did you do it right?' asked Anderson.

'Yes, I did,' answered Batten coldly. 'Is Mr Jeffries along here?'

'Fourth room down,' said Anderson, flicking his ID at a nurse who didn't bother to look – just as Walker had said.

Jeffries lay on the bed, snuggled up as if expecting an attack from somewhere, when the door opened. His eyes darted from Batten to Anderson and back again, like a condemned man's door being opened by the Lord High Executioner.

Anderson made introductions that were not needed, and hoped that Jeffries would not go back on his word. Amy's mum was in the building, David was still missing. He would let Jeffries know that. If the old DCI held the key to all this in his subconscious mind, he had no moral right to deny them access. Anderson had no real plan B if Jeffries spouted the same crap that Amy had. But the doctor didn't look that worried, so that in itself was indicative of something.

Jeffries eyed the psychologist for a long time. 'I recognize you, Dr Batten. I think I worked with you once.'

'You did. You told me I was talking a lot of shite. That I wasn't doing anything that wasn't bloody obvious to a five-year-old and that I should go back to my colouring in.' Batten's voice was jovial, totally free of rancour as if he was rather proud that his professional opinion had been dismissed in such a way.

'Sounds like me,' admitted Jeffries. 'And I bet I was wrong, not to accept them.'

Anderson pulled up a seat and looked around for another.

'Partially wrong. It's always the balance between the practical and the theoretical,' Batten conceded. 'How are you keeping? You had a pretty nasty trauma to the head? Are you up for this?'

'Well, I really want to tell both of you to fuck off but anything is better than lying here doing bugger all. You think I can help with this?' he asked, his professional instincts were kicking in. He wanted to be involved; he had a lifetime of it. Only this time, he was the one who had been victimized and humiliated.

'I do.'

'He's not going to make you dance like a chicken and give us your bank account details,' assured Anderson.

Jeffries smiled for the first time. 'I dance like a chicken anyway and it's my ex's bank account details you would need. You are welcome to my overdraft any day.'

'No ta, got one of my own,' said Batten, sitting down on the seat that Anderson had found.

The mood had lightened. 'So, to recap, if done properly, accurate memories can be recalled under hypnosis. This is only supporting evidence and none of it is going anywhere near a courtroom. We need to get into your injured head and find out what your subconscious can recall. It knows what happened to you and who did it. Colin here needs the details of that retrieved memory.'

The two detectives flicked a look at each other, a mutual nod of consent.

'And the fact that the only other survivor of these attacks has no memory at all means that you are our only hope. So no pressure. We are going to use a deep relaxation protocol.'

Batten did a countdown, telling Jeffries to allow his eyes to close. Anderson switched on the recorder and tried to listen closely, but found himself carried along, drifting slightly, relaxing deeper into the seat. It was suddenly very comfortable.

Batten talked through a pleasant memory first, a few wise-cracks going back and forth. Jeffries had his eyes closed but insisted his best memory was the day the police dog had chased the ACC up a tree. It was a well told story in the police force, so often told that nobody knew or cared if it was true. They had a laugh but Anderson noticed that Batten was gently nudging his subject into a deeper state of relaxation, talking about stuff away from work, his holidays. When Batten mentioned his family, tears ran down from the older man's eyes. Batten took him back to a happier time when the kids were young. Jeffries was talking about a beach and a camping trip, making sandcastles and hunting for crabs in the rock pools.

Even Anderson could see that Jeffries was totally at peace now. Batten nodded at Anderson, while his voice reinforced that Jeffries was relaxed, and happy. He was here in a safe place, thinking nice thoughts, and he told him that it was safe to remember. Batten then asked Jeffries to think of the time when he had got the scar on his elbow. Anderson hadn't even noticed it but Jeffries started giggling like a child. He had been running along a rocky beach with an ice cream and had fallen. He had cut his elbow badly and the ice cream had melted. In his hypnotic, relaxed state, it was obvious from the tone of his voice that he had been very young when this had happened. He had been more upset at the ice cream melting than the blood streaming from the cut, and the five stitches it had taken to heal it at a cottage hospital somewhere in the Western Isles that the two of them had never heard of. Batten shuffled in his seat, glancing at the recording device. Anderson heard somebody walk down the corridor coughing heavily as they went. If they weren't a patient in here they bloody well should be.

Batten was now telling Jeffries that he wanted to talk about the night he met his friends in the Rock. And if Jeffries was OK with that, he was to raise his finger.

The pink puffy finger lifted slightly on the blue bed cover.

'We want you to tell us the little details. Let them come to you when you are ready. You will become aware of what you saw, what you noticed, what you heard . . . or said . . . what you were feeling. That is a memory and you know that you are safe here. All this is just memory. You will remember everything of importance that there is to know, safe and comfortable in the knowledge that it is a memory and that all is well. The actual events are all in the past. You survived the event and you can survive the memory so, what happened when you were with your friends at the Rock? You were having a pint.'

'Billy was texting some bird. I was watching the tennis on Sky Sport.'

'Who was playing?'

'Federer, somebody unpronounceable,' came in the reply instantly.

'And then what happened?'

'I was on my fifth pint. I needed a piss. I went to the loo. It was hot. I went out to the beer garden. No,' he stopped himself. 'She was at the door. She stops me.'

Batten smiled at Anderson, the memory had moved into the present tense.

'She stops me, she asks for help.'

'Who?'

'Her name is Diana.'

'And you know her?'

Jeffries faltered, trying to think. He grimaced in his sleep-like state.

'What is she like, Diana?'

Jeffries was immediately back on track. 'Nice wee blonde, tasty wee bit of stuff, OK wee lassie, you know.'

'Who is Diana?' asked Batten at Anderson's prompt.

'I don't know but she had a flat tyre. She was nice, funny. She had had a wee bit to drink and she was joking about trying to change a tyre without getting a big man to come with a big wrench, and we walked away a little. We got talking, then she couldn't find her car.'

'Why not?'

'Others had parked, up the lane. We couldn't see it.'

'Did you see the car?'

He faltered, his face pulled a puzzled expression.

'You are OK, Alistair, relax. You are safe here in the hospital, all you are doing is recalling a memory. Did you see her car?'

'No, not the car, but she was very pally.' He giggled like a schoolboy copping a feel. 'And we started messing about a bit. Then . . . now I am feeling really peculiar. I thought I was going to get lucky, you know, like she was hitting on me. There was no car, there was no car,' he repeated. 'No car.' Then fell silent. 'I remember thinking that she might be a pro, or that it might be a set-up by the ex, you know.'

Batten and Anderson exchanged glances. How bad had the marriage break-up been?

'So you started feeling poorly? What did Diana do?'

'Diana is asking me if I am OK.'

'Why?'

'Because I felt ill, then I fell and she is trying to help me up. She's lifting me, trying to help me. Then she leaves. She leaves me lying on the pavement.'

'OK, can we go back to the car, can you see up the street, up the lane?'

'There's a red BMW. A white . . .'

Anderson leaned forward. The only thing Wendy could recall about the car was the colour: white.

'Dog shit on the pavement, there was a cat. It was very quiet. Only chit-chat from the pub. That's all.'

'And the cars?'

Anderson wrote down 'white car' with a question mark.

'Estate. Needed a new wing, rusty, don't see much of that these days. Blue respray job.'

'And across the way?'

'Across the way?' His eyelids moved as if he was looking round his brain for the answer. 'White car parked up the side, quite new.'

'Make?' asked Anderson. 'Number?'

'Newish white car. Fiat?'

'Did you notice the number?'

'Can't see it, the car was parked on the verge. There's grass over the plate.'

Anderson noted that. Visit the verge. That piece of info, if correct, could take them right to the location. To the trail of Blondie . . .

'And then I fell, I don't recall anything after that but coming here.' Jeffries had his eyes closed, the lids flickered, struggling for a memory. 'There was something. It scratched me. There are a lot of brambles along there, I must have brushed against them. Bloody sore it was. It was bloody sore then and it is bloody sore now.'

'And where did it prick you?'

'On my arse.' He turned over slightly in the bed and pulled up the bed clothes. He pulled up his hospital gown to reveal a small red mark. 'Right there, I got pricked right there.'

It was the injection site.

Batten turned to Anderson, everything had just fallen into place.

But Anderson had fallen asleep.

'Do you think that Alzheimer's might be catching? I forgot where I parked the Panda yesterday,' said Sandra.

'There's no hope for us if it is. Some of them are enough
to drive you round the bend. See that Chic, he has told me
the same joke for the last six months, at least three times a
day. Twice while I was washing him. I mean you don't really
want to hear the one about the sausage and the nun, not in
those circumstances. Not as if it was funny the first time,' said
Norma, flicking open the paper. 'Good God have you seen
this. They still haven't identified the body found at the end of
the road. What are the police doing?'

'Said on Facebook that he was folded into a box.'

'And they think that it's a serial killer. There's that wee
Paige lassie as well. I mean folk don't disappear off the streets
these days, do they?'

They can when they want to, thought Sandra, but said, 'No,
I don't suppose they do.' She looked out over the street from
the staff room, seeing the CCTV camera sitting on the light
like a vulture waiting. She couldn't help feeling a wee bit
superior.

She was becoming part of something here, something above
all this gossip about little people. Runaways like Paige, that's
where Sandra had come from but that was not where she was
going back to. She was moving on and up with Paolo, with
or without the Duchess. She let her colleagues chatter on, lost
in her own wee world, thinking of Paolo coming out the shower
yesterday, looking very handsome with a towel wrapped round
his waist. He said that he had to go somewhere important and
needed a quick freshen up. He had then asked Sandra what
sort of day she was having, not just casually. He asked her
like he was really interested.

Then before she left, he had called after her. 'Sandra?' he
had said, just like that he called her by her name. 'Sandra,
that lipstick is too dark for you. I'll buy you something better,
something more suited.'

And now she was here in the staffroom with the other carers,
the skanks, talking about how drunk they had been on a hen
weekend in Benidorm. She hadn't been invited. She wondered
where Paolo lived. Must be local if he didn't need his car; he
had given it to Sandra. He did odd hours so maybe he was a
doctor, and that might be why he had swung a disability badge

for the Panda even though the Duchess never went out. So near the old Western? Up on Byres Road or if he was really high up, like a consultant or something, then he might be along Westerton or Jordanhill.

'Paolo Girasole's not married, is he?' she asked, fishing for more information by casually dropping him into the conversation. She regretted it immediately as they started laughing. She was back again at the school in the playground, turning up for a new school term in a coat her mum had got from a charity shop. Halfway through playtime Isla Brodie had pointed at her, laughing, shrieking that the coat had just been chucked out by her mum. She felt sick at the memory. That would never happen to her again

'Him? No way, he's a right mummy's boy. I mean I think he likes his mother, you know, really likes her. All that dressing her up and doing all her personal care, that's not bloody normal. She's an old bag, rich old bag. Have you seen her clothes?'

'I mean, nobody gets to look at her underwear. He takes it all home, probably dresses up in it. Or he dresses her up in it and does it with her in the shower.'

'Couple of bloody weirdoes.'

Sandra felt herself blush.

'Do you fancy him, seriously? Really? Oh my God.' Lisa pointed at Sandra, her hand over her mouth laughing. 'He is *gay*, you prat!' And they laughed, and laughed, but not unkindly. They thought her rather unworldly. She was right back in the playground again.

Lisa took her by the arm and shook her a little. 'Come on, Sandra, you must have noticed.'

But Tracey wasn't for letting up, 'Jesus, you do fancy *him*?'

Then Lisa said, 'Watch yourself, Sandra, seriously. Watch yourself, if the boss finds out you will be out of here. Be careful, girl, don't even joke about that kind of thing. The management have no sense of humour. Paolo likes you, he thinks you are good for the Duchess but if they sack you, you will be out on your ear and there's not a damn thing you or he can do about it. Look at what happened to Becky. And Caroline. That was nasty. Her husband's on disability and they still sacked her. They are shit, them upstairs. James Kirkton is a shifty wee bastard, Pearcy is the same. It's all about the money for them. All the money in the world and not an ounce of compassion. I'm telling you.'

'I wasn't—' started Sandra but was interrupted.

'Oh you were, I've seen you come into work, all dolled up,' said Lisa, giggling.

Sandra reddened.

'And I saw you sneaking down the stairs,' added Norma.

'I wasn't.'

'I bloody saw you.'

No. No. No. No. No.

'Seriously, Sandra? Don't do that. It's private what goes on downstairs.' Lisa smiled mischievously. 'I noticed you had your hair coloured and red lipstick on. You won't get him that way, you'd need to be seventy years old and speak Italian, and sing Italian like a bloke with his nuts in a liquidizer.'

'Oh, I see,' said Sandra quietly, letting the conversation move on to more familiar topics.

Lisa was back looking at the face of Paige Riley, saying that she had probably been killed ages ago. Norma was chattering on about the minimum wage. Alison about the car park being too small and how they were always having to move cars about to get in and out, they left their car keys on a hook. It was all residential parking permits up here, so the care home allowed them to park on a small patch of gravel that was always full, so no wonder Sandra forgot where she had left the Panda.

'Did you read that arse Kirkton in the *WestEnder* yesterday, wittering on about the safer society. And I got my bike stolen for the third time,' complained Lisa.

'You mean that was the third bike you got stolen.'

'No, it was the same bike; I got it stolen three times. Next time I am going to tie my husband to it and hopefully they will take him as well.'

There was a contagious snort of laughter.

'Well I don't like it. The cops were in here yesterday. And Sunday. That Pippa is the procurator's missus you know.'

'Fuck, that's all we need, cops in here every two minutes.'

'The management won't like it either given what goes on downstairs,' said Janis, who talked like she knew.

Sandra fingered her lips as she listened to Janis yabber on, imagining herself living in that book with the gold-leafed drawings and the beautiful artwork. She could lose herself in the pages of that book, she could be the enchanting princess in search of her prince in the forest.

She excused herself, rinsed out her cup and left the staff room, seeing the owner, Dr Pearcy and the matron outside the door of the dayroom and stopped dead. She was scared? Too strong a word. She was caught standing in the hallway, hidden behind the main support of the stairs. She could see them clearly, but they couldn't see her. The matron looked her way and checked that the door to the staff kitchen was closed. The doctor went into the day room while the matron stayed in the hall. Sandra had noticed them doing that before and it had struck her then, as it did now, that the matron looked as though she was keeping guard. She looked at her watch, it was still break time for the staff. What was Pearcy doing in there? He played no part in the personal care, and in any case, any resident would be taken to their own room for that.

Paolo kept the management in line, maybe she should tell him about this clandestine behaviour outside the door of the main day room. He was good that way, Paolo. The management knew that they walked a thin line between the support for the independent lifestyle of the aged and turning a profit. If their families couldn't care tuppence for them, it was up to Sandra to do her best, and nick what she could or be nice and see what she might inherit.

She stayed still, thinking that she couldn't move now without the matron knowing that she had been watching them. And she knew guilty behaviour when she saw it. She leaned forward into the white pillar, placing her forehead against it and watched as Dr Pearcy came out of the day room, quiet words were said. He slipped something into his pocket, Matron looked one way then the other, a casual look up the stairs. Sandra took a breath in, kept stalk still, scared to breathe too loudly. She waited until they were out of sight through the fire doors and probably back in the office. Then she made

her way down the stairs, her Crocs quiet on the side of the
stair carpet, then she bounded into the day room, and looked
around, looking for what had changed. Kilpatrick was glaring
at her as he always did. The rest of them were totally out of
it. Pippa Walker slumped to the side, fast asleep, her book
still open on her lap, upside down.

'Are you still on duty?' It was the matron, behind her.

'I finished my tea break.' Sandra had always been a very
good liar. She had her hands on her pockets ready. 'I am
looking for my car keys, I'm sure I had them down here last.
Not seen them have you?'

Matron shook her head slowly, and stood to one side, wafting
Sandra out the room. 'That's why there is a board for the keys,
you should have left them there.'

'I thought I had.'

'Better go and see that the Duchess is OK. That is what
you are paid to do.'

'And write up my notes,' she added in what she hoped was
a friendly, helpful and explanatory way. She held her head
high as she went back up the stairs. That was a habit of the
Duchess she admired; holding the head high, being above it
all. And that had rubbed off on Sandra, she was the Duchess's
carer. Not one of those wee girls who wiped the backsides
and blew the noses of the guests on the first floor.

Sandra was back at her small flat, lying in her bed, alone at
night staring at the light blue paint on the ceiling. Three
different colours of test pots before she lost interest. She had
lost interest in the flat totally now. She had run out of food,
all her credit cards maxed out. She had even nicked Lisa's
contactless card and bought some stuff from Starbucks before
dumping the card. Lisa would think she had lost it.

She had her heart set on a future elsewhere. It's not where
you start, it's where you finish, as the song said. That was one
of her mantras.

She wondered what the Duchess's husband had been like,
the dark-eyed man in the photographs. Roman-nosed and
strong-jawed, saved from being ridiculously macho by the
long wavy hair and fine, elegant fingers. She wondered about

any history between Kilpatrick and the Duchess. He was an ugly toad now but might have been a handsome prince once. Was he the jazz saxophonist in some smoky underground nightclub as she sung her heart out to earn any pennies she could, killing them with her fabulous voice; torch songs from a tortured soul.

They must have lived around the West End, she would have grown up around here. They would have moved and lived within the same square mile so it was likely they would have come across each other at some time, moving in the same circles. Whatever had happened, there was still a great deal of ill feeling. Had it been something romantic, Sandra wondered, as she snuggled into her bed. Had the Duchess broken his heart, or had he betrayed her. He looked the type. The bigger issue was that Paolo was an only child. And only children tend to inherit everything. Well anything that was left after years in the Athole House Secure Living Facility. So, she reckoned, the quicker the Duchess was out of her way, the better.

FOUR

Wednesday 8 June

T he call came through at half past one; Anderson had been half asleep, despite his intention to read *On Liberty* by John Stewart Mill, and trying to find some hope for a humanity that seemed obsessed with stick-thin, thick-eyebrowed celebrities, their low morals and lower IQs. He picked up his phone and listened. OK, it was five minutes away. The sirens had registered somewhere deep in his psyche, but he had tuned it out, digesting the book and dozing with thoughts of utilitarianism. He had been far, far away.

He went upstairs to say goodbye to Claire but she was fast asleep, curled in her bed like a child, her hands clasped in the sincere prayer of the subconscious. So he scribbled a note for

her and left it on the table downstairs where he had all his
favourite photographs, Brenda and the kids, their wedding day
and, on the wall, his favourite picture of Helena. On the panel
of the door, the stained glass showed the goddess Ceres keeping
an eye on them. She was already twinkling with the lights of
the cityscape outside.

There had been a fire in the West End, some building that
was being restored and a workman had maybe got a bit too
handy with a welding torch, left it lying around when it was
still hot. The flames could have been brewing for the last few
hours in an old building stripped back to the original wooden
infrastructure. And it had simmered before taking hold. It
wouldn't be the first time. And it wouldn't be the last time if
it was an insurance job. So God knows why they had phoned
him. He was head of a major incident team . . . unless somebody had died in the fire and then, maybe, the fire was not so
accidental. He couldn't think of any other reason why he would
get the call.

Twenty minutes later, the car that had picked him up at the
house on the hill was dropping him off behind a fire appliance.
It was gridlock already, despite them trying to keep the area
clear of any vehicles that weren't directly involved in fighting
the inferno.

The car quickly pulled away, waved through a gap in the
traffic by a cop in high-vis who was trying, in vain, to keep
the access clear.

Anderson stood back and assessed the situation, people
everywhere in hard hats, burning bricks and smoking black
wood stinking the air out. He placed the crook of his elbow
over his nose and looked back down the main road. This was
Vinicombe Street, right where the boy had gone missing. Was
that the connection that the fire officers had made? And then
they felt the need to call him this early in the morning? He
felt that sickening feeling drop inside him. David? He turned
round; he could see the Zeitgeist Café from here, through the
drifting smoke. Had they found a body in the flames? To pre-
empt a rerun of Sunday he pulled out his mobile and rang
Irene. She answered instantly, her voice tense and reedy.

'I am telling you that there is no news, Irene. We have been called out to another incident purely because of its location.'

'Where? Athole Lane?'

'No, down in Vinicombe Street.'

There was silence on the line.

Eventually: 'I don't understand.'

'The computer flags these things up. We need to check out if there is even a remote chance of a connection. I don't want your friends Facebooking you and texting to ask if the incident is anything to do with your son. And God forbid if the press get onto you.'

'Oh thank you, thank you very much.'

He winced at the relief in her voice. 'If it is anything to do with David, I will tell you personally. Don't believe anything that anybody says until you have spoken to me.' He rang off hoping that his gut feeling was wrong. This was the less cruel of the two options.

The Zeitgeist Café was on the corner of Vinicombe Street. The ball in his stomach tightened.

'Interesting,' said the fire officer, walking up to Anderson but looking beyond him, to where the tail lights of the car had driven into the darkness. 'It's the refurb of that nightclub Insanity. It didn't last long enough to get its doors open.' He seemed casual, amused even.

Anderson had to ask, 'Do you have a body?' He couldn't look at him, he didn't want to hear the words. He didn't want to call that driver back and ask him to drive out to Irene's house and tell her face to face. *I have some bad news for you.*

Somebody shouted. The roar of the fire and the reverberating rumble of the hose spray crescendoed, as if somebody had opened a door in the sky. Anderson saw the grimy face of the fire officer and his blackened mouth opening and closing but Anderson couldn't hear, not now. The fire officer turned round and was pointing up, describing something that had happened, like in a silent film all the information came through with gestures.

'Sorry.' Anderson tapped him on the shoulder and pointed to his ear. 'Can't hear you. Is there a fatality?' he shouted.

The fire officer shook his head.

'No?'

'No,' he shouted back in confirmation. He took Anderson by the arm to the back of the appliance where they stood in a slow-flowing puddle that made little waves as it met and ran round the toes of Anderson's shoes.

He had to repeat it again, to make sure. 'No fatalities?'

'Nope. Close though.'

'Not the missing boy, David Kerr? Nineteen years old . . .?'

'It's the owner of the club. Kenny Fraser. He's already been identified. We suspect a wee bit more than smouldering insulation left after a welder who skived early. That was off the record by the way.'

The noise died down again, a crisis had passed. The fire-fighter looked up at the sky as if he had willed the wind to change direction and help them out. Conversation became possible again. 'Two takes on it, either the campaign to stop this Insanity nightclub opening has taken a violent turn, or Kenny Fraser has really pissed off somebody – which is more than possible. He was lucky to get out alive. He's at the Queen Elizabeth and has two of your boys with him. From the look of him, he was tied onto a pipe and the place was set on fire. Plastic ties, not nice. But functional. That poor bastard has got on the wrong side of somebody. Heard there was a bit of a turf war up in Castlemilk recently so that might be a connection. But we wanted to show you the film of the fire. This is, or was, the old Vinicombe Street Theatre.' He pointed. 'I'm told there have been shitloads of protests about its change of use. Christ knows why, it's been empty for years.'

'Oh right,' said Anderson, thinking that this had the sound of protection about it and it was not something his team could get involved in right now. Or was he being taken off the David Kerr case and nobody had had the balls to tell him yet. If this was organized crime then there was no connection with David Kerr.

Nothing at all.

'Fortunately we got to Fraser before the flames did.' The firefighter looked high into the flames. 'He fought a few legal battles to get this nightclub. And a few illegal ones.'

Anderson looked questioningly.

'Paid off a few folk, so the rumour goes . . .'

'Anything more than a rumour?'

'Not that you will hear from my lips.'

'Why was he here at this time of night? Of the morning?'

'The premises were broken into earlier.' He looked at his watch, his thick gloves pulling back the cuff of the faded yellow jacket to see his watch. 'Well, yesterday. I think that cop Graham said it's been broken into five times while it was lying empty.' He shrugged. 'Nothing worth nicking. So we have no idea why he was here. Fraser's story was too garbled but it's obvious he was attacked and was attached to the pipe. But he was dressed, you know, like he was going out on the town; with some lassie probably and he didn't want the missus finding out? That's what I think.'

'Your sins will find you out. How bad was he?' Anderson asked.

'His breathing was bad, the air is toxic in there. It's not too good out here either.'

Anderson looked round the end of the appliance and up to the overhead gargoyles and wooden straps and beams, the front glass smashed, the tiles up over the old theatre door, disrupting their sunflower pattern. The rafters, blackened and exposed, became visible through the drifts of smoke. It came back to him, as clear as day, a memory of it when he had been a kid, the front window with its red curtains and the Christmas display. Puppet reindeers and Santa belly laughing, a hundred moving pieces. How they animated the marionettes was a wonder to him as a boy and it still puzzled him now. It had enchanted him as a kid, it was a favourite stopping point as much as the Christmas lights and a visit to Santa's Grotto. He hadn't even noticed it had closed.

'Oh, the building will stay up. It has to, it's listed.'

'The old theatre? I remember looking at the big front window and my mum saying it was too expensive to go in.' Anderson turned round trying to get his bearings, through the swirling soot, the watchers, the emergency vehicles, the dying smoke that burled and clouded in the sky.

'Well, you can go over all your yesterdays in the pub later.' The fire officer nudged Anderson's arm. 'This is what I really wanted you to see, the video record of the fire. They stream it nowadays as well as film the things, everything in triplicate so we can't be criticized by everybody for not doing it right. First in the queue will be the right dishonourable tosspot Klingon Kirkton, I presume.'

'Join the club.'

'We'll either be done for wasting public money by protecting a listed building. Or not doing enough to protect a listed building.'

'Probably both. There are so many cops now investigating themselves it might be easier if everybody locked up the station and went home instead.' That was on the schedule for tomorrow, yet another meeting about cuts and funding while trying to keep a workforce awake for thirty-six hours a day with no loss of cognitive power.

'We suspected arson, wilful fire raising. So we filmed the crowd as well as filming the incident. Standard procedure nowadays.'

'As the arsonist very often comes back to view the outrage he has caused? A theory I've heard many times,' acknowledged Anderson.

'Truth be known, we film the crowd more than the fire these days, for all kinds of law and health and safety reasons.' The fire officer held up a smart phone, pulling his gloves off to reveal two very clean hands with neatly cut nails over delicate pink skin. He tilted the screen for Anderson to see. They leaned into the shadow of the fire appliance as the water jets cooled the sizzling rafters and bricks that had been destined to be the new nightclub. 'One of your guys spotted somebody in the crowd and we took a closer look. He said you had actioned a lookout for a blonde. We knew about the derelict buildings memo, thinking that wee Paige might be somewhere. But she's not here.'

Anderson looked at the sizzling shell of the building and hoped he was right.

'But who we do have is this lady, so we thought you might want to see this sooner rather than later. She was standing right up there. Wearing sunglasses at night.' He pointed a little up Vinicombe Lane. 'Watching everything that was going on.'

Anderson said, 'Not uncommon, rubberneckers on a hot summer night when the festival is on. But in sunglasses?'

'Look carefully, DCI Anderson.'

Colin nearly missed it, or nearly missed her, nearly swiped on too early. Then he saw it. She was crying, in tears. Terrible, terrible pain was etched in every inch of her face that was visible. The younger woman next to her turned round on the film, obviously asking her if she was OK. Anderson zoomed in on the image, seeing her face, black tear streaks down her cheek. The blonde bob cut that never changed. The lower part of her face covered by a scarf, her hand up over it, pressing it to her mouth, supposedly to keep the smoke out of her airways, the upper half covered by the glasses. She was hiding her face. Or wiping her tears.

Anderson was slipping his wet shoes off inside his front door, aware of the stink of smoke. He felt dirty and grimy and he realized that his trousers were soaked up to the knees. He looked at them for a long time, hearing the flames and the crashing of the fire. He held his hands out and realized he was shaking. That summer night on the loch came back to him. He recognized the feelings and he let the horror sweep over him, it was easier to roll with it. He had learned that the hard way. He let the sweat pour down his back, let the panic tighten his lungs. His brain would always make that link. Fire. Death. It hurt.

He was still staring at his trouser legs, thinking how to get up the stairs and across the plush cream carpet of the landing without making a mess. Helena immediately came to mind, her world view where white carpets were functional. It never bothered her. He supposed she always had the money to get them cleaned. Or did Alan, her husband, genuinely never feel really at home here. He was so rarely in. Maybe things were less ideal than he thought. Nobody ever really knew what was going on in anybody else's marriage.

'Where have you been?' The voice behind him was low and feminine, husky with sleep.

He jumped for a minute thinking that it was Helena standing on the stairs, but it was Claire, still dressed as she had been before. 'Where have you been? You smell of smoke, you been to the Vinicombe Street fire?'

'The aftermath of the fire. How do you know? Facebook?'

'Yip. Was it anything to do with David?'

'No. It's a bloody awful sight to see something like that go up in flames.'

Claire grunted in dismissive amusement. 'Tough shit. That arse only bought the place last year, and he didn't really want any of its artistic heritage. He wanted a nightclub. Like the West End needs another nightclub. He was ripping the guts out of the Vinicombe Street Theatre, so no, I don't feel all that sorry for him.' She gave him that teenage look when they encounter parental stupidity. 'He prevented the family taking their own stuff back, you know, the plans and the models made over the generations. He threw it all in a skip. Nice man not! So yeah, do we have the right to own our own art?' Then added: 'Actually.'

'Why are you so cynical?'

Claire shrugged. 'Me? Cynical? A hundred years' worth of art and craftsmanship and beauty. People who lived and breathed the stories, made them come to life. The artistic soul of the city is being ripped apart for another drug dealer's nightclub.'

Anderson was going to argue, then remembered the truth and the single-mindedness of youth, the certainty of their world view.

'OK, so a serial killer and a beautiful piece of art are both in a room and the room goes on fire. The work of art could disappear forever. Which one would you save?' She looked at him, arms crossed in confrontation. At times she was very like her mother.

'Human life above all else, Claire.'

'Crap. I'd let Ian Brady toast and save the Sunflowers. In fact I'd stand on his head to reach up to the Sunflowers. I bet Costello would agree with me.'

Anderson felt his mouth twitch and stifled a giggle. 'I don't doubt it but she's not exactly the voice of reason, is she?' He sat down on the stairs, pulling the wet fabric of his trouser leg away from the skin on the front of his shin.

She slid down the wall, and rested her weight on the step two above her dad. 'People got very upset by it, the whole Insanity thing.'

Anderson was thinking of the blonde woman in tears, heart-felt tears. 'Like who? Who are the kind of people who get upset by the whole Insanity thing?'

'Anybody with a soul.' Her brown eyes, deep as chestnuts, regarded the goddess Ceres. 'Without art we are animals, Dad, worse than animals. So get with the programme, go on Facebook and see the storm this Fraser idiot has created, some people have no respect. No respect for art, for work.' And with that she trotted upstairs. He got out his phone and put in a reminder to get Wyngate or Mulholland to check it out. At this time of night it was all beyond him. He didn't think the dawning of a new day was going to help him so he followed his daughter upstairs to ask her to log into her Facebook page for him. He wasn't going to get any sleep tonight anyway.

Claire set up her laptop and they settled down with Nesbit and a box of Jaffa Cakes. He scrolled through the Facebook page called The Vinicombe Street Children's Theatre. It had been set up by somebody called Pauline Gee, a real aficionado of all children's puppets and puppet shows. She had put up a special petition to stop the building being sold for redevelopment. He had flicked through photograph after photograph; Vinicombe Street in the sixties and seventies, up to the nineties. They scrolled through them together looking at the dragons, the dinosaurs, the grand dames and the principal boys, Bo Peep, Pinocchio and assorted dwarfs. All framed by the bright sunflower tiles he had seen darkened and fractured after the fire. He saw the big window, draped in red velvet curtains like a stage just as he remembered it. Across the top of the window was a forest of brightly coloured animals and birds, all individual, all beautifully crafted, all carefully numbered. There were a few pages of the production posters. It looked like it had been a little powerhouse of fun. He felt very melancholy all of a sudden, the world had got from this to gaming in a generation. Anderson looked closely at some of the marionettes, named and numbered as if the puppets themselves had been individuals. He had never liked puppets, tending to think that they were a bit creepy. Even folk walking around like the Thunderbirds gave him the willies. His sister was phobic about clowns. No wonder their mum and dad had never taken them to the circus. But he had enjoyed scrolling through the pictorial history of the Vinicombe Street Children's Theatre as it had been called in its heyday. It certainly looked a lot more wholesome than *Call of Duty*. And a lot more fun. Puppets were scary and most kids like to be scared witless.

At five a.m., Anderson was fed up trying to sleep in the heat, his mind drifting to counting the number of phobias he might gather as he got older. Lying here in the darkness it was the noises that were getting to him. But he knew that the flames, the cracking of burning wood, were not welcome companions and not conducive to sound slumber. They were memories, and memory is a mere construct of the mind; harmless. He was trying to silence the noises in his head by thinking about the events of the day and Vinicombe Street before it went on fire. He really would have to pass this on to another team; the guys in the good suits who worked out of West End Central.

He needed to track down Pauline Gee and with a bit of luck she'd have a blonde bob cut and a history of mental instability – but he doubted it. People didn't set things on fire because they were annoyed at planning permission being granted. People set things on fire for money.

He turned over, snuggling deep into the pillow but sleep was still elusive. His mind wandering here and there but always back to Vinicombe Street. It ran at right angles on to Byres Road. The junction was marked by a raised area of concrete that made the pavement continuous and hinted to drivers that there was no point in turning up there unless you had a well displayed and up-to-date resident's permit. Mentally he revisited the scene where the car had dropped him off last night. The tiny old theatre was right on the corner of Vinicombe Street and Vinicombe Lane, the next junction down was Byres Road, cross that and . . . Mentally he turned off the noise of the fire, the banging and the crashing. He tuned out the hiss and whoosh of the flames. In his mind's eye, the car drove away and left him alone, standing still in a silent world. Everybody frozen in time and space, flames jagged tongues into the dark night. He looked at what was to the left and to his right; Byres Road wound north to Queen Margaret Drive and south to the Expressway and the river. If he stood there and looked slightly north there was the gap between Waitrose and the posh hotel – whatever it was called nowadays – the locals still called it One Devonshire Gardens. That was the location of the CCTV camera that had given them the footage of David's abduction. The images floated through his mind. He tried to think where that lane went, but he couldn't quite get there. He had a vague suspicion but he needed to be sure.

He needed to go for a walk

By six a.m., he was walking in the cool, early morning air down the lane, the sky was clearing, it was going to be another scorcher of a day. He started at Byres Road. He passed through the concrete spike that stopped cars using it as a shortcut. He admired the neat little cottages, the rear of the huge tenements towering above. He walked through the dogleg and ahead of him saw the whitewashed building jutting out, where the body of Mr Hollister had been found, bent neatly into a tea chest, a tea chest that had been designed to transport delicate cargo. Nobody had reported *him* missing. O'Hare and Costello had made no more progress about his identity. He was unmissed, unloved. He had come and gone as an autumn leaf caught in the breeze.

He walked past the building, ignoring the bit of police tape that was left. The marks on the ground that showed where the InciTent had been. The boy in the chest had been almost forgotten, such was the impact of Irene Kerr on the case. *My boy, my boy.* The other boy was already dead, but there was still hope for her son. And Anderson couldn't say that his actions would be any different.

It was as if Mr Hollister had never come this way; he had left no footsteps in death, and none in life. None that they could follow anyway. The forensics team had proposed that this should be ruled as a disposition site, not the murder site, and as such, they were finished. Archie Walker, the fiscal, had agreed, with one eye on the budget. Little of evidential value present, he could hear Walker's clipped voice in his ear. Anderson paused at the end of the lane and looked up the hill, over Athole Gardens to the nursing home at the top of the hill. The fiscal's wife was in there now, probably being woken from a deep medicated sleep to be kept awake long enough to eat her breakfast, to then be given some sedatives to send her back to the land of nod.

He turned round and retraced his steps, back to his car. It would have been quicker walking up to the station from here but there was something troubling him, some link he wasn't seeing yet.

He drove up by the Rock to where Jeffries had been . . . well, what had he been? Stalked, then chatted up, then injected by Blondie who may or may not have a Facebook identity of Pauline Gee. Mulholland would be on the track of all the Pauline Gees in the area as soon as he stepped his bad leg into the office.

Anderson got out of the car and strolled up the lane to the side of the pub, concrete underfoot, broken wooden fencing to his left, trees with a few parked cars underneath to his right. Nothing to be seen, tyre marks of all kinds of cars, but he was getting a sense of it. People talking over the half fence, drifting in conversation. Jeffries drunk, the back door of the pub open on a warm summer night. She approached, she engaged him, asking him for help as she had done with David Kerr, and maybe Amy and Mr Hollister too. But Jeffries had fallen and knocked himself out. He was too big, too heavy, for her to move without some assistance from him. She wasn't stupid, she would have realized that. So why select him? Was it about *him*?

Was this personal to him?

Amy's thyroid condition might have affected her metabolism of the drug. Then Mr Hollister, what had gone wrong there? Then David Kerr, the first perfect victim. Anderson could see no connection.

He turned round to walk back to the Beamer, deep in thought. He saw a poster for Paige Riley, fixed to a lamp post, protected by a laminated screen that clicked slightly in the breeze. Paige Riley? Maybe David wasn't the first perfect victim.

By 7 a.m., Anderson was in his own office and the preliminary report on the theatre fire lay on his desk, but it was the brown envelope lying beside it that intrigued him more. He recognized Elvie McCulloch's precise heavy handwriting. The note was short and to the point. 'Ask them to think about Curarium. Paracurarium? Epicurarium? Used to relax smooth muscle under anaesthetic.'

He walked into the investigation room and wrote that up on the board, with a note for it to be actioned. They sounded like drugs for hospital use; that fitted some of their ideas about Blondie.

He looked at Amy's photograph. Amy was told by the alien to come and see him. So the abductor knew him; a cop. And the abductor knew her, which should narrow the search a bit surely. Then Alistair Jeffries? Another cop. Both DCIs. There was some kind of a circle there. Not as difficult as the old days though, now anybody could be found. A to B to Z was a matter of a few key strokes.

Amy was not a stupid girl. She woke up somewhere, her brain saw something, or somebody, and interpreted it as an alien. Somebody dressed in silver? Green above her? Out in the open somewhere? The fancy dress of parade day could easily explain that.

He wrote the name Diana on the board, under Blondie and Pauline Gee. Diana. The goddess of hunting.

He looked out of the window, the sky was darkening again after the early light. Maybe the thunder would be here today. It was needed to clear the air, it might help clear his head.

He went back into his own office and opened the fire investigation report. They had found an incendiary device on the floor of the old theatre. It was definitely arson. The delay on the device was familiar to Anderson; a small bundle of cigarettes to create a slow fuse and a box of matches to start a flame. The arsonist had left it on top of a pile of the banners that were still boxed for the opening of the new nightclub. The report went on to say that the job lot of publicity flyers had been made in China and did not fulfil the trading standard for fire retardation. The toxic fumes had contributed to Fraser's breathing difficulties at the scene and there was a footnote to the effect that he would not be available for interview for the foreseeable future. Don't call us, we'll call you.

Anderson looked at the ever-growing pile of paperwork and crowded wall space. An arsonist, a delay device and Fraser tied to a radiator. Attempted murder? Deliberate placing of the device on that box of banners? He texted Batten and told him to get there as soon as possible. He needed some expert advice on this.

By 9 a.m., Batten was giving Anderson, Wyngate and Mulholland a full lecture on arsonists, pulling his chair up to the big table and placing both hands on the top, palms down. 'Well, it's a fascinating field.'

'Not when it dragged me out of my comfy chair at one o'clock this morning,' said Anderson.

Costello wrestled the coffee pot onto the table one-handed, then took her own seat, cradling a can of coke in her elbow, her phone to her ear. On hold.

'Well, "profiled" arsonists, fire setters, have a below-normal IQ, usually between seventy and ninety. They tend to be both mentally retarded and very angry.'

'So not clever then?'

'That's the ones that have been profiled and studied. The clever ones get away with it for years. Arsonists are angry, white and they are male.'

'Not female?' asked Anderson.

'No, male. That tends to exclude females,' added Batten dryly. 'I doubt this is a woman. It'll be a man, an extremely bright man. As a wee boy he'd play with matches and turn it into a game. It's his illicit thrill, it's dangerous and he is told so. That ups the ante. It feeds his flame, if you pardon the pun. The fires themselves are the behaviour of a single individual. He'll have started when he was about fourteen or fifteen. You need to look at your timeline. You need to look at past fires.'

They all stared at him.

Wyngate suggested. 'We have the new Sherlock search engine.'

Costello, the phone still to her ear, started scrolling down a screen. Ears on this, eyes on that.

'So do we search for some fires? Then find a connection. How can we find that out when I don't know any questions to ask? It's all bloody beyond me,' said Anderson.

Wyngate pulled himself up in his chair. He looked like he had slept even less than Anderson; he had two young children. He had another fifteen years before he had to suffer the teenage nonsense of his boss. 'All we need to do is set some parameters,' he said quietly.

'So arsonists start early, it's a teenage thing.' Batten settled in the chair, his chain of thought clarifying. 'So if we think that your mystery blonde is associated with him, with whoever. What about between now and what? 1970? 1960?' They looked at Wyngate as he grandly pressed 'Enter'. And waited.

'Too many,' said Wyngate.

'OK. Let's narrow it down. What postcodes would you be wanting to look at. All G11 and G12s?' Wyngate typed it without waiting for an answer.

'There will be a pattern,' said Batten, reaching for the coffee pot. 'Look for targets that are public or abandoned buildings. Hospitals, churches, private garages and sheds, all that kind of thing.'

'But in this case, was the man the target? I mean him rather than the building. He was tethered to the radiator,' pointed out Anderson.

'Both,' said Batten, 'I would say both. They would be linked in the arsonist's mind.'

'That kind of victim selection suggests revenge of some kind . . .'

'So when he was younger, he was humiliated in the children's theatre? The singing kettle sang out of tune? The hungry caterpillar got a bellyful?'

'Your best guess, Mick, was this a man that did this?' asked Anderson.

'Yes, for many reasons,' Batten replied as he flicked a thumb at the wall.

'So who is Blondie then? Beside the building, crying her eyes out? Who is she?'

'Somebody adored? Here is my offering. I love you?' Batten said, 'Something like that. Look at her face.' He pointed at the still photograph from the fire officer's film. 'Her heart is breaking. It was a children's theatre. Look at the emotion here. She is hurting? I don't know. It seems very sane for an insane mind. So maybe she is the key but he is the arsonist. And he—' he emphasized the word – '*he* will live within a five-mile radius of the fire cluster – once Wyngate has isolated it. And *he* has been unable to resolve an issue with the man in the fire, something that he feels he can't tackle in any other way.'

'So ties him to a radiator to burn him in a fire?' Costello was failing to conceal her admiration.

'So Blondie has a close relationship with him? With the arsonist?'

'But not in a conventional sense. The relationship does not fulfil her. Her life is behind her somewhere. He is easier to profile than her. He's confident with fire and his family will be disrupted by divorce or separation; his life would have been chaotic. He might have been able to run free as a kid, and nothing destabilizes a kid more than having no boundaries. He would have been truant from school, a runaway from home. And a history of fire-play, a personal experience of fire. Fire to them has a symbolic significance. So look back to any record where the cause of the fire was suspect. One where there was a fatality. If they could tie this man onto the radiator, then he's fit. Below fifty. So go back forty years. In a five-mile radius of here. You will see the pattern.'

'Bloody hell, there have been ten.' Wyngate was scrolling through the computer.

'Ten?'

'OK, two of those were in a car that went on fire in the early seventies. Another two . . .' He leaned forward. 'That was a scum landlord—'

'Slum landlord,' corrected Batten.

'I choose my words carefully.'

'Oh yeah, I recall that. Early eighties, that was.'

'Yes, that was signed and sealed, then three . . . oh,' said Wyngate, 'I think this might be worth a closer look, hang on . . .' He typed again, Costello leaned forward as far as she could without pulling the land line off the desk.

'What?' asked Anderson.

'If we then type the word theatre, as that qualifies as a public building, it brings us back to this morning, back to the Vinicombe Street fire.'

'That's a long, long time to wait.'

'He has been angry for a long time.'

They watched as Wyngate's fingers started flying over the keyboard again.

Costello snuffled quietly from her desk where she had been scrolling without anybody noticing. 'What about the fire in Marchmont Terrace?' She spun in her chair. 'That might be a good place to start, seeing that was where Mr Hollister was found.' And she stood up to leave the room.

'Stop!' Anderson looked at her, coldness in his eyes, his voice was clipped. 'Where exactly?'

She pointed to the whiteboard, 'On there. Bloody read it, why don't you? I'm away to sort my nose out, I think it's going to start bleeding again.'

'Where Costello?'

She realized that they were all looking at her now. 'Here.' She marched across the room. 'Right here.' She tapped at the whiteboard. 'Athole Lane. Which runs along the back of the houses on Marchmont Terrace. O'Hare spotted it straight away. It was the rebuild after it went up in flames. Do a search on the name Marchmont fire and fatal, that will bring it up. OK?' And she walked out, still sniffing.

'Why did we not see that?'

'Why indeed? It was listed as accidental, not arson. Christmas candle set fire to a coat hanging on a hook.'

'There's a protection order covering the release of further information.' Anderson shook his head. 'I don't know what's worse. Costello on the ball or her not on the ball.'

'She looks like Coco the Clown with that bloody nose. At least the swelling hides her face. That must be some kind of improvement,' snapped Mulholland.

'OK,' warned Anderson, lifting his head up again, 'thank you Primary Four. What about Marchmont Terrace.'

Again Wyngate's fingers skimmed across the keyboard and Anderson wondered how somebody so unbelievably clumsy could be such a good typist.

'OK, so we have a fire in Marchmont Terrace on Christmas Eve, 1989, a candle, blah, blah, blah, all the usual. The couple, the McEwans, who owned the flat, died in the inferno. One victim, Alice Kilpatrick jumped from the window and died from her wounds later, and the other, Derek Kilpatrick, survived. A fire fighter died, Ally McGuigan.'

'And Mr Kilpatrick suffered terrible burns to his face and hands,' added Costello, returning with a fold of paper towel at her nose. 'He lives in the secure living facility with Pippa Walker. Which looks right down on to the scene. His room looks right over the gardens. In case I have to spell out everything now.'

'When was that fire?' asked Batten.

'1989, are you not listening?'

'Was there a child in the house? That would explain a privacy protection order, if there was a child?'

Wyngate skimmed through. 'They had thought there was, but no – not in the house at the time but they did have a son. And no extended family. It looks like he was then protected by the system, can't blame them for that.'

'OK, OK. So we have "a something" here.'

'The same case or something different? Costello, can you call up the original files?'

The phone went. Mulholland nodded, said thank you and put the phone down. 'Well, the Vinicombe Street fire is now a fatal fire. Kenny Fraser died twenty minutes ago. His lungs burned out . . .'

'Lungs burned out as Blondie cried? I need to think. Wyngate? Costello? Get that board up to date. Find out what happened to that boy, if he is now going out with his girl-friend, killing people and leaving them outside his favourite childhood haunts, then we need to know. I need it all simpli-fied for me when I get back. I am going out for breakfast. I need sugar.'

'Me too.'

Anderson's phone went. He answered it, said yes twice, looked at his watch and said yes again. Then put the phone back down. 'Seems I have been invited to breakfast with ACC Mitchum up at West Central.' He looked shocked.

'Is this about the cold case initiative?' asked Costello. 'With all this going on? That is not good news, Colin, not good at all. Just mind your Ps and Qs. And don't get egg yolk down your shirt.'

'Oh, you are so jealous,' said Anderson, standing up and pulling a tie from his jacket pocket, flicking it around to get the creases out.

The phone went again, Wyngate answered it. 'OK, yes, I will get to it right now. It was on my list of jobs to do.' He glanced at the DCI. 'No, he's not at his screen right now. Yes, I will tell him.' He put the phone down and started typing. 'Sir, you know I phoned down for the CCTV from Vinicombe Street last night. I won't bore you with the details but the FIO has told us to watch from eleven fifteen to eleven twenty. Blondie. Right there.'

Anderson came back from the door as the film was downloaded and prepared to play. They were crowded round Wyngate's screen.

Costello sniffily reminded Anderson that he was going to be late for the big bad boss. Anderson told Costello to stop her sniffing as it was getting on his nerves.

'I'm claiming industrial injury,' she muttered.

The images started moving. The street was dark, busy. They could almost hear the chink chink of glasses and the murmur of quiet conversation from those outside the bars, spilling up on to the outside of the theatre. It was a small building, double fronted windows, old wood behind the glass, and Art Deco sunflower tiles over the door. Anderson couldn't recall seeing that but it looked as though it had been covered in posters for local concerts and bands until very recently. Then the new owner had bought it and was starting renovations, revealing the old building behind the advertising.

'What is that down the side of the lane there?'

Wyngate, who was closest, pointed with the top of his pen.

'I think that is a skip, nothing unusual there. The place was being refurbished.'

Wyngate had stopped the film. 'Here – look.'

And there on the screen as clear as anything was Kenny Fraser standing in the doorway. With him was a woman, turned slightly towards the camera, her head tilted, the collar of her swing coat up to cover her mouth but the angle of her face, the tilt of her head suggested something coquettish, something flirtatious as she led Fraser through the door of the old theatre, picking her way through the tools and the rubble. She paused and pulled the dark glasses down slightly. She looked right at the camera.

Anderson leaned over towards the screen and paused it, freezing the frame.

'Hello, Blondie,' he said.

Sandra pulled off her uniform and pulled on her dressing gown before tucking the towel in round the collar. Then she started separating her hair for the dye. She was going blonder. All part of her plan to get out of this tiny council flat. If she was going to make any inroads to a decent life, she needed to get her plan in operation now. Otherwise nothing would ever change, she would always be wiping bottoms and cleaning toilets, folding up pants and unfolding incontinence pads. Used or otherwise.

She studied her face in the mirror. No idea if she looked like her father. She certainly didn't look like her mother.

It had started with her mother and her first broken hip. Initially she had been glad to move back to the family home after three years of independence – the family home, her mum's home. That had taken a few years, then Jimmy Pinkett from across the landing had suffered a stroke and his son immediately buggered off to Australia. Somehow Sandra had slid into caring for him as well. Then old Ina downstairs broke her hip; at least her son had asked Sandra formally to look after his mother, and paid her, giving her a day off a week on the day when he could make it over from his house in Stirling. And Sandra was good at looking after Ina. When she eventually went into a care home, Sandra promptly inherited Ina's wee sister, who lived round the corner. And when she passed away, Sandra started doing the shopping for her neighbour and so it went on . . . and her life slipped by. But Jimmy Pinkett was always the troublesome one. He gave her a look, a look that got more intense after Ina's sister passed away. As if he knew.

ACC Mitchum was not in a good mood. Anderson had not even sat down when the boss threw the early edition of the *Daily Record* over to him.

Claire's picture was on page four, full colour. Anderson sped-read the feature. His own daughter had played an important role in the abduction of the boy now identified as David Kerr. It made much of the story of her father and the fact that he had inherited the house on the hill. There was also a picture of Irene Kerr looking very attractive and vulnerable next to an old photograph of Anderson looking gaunt and tired. Anderson was described as having a troubled home life.

Anderson closed the newspaper and handed it back, seething quietly.

'As far as I know, there have been no legal issues over you inheriting the house on Kirklee Terrace on the death of Helena McAlpine, so I am now wondering who is stirring this up.' The ACC sat back, speculative, not his normal dominant style, almost chatty. 'And why?'

'Some people have very small lives. And smaller minds.'

'I wondered why that man was also vaguely suggesting that you, DCI Anderson, should be removed from this case. And now we have this in the paper.'

'Who?'

'James Kirkton.'

Anderson snorted.

'You do see that he has a point, you know. Dragging your daughter into all this.'

'She witnessed the abduction, it would be negligent if we didn't speak to her. You can't have it both ways.' Anderson snorted again. 'I can't help thinking what the hell it has to do with him—'

'Everything to do with him and his pursuit of the safer society. Kirkton is trying to ingratiate himself into Police

Scotland. He's already in at the fiscal's office, sitting on every committee. Now he's onto us. Or maybe onto you.'

'In what way?'

'It's about you. He wants you off the case.' ACC Mitchum swung back on his chair. 'And I can't figure out why. I think he's trying to derail your career. Is there something personal going on here that I should know about?'

'Not that I know of.' Anderson laughed slightly. 'No offence, sir, but it's rumoured that the cold case initiative is exactly that. Maybe not my career derailing but certainly putting it in a siding, so if he is so convinced I'm such a threat to his safer society, why not just let it be?'

Mitchum avoided the question. 'Stay on the case, that's an order. I really don't like politicians telling me how to do my job.' He indicated that Anderson should leave. As he was at the door, the boss said, 'And Colin, keep an eye on Claire, will you? That's another order.'

Costello's response to Anderson's relaying of the conversation was to put a picture of Kirkton on the whiteboard. They laughed and Wyngate reached up to take it down again.

'No, leave it there, Wingnut, that man has been all over this from the start, so he's involved somewhere. He's right in somebody's pocket, causing us problems,' Costello said.

Anderson collapsed into his seat. 'Where is David Kerr? What are we not seeing?'

'We are not doing anything wrong, Colin, it's that they are ahead of us and we can't get at them or her. We have no location, nothing. He, she, they have a property to keep them in, a property that has wee green men in the roof. Any ideas?'

'But there *is* something we are missing.'

'Like what?'

'If I knew we wouldn't be bloody missing it!' He ran his fingers through his hair. 'OK, back to basics. Wyngate? Mulholland? Stop stuffing your faces with toast and get Sherlock all over this, try and get something that is not nonsense. Pure fishing, but . . . hey ho . . .' The buzzer interrupted him. It was Graham from reception. 'Here's somebody who might have news for us. Mathilda McQueen, forensic scientist extraordinaire.'

Five minutes later, Mathilda, all four feet ten of her, had centre stage and was in full flow. 'Interesting DNA. The body's DNA is on the jumper, obviously.'

'Obviously.'

'And David's because it was his jumper. Then we tested the DNA on the upper sleeve as we see on the film quite clearly that Blondie grabbed him by the upper arm when he toppled off the chair. Pressure of contact was heavy but was for very swift duration. So it gave us enough recoverable DNA to match way back to a fire on Christmas Eve in 1989. A familial match, but that really means very little. Somebody who was at that house when it went on fire was related to somebody who may have brushed shoulders with David when he was wearing that jumper; it means no more than that. The only survivor of that fire lives in Athole House old folks' . . . sorry, secure living facility.'

'The one-eyed guy that gave me the creeps.'

'You did say that you thought there was more to him than meets the eye. If you pardon the expression,' said Mathilda with a smile. 'Basically it takes us nowhere. But it could prove the link; somebody in the house that went on fire, at some point touched that jumper. But it was a tiny trace.'

'And if you think about the fire up on Vinicombe Street, that connects the Blonde, surely?'

'Very tentatively. Nobody called Pauline Gee, or Pauline anything, fits the script for this.'

'No, but it was the sunflower theatre, so that must be a link surely, somewhere in all this.' She pointed at the board.

They looked at her. 'What do you mean?'

'It has sunflowers over the door.' She pointed to the wall, to the picture of David's phone.

'He must be related to them, the theatre people, in some way, surely?'

'Who? That's David's phone, it was found in the street. There's nothing on it to connect it.'

'Really?' said Mathilda, who looked very clever. 'The chap who found the phone, his name? Do none of you cook?' She looked rather exasperated. 'The Jerusalem artichoke is a bastardization of the words "sunflower artichoke". The Italian for sunflower is *girasole* . . . the *girasole* artichoke becomes the Jerusalem artichoke . . . so the children's theatre was run by the Girasoles. Hence the sunflowers outside.'

'Right round the front door,' said Anderson enlightened.

'In the Art Deco tiles? Yes. And then this young man, Mr Girasole, calls up and gives you the phone . . .?' She opened her hands. 'Don't you get it? He must be one of them.'

The mood in the room lifted.

Anderson got to his feet, then sat back down again. He closed his eyes. 'Wyngate, get that list of cold cases off my desk. Blue folder. Blue folder quickly!'

He flicked over the pages, running his finger down the list. 'There you go, I knew I had seen it somewhere. Wyngate? Girasole. Murdered. Try to find it . . .'

Wyngate hadn't even got as far as typing in the date of birth when the screen came alive. He watched as the computer made connections. Somebody called Pietro Giuseppe Girasole, aged nineteen, had been found dead, lying against a fence at the back of Ashton Lane. The file had remained open but not been active for many years, until selected for cold case status and a DNA review. The death was New Year's Eve 1999.

'*That was the night they were going to boogie,*' muttered Mulholland, then he remembered that Prince was dead as well.

Mulholland read the case summary, the only thing that was available to him. He noted that the original case file had been removed by none other than somebody called DI A. Jeffries. It had been signed in and out a few times over the years.

'So Alistair Jeffries had been on the case. Literally,' said Costello, 'and he knows Kirkton.'

'So we have a Pietro Girasole dead at nineteen, now we have an untraceable Pauline Gee who may or not be Blondie.

Mulholland updated them. 'Our Pauline Gee is not on any electoral register. The social media and the IT guys are now working on the basis that she's fictional and we're tracing URL addresses to find the location of the computer she's using. It's very easy to hide in the virtual world. She's doing all this Facebook crowd funding appeal stuff. And Batten said that Blondie is emotional and the emotion is turning vengeful. Pauline, however, is very, very angry. Some of her ranting on Facebook is bloody impressive.'

One was the act of a desperately sad woman but sane. The other? Batten had used a lot of big words.

'We do have a Mr Paolo Girasole who seems to be very honest. How was he when you interviewed him?' asked Anderson.

'OK. Just a normal guy. He did react a little when we showed him Blondie's picture.'

'So we bring him in again?' Costello got to her feet.

'No, let's talk to him but play nice. David's life could depend on us getting this right.'

Kirkton was on TV, annoying Costello with his big shiny face and long, drawn-out vowels, flicking that irritating fringe. To her there was a direct line of stinking contamination. Kirkton to Jeffries, who had removed the file about the death of a handsome young man called Pietro Girasole on the dawn of the new millennium. And, as soon as Anderson had started digging around, Kirkton appeared to muddy the waters. All that crap in the newspaper. He was such a media whore . . . but why was he interfering with this investigation? There was something about that case that Kirkton and Jeffries did not want them to find out. That would explain why he was discrediting this enquiry and blocking Anderson looking into the cold case. If the two cases were connected to each other and in some way to Kirkton himself . . . So she was going to do some digging herself. Somewhere at the bottom of all this mess was David Kerr, and the death of an innocent man not called Mr Hollister. She thought about Amy and Anderson, Jeffries and David Kerr. And Kirkton. There was a sequence there.

On the TV, MSP Kirkton stood with his wife and family. Tania, the daughter, was standing to one side. Their son, Giles, to the other. They looked like every family of any disgraced politician: here is my wife and the two products of my loins, he seemed to say as he beamed for the gathered press. He spoke about the importance of the family unit, and the tragedy of the missing young man David Kerr. Costello starting mimicking him at this point: *A nice respectable boy who lived with his mother and had two working parents, and was white*

and Protestant, for all these reasons I back the police all the
way to the hilt in their effort to secure a happy ending to the
boy's disappearance. Then she listened to Kirkton speak: . . .
which had been ruled to be an abduction and now they were
all united in working towards a happy result for the family. It
was to his sorrow that one of the senior investigation officers
in the case had taken the decision to involve his own child.
At that point Costello thought she could detect a smirk from
the lovely Tania. James Kirkton hoped that this would not
have tragic consequences as he, as a father, knew that he could
not have kept his mind on such a stressful job if his own
beautiful daughter, who was in fact a good friend of Claire
Anderson, was involved in this terrible crime. He wished DCI
Anderson and his team God speed in bringing the case to a
swift and happy resolution. He would ensure they had any
extra funding required.

Costello pressed the remote and silenced him mid-speech,
hearing the door open behind her.

'From what budget? And where in this mess do we find
David? Is Kirkton scared that we uncover what a horrible wee
bitch his daughter is? Or do we think that he was caught in
suspenders up a dark alley with a beer bottle up his arse when
he was a student and thinks we will find evidence of it back
in 1999? And do what? Sell it to the papers?' Costello threw
the remote onto the desk in front of her in disgust.

'That's what he would do. But it's a fact that he has not
been off our backs while this case has been on.' Anderson
started sifting through a sheaf of paper.

'Because the media is all over the place because of the
festival, so he's glad-handing with one hand and slapping us
with the other. He was on one channel yesterday hinting that
if David's parents hadn't been separated then he wouldn't have
been abducted. "The lack of strength in the family unit." Yeah,
that makes perfect sense.'

Anderson looked up, checking that she was being sarcastic.
'That's typical behaviour for any politician, there is nothing
special in that two-faced shite. What is unusual is that he is
not up at West End Central, they are the big boys. Why is he
down here, annoying us?'

'Because of the cold case initiative. I'm telling you.'
'But we haven't upset him in some way have we? Personally?'
'Not yet no. but it's time we did,' said Costello.

O'Hare was re-examining the cold case evidence at Anderson's request; well, he was trying to but none of it made much sense. It was only 1999, not that long ago. Everybody had the flu and the world was going to crash and burn with the millennium bug.

In the end he had given up trying to find the police copy of the PM report which had been signed out and in by DI Jeffries and had then disappeared. O'Hare called in a favour from the mortuary's own records. The suspicious death of Pietro Giuseppe Girasole was scanned and emailed over to him. He downloaded it, then deleted the email immediately. He would rather work here on his own desk at home than at the big hospital, and away from the big queue to get out the car park at this time of day. He had bits of the file all over his desk and a very large, black coffee; he was on call. Turning over page after page of the printout, he jotted down the odd note here and there. The Girasole murder's chief investigating officer was Alistair Jeffries and O'Hare knew he wasn't going anywhere soon.

It had been in 1999, the millennium street party in Ashton Lane, the body found in Lillybank. O'Hare had worked that Christmas shift and his colleague had worked New Year. He had been English, only stayed with the department for a couple of years before changing his mind about his career and gone to train with Médecins Sans Frontières. God, was it ten years since he had died, caught up in some epidemic in Africa somewhere. O'Hare closed his eyes and rubbed at his forehead. Was his memory really getting that bad? A young man he had worked alongside day by day for a couple of years. A young man who had sat opposite him, drank whisky with him, attended scenes with him, discussed difficult cases long into the night with him, and he couldn't even remember when he had died. Not long ago. God he was getting old.

He remembered where Pietro Girasole died though, right at the end of one of the walkways that ran from Lillybank Gardens and down on to Ashton Lane. At that time of year it had been full of revellers, people everywhere were good natured and celebrating.

And everybody was busy having a good time.

Nobody had seen Pietro or where he had come from, but his body had been found lying against the wall the next morning, dead. It appeared death was caused by a single punch. One punch that had sent him backwards into a doorway. It might have been an accident, young guys larking around. His parents identified his body the next day. O'Hare could remember another boy, probably a younger brother, holding on to his mother, though who was giving who support was difficult to say. He wondered if it was now considered racist to say it had been very Italian; a lot of wailing, and weeping.

The case had been left open but remained inactive, closed to all real purpose six months after the incident, the summer of that year. And that was it. O'Hare flicked back and forth, it was a shamefully slim file. The document index was all over the place. Somebody had been in, taken something out to read and lost it. It did happen, especially with unsolved investigations. Every so often a cold case review has another wee poke, and the sign-in, sign-out system worked, most of the time.

O'Hare read the post-mortem findings, noting those that didn't quite fit then but they might fit now.

He would ask Archie Walker for a full forensic review. They would have to put in the request for the documentation, the clothing, the forensic samples and the pathology to make it official and to keep it nice and tidy. O'Hare was looking for a connection, any connection between the events of 1999 and those of 2016.

But he never lost sight of the fact that a nineteen-year-old lad had died. He was a nice lad, much loved by his parents and his brother. He flicked round the page, the 1999 death. He remembered Pietro had been a joiner, but there was nothing written for occupation, so why did they think that? He reread the PM. Rough hands? Splinters? The victim had worked with raw wood, a little intuitive insertion by his colleague? O'Hare could not recall. Whatever he was, he had deserved a lot better than he got. O'Hare carried on clicking through the pictures thinking about the DNA and how far that had come in the seventeen years since the Girasole boy died. Anderson had said something in a report on Mr Hollister. The phone that had been lost by David Kerr had been handed in by . . . He flicked through the paperwork. Paolo Girasole? Was that the name of the Girasole boy's wee brother?

Maybe not as strange as it appeared, the man who found the phone might walk past that spot on Athole Square seven or eight times a day. The deposition site of the Athole Lane victim – Mr Hollister – right behind where the Marchmont fire had occurred, was the coincidence. It was starting to all look rather tasty. Two was a coincidence, three was a pattern.

As his mother used to say on Grand National Day, 'It was worth a punt.'

Dennis, his name was Dennis. It was coming back to him know. A case that they did not solve and he could now recall Dennis coming to him to talk about it. They had even gone to the scene together, on the pretence of going out for a bite to eat at The Chip. A young bloke, killed, one fatal punch. O'Hare closed his eyes, recalling slowly. It was common knowledge that the body had had an item of clothing removed. There was very little blood on the clothes that he had been found in. So some outer clothing had been removed, a jacket, a coat, a scarf. It had been a cold night. A clear cold night, somebody most likely removed an item of clothing because there had been DNA trace on it. And there had been no defence wounds on the body, nothing at all.

And that pricked his conscience. The name of the deceased was not a common one. Girasole. Sunflower. That was also the name of the old theatre: The Vinicombe Street Children's Theatre. And that had just burned down. He remembered listening to something on the radio about the protest, crowd funding and other stuff he didn't understand. The Pietro Girasole case had troubled Dennis, the murderer had got away. It had been a rage killing. They had come to the conclusion that Pietro had been frequenting the gay clubs around that part of town. He had gone up a back alley with somebody for whatever reason and ended up dead. Some inciting event had happened in that lane. Had he run into a gang of some sort in the wrong place at the wrong time? It must have been quick, for there to have been no time for him to defend himself. There was something else. The boy's face had been very clean; it had been cleansed. Dennis had commented on it. Somebody had removed some identifying mark or substance from his face. And had taken his shoes. That was bad enough, worse was the fact that they did that without going for help.

He was about to close the computer down, when he saw the name – that was the connection his brain had made, the name of the woman who had identified Pietro Girasole was Ilaria Girasole.

He needed a map. He needed to join dots. He was on call tonight so he did not bother going to bed, he walked into the kitchen and made himself another black coffee instead and thought who he could get to stick a fox in the chicken coup. He thought about who he could phone.

Costello had got the nod that James Kirkton would be visiting the station again. He would be asking for Mitchum or Anderson but Costello's nose was still sore so she was just in the mood for him.

She watched him from the open window in Anderson's office as he stood on the steps, still expounding the virtues of the family unit and not quite blaming mothers for failing to look after their own kids. He was getting a lot of media interest. What he was saying struck a chord with the populous, and that made him dangerous in Costello's eyes. She opened the window further and stayed close to the wall to listen. She overheard a veiled criticism of Irene Kerr, to all intents and purposes a single mother who had no idea where her son was. It might have been couched in terms of concern and 'my thoughts are with her at this difficult time', but the slur was still there. The actual facts of the case were missing. Irene Kerr generally knew exactly where her son was and it was his sudden disappearance from her radar that sparked the investigation so quickly. Boys like that did not change their plans for nothing. David had had his plans changed for him.

When Graham buzzed up that Kirkton had arrived in reception and wished to speak to Mitchum or Anderson, both were diplomatically unavailable. So he asked for Costello.

She bounced out of the locked door like a sycophant. Or a serial killer. He was nearly walking out himself before he actually noticed her. 'Costello. DI Costello. How are you?'

His voice was as smooth as ever, but she detected a little fear somewhere.

'Fine. How are you?' She looked around. 'Why don't you come upstairs and lend us your expertise. We have a clear desk policy, so you won't see anything that might . . . upset you.'

He said, with mild irritation, 'I thought I was going to talk to a senior officer.'

'Oh, Colin's around, you know Colin, don't you? And his daughter? Who is friends with *your* daughter? No wait, I got that wrong. Not exactly friends.' She let that lie. 'However, I am here to be your serf with regard to your capacity as czar. Policing czar. That's such an odd title they have given you, considering what happened to the czar.'

'I am here to help sort out the mess that is Police Scotland and this case.'

'Like Thatcher offering to help in the search for the Yorkshire Ripper?'

He pulled the A4 sheet of paper she was reading away from her. He had fat stubby hands, his wedding ring cut tight into the skin round the base of his finger. 'You can stop reading that. I want to talk to you.'

'To me?' She started up the stairs.

'I am talking to all of you, looking at ways to make the place more efficient.'

'Difficult to measure how efficient a police service can be but the best way I find is to leave us alone and let us get on with the job. We are a major investigation team, we have a murder and we are investigating. We don't help little old ladies across the road. We go where the evidence leads, in this case back to 1999.'

He winced.

'But we could herd all the murderers together so that we can catch them all at once? Would that help?'

Kirkton smiled, it was that easy smile of a politician. It didn't really go anywhere. Or mean anything.

She held the door open for him. Costello smiled back, knowing that easily doubled as a threat.

'How do you find working here?'

'Fine. How do you find working in your office? Here the coffee drinkers steal the tea drinkers' HobNobs.'

'Offices are the same the world over, I am sure.'

'Course they are.'

'You have a very productive unit here.'

'I don't, I am part of the team, of this unit.'

'And what do you put the success of this team down to?'

'The lack of interference from above.'

'Above?'

'The police are very hierarchical. ACC Mitchum keeps out of our way but is always there to support us. We try to keep within our budget, but that is because we have a very small geographical area to look after and only specific crime to look into, the other units give us the support that we need. It works well for us, but not something that would be practical to roll across the force.'

Kirkton nodded. 'I think there might be more to it than that.'

'In what way?'

'Well, your own dedication to the force.'

'Maybe that's because we are not just numbers to each other, we work well together.'

'You and Archibald Walker the fiscal work well together?'

'I think it is fair to say that he goes out of his way to help us in our investigations but, as I said, we are a major investigation team. Any MIT will have a fiscal on hand.'

Kirkton looked deep into her grey eyes, regretted it and looked away. 'And do you think his home life is impacting on his working life?'

'I do not really know. I think you would have to ask him that, but I do know that his wife has suffered from early onset Alzheimer's, so if there had been any impingement to his working life then I think it would have been before he placed her in a secure living facility, but you would know that. Seeing as you own it. Do you use a lot of drugs up there?' The question came at him, bullet fast.

'I suppose they do.'

'A drug called Paracurarium?'

He frowned in genuine confusion. 'I wouldn't know.' Then he changed the subject. 'You and DCI Anderson work particularly well together. Do you think that works well, a well-defined pairing like that?'

'I think having longevity in a team like that helps, but I am a typical DI and he is a typical DCI, we complement each other. I wouldn't want his paperwork and he likes being tied to the office,' she lied. 'In our past two major investigations, he has caught two killers who had evaded justice. So that might be an area for you to look at – maybe here prevention is better than cure. You know, catch them before they go on to kill a second time. I know it's not sexy and it doesn't grab headlines. You can't prove a negative. But it is something to think about,' she said, and flicked a sarcastic smile. 'Do you want to see the board? I know we can trust you. This is David. His mother . . .' She spread her hand, watching for a flicker on his face – and there was something there; a wee bit of something.

He changed the subject. 'How is Anderson coping?'

Her grey eyes turned cold beyond a January grave. 'Fine.'

'Must be difficult, living in the house of an ex-colleague. A dead colleague who gave his life in the service of his duty, well that is one version of what happened. One version.' Kirkton allowed himself a sly smile. 'Anderson's career is not going unnoticed. His relationships are not going unnoticed. He brought his daughter into danger in the case up at Inchgarten.' He put his hand up to stop Costello correcting him. 'And he seems to be getting his daughter involved in this case.'

Costello snorted dismissively. 'Hardly, she was right there when David Kerr keeled over. It would have been dereliction of duty not to interview her. He was there as her guardian, a responsible adult. It was me who did the interview.' She smiled at him. 'And you can't prove otherwise.'

'I don't need to.'

'And the fiscal was there. Not accusing him of any wrong-doing, are you?' She continued before he could answer, 'And logically, being an artist, she had a very good likeness in her head of what this abductor looked like.'

Kirkton seemed to wince again at that. 'I have a daughter same age as Claire and I don't think I would like her to be involved in any way at all.'

'Well, I think Claire sees it as a young man a couple of years older than her getting abducted and she was the main witness. I think she considers it her civic duty to help. But I think you are right, she probably does have a good sense of civic duty. Gets it from her dad. What does Tania get from you?'

'And what do you get from your father, DI Costello?'

He regretted saying it. As soon as the words left his lips he wished he hadn't spoken.

Costello leaned forward and looked at him, closely. And, as many people do, he pulled away slightly. The grey eyes, a light, light grey gave Costello an alien like appearance when viewed very close up, cold, clinical, inhuman. Qualities her voice had also. 'I know you have looked into my past, my family, Mr Kirkton.' She overemphasized his surname. 'You know exactly what my brother was. You really might not want to know how I think. I am very good at thinking like a killer. And I am going to find David Kerr alive. No matter what it takes. No matter who gets in my way.'

Kirkton smiled slightly, and sighed.

She felt she had made some mistake, her brain moved on to her next conclusion. 'Then we are going to move to Cold Case and review every one of those cases on the initiative. Every single one.'

That hit home. He stared right back at her, trying to keep his eyes steady. 'Well, good luck with that then.'

He left, leaving the door of the investigation room swinging back and forth.

The doorbell went, the deep tone rang long and clear down the hall of the house on the terrace. Nesbit pricked his ears up, sensed a friend and trotted down the hall towards the stained glass front door. Anderson opened it, surprised to find O'Hare standing there.

'Hi, come in.'

'I come bearing gifts,' said O'Hare, waggling a good bottle of Scotch in his hand.

'Not for me, thanks, but you are welcome.'

They walked through into the small sitting room, the log fire was on, although the night was warm. It was obvious that Anderson had been sitting by the fire, reading.

'Good God, man, you will be in your slippers before me. What are you reading?'

'I am trying to read *On Liberty*. Every time I think I understand it, I am interrupted by work.'

'Sorry,' said O'Hare, devoid of apology. 'I read that book once, in a previous life.' O'Hare settled himself into his seat. Took the glass that Anderson proffered and helped himself to a tot out of the Glenfiddich.

'This has always been a lovely house.'

'It has.'

'It feels comfortable now, so tranquil.' The air in the house was cool and still.

'Well, because of it, Kirkton is gunning for you, living here. He thinks that it is immoral. He's a tosser.'

'And he's putting Claire in the news which is something she could do without.' Anderson sat down, adjusted the air flow through the flames and leaned back. 'So is this a social call. Or are you going to tell me about the sad demise of Pietro Girasole?'

'Well no, you are getting that in an official email tomorrow. I want to talk to you off the record, run something past you, something so bizarre – so far off the scale . . .'

'OK, go on, I am listening.'

'I was looking at the joints on Mr Hollister, the way the body was bent over and dislocated, folded up into a lined box, like he was a human doll.'

'Well he was. But Amy was abducted by aliens, whereas Alistair and David both seem to have been involved with a blonde with good dress sense.'

'If you are thinking about aliens then it's just as well you

keep off the drink. But there are broken joints, butchery. I've
had a good chat to the orthopaedic chap who looked at Amy's
knee. Somebody tried to bend it backwards. I think somebody
was disarticulating these bodies. There were no cuts on the
skin of Mr Hollister, Alistair or Amy. I agree with you about
an injection being given, to make the body compliant in some
way. Some form of extreme muscle relaxant. Like you get before
you are operated on, if you have no general. So Blondie knows
medicine, she can get her hand on drugs. And here somebody,
some person, was breaking the joints to get more movement
than the natural anatomy of the joint would allow.'

'So they could be folded up and put in the box, as you said.'

'But maybe not. Maybe he was put in the box because he
had died while having his joints dislocated. He had bled. But
had he fulfilled his purpose? Why are they drugged?'

'Because the perp is a woman?'

'She got a wheelchair for David, didn't she? And Amy's
thyroid issues meant she metabolized the drug differently.
Blondie tries with Jeffries but he is so drunk that the injection
makes him incapable of movement, he falls and cracks his
skull.'

'He was so pissed he thought the injection was a jab from
a bramble.' Anderson was thinking hard. 'And Mr Hollister?'

'It all went to plan until he choked on his own vomit. Which
suggests that Blondie is not that skilled at medicine. You don't
paralyse muscle then let the airway get blocked. When he
died, she had to find somebody else. She's working to a time-
table. The clock is ticking for her, and Colin, we need to find
David. I am very fearful for what he might be going through.'

'So who is Blondie?'

'Somebody with pharmaceutical knowledge rather than
medical? A chemist or a pharmacist but not a doctor, not a
nurse. But think of the physicality of the injuries? She is
breaking these people; breaking them and making them pliable
and bendy. I was looking at the death of Pietro in Ashton Lane
in 1999. He was a woodworker, odd in one so young, long
term use of wood on his hands, hard hands like a carpenter
who had been doing the job for thirty years. So the Girasole
boy who died, the theatre that burned down. Wooden puppets?

Was the Girasole boy a puppet maker? All it says is he worked in the family business. I have no idea what she is up to, but,' he grimaced as if he could not believe what he was about to say, 'is she making human dolls? Human puppets?'

Anderson patted Nesbit on the head, looking into the deep brown eyes for a long, long time. 'Can I have a drink of that whisky now? I think I need it.'

FIVE

Thursday 9 June

Sandra was ready to leave. It had been a busy morning and her feet were aching. The home was full of warm, heavy air that induced lethargy. But she couldn't find her car keys. They were not on the hook where they were supposed to be left when someone borrowed them to move the vehicle, and that suited her usually. Then she was told by Lisa that 'her boyfriend' was upstairs. So she smoothed out her hair and checked her breath. She went up to Tosca, as if she was going to say goodbye to the Duchess.

He didn't seem annoyed by her interruption, if anything he was rather pleased.

'So sorry, I was going to say goodbye.'

'You would have a hard job leaving,' laughed Paolo. 'You left your car keys on the dressing table over there.'

That was a big mistake. *She* had left them here. 'Oh thank you. I think I am losing the plot at the moment.' But she didn't leave, the Duchess seemed happy to see her although she felt that she had walked in on something. Their politeness was covering up their uneasiness at nearly being caught. But that might be her own interpretation.

'Nice hair, I meant to say yesterday. It suits you. Being blonde,' he said, looking at her, as if he knew. 'Suits your brown eyes.'

Sandra felt her stomach jump, she was nineteen again. 'How is she doing?'

He didn't let Sandra wait for an answer, guiding her to the corner of the room.

'Can I ask you a delicate question?'

'Oh.' Sandra bit her lip and opened her big brown eyes wide.

'Have you been going through the Duchess's clothes?' He didn't seem angry.

'I was looking at them, yes,' she answered honestly, 'it's that they are so beautiful, so well crafted. How do they get like that, I mean, where do you buy them?'

'Not all of them are bought. In the old days she used to get all her clothes made for her. The blue dress, the one she likes to wear, the Sunday dress? I have taken that dress apart and made a pattern from it so I can make more in the same style as she loses weight, as she gets a little . . .' He was about to say stooped.

'Frail?' suggested Sandra.

'Yes. She would not be happy unless she looked her best. What do you wear when you go out on the town? Out with your friends?'

She let the question pass, having no answer. 'How did you learn to do all that make-up stuff, sewing? You really are very good at it.'

He smiled at her, his Paul Newman eyes creased up. 'Growing up in the theatre, I had very good training. The best. I can make anybody look like anybody else. It's more about having the knack of seeing what you see, seeing what the person has that you can make stand out. When you are on stage, people don't see a face. They see an expression, a re-action, and that is what registers with them. It's all about using the face to communicate.'

'Oh,' she said. Noticing that he was closing the make-up bag, ready to go and she did not want him to go. She was hit by a sudden impulse to keep him there. She walked towards the door and stood there in what she hoped was a laid-back fashion, as if it was the kind of thing she did all the time; hang about and lean against walls. 'Is it what you do now?'

'No, now I have the most boring job the world has ever seen. I work at the council and I sit all day and bang numbers into a computer for so long that it makes my brain ache, but you, you have a great job surrounded by this life and this wealth of experience.'

She stared at him not really believing him. He was a doctor, a lawyer, not somebody who worked in the council. Was he having her on?

He seemed to read her mind.

'A job is a job. The money I get does not reflect what use I am to society. Look at what you do, you're really valued by people, Sandra. You are so valued. What could be better than that?' He placed a hand on her shoulder.

Surrounded by bed pans and incontinence pads, thought Sandra. Paolo had a point. And some folk who worked in the council get paid mega bucks. 'Not all our guests are as lovely as your mother,' she said.

'The Duchess,' corrected Paolo, something that he did automatically. 'Please, come and sit.'

She sat on the stool in front of the mirror, trying not to pull a face different to her own. He pulled her hair back and adjusted the neck of her jumper slightly, making a collar round her throat so he could see the outline of her face, her jawline and the curve of her cheekbones.

He then took out a lipstick. 'I bought this for you. It will match your complexion, and your new blonde hair. You don't make the best of yourself, Sandra. You don't realize that you have cheekbones that could knock people out.'

'Would you do my face, you know, if I paid you? Like you do with your . . . with the Duchess?'

He looked at her, his head to one side, then looked at his watch. 'Let me think about that.'

He was embarrassed. He did not want to say no and now he was desperate to get away from her. He looked over at the door.

'I'm sorry, I didn't think. I shouldn't have asked. It's not something I've had the chance of before.' At least that was true.

'No, no, it's fine.' He was apologetic. 'I was just thinking that my flexi will nearly be up. I need to get back to work.'

'Oh,' she said, 'I had better not keep you.'

The moment was gone, he picked up his jacket and slid one arm in, then the other. He lifted the satchel he always wore over his shoulder and the laundry canvas bag, then he walked to the door. Sandra's heart was breaking as she opened the door for him, wondering if he thought she was acting strangely; out of the ordinary now that she knew he was ordinary. He paused as he was about to go through the door, and put the canvas bag down. He stood in front of her and pulled her collar back, both hands, firm but gentle against the side of her head, fingering the strands of hair from her face.

'Sandra?'

He had never said her name before. Not like that.

'Yes?'

'Why don't we meet later tonight?'

'OK,' she whispered.

'Then I shall come back tonight.'

She thought about the princess in the book, her arched eyebrows and porcelain skin. Rapunzel. 'And you can make me beautiful?'

He placed his lips lightly on her forehead. 'It's not such a hard task, Sandra.'

Anderson was trying to have a fruitful morning in his office. He knew they were getting close.

Wyngate had looked into the past of the Girasole family; not so extraordinary, theatre people. The Girasoles of the Vinicombe Street Children's Theatre. He thought back to the windows he had seen, colourful and magical scenes of goblins and elves, draped in dark red curtains. There was skill, a theatrical skill of showmanship. And of misdirection.

They were a normal family who had lost a son and the aging mother was now in a care home, an expensive care home that showed how just how financially successful the family business had been.

He had spent some of the previous night with Alistair Jeffries. It had not been pleasant. No police officer enjoyed questioning another police officer, but Jeffries had been the victim of an attempted abduction. And there was the small matter of some missing files from the 1999 fire. Not an unusual occurrence, but too much of a coincidence.

Was there a link?

Jeffries had thought about answering, then told Anderson to go ahead and review everything in the cold case file. It had all been fully investigated in early 2000. Pietro Girasole had been found dead, and nobody had any idea how he got up Lillybank Lane.

So Anderson left him with the picture of Pietro, dead on a slab. His aquiline profile was one Jeffries should have been very familiar with.

As good as his word, back at the station, they were reviewing the 1999 tape. Jeffries was right. There was no sign of Pietro coming out of any of the nightclubs or pubs along that way. Nothing. He had just turned up dead in the lane. It had been a clear night with a full bright moon, easy to see, except that a young man in blue jeans and a white, short-sleeved T-shirt was hardly unique. Too hardy in his youth to feel the cold. Or too drunk. Or had some of his clothes been taken?

The only areas being monitored were the university and Byres Road in those days and there were experimental cameras around the Ashton Lane area, luckily for them. At that time there was a parliamentary report about the efficiency of CCTV in deterring or solving crime, so much of the tape from that time was kept. Almost every movement of the millennium celebration in the area around Byres Road was caught on film and stored safely, hour upon hour of it.

At the time the film had been watched frame by frame, looking for Pietro Girasole to appear somewhere and meet his murderer. And he had not. All the same, Anderson was not downhearted. Obviously something had been missed. It was an overnight case at New Year. The major investigation team from 2000 were not incompetents from the dark ages; they had been a good, reliable squad; cops he had known personally. The advantage that Anderson's team had was that he knew about Blondie. They knew who they were looking for. He also told the ten-man team who were viewing the footage that they were looking for a woman acting strangely. A blonde in a nice frock with a neat bob. And a young man in blue jeans. 'Keep an eye out for her, that's all.' The images they had of her were all up on the wall.

'How do you know she has a neat bob?' asked one, a neat-boned Asian woman.

'I doubt she has changed her style in the last twenty years. Or she has returned to it now. She's revisiting it all; lock, stock and barrel. Haircut included.'

They were working away. Anderson was flicking over the written reports as they emptied the boxes, everything sealed in plastic bags, everything tagged and labelled, the complexity of the evidential chain shown by thirty or more signatures.

'There is one thing that makes me think that we are barking up the wrong tree. They never found Pietro Girasole on the tapes did they? He was found dead the next morning, which technically was the next year, but nobody saw him and his murderer together. So why are we looking for her?' Wyngate contemplated. 'We can't even find him.'

'Let's ask her when we find her. And if we see her on the tape, we might see him. She's easier to spot. Nobody saw Amy with anybody, nobody saw Alistair Jeffries with anybody,' Anderson pointed out.

Wyngate asked, 'So are we looking for a woman? Or a man?'

'One or the other, Gordon.'

'Just that Batten said arsonists were male. But we are looking for Blondie, yes . . .?'

'And her male accomplice, Wyngate.'

Anderson was watching the film thinking about something else Batten had once said about the difference between actors and impersonators. The impersonator takes the actions of another upon themselves, and they merge. But the original is still there, perfectly visible. A good actor becomes that other person.

Anderson went into the sanctity of his own office to read the contents of O'Hare's email. The old pathologist seemed obsessed with Pietro's fingers. They were the anomaly. What did he actually do for a living? The analysis of the skin swabs had revealed lotion on his skin and something that resembled make-up remover. O'Hare had highlighted this to see later.

Anderson looked at the pictures of the face on the CD, easing his fingers apart on the screen to magnify the image, then looked deeply at the eyelashes, the base of the eyelashes, then at the mouth, around the mouth, the outline of the lips, nothing there. The body was smooth of hair. He had a thin, lithe build and it was not unusual for men who go to the gym to get a chest wax, a buttock wax. What was it they called it? A back, crack and sack? Anderson juddered at the thought and moved on. Pietro had smooth legs. Smooth feet. He had been epilated. The pathologist at the time had placed a question mark there. Because he was gay?

He went back to the photograph of the body lying before the post-mortem had started, lying as if he was sleeping. Peaceful, extremely . . . pretty was the word that came to Anderson's mind. Pietro had looked like some actor, a young Jude Law maybe.

Pietro had been five feet seven, had weighed nine and a half stone, with slim, well-defined muscle, when he died. Anderson stared at that picture for a long time, looking at the eyelashes. Some men were blessed with very long eyelashes, his wife had remarked on that often. But his beard line was non-existent. Were there metrosexual men in the last millennium?

So what was Pietro Girasole doing? Out enjoying the New Year celebrations. Then what? He looked back at the bare feet. He needed to get those clothes up from the productions archived store as soon as possible.

He went back to the body of the email.

It was postulated that the body was undressed after he was murdered and then redressed in clothes that were not his – the white T-shirt, the jeans. That had echoes of Mr Hollister. Right down to the lack of shoes. And if they could . . .

The door burst open, it was Mulholland looking uncharacteristically excited. 'Sir, you need to see this—' he pointed at his own monitor – 'on the CCTV coming out of the Auditorium, which was a nightclub up near where Oran Mor is now. The film is black and white and as gritty as anything . . . But there she is. Blondie. And she's heading down towards Ashton Lane.'

Anderson sat down on his sergeant's vacated seat. 'With this guy. Who's he? Too tall to be Pietro. Much bigger build.'

'And once we move on down the road, she gets very pally with him.'

'Let's isolate that bit of film.'

'He looks sober, he has his arm round her shoulder at this point. But then she kind of shrugs it off, and here he adjusts his hair, preening, all to look good for Blondie . . .' said Mulholland.

'OK, he's interesting but she is the one of interest. Follow her all the way, sooner or later, she will walk into Pietro Girasole. Sooner or later . . .'

'She's a rather grand lady, do you get a lot of them in here? You know, actresses all swanning around being lovely, the old guy in the front room? What happened to him exactly? And don't even try to pull the confidentiality trick this time.' Costello smiled, sweetly.

'Oh, I don't know if I can tell you that,' said Matron Nicholson, looking very starchy and efficient in an office that was pleasingly chaotic.

'I am a police officer,' said Costello, which had no relevance whatsoever in the case of Deke Kilpatrick but it often did the trick, that and the fact she could see the matron of the home was desperate to talk about something.

'He was burned in a fire. Just over there.'

'Marchmont Terrace? 1989?'

She looked surprised. 'Goodness, that long ago? Yes, I think so.'

'And the Duchess, does she ever speak? Could she be interviewed?'

The matron looked a little confused at the sudden change of subject. 'Doubt it, she just speaks the odd word here and there. In Italian.'

'Do the Duchess and Mr Kilpatrick ever communicate?'

'No. They really don't like each other, they are like kids.'

'Yes, I noticed. The way they glare at each other. Do you think they knew each other from before?'

'They might have done. They were both from round this

area. The Girasoles were theatre people and he was a singer, no a saxophone player, I think. His wife was an actress. Or a dancer. She died in the fire, so sad.'

Costello held her stare for a long time.

'So what's her name? The Italian with the opera diva hair?'

'Everybody just calls her the Duchess, it's one of the few names that she actually responds to.'

'Her real name?'

'Ilaria. Ilaria Concetta Girasole.'

'Her son died.'

'When? That's terrible.' The matron looked shocked, her breath went as though she had been punched in the stomach. She sat back on the edge of her crowded desk. 'That's terrible. He was here only . . . well, an hour ago . . .'

'No, I mean her other son.'

'She only has one son.'

'I mean Pietro. He was killed in 1999.'

The matron looked a little puzzled, 'Oh, thank God. I thought you meant Paolo. I thought he was an only child and he was here this morning, alive as anything. Nice boy, very nice boy.'

'Paolo? I think he's a cousin.' Costello sat on the edge of the single armchair in the office, inviting more chit chat. 'He helped her identify Pietro's body. I think over the years, they have grown close.'

The matron smiled, then her eyes flitted round the room, as if she had just remembered something very unpleasant. She stood up and straightened her uniform. 'God, that's sad, maybe it does explain why they are so close. But not in a mother to son way. But he does everything for her; he pays all her bills.'

'And Deke Kilpatrick? No family for him?'

'No, not him. No visitors. He has very little memory nowadays.'

'Can I have a word with him?'

'If you think it'll do any good, of course. He's in his room. Come on, I will take you there.'

Costello followed her, with her neat little nurse's walk, along the lower-floor corridor to a small single room.

Deke was lying on the bed, a thin blanket over him. He tried to move slightly as the two women came in, trying to wriggle away from them. The dark eye looked ahead, then followed after the matron when she left, leaving the door open. He was suspecting an attack was coming from somewhere but had no idea where from.

'Hi. I think you know that I am a police officer.' She placed her warrant card right in front of his good eye. 'I want to talk to you.' She picked up a few records and flicked through them. 'Dexter Gordon? You rate him? I'm more of a Julie London fan. Lena Horn, Stormy Weather and all that.' She pulled out her mobile, turned on the media player and flicked down. 'You recognize this?' She pressed play. '"The Blue Bossa", you like it?'

The dark eye stared straight ahead, but he didn't slide away. If anything he leaned in a little closer, listening to the slightly tinny noise coming from the phone speaker. She sat beside him, nodding her head along, not really wanting to say that this wasn't really her thing. Derek 'Deke' Kilpatrick was a real jazz musico and to do anything but listen in silence to a jazz blues classic would be sacrilege. The track finished, she turned it off. The head stayed inclined, but turned away slightly. She leaned forward to see into his face better. The face turned away ever so slightly, but not before she had seen the tear.

'I want to talk to you,' she said, 'and I think you want to talk to me.'

The eye opened, looked straight at her.

'When I first saw you I thought you had committed a crime. But I was wrong; you have been the victim of a crime. And now, there's nobody looking out for you. You are on your own. I've looked into your background.' She pulled out a small buff envelope. 'I found some of these, maybe if you looked through them? Some are from the internet, just pictures I pulled out. Some of the jazz clubs around Glasgow. My friend was a fan of yours, imagine. And here is one of you and Alice.' She placed that into his hand; he tried to turn it over. 'She died after the Marchmont Terrace fire, didn't she?'

She could swear that he nodded. She took a tissue from her pocket and dabbed at his eye. The black eye had a jagged line across it. The other eye was a bright blue, solid yet marled. Another scar from the Marchmont Terrace fire.

But his body language had changed. The hand moved forward and reached out to her. Just one simple movement.

'When you saw me, you knew I was a cop, didn't you?' Her eyes held his steady, watching for a response. 'Why was that? Do you have something you want to tell me?' The hand tightened on hers a little. 'You want to tell me something? About your wife? About the fire? About the McEwans? Did they start the fire? Did they do something deliberate? Did the boy?'

That got a response.

'Do you know where the boy is?'

She thought she saw a smile play round his lips. A faint movement of the finger, trying to point.

'Has he been here?'

Another slant of a smile.

'Ah,' was all Costello could say. And played "The Blue Bossa" again. She thought she might get to like it.

Paolo sat down, the fiscal and Costello sat opposite him in the small visitors' area on the first floor. He had left the Duchess in her room. They could hear the soft flow of opera coming out from behind it.

Paolo didn't look troubled. Just a little nervous; enough for an honest citizen, not brazen like the guilty.

'Can you confirm your relationship to Ilaria Girasole, please?'

He laughed lightly. 'I wish I could. I have the same surname and as kids Pietro and I naturally gravitated to each other. I was told I came over from Italy young, grew up in care, you can check all that out. I ended up going to the same school as Pietro. The name brought us together and if anybody asks I say I am a cousin, a distant cousin. And I think I have been saying that for so long, I believe it. The Duchess does. I would have said that when I identified Pietro's body. And deep down, I think the Duchess knows who my mother was. I think she might have guessed who my father was. Her husband was a bit of a lad when he was alive. You get the picture?' He made a very Italian gesture with his hands. 'All I know is that the Duchess, and old Guido, bless him, have always looked out for me. Treated me the same as their own child.'

'So where were you on the night of the millennium?'

'In bed with flu. I know that very well. I remember trying to get out of bed when the Duchess got the news. If I had been there, it wouldn't have happened.' He opened his big blue eyes very wide. 'The Duchess isn't one for turning back the clock. My own mother left me, I was brought up in the Nazarene care system. So I was always very glad to go to the Girasoles. The Duchess has never got over the shock of Pietro.' He started to cry.

Costello went to the toilet and brought him back some tissue.

'I'm sorry, the Duchess is very ill. Some things just bring it all back. The incident at the end of the lane, the unknown boy? That really got to me.' He shook his head.

'I'm sorry. We didn't know she was unwell.'

'I forget her age. You believe some people are going to go on for ever.'

'So who is this then?' She held out the picture of Blondie again.

Paolo wasn't fazed. 'Like I said, she looks like somebody Pietro knew. His girlfriend would be putting it a bit too strongly. Oh, I don't know. He never said.' Paolo rubbed his eyes, tired suddenly, the emotion too much for him.

'But you two were close.'

'Time is a river that rolls on, it takes you where it takes you. I was growing into his family. Maybe Pietro was growing away from his, as boys of that age should do. I think he met a girl and didn't tell me or the family. I think that's her but I thought she was older than that. She never came to the funeral. She never came near the family once, not once.'

'What was her name?'

Paolo looked at the picture and shook his head. 'I have no idea.'

'What did the family do, Ilaria's family?'

'The Girasoles ran the Vinicombe Street Children's Theatre. Just like the one in Central Park in New York. I saw it had burned down. I'm trying to stop the Duchess from reading that or hearing about it. I feel like everything I have is being taken away.' He looked at the ceiling. He was a beautiful man, a young God. 'I used to like looking in that window when I was a boy. So maybe I knew it was in my blood. Then Pietro died. His father died. We lost the theatre. And I had to get a job in the council.'

'Do you know about the Facebook campaign for the theatre? It was very active.'

'Oh yes, but it's more about politics than puppets. I don't know Pauline Gee. She doesn't know the Duchess. Or me. So go figure.' He shrugged.

'OK, we will leave it there; I hope the Duchess feels a wee bit better.' Costello stood up.

They left, walking slowly along the carpet before turning to go down the wide sweeping stairway. They passed within inches of Sandra hiding against the corner wall, where she had been for the duration. She counted to a hundred then walked neatly round the corner carrying her bundle of towels and did a good act of stopping dead in surprise when she saw Paolo.

'Has anything happened to the Duchess?'

'No. Sorry. I need to go into work. I don't want to talk about it.' Then he relented. 'Well. Not now. We'll go out for something later.'

She smiled her widest smile, straightened up his collar and sent him on his way saying that she would stay with the Duchess. She walked into the room closing the door behind her. The old woman was sitting in the bay of the window, looking out.

Sandra sat on the bed and looked at herself in the mirror, trying not to get excited. She recognized that nervousness. He wasn't upset, he was nervous they were going to find out a secret. She turned her head so she could see the Duchess, and looked round the room. He was a cousin, the son had been killed. Nobody knew who by. And Paolo claimed to have been in his bed with the flu. And who benefited from all that? One person. Only one person. Paolo. He would have all this. Sandra doubted he worked for the council, he was never there. He had given her a car. He had money. He let the mad old bitch think that he was Pietro. She had called him that at least twice in Sandra's earshot and he had not corrected her. And he had all this. No wonder he was so nice to the old cow. It was guilt.

And maybe that was why Paolo liked her. Did he sense the same thing in her?

'Game on,' she thought, 'Game on.'

Costello walked down the hill past the gardens and into the lane. It was empty, but of course it would be. She had arranged for Rosemary Lucas and Eddy Urquhart to meet her at the site of the fire. Not in the lane behind it. She retreated back out of the lane, the chill in the air eating into her bones. The sky was getting heavier by the hour. She looked up at the oppressive clouds, the same slate grey as the roof of Athole House, almost blending together.

Rosemary Lucas was standing there, looking at her watch. Middle-aged now, a neat haircut with blonde covering the grey, dressed in an old-fashioned, light raincoat that would be rolled back up into her bag if the rain stayed away. It rustled as she walked. She had on Pavers shoes, a slight swelling of the ankle carrying an overhang. She looked like a woman who would still go to church and mean it.

'Rosemary? DI Costello. Thank you for coming along. Sorry if I am going to stir up bad memories.'

Rosemary Lucas nodded, nervously. They shook hands.

'I'll be as brief as possible. I hope the rain stays off. It's going to be a downpour.'

They were silent in tacit acknowledgement that Scottish weather was a law unto itself.

'So, Rosemary, do you recall the night well?'

'Of course I do. I was just over there when I heard the crash. That was the first thing we heard, my husband and I. We were walking home after the midnight mass, it was snowing lightly. All very romantic and Dickensian. There was a smell of smoke in the air but it was very pleasant. Like wood smoke, not like burning plastic.' She spoke well, clearly. Costello let her speak. 'And there was the heat, never felt anything like it.'

Rosemary bit her lower lip, looking round her. 'We ran round the corner. We were in hell. The paint on the front door of the house was melting right in front of my eyes. There was a man behind the glass, trapped. The smoke kept burling round

and round, sometimes I could see him, sometimes not. I tried
to reach him. God knows I tried.'

'Deke Kilpatrick.'

'Yes, then the . . .' She turned at the sound of shuffling
footsteps of an old man walking slowly along Marchmont
Terrace, waving a magazine in front of his face, trying to give
life to the dead air. Rosemary sidestepped to let him pass. But
he stopped and looked at both the women.

'Rosemary Lucas?' he asked, extending an old, liver-spotted
hand.

'Yes?' she replied.

The old firefighter was struggling a little, emotional and
breathless. A hand under his red rheumy eyes wiped away a
light tear. Costello stood back, letting them compose themselves. They were standing on the pavement, shaking hands.
He held on to hers far longer than was polite. Then Rosemary
gave him a hug that was strong and heartfelt.

Costello wondered if firefighters ever met their successes.
Of if they were eternally haunted by their mistakes? This man
had sent another man to his death. Not an easy thing to deal
with. Costello knew that.

She waited until they broke up. 'Thank you both for coming.
I know it can't be easy.'

'It's refreshing to know that you are still trying to get to
the bottom of it.' Urquhart's voice was rough.

'It was an accident, surely,' said Rosemary. 'The boy? That
poor wee boy who was taken away, kept from the public eye,
poor child.'

Eddy Urquhart snuffled in what might have been a snort of
disbelief.

'Did you know him? The family?' Costello directed the
question to Rosemary.

'Yes, I knew him. Paul. Used to wear a sunflower yellow
duffle coat. He walked back and forth to school in it. Nice
wee kid, I used to feel a bit sorry for him. He was a lonely
child. Always on his own. No other family. No friends. Nobody
at all, not afterwards.'

'Happy child?'

'Not a word I'd use.'

'Maybe that was why he did what he did,' said Eddie, looking up at the new build.

'Do you think it was deliberate?' Costello asked.

'Oh he did it. No wonder social services took him away. Hope he never found out what he actually did.' There was bitterness in his voice. 'I sent a man in there to look for the kid. He lost his life. The boy wasn't there. We found Ally's body in the boy's bedroom.' Eddy looked away, slow gentle tears coursed down his lined face. 'I sent him back in. I had been told the boy was in there.'

'You couldn't have known,' Costello said.

'We got the bodies out. Barry McEwan had tried to get out the back door, he was found in the kitchen. The wife was found in the upstairs toilet. Totally untouched by flames, the smoke got her just like Kenny Fraser. It happens all the time. Then Alice Kilpatrick got trapped out on the ledge. She couldn't get back in, so she jumped. We got Deke out from behind the front door alive. We had to stop Rosemary here from rescuing him.' A memory halted him in his tracks.

'And Paul?' Costello nudged him.

'We were led to believe he was still inside. Ally was in there as we heard the roof come down. I tell you, hen, there is no other sound in the world as horrible as that. Terrifying. His fault, you know. That wee lad. He left. And before he left he set fire to the house. Out the front door as smart as you like, started the fire with the candle on the coat stand. His room was downstairs – right at the front door. Oh, I think he did it.' The old man nodded. 'Oh yeah, he did it.'

'You can't mean that.' Rosemary was shocked.

'So why is he being protected now?' The old man turned to look at Costello. 'Find him and ask him.'

Back in the station, Costello leaned back in her seat and looked at the ceiling. 'I am trying to follow your thinking here, Colin. You seem to be spending a huge amount of money for no gain. Pietro Girasole was in a nightclub. He left although nobody saw him. He must have gone out a back door, then went up the back alley with or without a blonde who may or may not be our blonde and then his body was found. And the

Blonde disappeared into fresh air, the same way that this blonde has disappeared into fresh air.'

'I think that's what connects it in my mind, now you see her, now you don't.'

She turned to look at her boss for reassurance. 'Is she some kind of White Widow? Colin, can we do a full media blowout? Just find her. Cut the crap. We ask her if she had anything to do with that murder all those years ago. Or do you think she will hurt David if we do that? And David will slip through our fingers?'

'To tell you the truth, Costello, I have no idea and—' The door bounced open. ACC Mitchum came in, closely followed by James Kirkton. The local member of the Scottish Parliament did not look like himself, the veneer of smugness and the arrogance was gone. Costello and Anderson exchanged glances before Mitchum said, 'You two, Anderson's office. Now!'

The four of them squeezed into the small room, Mitchum taking pride of place behind Colin's desk. He wasted no time in getting to the point.

'Tania Kirkton didn't come home last night. She was out at a garden party over in Kelvinside and her mother got a text from her about half ten to say that she would be staying over.'

Anderson had that dreadful feeling of déjà vu. 'Just a text, your wife didn't speak to her in person?'

Kirkton shook his head but didn't manage to look Anderson in the eye. Mitchum explained that he had already sent out the local police to investigate discreetly and that for now they wanted it all kept under wraps.

'But how can we?' asked Costello, 'with all that going on out there. How long has she been away for? Eighteen hours now and there has been no sign or sight of her?'

'I think we have to prepare for the worst and presume that she has come to the same fate as David Kerr,' said Mitchum brutally.

'So I want every resource you have available on this task-force. I want to know exactly where this investigation is going. I want my daughter back and that is the most important thing.' Kirkton's face looked grey, yet it couldn't be from lack of sleep. They'd had no real idea there was anything wrong until

Tania failed to return that morning. They had believed she had stayed over.

Anderson and Mitchum both knew it would be Costello who said it. 'And I am sure the most important thing for Irene Kerr is getting David back. Your daughter is no more important than anyone else's child and you will get the same resources and endeavour that everybody else gets. After all, we are all committed to the safer society.'

Wyngate was wondering how dark and humid it would get before it finally started to rain. The clouds that rolled in were more black than grey. The city was a very uncomfortable place to be. He hoped it would have its downpour and clear the air.

He was walking up Byres Road after a rather nasty emergency root canal, still in pain but a different pain to the one he had had before; instead of the daggers of agony shooting through his jaw that were so painful it almost made him pass out, there was now a dull throb that was responding to paracetamol. He was going up to Boots to collect a prescription for antibiotics. He walked with his jacket collar pulled up over the side of his face as his tongue probed at the gap, gently feeling its way round where the dentist had performed his surgery. It felt . . . Wyngate stopped.

There she was.

Walking down Byres Road, lilac raincoat swinging open, small heels, blonde hair and dark glasses. A large black handbag swung from the crook of her arm. She was walking quickly like she was in a hurry but was too cool to run. He slipped into the crowd walking behind her. Byres Road was busy. People were sitting out drinking coffee, looking at the sky as if the weather of the next half hour was going to be an event. At the corner of the Hilton she slipped up the small lane that led from the Waitrose car park and beyond through the pike that prevented vehicular traffic through to the service lane beyond. Wyngate thought that if his geography was right, this would take him out at Athole Lane, where Mr Hollister had been found. He got out his phone, held it to his ear as if he was making a call. She had slowed slightly and he did not want her to turn round. Her shoes seemed to be causing her

a little difficulty on the rough surface of the lane so Wyngate
was forced to slow down. He ambled along, one hand on the
phone at his ear, one hand in his pocket, appearing casual
while his heart thumped like a piston. The walls of the tenements to the left and the right, four- or five-storey high buildings on either side, cut out the noise from the city. They could
have been anywhere, locked in a world of their own walking
along. She was going quicker now as the lane surface became
well repaired concrete. She went past a skip. There was a car
half-parked to the side, well tucked in to let other vehicles
squeeze past. He leant on the skip, scared of getting too close,
and took a photograph of the figure in the lilac coat. Her gait
had changed, walking slower now, as if she was enjoying
herself or as if she had found out that she was early for an
appointment after an initial panic. He phoned Vik Mulholland
back at the station and tried to keep his voice calm.

'Vik? I think I have a visual on Blondie . . . she's walking
along Athole Lane. Right in front of me.'

'Really?'

'Yes, heading south. Do you know how many exits there
are?'

He heard Vik typing away, calling up a map. 'Gordon, there
are loads of ground troops out there. Do you want me to send
somebody to see where she goes in case you lose her?'

Wyngate heard the noise of typing. 'Yes.'

'The lane ends in a T-junction with Bowmont Gardens, so
she can go north or south. If we get a patrol to Saltoun Street,
they will see her at the other end and see what way she goes.
You can't afford to lose sight of her and you will at the dogleg.
This is the closest we have got to her. We need . . .'

Wyngate could hear the panic in his voice; not like
Mulholland to get carried away like this. 'What's happened,
Vik?'

'Tania Kirkton has gone missing.'

'Oh God. I need some help here, Vik, she's moving fast
again. Get back up, she's easy to spot. Blonde. Aviator
sunglasses. Same bob cut. Lilac coat.' He moved out from
behind the skip, in pursuit once again. The lane doglegged to
the left then the right. He lost sight of her for a moment. When

he walked on to the straight stretch, she had disappeared. He turned round making sure that he had not missed her.

That wasn't possible. There were six doors in the walls on either side, old wooden garden doors that allowed access from the lane into the rear courts of the tenements. He pushed at the first one, painted bright red. Locked. The second one, its peeling black paint formed a bond over the frame. It had not been opened for years.

No, no, no, no, no. He couldn't have lost her. He jogged on. Not believing it, his toothache forgotten. He eyes searching, looking for a hidden little place, any other pathway or doorway where she might have gone.

He redialled. 'Vik, are you looking at a map? Is there any other way out of this lane, right at the dogleg, right here? I can't see her at all.'

'I have the map right in front of me and there are two doglegs but no way out until the fork at the end. Surely each garden has a back door that opens on to the lane. She'll have gone in there. Did she go left or right?'

'I don't know,' Wyngate said.

Silence, then: 'What do you mean, you don't know?'

'I mean that, I really don't know.'

Wyngate closed the phone and cut the call. He needed to think. He walked back to the bright red door, closest to where he had last seen her and tried the handle. It was securely locked on the inside. He stood in the lane looking behind the wheelie bins as if she might be hiding there like a kitten, ready to jump out at him.

But she wasn't.

He walked up to the next door, newly painted with a serious padlock on a metal clasp. He thought it had given way, then he heard a lock turn. A young man with dark spikey hair and a smear of earth on his tanned face stuck his head out the red door; the one he had first tried.

'Can I help you?' The voice was clear, clipped and very Edinburgh. The suggestion, politely put, was that he was going to be arrested if he didn't have a very good reason for trying the door.

'I am a police officer.' Wyngate searched for his warrant

card, dropping his phone in the process. The man watched him bend down to pick it up, with a look of slight amusement. The door opened a little more to reveal a long dirty shirt and baggy trousers, a pair of secateurs in his dirty gloved hand which he raised to backhand sweat from his forehead. He had been busy pruning.

'Are you sure?'

'Well, I was when I left the station this afternoon,' he joked.

'And do you have a reason to be sneaking about here? I was watching you from the house.' The man waggled a finger at the door. 'Is it to do with the body found out there?'

'Yes.' Wyngate gestured to his right, the direction the Blonde had walked off in. 'I was following somebody who we would like to talk to. Just caught sight of her, then lost her.'

'Who?' He seemed more interested now, the door was opened a little more. His large dark brown eyes flickered down the lane.

'I just want to know where they went, or if they live round here. Blonde lady. Lilac coat, well dressed.'

He looked up the lane. 'I don't recognize that description. A lot of folk use it as a shortcut though.'

'Does anybody here keep their door open? Where she could have got in? I would really like to talk to them.'

He glanced back at the ID, rubbing his eyebrow with the back of his glove, leaving another smear of dirt on his face, then said, 'Shona, maybe? That black door there. They have young kids that play up and down here on their bikes. That might be a place to start. I'll phone her and let her know that you are coming. After all that's been going on, she might be a wee bit reluctant to open her door. We are all a bit jumpy after that boy was found.' He put the rusty secateurs on the ground and patted his pockets, presumably looking for his mobile. 'Are you any further ahead with that?'

'We are looking into a few leads. So over here, behind the black door?'

'Yes, it will be open. You should tell us what's going on. We might be of some help.'

'I'll pass that on to community liaison. Thanks. And your name is?'

'Hodge. Richard Hodge. 27 Marchmont Terrace. Secretary of the local Neighbourhood Watch. You can pass that on to James Kirkton. We like to police ourselves here.' The door closed in his face.

Wyngate turned round, checking the lane again, a strange chill flickered in the heat. None of this made sense. He pushed in the newly painted black door. It opened to reveal a neat back garden with stone inlay patio, a table with four wrought iron seats and a neat old-fashioned clothes line with four posts and a flower border as straight as sentinels. Wyngate walked up the path to what would be the rear door of the close in the old days. It was locked as well. So if she had come in here then she must know the code.

He walked to the rear window, tiptoeing through the border of red gravel to see a woman talking on the phone as she folded something on the ironing board. His face at her kitchen window startled her. She put her hand to her chest and then held it out; recognition as he held up his warrant card. She cut the call and left the room appearing at the rear door of the close less than thirty seconds later; the security pad protected the rear door. She was not happy. 'Yes? Can I help you?'

He repeated the story of the blonde woman.

She looked at him as if he was mad, shaking her head. 'Nobody here of that description. And nobody can get through. See, even if the door was open you need the code to get in to the close in order to get access to the front. I would have thought that was obvious.'

'Always?'

'Yes always. And I can hear that door open and shut so would have known.'

'Oh, it's just that the man across there said that you were the likely one, he must think that your door goes all the way through,' he ended lamely. He felt his heart sink. 'Are you called Shona?'

'No, who's Shona? There's nobody round here called Shona.'

'And there's nobody round here called Richard Hodge either is there?' At that point Wyngate started swearing quietly to himself, looking at the red door, banging gently in the wind.

*   *   *

'Why do you have dirt on your face?' asked Paolo, pointing at Sandra's eyebrow.

'Do I?' She lifted her hand to her face. 'I picked up that bloody cat. He gets everywhere. Wee Piero, he's been rolling in the garden. I think he's trying to cool down. This weather is awful, too clammy.'

Sandra sat facing the mirror on the dressing-table stool that the Duchess used to use before her balance got too bad. Paolo had pinned her hair back and wrapped a towel round her neck. He worked intensely. He was concentrating but soon she too was totally immersed in what was happening to her face. Her skin, red and blotchy, was evened out with pale green cream rubbed in so finely that it disappeared and her face, for a moment, was almost translucent with the subtle gloss of a pearl. He dotted on vanilla coloured cream, and smoothed it over her skin with firm pressure, fine deft strokes as if he was painting. Her face became a doll's face, all the imperfections of humanity gone; her eyebrows were beautifully pencilled back in, then the fine thick black eyeliner shadowed her eyes, which looked garish against the milk white of the rest of her face. As he worked his hands creamed on her cheek, brushing white powder one way and brown powder the other, contouring her face. He held her head delicately so she kept still and did not pull away and spoil it.

When he said 'close your eyes', she did. She did not want to open them again.

At some point he put on some opera; she wondered what it was.

Sandra let herself relax along with the music. This was what the Duchess listened to. The young man crying his heart out for the love of women who didn't want to know him because he is poor.

'Does this mean a lot to your mother? She listens to this so often.'

'Do not speak,' he said and gently pressed his lips against the top of her head.

She was transported, not aware of the brushes on her skin. It seemed easy to allow him to slip off her clothes, pulling the rough nylon tunic up over her head, then something else,

softer and warm-flowing down over her shoulders. The stiff
trousers came down, she held her hand out to steady herself
as she stepped out of them and felt something cascading down
her back, stockings being rolled on her feet, her feet being
slipped into shoes. Her hair released from its binding. His
fingers through it and pulling her fringe this way and that.
Then she was pulled back onto her feet. She could feel his
breath close to her ear, she didn't want to look. She wanted
to hold on to the feeling of being beautiful, of being
treasured.

'Open your eyes,' he said and she did slowly, feeling the
weight of individual eyelashes on her eyelids. She looked at
herself in the mirror. Another face looked back at her; a perfect
version of herself. Paolo stood behind her and rested his chin
on the top of her head as they looked into the mirror together.

She smiled at him. 'Oh thank you very much. Thank you
so very, very much.' And she felt truly grateful. He looked
absolutely smitten as his gaze drifted over the reflection of
her features.

Now she had him where she wanted him.

Wyngate felt wretched; his misery was deep and all consuming.
And so obvious, nobody was taking the piss. Not even
Mulholland. He had always been the back room boy, sitting
at the computer and doing what he could to support the team
and he excelled in that. But he had always harboured thoughts
to go operational in the field. So far he had been out twice.

And messed it up twice.

It wasn't his forte. He was not good with people. He was
not sharp like Costello or empathetic like Anderson, not bright
like Mulholland or worthy like Walker. He did not have the
gravitas of O'Hare. But when Vik had to go in for his second
operation on his leg, it had seemed perfectly logical, instead
of recruiting another member to the team, to swap roles. Or
swap part of the roles. It had been Wyngate's job to show Vik
how to input data and how to get the best out of the
databases.

He *had* done the right thing; he had followed the Blonde
when he saw her. He had phoned in and asked for help when

it was unclear which way she was going to go, and the path might have taken her a way that he could not confidently follow. That was right. Only, she had just disappeared.

His colleagues had not said anything but he sensed their disappointment, and their frustration. He had held her in his sight and he had lost her. Their big lead was gone. It had reached the ears of the ACC and now they would have to close ranks, especially with Tania Kirkton missing.

How could he have messed it up so badly? But she *had* disappeared into thin air. As Costello had put it, he had ballsed it up totally – except he knew he hadn't.

He sat and nursed his ego and his cup of tea, then had an idea.

Anderson stood at the wall, looking at Mulholland's efforts at making sense of the case. David was still missing. So was Tania.

The Blonde had now moved centre stage, she was at the top of the board with a map of her last known movements. They had no idea who she was. They had no idea who Pauline Gee was either, but a trace of her IP address, the only one that related to the Facebook page, was registered to Athole House Secure Living Facility. The clustering of activity suggested that 'Pauline' had a job that allowed her access to the computer daily but only in small intervals. The pattern of a shift worker.

So tomorrow they were going to make a move on Paolo Girasole, ask him about the original fire and have a chat about the Vinicombe Street fire. Then ask him again who Blondie was. Tonight they were going to prepare the case for the interview. They wanted his DNA and they wanted some leverage on him. Was he the 'Paul McEwan' who had disappeared at nine years old on the night of the fire? Paul could be anywhere in the world by now, living a life without any criminality. He may have grown up into a man with a different life, keen to leave the tragedy of the Marchmont fire behind.

Or he might be three minutes away.

And 'Paolo Girasole' had appeared from nowhere. There was no record of somebody of that name working at the council and no record of him living at any Manchester Avenue address. If nothing else, he had some explaining to do.

It was the Blonde they really wanted to speak to. Costello had pointed out the oddity of a woman who didn't change her hairstyle for years. Princess Anne was the only one she could think of. She thought if it was a wig, it was a very good one. Even if it was the same wig, it didn't mean it was the same person.

One thing they had confirmed was that Pietro Girasole was dead and buried, lying in the Linn cemetery. So at least they knew where he was.

The phone went. Everybody looked at Anderson, knowing it would be Irene Kerr. They knew that time was running short. If it hadn't already run out.

So they ignored it.

Sandra had relished the meal and the company, the music and the ambiance accompanied by the satisfaction of a plan coming together. Paolo had taken her to Café Russo. She had walked past the front door many times, not knowing that a beautiful little Italian restaurant existed upstairs, all checkered table-cloths and dripping candles in raffia-clad bottles. The lighting was very subtle.

Paolo had booked them for the pre-theatre timeslot, sort of implying that he had plans to take her somewhere else but didn't say what or where.

He was lovely. Younger than her, obviously, but he had enough maturity to look after his mother, look after her because she was precious to him, through choice not obligation. Or were there darker reasons? She tried to find out exactly how old he was; he looked young. He could be young enough to be the Duchess's grandchild. She tried a few gambits to try and figure out exactly how old he was. Her favourite one was 'who was your favourite Dr Who?' as inevitably, the answer would be the one that they had watched as a child. In the early days, when Dr Who actors stuck with the character for more than one series before Hollywood called. The answer might get her within a vague age bracket, but Paolo's answer was typically theatrical. He liked them all. They all gave something to the part. She had to understand that they were not comparing like with like. He spoke about the special effects, the costumes and the standard of writing and how an actor can live the part so much more when good writing and imagination is not hemmed in by budgets.

'So were you ever an actor?' she asked, refusing another top up of Pinot Grigio but glad to see that he was swigging it down. She needed a clear head, to be in control.

'I was never an actor although in some ways I consider myself the greatest actor the world has ever seen.' He took a mouthful of the gnocchi and laughed. 'I mean I go to the council every day and act like I enjoy my work. I talk to people I despise. I go to meetings as if I'm paying attention when my mind is really writing the next play or designing this or that. The art of the theatre is what I love in my head. So yes, I think I am the greatest actor the world has ever known.' He was sincere, scarily sincere.

She thought about swimming in the blueness of his eyes. He stared back at her for what seemed a very long time, the intensity was palpable. She began to feel very nervous, like he could see inside her soul. She looked away.

Then he laughed. 'You see what a good actor I am. You loved all that shit, didn't you?' He had a captivating laugh.

And she laughed too. Glad that she had been caught out. She took a large slug of wine, trying to rid herself of the feeling that she was back at school and everybody was laughing at her. She was wearing someone else's coat. A hand-me-down. Second class. Second rate.

'Are you having a good time?' he asked.

'Yes. I am, I really am.' She raised her glass to him and they toasted each other. He excused himself and went to the loo. She watched him go up the stairs; a hunter watching its prey. He wasn't a big man, rather insubstantial with thin, narrow shoulders. There was not a lot of power there.

He had the biggest blue eyes she had ever seen, large pale blue moons, just like those of the Duchess. But diluted, washed out as if he had been crying for a whole lifetime. He had a small nose on his handsome face. That was a sign of moral weakness. She hoped.

She saw him come out the toilet, pause at the top of the stairs and look round for her, smiling when their eyes met. A nice, open smile.

She knew he would pay the bill. She knew he would ask her if she had enjoyed the night. She would say she had. She knew he would suggest going for a walk, head off for somewhere quiet he had in mind. And she would let him think it was his idea.

SIX

Friday 10th June

A nderson hadn't even sat down at his desk before his phone rang. It was the ACC. He was curt and to the point.

'I'm not sure if it is a blackmail demand but James Kirkton has had a letter through his door during the night, telling him to show up on Elean Street, at the corner where the garage is; the wee antique mall?'

'Yes I know it, all back alleys and footpaths. That's difficult.' His respect for Blondie was growing.

'We can think that through. The letter has the middle name of Kirkton's wife which is something very few people know; Priscilla,' he added. 'And that is some kind of proof that whoever wrote the letter, might have had Tania sitting in front of him. Kirkton wants nothing done.'

'So why did he contact you then?' snapped Anderson.

'I suppose he's conflicted. The note says don't tell the police and he was telling me as a friend so that if we got wind of it, he wanted nothing done. But that's not his call and he damn well knows that. Which is why he phoned me in the first place. I think a low-key presence following Kirkton might be of use but you need to get your skates on. The note was put through his door by hand overnight and he has to be there this evening. I don't need to tell you the importance of this, Anderson. He has been an irritating thorn in our side all year but this could silence him forever. If you know what I mean. You will have all my support, whatever you need.'

'And what if David is in there? We can't have a low-key, fast-action response team. We either do or we don't. Ask Batten and see what he says?'

'Do that. And I know what Batten will say.'

'Talk her round? She's angry, emotional and hurting.'

'So that's just your thing, you and your emotional IQ. And, you know Paolo Girasole doesn't have a driving licence or a car. So Blondie is the driver. Stick him on the back burner for now.'

It was a not-so-subtle command from a superior officer. Anderson wondered who had told Mitchum that, but had neglected to tell him. Mulholland. It would be Mulholland.

'Kirkton will be your way in. And use your intelligence, Anderson. This is a woman who can be talked round, maybe a killer, or a killer's accomplice. No big stuff. Whoever she is, she wants you to know about it. She, or her accomplice, told Amy to tell you, so there is some connection there. We don't know if David and Tania are there. We need to do as she wants. For now. You want Costello with you? I'd rather you kept her out of it.'

'Blondie needs to separate her victims from the pack. I trust Costello to stick to me. She's my defence.'

Mitchum was quiet for a long time, mulling this over. Then agreed and hung up.

In the station, Anderson called a meeting for a full briefing at ten a.m. The case was subject to a media blackout. The DCI listened as Costello gave them the details of the Elean Street rendezvous. Her meeting with the fire officer who had attended the Marchmont Terrace was history now. He could tell by the way she was talking that she was going through the motions, her mind was already running through the various outcomes of that evening. Even the worst.

Batten was sitting at the back, working out a strategy of what to say and how to talk Blondie down. He did point out that they didn't know who had actually written the letter, what part they were playing. But his advice was the same. Blondie was angry about something, and she wanted them to listen and empathize. No matter what she said. They were going on the principle that the letter writer was Blondie, a female arsonist with some connection, probably a childhood connection, to the Vinicombe Street Theatre. She was making dolls of people. If they died in that process, so be it. She needed help. But she was very, very angry about something.

And they had to diffuse that by talking. Any show of force would make her worse. And – the big *and*, – she was not stupid.

Costello was now talking about the fire at Marchmont Terrace as the logistic guys from West End Central made their electronic plans in the room next door. She pointed to the photographs on the board. Barry McEwan had burned to death trying to get out the back. His wife Diane was found in the upstairs toilet, untouched by flames, having succumbed to smoke inhalation. Alice Patricia Kilpatrick, Deke's wife, was the only victim of the Marchmont Terrace with a definitive time of death as she had survived the flames, the damage to her lungs, the fall and the collision with the Victorian birdbath that shattered her spleen. She had survived the fracture to her skull on landing only to die two weeks later of a chest infection. Her husband Derek Kilpatrick had survived his injuries but was left partially sighted, disabled and disfigured. His own opinion was that his life was not worth saving as it was not worth living. He had been staying at the Athole care home for the last twenty years, under an antidepressant and analgesic regime of medication.

The fire had been started by a candle placed under a coat rack, deliberately according to the chief fire officer at the time. 'And somewhere in that, in all that tragedy,' said Costello, 'is the reason why Blondie is so angry.' She then pointed to the DNA coding on the wall. 'That DNA links the two scenes.'

'So it must be Paolo.'

'Or Deke.'

'It's male, that's all we know for sure.'

'Well, it's not Blondie then. Which gets us nowhere.'

*   *   *

Wyngate sat down in Anderson's office. Batten sat beside him, asking him if he was comfortable. Wyngate said no, his tooth-ache was still bothering him. He was keen, he wanted it to be shown that he had not lost Blondie, that she had vanished into thin air. And if he needed hypnosis to prove that, then so be it. He was so sure, he wanted it on tape.

Batten began by asking Wyngate if he was relaxing now, calling him Gordon, repeating a few phrases over and over.

Wyngate closed his eyes, his breathing slowed down, his shoulders dropped a little. Batten asked him to lift his finger. Wyngate's hands were placed on top of his own knees, like he was ready for a hard question at an interview and wanted to keep his hands from betraying any nervousness.

His finger rose but Wyngate's eyes remained closed. Batten talked him through it one more time saying the same words in a deep calm voice. The phone rang outside. Costello moved to tell them to silence it but Batten held up his hand. There was no point. Wyngate relaxed, his conscious could be aware of all the noise in Christendom but it was the subconscious that Batten was talking to.

Batten asked him for a few points of reference. Wyngate knew where he was and he knew what day it was. Costello commented that that in itself was a first.

Batten asked if Wyngate recalled what had happened the day before.

'Many things, the usual things. Sam had been sick that morning. He eats his food too quickly.' Wyngate spoke about his wife cleaning the mess up. It had been all over the baby's face. She had taken cloths and wiped him, then Wyngate wiped his face with an imaginary cloth, then nodded. That was the end of it.

Anderson looked at Costello and shrugged, no idea what was going on here.

'So you went to the dentist? Where did you go?'

'Walter Armstrong, Byres Road.'

'And did you see anybody you recognized?'

'The Blonde.'

'And what was she wearing?'

'Lilac coat, black shoes.'

'Was she carrying anything?'

'A black bag, like an overnight bag thing. Big handbag.' His hands indicated the size of the bag. His subconscious had noticed it.

'And what did you do when you saw her?'

'I followed her.'

'And where did she go?'

'Up Athole Lane. Where Mr Hollister was found.' Wyngate got quite animated, his breathing quickened, his feet started twitching as if he was running. 'I phoned Mulholland. I didn't know where she might go at the other end. Left or right or straight on. I might not get there in time.'

'Why might you not get there?'

'I didn't want to follow her too closely as she would see me, so I held back. I stayed out of sight.' His hands waved at his side. 'There was a skip here so I stood behind that and pretended I was on my phone, then I stood in a doorway. The lane turns left then right. She walked round the corner and by the time I got there, she was gone. She was not there.' It was said calmly but definitely.

'Where did she go?' asked Batten.

'I don't know.'

'You didn't see where she went?'

'I did not.'

'What did you do?'

He started moving his right hand, knuckles tight trying to get a door handle open. 'I am opening the garden doors, to get access. She must have gone into a garden. But there was only one unlocked. But the lassie who was not Shona did not hear her door open or shut. The close door is locked so the Blonde did not go through her close.'

'And you believe her?'

'I do.'

'Why did you call her "the woman who was not Shona"?'

'The man said that she was called Shona. But she was not.'

'What man?'

'Richard Hodge.'

'OK, where was she when you first saw the woman who is not Shona?'

'In her house on her phone, she saw me out the window.'

'Did she come out to get you?'

'Yes,' Wyngate said straight away. 'Yes, but I had to wait until she went out the door of her flat, then came to the back door of the close, then out to me.'

'And what did you do?'

'I waited.'

'For how long?'

'This long.' He paused. 'About that length of time.'

'And who else did you speak to?'

'No one.'

'Let's go back to the man called Richard Hodge.'

'He's behind the red door. He heard me try the handle, he came out to see what I was doing.'

'Was he in the house?'

'He was gardening.'

'Why do you say that?'

'He was dirty, holding secateurs.'

Batten leaned forward, checking that the machine was recording. 'When you were talking to him, was his close door open or shut?'

'Shut.'

'And you are at the bottom of the garden? How far is it to the door at the back of the close?'

'About thirty metres. They have very long back gardens.'

Everybody in the room knew that they did.

'And who is Richard?'

'He lived there.'

'Do you know that?'

'No, I do not. That was what he said.'

'How was he breathing?'

'He was out of breath.'

'And the back door of the close was shut?' he repeated.

'Yes.'

'Can you describe Richard?'

'Shiny face,' came the reply. Then Wyngate started to talk. 'He had short dark hair, slicked back against his head and dirt on his cheek.'

'How old was he?'

'Twenties maybe thirties, maybe older. Edinburgh accent.'

'Eye colour?'

'Brown eyes.'

'Did you know him?'

'I did not.'

'Had you seen him before?'

A pause. 'I had not.'

They looked at each other.

Batten leaned in.

'Did you recognize him?'

Wyngate's eyelids flickered. The question created conflict.

'He said . . .'

'Yes?'

'He said, "And you can pass it on to James Kirkton. We like to police ourselves."'

The room fell quiet.

Batten went on. 'So he saw you from the house, but suddenly appeared at the door at the end of the garden. Was there enough time?'

'There was not.'

'Did he say he was in the garden?'

'No, he did not. He said he was in the house.'

Batten paused for a while, looked over to the other two then asked, 'What was he wearing?'

'Long dirty white shirt, old black trousers.'

'And on his feet?'

'Black shoes.' Wyngate seemed to pause. He shook his head. 'His laces were undone.'

'OK, what did you think when you saw his face. Damp like that?'

'He reminded me of Sam after we had wiped the beans from his face.'

'And the trousers, how did they look at the bottom?'

'Creased. Been folded.'

He counted him back out of his relaxed state. Wyngate opened his eyes and looked around hopefully. 'So was that of any use?'

'Yeah, we know your kid rubs beans on his face and that

you are a shoe fetishist, so no, no bloody use,' joked Costello but the whole room had relaxed.

They knew.

Batten pulled a photograph from the wall, the picture of Blondie at the fire where bright flames cast shadows on her face, highlighting her cheekbones, darkening the hollows. The huge dark glasses that covered her eyes were a canvas for the reflection of the bright jagged flames.

Batten placed the photograph next to the computer screen. 'OK, Vik work your magic, change the hair in that to brown, slick it back like Wyngate described.'

'You want me to turn her into some bloke that Wyngate met in Athole Lane behind the door?'

'Yes,' said Batten blankly. 'And take all that make-up off him, take off that lipstick. Give it a little more masculine hair line, a widow's peak. Take the scarf away. Now the glasses. Wyngate? Describe his eyes.'

'Large, very open.' Wyngate pulled his own eyes very wide. 'And a deep, deep brown.'

Vik shrugged but did it. The face grew in familiarity.

'But doesn't that just look like him because I am making it so.'

'There are many bits she can't change; the shape, the nose, the lips.'

'Shades of Pietro though, that cleansing of the face?' said Costello. 'Paolo has very big blue eyes. Not brown.'

'And no driving licence,' said Anderson bitterly.

'Are we saying that Wyngate was talking to a woman and didn't notice?'

'Who wears a coat in high summer? Big bag? Do you think she might have been carrying her alter ego around in there? Miss Blondie . . . No wonder we can't find you anywhere, you don't bloody exist. She just goes around then slips in somewhere. Coat off, wig off, changes shoes. But in this case had no time to tie the laces.'

'Why didn't she stay there behind the wall? Wyngate would have walked off.'

'Well anybody could have looked out those windows at any time. And she would have heard Wyngate phone for back up. The place was going to be full of cops. She, he might have even passed Wyngate as she walked out.' Batten sat back thinking this through.

'Weird? Absolutely. Clever? Absolutely. But that sense of theatre, of acting.' He pointed to the picture of the Vinicombe Street Theatre on the board. 'And it all goes back to there.'

David wondered what had happened to the girl he had tried to talk to. There was something that he was not seeing, and something that he was missing. The woman had come out and adjusted the drip in his arm. He had passed out, drifting out to the white place where nothing annoyed him and all was good. It wasn't heaven but it was pretty close to it, as close as his imagination could get. There, walking around, he saw his mum and dad back together again. The dog was a playful puppy. He was younger, he must have been because Granny and Granddad were there. It was Christmas but they were all out in the garden. He had heard them talk, talk about him and what a shame it was.

He was trying to tell them that he was OK. But his mouth wouldn't move. Nothing would move.

Then he was up on his feet. A clanking from above was pulling him up by the shoulders. His arms moved without any effort on his part. He could only feel a little pain as he was suspended from the brace across his chest, his feet not on the ground. His arms now falling uselessly by his side. He could see them but could not move them. There was a tight wire fixed to his wrists, so deep in, the tight, swollen skin was cut through. His fingers were somebody else's thick black fingers. Then his hand moved. He tried to raise the right hand to look more closely but it was the left hand that moved.

He attempted to look down. He couldn't, something was holding his chin up. In front of him was a huge nothing, just blackness. The noise was the same, but the smell was different. Using only his eyes, he strained to look above him. Branches, leaves, trees, all bright green and false. He could see somebody up there, crawling through metal girders, a faint and silvery will-o-the-wisp through the darkness.

There was a creak and he felt his neck snap. His chin fell onto his chest. Now, at least, he could look down to the dark, stained concrete floor. But he was standing on wooden floor-boards. Beyond that were tea chests, stacked up.

He was on stage.

He was waiting for his audience.

And at that minute, he knew he would die.

He thought about his mum. And Winston's dog. Strange thoughts with no tears.

He thought about that pretty girl with the dark hair, the one with the flower. Had she been part of this? Part of the lure? The woman who had come back and stabbed him in the arm so he lost control and she could bundle him away into a car. Had they been part of it all? He closed his eyes, thinking of her smile; a Judas smile.

Sandra woke up. Something lovely had happened. Mentally she snuggled down deep in the duvet that honeycombed round her. Paolo had been lovely. So lovely. He had taken her to a small Italian restaurant, upstairs somewhere on Byres Road, a small intimate place where he spoke Italian to the waiters and they greeted him like a long-lost family member. She was included in their hugs and kisses. She hadn't recognized any dishes on the menu but he had asked her what she liked and he had chosen for her. They had drunk wine, far too much wine. She was wearing a dress that belonged to the Duchess, while silk, simply cut that cascaded from the cowl round her neck down in soft waves to mid-calf. Nothing she hadn't worn before, it was one of her favourites but Paolo was not to know that. Or if he did, he didn't mind. The leather of the Duchess's handmade shoes was so soft it caressed her feet as she climbed the stairs. After that things got a little hazy, she remembered going down the stairs, back to the street. The cool wind on her new, lovely face. Rain was on the way at last. They walked across the road towards the car. Paolo had taken the keys, insisting on driving. And she remem-bered getting back in it, drowsy with the drink, then she couldn't recall any more but that didn't matter as her plan was coming together. And as the Proclaimers song said, she was on her way from misery to happiness.

She told Paolo where to drive, not noticing where he was going, and now she was snuggled up, looking up at the sky, the trees and the green little animals hanging off them. So pretty.

Sleep came quickly. She had some thinking to do about part two of her plan. It was all going so well.

Wyngate was back at the dentist late that afternoon. His root canal was starting to feel very hot and painful. Then it started to throb and Anderson had told him to go round and get something done with it. In truth Wyngate was happy to walk away. They hadn't really said anything but he felt guilty. If he had had his wits about him, would they now have Blondie in custody?

And what about him? Wyngate knew it had been a bloke he had talked to. And it was a woman he had been following. He could tell the difference. His subconscious mind had told his colleagues what he knew they wanted to hear; that was the problem with hypnosis. He was mulling it over, wanting to prove himself right but seeing no way to do it. He was walking down towards the bottom of Byres Road, out of the dentist and heading towards Elean Lane which would take him up to Elean Street. He had lost her once before, but he was going to be ahead of the game this time. He was fed up with Mulholland's sly glances. He pulled his hood up against the light drizzle that was threatening, at any moment, to turn into a downpour. He continued up past the Cambodian restaurant with its three scooters neatly parked outside, under a canopy in preparation of rain. The cobbles underfoot were slippy, oily after so many days of blistering heat. He looked round, searching for any sign of a low key operation being underway. By now, they would have some covert surveillance on the situation. But to him it appeared to be office workers hurrying back and forth, the odd shopper, all moving quickly to get inside before the heavens opened. He looked at the angry black clouds, grinding their way across the sky, charging into each other. He scanned the roof of the single-storey garage with the double-storey central workshop. There were no Sky men, no BT engineers, no roofers, nobody that might be a surveillance unit. There was an arcade or something here, an antique shop, bric-a-brac, a warren through the old single-storey buildings.

Of course, anybody on a roof would be highly suspicious with the amber weather warnings currently in existence. Was Blondie merely lucky or had she moved quickly on Tania Kirkton to take advantage of the weather?

She was not a lady to be underestimated.

Wyngate stood in the middle of the crossroads. Cobbled lanes, four of them at this point, five or six if you counted those offshoots within a twenty-feet radius. It was a clever place for a meet, easy to lure him here, easy to see him without being seen. But then what? Lure Kirkton away with a phone call? Then Wyngate realized that he himself was acting suspiciously. So he pulled out his phone, easing himself on to the wall of the disused garage; the old Elean Lane Car Repair and Body workshop. The vehicle entrance was roller shuttered, closed tight. It hadn't been used for years this place, but it had an overhanging roof which gave him a good eighteen inches of protection from the rain. He too was going to take advantage of the weather, and shelter under the roof. A young man, on his mobile. Nothing suspicious there.

His tongue was back at his tooth, probing the numbness of his cheek, wondering if it had stopped bleeding at last. The door behind him opened, then closed. Quietly, as if nobody was supposed to notice.

Then it opened and closed again, nothing more than a little bang and a bounce. As if somebody was checking he was gone before they came out.

He looked round, then tapped roughly on the door with his knuckle. He placed his hand against it, it opened easily; just an old wooden door with the wood at the bottom frayed, eaten through by damp.

This would be a good place for the homeless to sleep. Were they gathering here in readiness for the onslaught of weather? It looked like the Met Office might have got their timing right this time. A chill of wind pushed the warm air from the narrow channel of Elean Street as he stepped inside. He shouldered open the door as it caught on the rough concrete.

And he was in an office, a dusty old office with a flagstone

floor and an ancient desk, a tattered and curling Pirelli calendar
above it. It was dark in here. It was getting dark outside, the
sky blackening by the minute. He left the door open to get
some fresh air in. He called out, *'Hello?'* This would be a
good place to view the crossroads outside. He called out again.

No answer. There was no real furniture, just a rusty cabinet
like a wardrobe, and an old filing cabinet, both drawers slightly
open. He didn't investigate closer.

'Anybody here?' He got his warrant card out, pulled down
his hood. The metal cabinet was locked. There was another
wooden door, presumably into the mechanics bay and the main
workshop of the garage. At the far end of that were the big
double roller shutters that opened on to the other side of the
lane. Another good viewpoint.

He opened the door, and stepped through into a stone floored
corridor. The place was bigger than he thought. The left-hand
wall had a huge mirror, somebody here was either very vain
or it was some kind of two-way mirror for the workman to
see who was going in and out of the office.

There was no sign of anybody about, but there was a sense
of there being life here. Paige Riley would run to a place like
this. Wyngate knew this area was on their watch list for beggars.
He opened another door, just a cupboard, old shelves. He
disturbed something that scurried away with a flash of silver.

He closed the door. There were another two, one double, a
single and one of them, he presumed, must take him on to the
floor of the workshop.

David watched him through the big window, his heart striking
a military beat. So close. So close. He could see the man in
his hooded anorak opening and closing the doors behind the
window, could see the individual crystals of rain on his shoulders. So it was raining out there. He could hear the drumming
on the roof that was a few feet above him, but sounded so far
away. Was this somebody coming to look for him? This thin
man who walked nervously, opening cupboard doors, here and
there, peeking in like he was playing hide and seek and he
was seek.

David knew he was hidden, behind the mirror, swinging.

He was dangling in mid-air, swaying slowly with an invisible momentum, suspended by the bands round his groin, his waist and under his shoulders. He could see his own wrist, the tight wire wound round it that disappeared into thin air even though it was slack now and his wrist dangled at his side. Earlier, the wire had been tight and had been tightened further, moving his arm up by jerky movement, accompanied by a mechanical clunking and grinding from above him, from up in the trees somewhere.

But he couldn't move or shout. All he could do was watch.

He looked over to his left. The girl came into view every now and then, a frail wispy creature who floated through the air on her gossamer wings. She had been noisy at first, then bleeding. Now she was silent. And the bleeding had stopped.

Wyngate could hear the rain battering down on the flat roof, it rattled like a drum-core. He opened another door, just a storage room, no sign of anybody living there. Strange when the door was unlocked. Surely some desperate soul would have discovered this.

He opened the double door, and took two steps back. A rack of little people hanging one by one, neatly arranged. To one side was a frame with clothes hanging. Shelf upon shelf of fabric, wire, tools, small pieces of wood, turned and smooth. The largest single item was a yellow duffle coat, too small to fit an adult but much bigger than any of the other dolls clothes.

On the side of the door were separate sheets of paper, pinned many layers thick, numbers listed with beautiful italic writing, four sets of numbers again and again. And on the inside of the wooden door, much older paper but the writing was of the same style, the same pattern.

He saw pairs of tiny shoes, polished to perfection. And a rolled-up futon.

A clean, rolled-up futon. And a neat pile of folded clothes.

So somebody had been sleeping here. Somebody who loved dolls and puppets, and made dolls and puppets.

Was Tania here? David?

He saw a case, like an artist's case with pockets and drawers. Full of make-up. And on top of that a familiar little case; blue

circle on one side, white on the other. Contact lenses. He bent
down to pick them up, unscrewing the top. Brown-coloured
lenses.

Don't it turn my brown eyes blue, so the song went. Or
was it vice versa?

He thought about searching the rest of the place but this
was no time for bravado. He was going back out to the street
to call for back-up. He jumped at a noise, like a cough or a
muffled shout, and turned round. He placed his ear against the
wood of the big door. He was sure this was the door going
back into the workshop. He opened it slowly. The smell that
assaulted him was recognizable. And human. Human decom-
position. He lifted his phone to use the light. Then he hit the
floor.

David couldn't turn his head. But he heard her. The click click
of those heels on the concrete floor as she walked across the
floor beneath him, heading for the single door. She was going
for the man in the anorak. He had taken his hood off now, he
was moving very slowly and taking his time as he walked up
to the big double cupboard. Why was he on his own? Why
was he being so slow? She would be here soon, shadowing
around in that suit that rendered her invisible in this dull light.
He wouldn't see her or hear her. David watched helpless, his
heart sinking. He knew she was going to open the door and
the man in the hood would be too late turning round.

David swung, back and forth, dangling from his four wires
and he knew blackness and despair.

They looked at each other in the mirror. One chin resting on
the head of the other. Identical. Like a sculpture. Blonde on
Blonde. Naked.

Lips parted. One in pleasure. One in fear.

Four eyes wide open.

A gloved hand side-shifted a few stray hairs from the fringe.
So they matched. Precisely.

Pale skin. Dark eyes. Perfect arched eyebrows.

Ruby red lips.

Blood red lips.

And he had said that colour was too dark for her.

Two hands came to settle round a neck, giving the sculpture a base, two serpents of forearms and fingers wound and twisted.

A kiss from ruby lips to a nest of blonde hair.

One face leaned back to scrutinize the other in the mirror.

There had been alcohol and sleep. And now this.

Lips kissed the top of a head again.

This was a game.

It was going to be OK.

Just a game.

They were Greek gods.

One body, two faces.

The dark eyes studied the image, examining its every pore, as if they were a sculpture of great value, of great beauty.

The work of art was admired by its creator. And vice versa.

So close, so very close.

Then a wave of hot breath over skin. The scalpel came up slowly.

The blade pressed against the skin just under the ear and pierced the flesh creating a single bubble of ruby red. The edge worked its way round the jaw line. Not going deep, just slicing under the skin, peeling it off as it cut its path.

The gloved fingers eased the skin off the underlying tissue, loosening it so the face could come away in one piece.

There was no pain. Just a bubble of ruby red that turned into a crack of crimson, that formed a rose that veined and spread to give a cerise collar on the perfect white skin.

It was raining by the time the police gathered, covertly, in the cobbled junction of Elean Street, Elean Lane and a very narrow walkway called the Potters. Kirkton was making himself very obvious, walking up and down, a slight march rather than a leisurely stroll. They had not wired him. Colin Anderson, in a beanie hat, was watching the doorway of the antique mall, doing a good impersonation of a hungry husband waiting for a wife to take him to dinner. Costello was studying the menu in the door of the Cambodian restaurant, giving her a good side view of the area. She thought she could see a couple of members of the tactical deployment team, but maybe not. They should not be obvious.

Batten had assured them that it would not come to that. Blondie was angry, she wanted to be heard and their best weapon was to listen. He pointed out that this was a public place, obvious, with no easy get out. His reason for this was that this was her end game, she wanted to finish it here. They just had to make sure that the end was on their terms not hers. He had suggested that Blondie had a previous rapport of some kind with Anderson, something so slight it had meant nothing to him but had significance for her. So he needed to work on that. Batten had spent a couple of hours with Anderson going through tactics, the deployment team had kept to themselves, Mitchum being the liaison back and forth, only telling them what they needed to know. Costello was wired and had a baton. They both had a camera, they both had Kevlar. Slash proof but not stab proof. The jury was out about hypodermics.

Anderson was watching Kirkton, knowing that he should feel a degree of pity for the man, but couldn't quite shrug off the feeling that the politician had brought this on himself. There was something he was not saying, some reason why he didn't want Anderson on that cold case team. And had that made him a target? Well, they would get his daughter back and sort out the devil in the detail later.

Anderson was keeping an eye on the garage diagonally across from him. Costello was watching the antique arcade behind him. She looked like a tourist waiting for a friend, caught out by a Glasgow downpour and amusing herself by looking at all the menus.

Anderson saw Costello go walkabout, casually taking in the doors of the garage, the single door that was almost rotten away. She then looked down the cobbled lane, a wine merchant and two hairdressers, a shop for vintage clothes – all their wares pulled tight under a canopy for the forecasted cloud-burst. It was strange to watch people walk about, looking at the sky. Costello herself was looking at the big roller doors, covertly looking at the rust, seeing if they had been opened recently. They hadn't.

Whoever Blondie was, she knew the city well. This was

somebody who had spent a lifetime walking round here, Costello mused.

Anderson coughed. Costello strolled back to her position at the restaurant, hidden from anybody coming down the lane. Kirkton had reacted to something. Costello saw him turn. There was a subtle flow of a signal from the couple who were eating chips in the doorway of the printers, to the man talking to nobody on his mobile phone, to the older man reading the menu in the window of the Italian restaurant then to a joiner fixing a lock on a door of an office. He spoke into a radio clipped on his collar. The rain got a little heavier, everybody moved on.

A few nods. Everybody in position. One radio directive. Seven answers. Nobody was going to get out of this building, no matter how she was dressed.

Then Kirkton moved, a definitive step to the side. A door had opened welcoming him in. He closed his umbrella, shaking it out before he entered through the door with the rotten lower planks.

The door closed.

Taking a deep breath Anderson signalled to Costello. 'Let's do it.'

Costello took a last sweeping look round the crossroads and hoped that those who should have been watching were watching.

Anderson opened the door. Costello followed him into the small outer office. Kirkton was standing in the middle, trying to be brave but they could see the relief in his eyes.

'The door was open,' he said.

'The door was opened,' Costello corrected, looking round her, 'for you, so there is somebody here.' She looked at him with a degree of suspicion, for a moment she wondered who was following who. Her hand rested on her baton. Then she recognized the scent in the air, above the stink of damp and rotting wood, were the high notes of Fracas.

'What now?' Kirkton asked.

They were standing in a tiny wood panelled hall. The single door in off the lane was battered and old. There was another door, a small dusty desk. An old Pirelli calendar on the wall, browning and curled. There was no natural light at all, except some filtering through from the slightly open door and a small glow from somewhere else, but the shadowing patterns were confusing.

'I guess you should go in, that's the way the sign points.' Costello held her mobile phone in her hand, and opened the door slightly. 'We will be right behind you, working towards a safer society. Couldn't possibly leave you alone in a place like this. Anything could happen to you.'

Kirkton stood his ground. For a minute Anderson thought he was going to bluster.

Then the room darkened.

The three of them stood, knowing that they were not alone but their company was not in this reception area. Anderson tried the light switch. Nothing happened. The door that led into the main part of the garage opened with the same slow squeak that is a cliché in any horror film, but is truly blood-curdling in real life. It moved with more strength than could be caused by a breeze. In the dark. A gentle light came on in the room beyond. Anderson could hear Costello breathing and felt her fingers curl round the bottom of his jacket just to make sure they didn't lose each other. Or if one took a syringe stab, the other one would know. There was a sharp clunk, deafening in the silence. That was the door behind them locking.

'What was that?' asked Kirkton, the voice coming from the blackness behind Anderson.

'Our escape route,' said Costello. There was the noise of movement, shuffling of feet, as Costello told the politician to stay close.

They all jumped as the discordant harmony of funfair music started. Barrel organ deafeningly loud, small bright lights started dancing in the darkness. Head splitting volume, the colours disorientating. Costello extended her baton. Nobody was coming near her with a hypodermic without getting a battering.

'Theatre people,' muttered Anderson, by way of explanation of the macabre sideshow. He pointed to a rotating disco light in the ceiling. Cheap. Simple. The music quietened, to that of a child's music box somewhere in the next room where the music would always be just out of their reach. Anderson felt behind him for Costello's hand and gave it a gentle squeeze. He was going to walk forward. Costello dropped the baton onto its wrist loop, and switched on the phone torch.

She heard Kirkton mutter one word. 'Tania.'

The three of them walked forward into a narrow corridor with several doors on the left, a big mirror to the right, reflecting them moving slowly in a single line, second rate Keystone Cops. There was a door open at the end, to the right, to the area behind the mirror. Anderson tried to get his bearings, that would be to the mechanics bay.

They went through, three of them; Anderson in front, Costello at the rear. The circus music was louder here, more flashing lights in bright colours spun past them, faster and faster. Anderson thought they were in some house of horror cakewalk.

This was pure theatre.

Anderson had paused with his back against the black painted wall of the old garage and he pointed at the row of tea chests banked up high, decreasing in number as they went towards the front, forming a theatre, an auditorium.

Auditorium. The club where Blondie had been in 1999.

Tea chest. Just like Mr Hollister.

They edged along the narrow gap. The seats appeared to be occupied but the only light in the room were the dancing flickers that kaleidoscoped around the room, making it difficult to work out shapes with any precision and making it impossible to ascertain any movement. Or if anybody was there at all.

In the front, beyond the lights, was darkness, too black to be merely the absence of light. That was the backdrop of a stage.

Costello kept her back to the solid concrete wall, thinking about going back and closing that door that left them exposed. All those films she had seen, the good guy at the back copped it first.

They moved in timid single file along the narrow gap between the wall and the tea chests. Costello swung the narrow beam of the torch around, picking out shoes and bits of legs and trousers of an audience that were deadly still and deadly quiet. The air was cold and rank. Sitting in the middle of the lowest row of tea chests sat a figure blocking the light from the stage beyond. The silhouette was a circle on a box. Perfect round hair on a pair of narrow shoulders. Costello caught the sight of jet black hair and a handle. Then the flash of a white bony hand raised in mid-air, playing a silent piano, a mosaic as the kaleidoscope colour whizzed round them, flinging bright patterns on the wall; reds and yellows. Like a roundabout. But they were standing still.

She could make out, in the flickering, the Duchess in a deep pink evening gown and her rolled up black hair, the lights tinkling and glinting off her tiara. Or her crown.

Costello swore quietly.

In the back of the Italian restaurant they were following the images on two laptops, relayed from the cameras on Anderson's jacket and Costello's lapel. The command had all kinds of earpieces, talking quietly to each other but not to the two detectives who had gone into the garage.

Batten and Mulholland were watching the same feed at the station, both anxious. Costello was wearing a wire and had two panic buttons, but Batten had told them to be as unobtrusive as possible. If the images through the lightshow were what they appeared to be, Blondie was putting on a show for them.

Once she had her say, she would be a different creature.

Mulholland watched until he saw the stage in the old garage. It was a hidden corner of the West End with tiny antique shops and a couple of very good restaurants that he could no longer afford. He knew the area, he should have been there, but they thought him unfit because of this leg and his fracture that kept fracturing. So they trusted that arsehole Wyngate now. Wingnut Wyngate with his sticky out ears and his little rucksack that went everywhere with him. Mulholland looked round at the coat stand. Wyngate's anorak was gone but his rucksack was still there. He had gone back to the dentist. Anderson was fed up with him and Costello having a 'who has the sorest face competition'.

He stood at the whiteboard, looking at the stills from the various videos and the CCTV screen shots. The picture of Kirkton that Costello had put up on the board. A victim now surely that Tania had gone missing. Mulholland turned back to make sure that Wyngate's rucksack was still there, then phoned Graham downstairs, confirming that the constable had left but not yet returned. Mulholland phoned Wyngate's phone. Switched off.

So he was held up at the dentist. Nothing more. Trust him to be away when all the excitement was going on.

He settled back to look across at the footage streaming in, just colours and lights, but the movement of the camera suggested someone walking slowly. Both trackers said the same, Anderson and Costello were moving and were still together.

He wished them well and looked at the photograph of David. He reached out and touched it, his fingertip on the boy's cheek. He hoped he was there, alive. His mother had not been told of the operation today; she couldn't be trusted on social media and there was a media blackout. He looked at David's hair, spikey, high up off his forehead. And then James Kirkton with his big floppy fringe like a poor man's Boris Johnson. The picture had caught him with that tic of his, third finger of the left hand pulled through his hair like a snowplough. He had seen that before.

The circus music stopped, the barrel organ wheezed to silence.

The soaring strains of *Madame Butterfly* filled the room. Darkness fell. The swirling lights slowed and slowed, spinning to a standstill.

For a moment Anderson held his breath, he flicked his eyes down to the small camera, hoping it was still working.

Then a voice, quiet and perfectly harmonic with no distortion through the sound system, asked them very politely to 'Take a seat. All of you.'

'Well, she knows fine that we are here.'

'I think she knew that all along. And I don't think she is going to mind a bigger audience than she invited. Theatre folk never mind that, do they?'

Kirkton, now in-between the other two, hissed at them. 'If this, any of this, means that I will not get my daughter back then . . .'

'There will only be one person responsible for you not getting your daughter back. And right now, she's calling the shots.'

Madame Butterfly got a little louder. A spotlight settled on one empty tea chest, crudely rigged up to look like a chair with red velvet cushions. The seat was next to the Duchess's wheelchair.

If it were for James Kirkton, then the member of the Scottish Parliament had the best seat in the house.

Costello said quietly into the ear of James Kirkton, 'Go and take your seat.'

As the politician did so, a single spotlight danced around him. Anderson tried to look up to the stage, to see if there was somebody present. Not all of this was pre-recorded. Kirkton's every movement was being illuminated and there was no way that could have been predicted unless there was a motion sensor motor on the light. This technology was impressive, and beyond the profile they had of Blondie. ˙

Had they got this wrong?

However, the light followed Kirkton and only him. Leaving us in the dark, thought Anderson, hoping the words were not significant.

The music changed to a song Anderson vaguely recognized. He recognized the female voices. Abba. When they sung the lyric 'Happy New Year', Kirkton nearly jumped out his seat, looking around him. Feral fear now gripped his face, all thoughts of his daughter had gone. He was up, ready to leave.

Costello gripped Anderson's upper arm.

'I saw that.'

The red curtains rose inch by slow inch. The music dampened down, but the bass remained full and throbbing as if somebody had closed a thick door over, creating a barrier.

It took a moment but Anderson recognized the scene that had been expertly painted on the backdrop on stage. He had looked at it often enough in the last twenty-four hours. And he had seen it in the cold case file. The small alley at the back of Ashton Lane; Lillybank.

Mulholland looked at the photograph on the wall for a long time. He had seen that, in motion, recently, that weird tic of Kirkton's. He ran the CCTV over in his mind. His memory trying to reach for the colour but not getting it. It would only come back to him in black and white. Was it from the CCTV footage from 1999?

He looked around him, there was no free computer in the room. The hub of the tactical squad had taken over so he walked over to Anderson's office, pushed at the door to see if it was locked. It rarely was. He then sat at his boss's desk and fired up the computer, logging in. He glanced at the photographs in their silver frames; Claire and Peter, both growing up so fast. Vik felt very old.

Then he started to search for the files on the CCTV footage of 1999, Byres Road. The old nightclub near where Oran Mor was now, what had it been called? Auditorium? He pressed play and watched. Anderson's file only held the edited high-lights, starting at the point when Blondie walked into view, the tall man beside her with his arm over her shoulder. She moved to one side. He moved the other way. They laughed. Mulholland wondered if they said bread and butter when they joined hands again. The man's black fringe fell forward and he swept it back over his forehead. Third finger left hand.

Tania Kirkton walked on the stage, eyes open, mouth open. She was drooling. Her walk was ungainly, slow and mechanical. Her elbows held high, her hands swung as her body moved in response to the tension of the fine wires that ran up to the darkness. On her head, brilliant gold in the lights, was a blonde wig, bob cut. Kirkton moved towards the stage.

The music stopped instantly.

Tania stopped moving, only her right hand, dangling free shook a little.

Batten was right, Blondie wanted to have her say. They had to listen and watch.

Anderson narrowed his eyes, trying to see what was behind

the curtains. He could hear a gentle grinding, like fine meshed gears. Was this some mechanical system, ran by a computer in synch with the music?

Or was that too high tech for her?

He looked back at Kirkton. The politician's demeanour had changed, as if some new and terrifying realization had just dawned upon him.

He knew what all this was about. 'Tania' was now standing up. The crude noose that ran under her chin to the top of her head pulled her face up so she had sight of her select and noiseless audience. Anderson could see someone else lying on the stage, curled behind her, on a piece of backdrop painted as a back doorway. Tania looked into the audience and saw her own father. Tears rolled down her face, her eyes red and swollen, her nose puffy she tried to shake her head. Pleading.

In desperation.

In pain.

Anderson watched, hating himself for hearing Claire's small voice in his head, distressed about the bullying. Tania was the victim now. And he despised himself for the little quiver of pleasure he felt.

He concentrated on the horrific tableau being created in front of him, trying to figure out how many people were there. Did Blondie have an accomplice? If so, which one was the dangerous one?

Another figure hobbled on from stage right, a mechanical clunking accompanying every lift of his leg, left and right being dragged up by the knee. His feet not touching the ground in a slow motion parody of Irish dancing. Then Anderson looked up at the hair, the bruised and bloodied face. The ill-fitting leather jacket swung round him, puckered at the collar where the underlying wires, now weight-bearing, pulled taut. He recognized the face, Gordon Wyngate. He heard Costello swear behind him. The strains of Agnetha and Frida, singing about a world where every neighbour is a friend, echoed round the walls.

They watched in macabre fascination as Wyngate's mario-nette walked up to Tania's. The faces came together. Arms flew out, heads spun. Knees lifted off the ground. A shoulder moved too far from the chest wall. Dislocated.

Their heads locked.

It would be laughable if it wasn't so awful.

Anderson was trying to count the wires that ran high into the darkness above the stage. More than one set, more than two . . . there had to be more than one puppeteer then.

Costello pressed the alert on her phone. She'd had enough, no matter what Batten said. Now was the time for back-up to arrive.

'Wyngate' had his arm pulled back, elbow first and he threw a wild comedy punch that went all round the houses. Tania crumpled, dropping as if her strings had been cut, and lay on the stage, folded, limbs lying at strange angles. Then Anderson noticed the shadow of the other puppet rising, the dark outline first. Then the actual form of a human being, a ghastly creation with a blonde wig and a terrible blood-smeared face.

'Oh my God,' Costello muttered.

Anderson felt her recoil. This shadow marionette had had its face removed. The mask it wore had a fine wire of its own, barely visible. The puppet tried to step over the body of Tania but didn't manage to lift its foot clear and the body dangled, lurching back and forth, the knee held high and the lunar trainer swinging loose. And its further progress was blocked. Anderson looked at the shoes, the misshapen shoulders and the height of this marionette next to that of his colleague. This puppet was a man.

The marionette stayed where it was, swaying slightly, elbows high. The skin of the face slid loose and floated away like a bird, suspended on a fine wire that fluttered it heavenward.

'Call for back-up,' whispered Anderson.

'Already have.'

He heard Costello click her baton to full length.

Kirkton was on his feet, screaming, the music got louder; all three at once now, *Madame Butterfly* and Prince made up a rabble that was deafening. Then Anderson heard, or felt, a gasp from Costello, as the shadow marionette lifted his hand and swung for Wyngate's marionette which promptly collapsed as well. His body hit the floor with a resounding thud that

echoed over the blaring racket. Then it quietened. A waif in
the air, dropping down on gossamer wings was flying towards
the bloody-faced marionette. It outstretched one thin, fragile
arm and the stage was obscured by a star shower in gold and
silver. The shadow marionette rose from the ground, slowly
up and up into a cloud of dry ice that billowed from the ceiling
somewhere.

The music stopped dead.

Everything stopped.

They could hear the rain batter on the roof, the sound of
footsteps outside somewhere. Quiet.

Then gentle words floated round the theatre.

'*Bravo, bravo.*' The Duchess gave a slow handclap.

The curtain fell and a single spotlight highlighted central
stage. A lone figure taking a bow. A blonde with a bob cut,
dressed in a black and grey baggy boiler suit, silvery striped.
It distorted her outline. It covered every part of her body apart
from her face, her blonde bob was in place, and her make-up
was immaculate.

She had her arms out, absorbing her applause, then she
curtsied.

'*Bella, bella.*'

She slithered off the stage towards Kirkton who retreated
quickly. Costello stepped forward, baton raised, calculating
how quick she could get there but two steps took the Blonde
to the Duchess, an embrace. The doors opened and the back-up
flooded the room with light. Nobody moved. For a minute
everybody was standing still, caught in a snapshot.

Blondie was quick. She jumped back on the stage and out
of sight. Then reappeared, climbing like a monkey. Anderson
reacted first and bounded onto the stage, after her. He climbed,
trying to keep clear of the maze of tight wires, looking up
into the swirling darkness, seeing the small skylight, the forest
above. The animals on the tree branches danced and quivered
in the draft from the open door. Anderson was climbing high
on an internal steel stairway, getting a better view of the gantry
as he gained height. Blondie had stepped onto a giant metal
grid, like a huge weaving loom. She wormed her way through,
keeping clear of the taut strong wires that could hold a man's

weight and would probably slice off a limb if it caught it. She clipped herself onto a wire, and used that to pull herself up; she was an alien, *the* alien, attached to her wires, just as Amy had said. It allowed her to climb. She was getting away.

Anderson looked down, and held on. Thinking what he was going to do now. She had nowhere to go. What use was this? He was near the top of the garage, right at the ceiling two floors up. It was a long way down. He leaned over to see what was happening below. The stairway squeaked clear of its bolts on the wall and swung out alarmingly. He leaned in quickly, keeping his body weight close to the wall. He could taste fear but he saw torch beams on the ground below him, moving slowly, no panic. The tactical team were in recovery mode.

It was over.

He allowed himself a long slow breath and decided that somebody else could be a hero today. He was too old and for this particular stairway, he was too heavy.

Anderson heard the hammering of heavy rain on the flat roof. He could see the little paper animals that Amy had seen, quivering with the vibrations of the thunderstorm. Below, the beams of torch light played over the floor. He saw a patch of red, ever increasing, from under the Duchess's wheelchair. Somebody was shouting. He could hear sirens approach through the battering of the downpour. Kirkton was on the stage cradling his daughter's head. Costello was kneeling beside a pair of gossamer wings, her baton discarded.

He followed a torch beam as it highlighted the audience. All stuffed people, false heads, big puppets, small puppets, misshapen, every one of them dressed up. He heard somebody shout for the ambulance to 'bloody hurry up'. He closed his eyes at the thought of Wyngate. Or David. Then heard the words, 'It's the Riley girl.'

'Paige?'

He looked down at the swarm around Wyngate, somebody was telling him not to move. Anderson tried to find a foothold to steady himself, when he flinched at a bright spotlight. The spotlight whirled and went back to centre stage.

Everybody fell silent.

Nobody moved.

She was beautiful, her blonde hair, her pale, pale skin and ruby red lips against the black backdrop. Dali's 'Christ of St John' high above the stage.

Then slowly, imperceptibly, she took a step forward. She hung for a moment in the bright light and then joined the glitter flakes falling.

Falling.

Falling.

By the time Anderson had climbed gingerly down the stairway, Costello was already helping Wyngate onto a stretcher. One of the response team had found some wire cutters, but even he was having difficulty cutting them free. At the secure points, the wire had cut into the skin, bleeding and blistered. Another scar he would have for life.

Costello was busy unwinding the wire that ran under Wyngate's jacket, another cop pulling on it to give some slack. She repeated his name over and over, telling him that he would be all right and that his wife would meet him at the Queen Elizabeth. The paramedics were already here, prioritizing.

'We think he might have been given something called Paracurarium,' she said.

Anderson now stood in the middle of it all. Blondie was lying in her silvery black outfit that shimmered every time the light hit her. Her mouth was open slightly, a single trickle of blood ran from the corner of her lips but her body seemed to melt into the stage. Some kind of backstage material necessary for a puppeteer. It blurred their outline, making them invisible. The silver alien, just as Amy had said.

An older paramedic had his fingers at the Duchess's throat, leaning over to avoid standing in the pool of her blood. He straightened up and closed her eyelids, wrapping her shawl round the narrow shoulders, as if he was closing a book. He turned round and walked away.

Costello came over, blood smeared down her cheek. 'Not an opera singer then, she was a puppet master. She did that thing with her hand all the time at the care home. God, what a mess.'

'How's Wyngate?'

'God knows, they are getting him to hospital.' She pointed to the puppet lying on the floor of the stage, hands up over his bloodied face. 'David, he is conscious, still crying for her to leave him alone; Christ knows what she had been doing to him. They are getting him out of here. His face has been butchered. What the hell has been going on here?'

'Did I hear somebody say Paige Riley?'

'Yes. That was her in the clouds, the damage from those wires is very deep, and infected. She's emaciated. And not conscious.'

Anderson stepped over the commotion on the stage. 'Mr Kirkton, you may accompany Tania to the hospital and stay there for as long as you wish. Then come to the station and tell me exactly what happened that night in 1999. Somebody has to make sense of all this.'

The politician was kneeling on the ground beside Tania, sobbing. She was bleeding a little. Her hair pulled back in a white skull cap, the make-up made her look like a clown.

'But right now, in front of these witnesses, admit that you killed Pietro Girasole.'

He was crying, he nodded, sniffling. 'I didn't know. I didn't know.' He dissolved into tears, shoulders shaking.

'Didn't know what?'

But the answer was interrupted by a paramedic with a stretcher. 'What the hell has been going on here?'

'Long story,' answered Anderson backing off and picking his way over wires, limbs and medical equipment to Blondie, lying on her back. A young male paramedic was feeling the movement of the bones in her neck.

'Is she dead?' he asked, not knowing what he wanted the answer to be.

'Who?'

'Her?' He pointed to the Blonde.

'Him,' he corrected. 'No, he's alive.'

'Sir? You might want to see this?' A voice shouted, a few faces turned to look at him. Four of them. One response team member, one crime scene and two paramedics were looking at the ground. The paramedic was pointing backstage, to a pale pink fold of damp paper . . . or was it?

'I think that's somebody's face.' The paramedic swallowed hard. 'So if we have a face there, then there is somebody missing a face . . .' Her voice tailed off. She went very pale in the harsh glare of a spotlight.

'Would somebody survive that?' asked Anderson.

'I bloody hope so.' The paramedic replied as she paled further.

'Come on, Colin,' said Costello, 'we need to search this place. There is somebody else here. This lot are getting the help they need.' Then she relented. 'Do you want to phone Irene first? David will be next in the ambulance.'

'She can wait.' He turned to the paramedic. 'Can I borrow your torch?'

They walked away from the mayhem, back into the hall and looked in the cupboards just as Wyngate had done. They came to the big wooden cupboard, the crèche for the mario-nettes, the little numbers on the side.

'Measurements for the puppets, their clothes? What kind of fascination is this?' she answered herself. 'Tragic.'

They moved on in silence, keeping together. Costello reunited with her baton, Anderson wielding a torch. They found the futon, the clothes, evidence of food, a small burner, water bottles. Somebody had been living here, alone. Surviving.

Then under the big mirror was a bin bag, they could recog-nise the smooth curves of a hip, the point of a flexed elbow. Costello held the torch in one hand, the baton ready in the other. Anderson tucked his torch under his arm and opened the bag and looked in, and quickly pulled back.

'Jesus, get one of those ambulances here now.'

'Who is it?'

'Don't know. They don't have a face.'

Anderson walked up to the whiteboard and looked at the smiling face of David Kerr. He was safe now and he would recover. He had his whole life ahead of him which was looking unlikely for Sandra Ryme; she was fighting hard though.

Tomorrow the boys would start looking into her background

although there was information coming up on the system already; some blackmail, some theft; a highly suspicious death of an old woman she was looking after.

Sandra Ryme.

People had liked her. She wasn't the brightest and had made a lot of bad choices. Going to work at Athole House was one of them. She had met Paul McEwan there, Paolo as he called himself. He looked at his watch. Batten was going to interview Paolo at the hospital. Anderson was going to have a chat with Kirkton. At some point.

Tania and her mother had been very quickly debriefed and had flown off to a special clinic in London to get her shoulder operated on. And to keep out of the eye of the media. The police czar was in the headlines now for all the wrong reasons, and he was keeping Archie Walker busy, listing the charges the politician would face. Murder was at the top of that list.

Two incidents tragically linked. One on Christmas Eve 1989 when a nine-year-old boy had set fire to his parents' house. The second when a married rising star of politics succumbed to the charms of a beautiful young blonde in the Auditorium nightclub. She was celebrating the millennium. He was celebrating the birth of his son. He was pretending to be single.

She was pretending to be a she.

This time Costello walked confidently up the worn steps of Athole House Secure Living Facility for the retired stars of stage and screen. As she waited for Mulholland to drag his bad leg up behind him, she rang the bell and didn't resist the temptation to look through the letterbox. She saw Piero the cat sitting on the bottom step of the carpeted stairs, tail jerking back and forth. The cat hair. The black and white long cat hair. Piero's expression said, 'You should have asked me, I've known all along.'

'My leg hurts,' Mulholland moaned.

'Well it'll stop once you see this matron, she graduated from the Lucretia Borgia school of nursing.'

'Matron? Christ!'

Eventually, they heard the rattle of the door opening.

'Hello. Matron Nicholson. Elizabeth, isn't it?' asked Costello.

'Hello.' She looked past Costello to the two men behind her, one with a bad limp and the other a uniformed police officer. 'I'm not sure that this is the best time, you know. We are a care facility.'

'Well, this time, it doesn't really matter what you think. We are coming in to look around.' Costello stepped into the hall. 'It's all on official business. Ours, not yours.'

The matron looked at Costello in her navy blue suit, the flat black boots. She thought for a moment, then straightened herself up. 'I think you need a warrant.'

Costello gestured to the uniform who handed over the papers.

She looked them over briefly. 'OK, I'll go and speak to Dr Pearcy.'

'Yes, of course. But you are taking PC Graham here with you. Just so nothing happens to you. You no longer have Kirkton to protect you with his Safer Society.'

That got a reaction. Matron looked at the young constable in horror. He smiled obligingly.

As they walked away along the carpeted corridor to the main office, Costello took Mulholland down the stairs to the green door. 'I really want to know what is behind here. Archie is convinced this is where the Paracurarium might come from.'

'It's locked,' said Mulholland, trying the door.

'Yes. I can see that, Sherlock. But can you get it open?'

'Nope, it's an electronic lock. We need the code.'

Matron found them ten minutes later, her hands were shaking.

Costello was very helpful. 'Under the terms of the search warrant you have to open the door and show us what's behind it.'

'I don't think I have to do anything of the kind.' The words held more defiance than her voice.

Costello sensed victory. The woman was caught between a rock and a very hard place. Cooperation was her only way out.

The matron swallowed hard and for a minute her eyes drifted to the keypad.

'Look,' said Costello, 'you've got yourself involved in something here. You probably had no idea what it would lead to. People have died and you are an accessory before and after the—'

The matron was already shaking her head. 'No, no, no. It was nothing like that, not at all.' Her perfect little hat fell to one side.

On a roll, Costello could lie with the best of them. 'Why do you think the fiscal got his wife in here? She's never been an actress, never set foot on the stage in her life. But Mr Walker was very insistent. And why do you think I've been here pretending to visit Mrs Walker? We know all about it so open the door.'

The matron's hands were trembling that much she couldn't have pressed the buttons if her life depended on it. She gave the detectives her six-figured code quietly in one breath and then held her hands over her face and slid down the wall into a sobbing heap on the floor. Mulholland was already entering the buttons on the pad. There was a click. Both of them hesitated before they pushed the green door open. Mulholland walked in first, getting one step inside the room. Then he stopped so abruptly that Costello walked into the back of him.

Mulholland spoke three short words, but took his time over every syllable. 'Oh. My. God.'

Twelve people lay in beds, jammed packed, the air fetid and stale. It was a basic dormitory ward, nothing more. Nothing less. Leading off it were two of three other rooms, each full of five or six beds, each bed had an occupant. Then it struck Costello that nobody had turned when they came in, nobody had batted an eyelid. These residents were zombies.

'OK,' said Costello, turning to the matron. 'We are going to get our own medical team down here. Do you want to save us the time and money and tell us about the Paracurarium?'

Matron Elizabeth Nicolson nodded in resignation and pulled another key from her belt. She handed it to Mulholland and pointed to a door in the far corner. 'It's all in there.'

'And did you supply Paolo Girasole with the drug?'

She shook her head. 'But I knew it was going on.' She blinked, very close to tears.

'Give us the quick version,' asked Costello, not able to look at the skeleton staring at the strip lights, or the wizened paper thin woman holding a baby doll in her withered arms.

'Dr Pearcy. Paolo said he needed it for the Duchess.'

'But he didn't.'

'No. We sometimes use it here to relax the muscles in the throat but Paolo was blackmailing James and Rodney, Mr Kirkton and Dr Pearcy.' She corrected herself. 'Well, it wasn't exactly blackmail. He wanted the drug, and it is available for institutions like this. He just wanted the best room for Ilaria. That was all. Once he found out we had residents down here, paying and . . . well, not getting the service they are paying for.'

'Where are their relatives? Does nobody visit? The care commission?' Costello was horrified, but not surprised at Nicolson's answer.

'Nobody comes near them. Even if somebody does visit, it doesn't take long to take them upstairs to a nice room, and pretend it's theirs. Nobody cares. We feed them, clean them and keep them drugged. They aren't even on the radar.'

'And you charge them full care fees?' Costello looked round at each face staring at the ceiling. No response, not awake, not asleep. Just staring. Like Pippa. 'Poor bastards.'

SEVEN

Saturday 11 June

Batten was having trouble keeping up. Paul had waited a long time to tell somebody his story. He wasn't going to hold back now. He had spent everything he had on keeping the Duchess in silks and finery while he lived in a garage like a homeless man. Then the money ran out, and the diagnosis of her cancer came through.

So he had scripted the end and he now had an audience

for the whole story. The eloquence of the delivery was sublime. The actor had learned his part well.

Batten had asked him to start at the beginning. The night of the fire. He made sure the recording machine was on, and listened without interruption.

'I couldn't get to sleep. I never could when my parents had dinner parties, well, drinking sessions. Their carry-on echoed down the old chimney on the wall beside my bed. I'd ram my ears into my pillow, but I could still hear it. They got louder as they got drunker.

'That night, that Christmas Eve, they were well pissed. I had made my den, in the floor of my walk-in wardrobe and lay there, listening. They were talking about me, singing the song from *Pinocchio*, the one about having no strings to hold me down. They were taking the piss out of me.

'There were snowflakes outside, falling outside my window, so I slipped my yellow duffle coat over my pyjamas and in the hall, I tried to get my hat down from the upper hook of the coat stand. I couldn't reach it so I moved the advent calendar and the candlestick to one side.

'And I climbed up.

'I've often wondered if I left the candlestick there on purpose.

'The snow was light and fluffy. I remember the snowdrops tickling my face and the cold air nipping my nose. I ran and ran. Ended up at Vinicombe Street, at the theatre. The front doors with the sunflowers were closed. I started to cry. I was so alone. The tears were icy on my cheek. But I could smell hot cinnamon buns. I went round the side and the stage door was slightly open, as if they were waiting for me and I could hear them laughing. I crept closer and the smell of the toasted buns made my stomach hurt. Mum had forgotten to give me any tea.

'I stepped into another world.

'The next day I found my house had burned down. I sort of stayed. I never left. Pietro and I grew up together. We were Pietro and Paolo, Peter and Paul. Flyaway Peter, flyaway Paul. We were together. I became the Duchess's son. They told a story of how much they loved me, I was allowed to stay, eventually.

'But by his teens Pietro wanted a different life. He wanted a life as a girl. Then he became a different person. Paula. I used to hang about with Paula. She was so beautiful. Nobody knew. Not even the Duchess, that would have broken her heart.

'It was when we were out celebrating the millennium, we got separated. We'd had a bit of an argument and she went off with some bloke. I had been ill with the flu and wanted to go home but she was keen to party. It took me a while to catch up with them. They were having a snog just off Ashton Lane, it was busy. There was a bit of a carry on. It didn't look much, Paula should have been able to take a punch, but it was so quick. The bloke had realized, fumbling about, that he was snogging another man. So he lashed out. She laughed, and she really would have laughed at him. Then he punched her. She went down, he ran away. James bastard Kirkton. He just ran away. He left her there, dead.

'I couldn't let anybody know about Paula. Not his parents. That would have killed them. Guido died of grief six months later.

'But at the time I carried her back to the theatre, it wasn't far. I dressed him in my clothes, took his make-up off, his blonde wig. Paula stayed with me and I put Pietro back, he died as Pietro. His arm round my shoulder, I sang as I walked him back. Just a pissed pal being helped home. It was so easy.

'So soon it was just me and the Duchess. She never spoke again. Not really, so I wasn't really as good as the real thing, was I?

'But second best was better than what I had before. I forgot all about Paul McEwan.

'Then the dementia struck. I didn't know what to do. They sold her property from underneath me to pay her fees at Athole House. The puppet theatre had to go as well. I wasn't her son. None of it was mine.

'I tried to start a campaign – just to get the dolls, the patterns, but no . . . Kenny Fraser put them in a skip. Lying in the rain, twisted and broken, my marionettes, my fractured little dolls that had been handcrafted and so loved by my family. I had to pull the velvet red curtains out during a downpour, a drunk had been sick on them.

'Then I knew the end was coming, as it always does.

'I thought, why not give her Pietro back? That's what she wanted. Her favourite story was called *The Enchantress*, it had been hand drawn by Guido. He used to be a fire eater before he became a puppeteer, you know. God I find normal people so boring. I do like flames though. Flames and puppets.

'And I am a very good actor. I can be anything, do anything. I had about four minutes to change from Paula to Paolo before I met that cop in Athole Lane. I had been talking to him face to face when I handed him the phone but a different setting, accent, pulled my hair back and a dirty face and he had no idea who I was.

'None at all.

'That's how good an actor I am.

'It was easy for me to think about bringing Pietro back. I needed an Enchantress. That wee girl. I don't know her name, was so thin and so pathetic. I just picked her up off the street. She needed to be light, less strain on the wire. I was going to re-enact it and give the Duchess a different ending, her ending. I had seen Kirkton on the news. I knew it was him. I had watched him walk away from Paula, leaving her slumped against the wall, dying, her brain bleeding.

'And now the Duchess was dying. She was sitting in that care home in her piss and shit. I wasn't having that, not for her.

'I made a list of my cast, my props. I knew they were abusing Paracuraium, easy to get them to give it to me. Taking the people was easy but that other girl just wouldn't pass out, so I let her go with a message to go and speak to Anderson. I had met him once, and had read about the cold case unit. And then the first boy, he passed out too quickly and died. He choked. The cop was too drunk and fell over, I couldn't get him up.

'The second boy was easier though. And Sandra was my project. She looked a bit like Pietro, same face shape. And she so thought she had me, but I had her . . .

'I bought her a car so I could use it without her knowledge. At Athole House the staff hang all their car keys on a rack. The fact I found jewellery she had been stealing in the boot

just made it sweeter. She never, ever stole from the Duchess
though.

'Then I thought, why not take it further. I could catch
Kirkton, I knew I could. And like I said, I had met that nice
cop once at an art gallery. I remembered him. He was a
friend of Helena Farrell and I had a vague notion of his
name. A junior police officer came to see the Duchess about
the possibility of Pietro's case being reviewed. And DCI
Colin Anderson was named by them. I took that as an omen.
From that minute on I had Kirkton in my sights. I wanted
to destroy him.

'So I did.'

Anderson was waiting for the lift, looking over the vast atrium
of the Queen Elizabeth II University Hospital. On the way up
to Jeffries' room he had heard two patients refer to it as Sweaty
Betty's, and the hospital was living up to its name in this
stinking hot weather. He looked out to the floors below, wheel-
chairs, queues, coffee drinkers and at the newsagents near the
front door, every front page was about the arrest of James
Kirkton for the murder of Pietro Girasole. The tabloids were
making much of the irony of the safer society. His wife was
standing by him, but from a distance as she was still in London
with Tania.

Anderson had just finished interviewing Jeffries before the
case would be passed over to the complaints team for an
internal investigation, and Anderson could have written the
script for that story himself. Jeffries, a DI, had been casual
friends with Kirkton. It was natural for Kirkton to turn to him
for help when he had punched Pietro, thinking he was Paula.
It was a shock, he hadn't meant it. Jeffries' macho persona
had swallowed that. At first, he was just turning a blind eye.
But deceit had led to bigger deceits over the years, covering
his own tracks as well as Kirkton's. He had interviewed Paolo
at the time and 'Paolo' had remembered. Over the years the
case file had been requested from records, tweaked, pages lost,
deleted, all on the pretence of reviewing the evidence in case
something came up. Jeffries was a good cop who had got lost
somewhere along the line, hiding in the dangerous coat-tails

of James Kirkton. Why should a cop and the self-appointed police czar not be the best of friends?

The lift came, the doors slid silently open. It was full, Anderson waved it away, he would take the stairs. He thought that he might never get out of the hospital. He had already visited Wyngate, post-surgery for ligament damage to both his shoulders – he was going to be out of action for months. Baby Sam had been crawling over his dad's bed, reaching for the games on the screen. Anderson was intensely aware of Wyngate's wife's scrutiny. Twice he had been operational in the field and twice he had been seriously injured. It wasn't a debate he wanted to get into at that moment but he knew Wyngate's wife had already mentally written his letter of resignation.

Walking down the corridor, to the room in HD, where another life hung in the balance, thinking about Mr Hollister; young and strong, had his life taken from him and nobody had noticed, nobody had come looking for him. Despite Costello and O'Hare's best efforts, he remained unidentified. He was a body in cold storage and a selection of tissue samples on glass slides. Not much to show for a life. He allowed himself a wry smile at the thought of the Kilpatrick O'Hare reunion, jazz records playing at the care home, two aficionados doing their cool stuff. Good luck to them, two lonely souls had found some solace in all this mess.

'Bloody hell,' Anderson looked into the room, tubes and pipes and monitors everywhere. The body lay on the bed covered in a very light white sheet, the window at the side of the bed gave little light. There was an observation window that they were looking through now. Above the door, visible to those in the nursing bay was a series of lights. All of them quiet, no buzzers going off, no emergency going on. Life was ticking over slowly. In the room a ghost dressed all in white moved around. The outfit reminded Anderson of the scene of crime officers. There was some irony there, that those on the precipice of death were served by the same rules as those who had recently fallen over it.

Sandra Ryme would be very lucky if she made it. Or unlucky, as Costello had said. Unusually moved for her, her voice had

broken slightly because it was such a horrible thing to happen
to anybody, or any other woman, or because it had brought
back some terrible memories for herself. That little scar on her
forehead, and probably now another on her cheek on the
opposite side to match it, courtesy of Mrs Kerr. Now David
was back and relatively safe except a few psychological scars,
and a dislocated shoulder, knee and ankle. The reunion had been
tearful. Anderson had stood on the corner unashamedly tearful
himself. Duncan Kerr had been left very much on the sidelines.
Colin couldn't help himself, he took the dad to one side and told
him not to give up on his boy. He needed to be there for his
son, kids are always kids, no matter how old they are. The man,
tearful himself, had nodded. The marriage might have gone but
that umbilical cord is never really broken. He wished he had
been given that advice. Duncan Kerr had turned away and
Anderson asked him if he wanted to go and sit outside, have
a coffee from the machine and leave David with his mum.
She deserved that.

And so Colin Anderson and Duncan Kerr moaned about the
younger generation like two old codgers in the pub.

'Funny, how when you work away, you know so little about
them.'

'Believe me, living with them doesn't help.'

'I never knew he had a girlfriend.'

'He doesn't. I turned your son's life upside down and he
does not have a girlfriend.' Anderson took a sip of his coffee.

'Ah, so his mum doesn't know either. I felt rather proud of
him. He kept his young lady a secret.'

'Like father, like son?'

Duncan Kerr laughed grimly. 'I guess I asked for that. But
it proves you can't trust them, no matter what you do.' He
smiled to himself. 'Yeah, nice girl, long dark brown hair. Well
spoken. She came into his room yesterday and gave him this
crumpled up old bit of tissue, all red and dirty. Young romance,
eh? It obviously meant something to them.'

'Long dark hair?' asked Anderson.

'Yes, do you know her?'

'Does anybody know anyone?' asked Anderson, smiling to
himself. One day he would get the hang of this parenting lark.

EPILOGUE

Anderson wasn't so sure that it has been a good idea, but he could see the sense behind it and the emotion that drove it. David and Amy would both, hopefully, make a full recovery eventually. They needed surgery and a lot of physio. They needed to attend their lectures at university, different lectures but at the same place. They needed a little help if they wanted to stay there and not drop a year. Anderson didn't know which one of the three had come up with the idea but he hoped Claire had something to do with it.

Paige Riley was given the job of running them around, pushing them up kerbs and holding onto the chairs as they rolled down. Amy's operation was on one knee but David was looking forward to all kinds of bilateral surgery to get any kind of functional movement back. Anderson thought that Paige would be through their pockets and over the horizon before they could say borstal but something had happened to Paige. Maybe it was the way Amy and Claire made a friend out of her. They went for coffee. David joined them, Claire pushing one chair, Paige the other. Or maybe it was the fact that Paige had seen death up close. And she had seen life, the life of parents, children, getting on and believing in yourself. The last Anderson heard about her, she was thinking about moving on once Amy and David got back on their feet. She was thinking of going to college, and taking her Nat fours. Then maybe, going for an HNC in care.

Anderson hoped she made better choices in life than Sandra Ryme.